She shook her hea...

"Zoe, listen." His voice dropped, brittle and urgent. "I'll find a way to get it done. But I can't lose my job, which means you can't boot me. *Please.*"

The words took a straight path to her sternum, kicking the air from her lungs without the argument she'd intended to use it for. Alex's eyes glittered, dark blue and determined in the dusky light shining down from the bare bulb over their heads. His normally cocksure demeanor was nowhere to be seen, replaced instead by an expression so oddly intense, Zoe's pulse sped even faster through her veins.

For just a stop-time sliver of a second, Alex Donovan was vulnerable.

And she could either give him one last chance, or she could sign his walking papers out of her kitchen.

RECKLESS

KIMBERLY KINCAID

ZEBRA BOOKS
KENSINGTON PUBLISHING CORP.
http://www.kensingtonbooks.com

First Printing: February 2016
ISBN-13: 978-1-4201-3773-6
ISBN-10: 1-4201-3773-5

eISBN-13: 978-1-4201-3774-3
eISBN-10: 1-4201-3774-3

10 9 8 7 6 5 4 3 2 1

Printed in the United States of America

Every once in a while,
someone comes along who is an integral part of
helping me take a book from concept to reality.
You know who you are.
This one never would've happened without you!

ACKNOWLEDGMENTS

I cannot even explain how excited I was to write this book, but it definitely wasn't a solo endeavor. First and foremost, I have to give a huge shout-out to the unbelievably patient men on C shift at Station Four in Atlanta, Georgia, specifically Captain Williams, Lieutenant Nour, Clark, Jason, Jordan, and Peter. Showing a romance author the ropes (and Halligan bars and obstacle courses) for a full twenty-four hours was a tall order, and you all taught me so much more than you know. Any mistakes or liberties taken for the sake of fiction writing are purely mine, while the awesome? Yeah, that's all you guys.

Alyssa Alexander, Tracy Brogan, Robin Covington, Avery Flynn, and Jennifer McQuiston . . . you are simply the best friends I could ever, ever ask for. Your encouragement, your laughter, your wisdom, and your solidarity get me through every day.

To Liliana Hart and Bella Andre, thank you for your kindness, both professional and personal. I don't know anyone with more sass and savvy than you.

To the fabulous Tina Payne, for "loaning" me your name, and the also fabulous Pamela Clare, for showing me what endurance and strength of spirit look like.

To Reader Girl, Smarty Pants, and Tiny Dancer, who are funny, fantastic girls, I'm so very proud to be your mom, even when you tell your teachers that I "write really inappropriate books for a living."

And oh, Mr. K. Where would I be without your unending patience, love, and support? Spoiler alert: not here, doing my dream job and writing about the happily-ever-after I know exists.

Lastly, the biggest thank-you goes to you, my readers! From my die-hard street teamers (woo-hoo, Taste Testers!) to my very newest fan, I simply couldn't write if you weren't so excited to read. I am thrilled and honored that this book is in your hands. I hope you love it as much as I loved writing it.

Chapter One

Two things in firefighter Alex Donovan's life were dead certain. The first was where there was smoke, you could bet your lunch money there was going to be fire. The second was wherever there was fire, Alex wanted in.

No contest. No question.

"Okay, listen up, boys, 'cause it looks like we've got a live one," Alex's lieutenant, Paul Crews, hollered over the headset from the officer's seat in the front of Engine Eight, scrolling through the confetti-colored display from dispatch with a series of clacks. "Dispatch is reporting a business fire, with smoke issuing from the windows at a warehouse for a chemical supply company on Roosevelt Avenue. Looks like the place has been abandoned since the company went under last year."

"Is that down in the industrial park by the docks?" His best friend Cole Everett's tried-and-true smile disappeared as he reached down from the seat next to Alex to yank his turnout gear over his navy-blue uniform pants, and yeah. This wasn't going to be your average cat stuck in a tree scenario.

"Yup. Nearest cross street is Euclid, which puts it four

blocks up from the water and smack in the middle of Industrial Row." Crews looked over his shoulder and into the back step of the engine, jerking his chin at the two of them in an unspoken *get your asses in gear,* and hell if Alex needed the message twice.

"Pretty shitty part of town," he said, his pulse jacking up a notch even though he reached for the SCBA tank in the storage compartment behind his seat with ease that bordered on ho-hum. Not that his adrenaline wasn't doing the hey-now all the way through his system, because it sure as shit was. But getting torqued over a promissory note from dispatch without seeing the reality of flames only wasted precious energy. He'd learned that well enough as a candidate eight years ago.

Plus, there would be plenty of time to go yippy-ki-yay once shit started burning down.

"Does it matter that we're headed into Fairview's projects?" Mike Jones asked from Alex's other side, yanking his coat closed over his turnout gear with more attitude than anyone with three weeks' experience had a right to.

Hello. The candidate has a sore spot. Not that it would change Alex's response, or his delivery. Sugarcoating things was for ass-kissers and candy store owners, and neither title was ever going to go on his résumé.

He fixed Jones with a hard stare. "It does when there are probably squatters inside the building, Einstein. How do you think a fire starts in an abandoned warehouse anyway?" Even money said the place hadn't seen running electricity in a dog's age, and with the city still in the tail end of winter's hard grip, there was a zero percent chance this call site had nobody home.

"Oh." Jonesey dropped his chin for just a split second before picking up the rest of his gear. "Guess I wasn't thinking of it like that."

But Alex just shrugged. He'd never been one for getting his boxers in a wad, let alone keeping 'em that way. Especially over the small stuff.

After all, life was too short. And hell if he didn't know *that,* up close and personal.

"Gotta use it for more than a hat rack, rookie." Alex tossed back the emotion in his chest like a double shot of Crown Royal, and it burned just the same as he slapped the kid's helmet with a gloved hand. "You'll learn."

Crews eighty-sixed his smile just a second too late for Alex to miss it, the wail of the overhead sirens competing with the lieutenant's voice over the headset as he blanked the momentary blip of amusement from his face. "There's no reported entrapment, but Teflon's right. An abandoned warehouse in a neighborhood like this is ripe for squatters, even in the daytime. Plus—" Crews broke off, the seriousness in his voice going full-on grim. "We don't know what kind of chemicals might've been left in the place. We need to go by the book on this one. Thirteen's already on scene."

"Outstanding," Cole muttered, tacking on a few choice words to the contrary about their rival house, and Alex's gut nose-dived in agreement.

"Those guys are a bag full of dicks." Not to mention their captain was a douche bag of unrivaled proportions. Alex might not stay mad at most people for long, but he sure as hell knew a jackass when he laid eyes on one.

"I mean it, Teflon." Crews's warning went from dark to dangerous in the span of half a breath. "I don't like those assclowns at Thirteen any more than you do, but a call's a call. Head up, eyes forward."

"Yeah, yeah. Copy that." Alex took off his headset, his mutter falling prey to the combination of Engine Eight's growl and the rush of noise that accompanied the final prep for a real-deal call. He went the inhale-exhale route as he triple-checked his gear, monitoring his breath along with the time as they approached the edge of town leading into Fairview's shabbier waterside neighborhoods.

"So, um, how come your nickname is Teflon?" Jones shifted against the SCBA tank already strapped to his back, the heel of one boot doing a steady bounce against the scuffed black floor of the engine.

Alex's laugh welled up from behind his sternum, and what the hell. The rookie might be ten pounds of nerves stuffed into a five-pound bag, but at least he was curious, too. "I guess you could say it's because I've got special talents."

Jones's head jerked back. "You cook?"

Cole flipped the mouthpiece of his headset upward, tugging the thing off one ear to interject. "Hell no," he said, his tone coupling with his laugh to cancel out any heat from the words. "Clearly, you didn't partake in dinner last week when he was on KP."

"Hey," Alex argued, although he had a whole lot of nothing to back it up. He was a single guy who'd lived all by his lonesome for twelve years. Sue him for not being a gourmet chef. "Dinner wasn't that bad."

"Dude. You fucked up spaghetti."

"Italian cuisine can be extremely tricky." He tried on his very best cocky smile, the one that got him out of speeding tickets and into the panties of every pretty woman he set his sights on, but of course, Mr. Calm, Cool, and Buzzkill just snorted.

"The directions are on the freaking box." Cole lifted a hand to stop Alex from going for round two, turning his attention back to Jones. "To answer your question, Donovan here got his nickname for exactly what you just witnessed."

The candidate's blond brows lifted upward, nearly disappearing beneath the still-shiny visor on his helmet. "Which is . . . ?"

"He's slick enough to sell a cape to Superman. No matter what he gets himself into—and believe me, I've seen him get into some high-level shit—he talks his way right out of it. Trouble always slides right off him."

"Ah." Understanding dawned on Jones's face, and he swung his gaze from Cole to Alex. "Nothing ever sticks to Teflon."

"Nope," Alex said with a grin. Going through life on a bunch of should-haves and maybes was about as appealing as a prostate exam with a root canal chaser. If he wanted something, he did it without hesitation. Dealing with consequences was for after the fact, and despite Cole's smart-ass delivery, he wasn't wrong. Alex could handle anything that came his way, no matter how big, how bad, or how dangerous.

And he tempted all three on a regular frickin' basis.

"Gentlemen!" The staccato clip of Crews's already serious voice popped him back to full attention in the back of Engine Eight, and Alex replaced his headset with a swift tug. "We'll be on-scene in two minutes. Squad is right in front of us, and O'Keefe and Rachel are in the ambo directly behind, but we need to be ready for anything. Look sharp and be on point to set up water lines if Thirteen needs an assist. Let's get ready to work."

Alex shot a gaze out the window, balancing the now palpable push of adrenaline in his veins as he used all five senses to calculate and categorize. Getting a good line of vision on the call site was impossible with the rows of tightly packed factories and warehouses on either side of the street, but even though he couldn't get his eyes on the telltale column of smoke that always marked an active fire, the acrid bite of something burning filled his nose, growing stronger as they approached the heart of Fairview's industrial park. Squat, boxy buildings in various states of dingy and decrepit lined either side of the street, and when

Engine Eight screeched to a stop in front of one of the filthier suspects, Alex didn't even burn an unnecessary nanosecond hitting the pavement to get a better visual.

"Whoa." Even from the opposite side of the street, the warehouse was a nightmare waiting to shake out. Although access to the block had been cut off by the imposing presence of all the emergency response vehicles, a smattering of onlookers dotted the perimeter of the scene. Dark gray smoke chuffed from the partially boarded front windows of the shabby warehouse, painting a thick layer of haze over the bright early-morning sky. Thin ribbons of orange firelight glowed behind the few surviving windowpanes on the Alpha side of the warehouse, but instead of staring at the flames, Alex focused on his assessment.

The fire wasn't always where the biggest problem lay. Or the biggest threat.

"Nice of you girls to show," came an obnoxious drawl from his left, and great. Looked like it was time to play Name That Asshole.

"Captain McManus," Crews deadpanned, all business. "What've we got?"

McManus jabbed his pointy chin toward the dilapidated warehouse. "*We've* got a warehouse fire, Lieutenant. Showing flames on the Alpha side, second floor, roof intact. My men are trying to set up water lines, but the goddamn hydrant's stripped."

"You're not going to search ahead of the water?" Alex asked, and McManus turned to pin him with a stare, his lips pressing into a thin, white line of *screw you*.

"Use the big head for thinking, would you, Donovan? This warehouse is abandoned. As in, no one's inside."

He straightened, pegging McManus with the irritation free-flowing beneath his sternum. "Nothing's abandoned in the projects." Come on, this was Common Sense 101. Not that McManus's overprivileged and underachieving ass seemed to care.

"Dispatch says this place is, and I'm not inclined to disagree." The guy stepped up, his chest barely inches away from Alex's. "A search isn't necessary in this situation."

Only if you're too chickenshit to do one. Alex opened his mouth to tell McManus exactly where to shove his "situation," but Crews shouldered between them, decisive and quick.

"Captain McManus, can you advise?"

A smug smile twisted the man's lips into an expression that was all teeth. "Let's get Squad Eight on the roof for a vent. Engine Eight can run backup water lines if Thirteen needs an assist. You can clean up whatever my men don't catch."

The muscle over Crews's jaw gave a single twitch. Alex silently begged the guy to argue, to tell McManus to get bent, to do *something* other than fall in line.

But then Crews's expression went blank. "Copy that. Jones, you come with me to ready the hoses from Eight in case we need them." He turned, snapping Alex's brewing protest in half with a don't-fuck-with-me frown. "*If* we see any evidence of entrapment, I'm sure we'll reevaluate the need for a search. Until then, Donovan, you and Everett stand by. Clear?"

"Crystal," Cole said, walking Alex out of McManus's earshot before either of them could respond.

"This is bullshit," Alex hissed, grinding his molars hard enough to test the limits of their integrity. "The fire's not fully involved, and the roof is sound. You and I both know if we'd been first on scene, Westin would've had us in that warehouse looking for squatters while squad vented the roof."

"I do." Cole stepped in, his voice low and level. "But I also know that's a judgment call, and someone who outranks me made it. I want to make sure that building is clear just like you, Donovan, but as much as it sucks, we have no way of knowing what's inside. Or more to the point, what's not."

Anger ricocheted through Alex's chest, leaving a bitter exit path in his mouth as he exhaled. "Someone could be trapped in there."

"And the second we see evidence that someone is, we'll go in and get them out."

Alex swore roundly under his breath, channeling his irritation into examining the scene again to look for any signs of life inside the building. The front doors were old and unchained, and although they were likely locked, it was nothing five seconds with his Halligan bar wouldn't take care of. Heat blurred the edges of the dirty wooden window casings, escaping beneath the splintered boards nailed over the openings from the inside. Smoke poured from the building in thicker bursts, indicating the fire was growing, and God damn it, this warehouse had shit for visibility in or viable exits out. Not to mention that their chances of getting anyone *to* those limited exits were circling the drain with each passing second.

Alex's boots had him on a trajectory for the building before the movement made it all the way up the chain of command to his brain.

"Hey!" Captain McManus scrambled forward to step directly in front of Alex, puffing out his narrow chest as his face turned the color of the fire truck blocking the street behind them. "What the hell do you think you're doing?"

"I'm going into that warehouse to do a search," he said, and what do you know, it wasn't a question. He'd have plenty of time to make nice with McManus later. Right now, he needed to do his job. His way.

No hesitation.

"Your level of fuck-uppery knows no bounds, Donovan. You're not going anywhere." McManus refused to budge, crossing his arms as if awaiting an argument. But Alex was done yapping, and he moved to just sidestep the guy so he could get on with what mattered.

"I said stand down, you little punk," the captain spat, matching Alex's lateral movement as he poked a finger into his chest. Although the sensation barely made it past all the reinforced protection of his turnout gear, the contact sent a hot, unrelenting pulse of oh-hell-no all the way through his blood.

He dropped his gaze toward the offending digit for only a split second before returning it to McManus's beady eyes. "Take. Your hands. Off me."

Testosterone collided with the uncut adrenaline coursing through Alex's veins, creating a *whoosh* of white noise in his ears. He was vaguely aware of the thud of boots over pavement, another voice adding to the distant, muffled sounds beyond the anger making a spin cycle out of his gut. But the only thing he heard with any clarity was the irrefutable challenge of Captain McManus's reply.

"Or what, son?"

His body went subarctic despite the heat rolling off the building in front of him. "What did you call me?"

McManus's upper lip curled, his finger pressing harder as he hissed, "I said stand down. You're out of your league. *Son.*"

In one scissor-sharp instant, Alex's last thread of control spontaneously combusted.

His stiff-arm found McManus's center mass in less than a breath, reopening the direct avenue of daylight between him and the warehouse's closest point of entry. His legs made quick work of the distance, while a punishing kick eliminated the barrier of the door. Heat and smoke met him in a one-two punch of hot and nasty, and he yanked his mask over his face with a swift tug.

"I'm pretty sure that's less cordial than McManus is used

to," Cole said in a half holler, and Alex wheeled around just in time to see his best friend pull his own mask into place. Shock took a potshot at his rib cage, but the sensation didn't last. Station Eight's golden rule was to have each other's backs above all else. Of course Cole hadn't broken ranks. Just like Alex wouldn't have if the situation were reversed.

After all, there was no *I* in *team.*

"I'll deal with that weasel-faced asshat later," Alex said, pointing to the dimly lit corridor in front of them. "Right now, we need to make sure this place is empty, from the top down."

"Copy that." Cole snapped on his flashlight, jerking his helmet at the rusty door marked STAIRS. "Let's go to work."

Alex flipped directly to go-mode, the echo of his boots on the concrete steps alternating with his deep-lunged shouts for anyone within earshot to call out. He and Cole divided the third-floor office space down the center of the smoke-stained hallway, checking the offices at the far end with an economy of movement. The first few rooms turned up enough discarded food wrappers and empty liquor bottles to send Alex's hackles into high alert, and he slammed the doors shut in his wake to hold off the spread of heat and smoke pushing up from below.

Someone was in here. And time was running out to find them.

"Fire department! We're here to help you. Call out!" He tore a path to the next office, swinging his flashlight over the littered floor. The beam caught on a pile of rumpled fabric in the corner, and Alex's heart knocked against his ribs like an MMA fighter in a cage match as he raced over the dirt-streaked linoleum.

A stuffed rabbit the color of grime tumbled from the empty sleeping bag.

"Command to Donovan," crackled the radio on Alex's

shoulder, and shit. Guess Crews had gotten the news flash on his whereabouts. "Get your ass out of that warehouse. *Now.*"

"No can do, Lieu." Alex stuck as much respect as he could to the words, but no way was he leaving this party with only half his dance card punched, especially now. He scanned the rest of the office, pulling the door snug within its frame as he moved back into the hallway. "We've got definite signs of squatters in here. I'm finishing this sweep."

Crews switched tactics on a dime, although his tone was no less pissed. "Command to Everett. I want you both to fall out immediately, if not sooner. Do you copy?"

"Affirmative, sir," Cole said, swinging his flashlight back toward the stairwell door as he signaled to Alex that his side of the floor was clear. "But with all due respect, if Donovan's finishing this search, I've got his six."

Crews unleashed a string of upper-level curse words through the radio before continuing. "You're in a world of goddamn hurt when you get out of there, Donovan."

But as much as getting chewed out by Crews was going to suck in Technicolor 3-D, taking the hit in order to do his job right was worth every syllable.

"Copy that. But I'm not leaving 'til the rest of this building is clear."

Alex double-timed it to the second floor with Cole on his heels. Smoke clogged the hallways and larger storage rooms, turning their visibility to jack with a side of shit. In the handful of minutes they'd been in the building, the flames had rolled out to cover the entire north side of the second floor. Damn it, this scene was getting sketchier by the second.

"Fire department! Call out!" Alex's bellow thundered past his lips. Sweat trailed between his shoulder blades and over his eyebrows, his breath tearing a path through his lungs in spite of the mask regulating his air flow from the

SCBA tank on his back. He repeated the yell in every door frame, searching each smoke-filled corner with growing despair.

No one answered.

"Donovan!" Cole hunched at the waist in the main hallway, planting himself in Alex's line of vision with a tight shake of his head. "Looks like anyone who was in here took off. Squad's gotta be close to done venting the roof, and this fire's getting out of hand, fast."

Alex squinted through the haze of smoke and soot, sweat pouring down to sting his eyes beneath his mask. Shit—*shit*—Cole wasn't wrong. Alex might jump the gun and the rest of the arsenal along with it sometimes, but that didn't mean he had a death wish.

"Okay," he said. "Let's hit the ground level and make sure no one got lost on their way to daylight. Go."

He and Cole pivoted toward the stairwell in tandem, their boots competing with the whooshing rush of the flames as they carved an exit path. They retraced their steps to the first floor, and Alex swung the beam of his flashlight through the thick waves of falling ash in a quick check of the cavernous ground-level space before following Cole through the front door. Sunlight blasted his retinas, momentarily French-frying his vision as he clambered back into the full reach of daylight, and he squeezed his eyes shut against the brightness overload.

When he opened them a few seconds later, the first thing Alex saw was his boss, Captain Robert Westin.

And the man was downright furious.

Alex reached up, relieving himself of his helmet and mask combo as his gut plummeted toward the cracked and dusty pavement of Roosevelt Avenue. Although Captain Westin was a pretty hands-on boss—not to mention an extremely dedicated firefighter—he almost never showed up when another captain had already called the ball at a scene.

Which meant someone had radioed him in. And Westin stuck to protocol hard and fast. Christ, Alex was going to need to work up more damage control than he'd thought in order to get out of this.

"Cap, I—"

"Do you need medical attention, Donovan?" A muscle pulled tight over Westin's clean-shaven jaw, telling Alex in no uncertain terms to offer nothing but an answer to the question.

"No, sir."

"Good." The captain shifted to look at Crews for just a split-second's worth of eye contact before pile-driving Alex with a cold, flat stare. "Then store your gear in the engine and get in my vehicle. You're going back to Eight with me."

Just like that, damage control became the understatement of the millennium.

Alex unshouldered his SCBA tank, the blast of cool air that accompanied the removal of his hood and coat barely registering as he replaced his gear in his allotted storage space. He walked a straight line to the captain's red and white department-issued Suburban, parking himself in the passenger seat as he shut the door and braced for impact.

It didn't come.

The entire fifteen-minute drive back to Station Eight was filled with nothing but the intermittent squawk of the radio on Captain Westin's shoulder and the low, rhythmic rumble of the Suburban's engine. Although Alex was tempted to jump in and rip the Band-Aid off the conversation just to get it over with, he trapped his tongue between his teeth instead. Westin might be a great captain—one of the best, even—but he could be a salty old guy when he set his mind to it. Alex had seen Westin pissed enough to swear at, suspend, even sanction his firefighters if the spirit moved him.

But only once in eight years had he seen the guy go for the full-out silent treatment, and yeah. Alex was going to have to play things just right in order to keep this little come to Jesus meeting from leaving a mark.

Westin pulled the Suburban into the oversized garage bay on the far left of the two-story brick building, his precision barely a half step from surgical as he got out and shut the door. Alex ran a hand first over his helmet-matted blond hair, then the sweat-damp T-shirt he'd worn beneath his turnout gear, the impenetrable bite of smoke clinging to the bunker pants and suspenders he still had on over the rest of his uniform. His stomach knotted as he followed a still-silent Westin through the equally quiet hallways of Station Eight, passing the locker room and the house's common space before cutting across to the back of the building where the captain's office stood.

Captain Westin pushed the door shut with a *snick*, finally breaking the silence. "Tell me, Donovan. In your eight-year tenure as a firefighter, have you ever been told that the chain of command is optional?"

Alex cemented his feet to the linoleum to stand at complete attention, despite the fact that his vitals had just spiked up to oh-shit territory. "No, sir."

"Really?" Westin's gray-blond brows winged upward, his arms flexing tight as he knotted them over the front of his crisply pressed uniform shirt. "Did you get a recent promotion I don't know about, then? Because last I checked, both Captain McManus and Lieutenant Crews outrank the shit out of you."

"I can explain," Alex started, but Westin cut him off with no more than a single shake of his head.

"You shoved a superior officer to the ground before disregarding his command to stand down at the scene of an active fire, and then you disobeyed a direct order from a lieutenant in this house to fall out. You are going to have to do a hell of a lot more than explain to get yourself out of this."

Shock combined with realization to form a cocktail of fuck-me in his veins. "I didn't mean to knock McManus down."

"Your intentions don't mean a thing in the face of your actions," Westin popped back, his stare going thermo-nuclear and wedging the rest of the story in Alex's throat. "Every time you try to clean up a mess, the only thing you do is end up filthy. And it is getting harder and harder for me to keep hosing you off."

Anger snapped up from Alex's chest, and it blew past his already questionable brain-to-mouth filter in one swift gust. "I only wanted to get around the guy, and anyway, he put his hands on me first."

"But you upped the stakes when you retaliated, not to mention when you ran into that building. McManus wants your head on a Thanksgiving platter, Donovan. But since I'm pretty sure he'll settle for your job, you might want to change your tune."

Icy fingers of dread slithered between Alex's ribs, digging in hard. "You can't be serious," he breathed. Being a firefighter was the axis that had kept his world spinning for the last eight years. The job wasn't what Alex did, it was who he *was,* as much a part of him as his blood or breath or bones. He could not—under any circumstances—lose it.

This house was the only family Alex had.

"There has to be a way I can get around this," he said, channeling all his effort into a level voice even though his pulse had surpassed warp speed. "I might not always go by the book, but come on, Cap. I belong here. I'm a good fire-fighter."

"You are a good firefighter," Westin agreed, the surprise

in Alex's chest morphing quickly into trepidation as the captain added, "But lately I've got to wonder if you're forgetting the difference between bravery and recklessness. We lost a good man from this house two and a half years ago." His gaze shot through the window to the wall outside the office door, where a framed photo of Mason Watts hung in silent memorial, and Alex's gut went for the full free fall. "I won't lose another, especially not over something that can and should be controlled."

He scraped in a breath, unable to keep his exhale from going hoarse over his words. "I can't lose this job, Captain Westin. You know I can't. . . ." He broke off. Sucked in a breath. "I'll do whatever it takes."

Westin paused for a minute that lasted a month. "According to the personal conduct policy, there is one option."

"Name it."

"As your captain, I can recommend you for a remediation program. You'd have to agree to perform four weeks of community service, done concurrently with an unpaid leave of absence from the house. After that, the fire chief will review your case and decide whether or not to reinstate you to active duty."

Alex's jaw took a one-way trip south. "You want me to ride the pine for four *weeks*?" Christ, those rule-writing desk jockeys knew exactly how to send the slap shot where it would hurt the most.

Westin measured him with a brows-up frown, the gesture pulling the angry red scar that ran from his neck to the back of his ear into sharp relief. "You may be a good firefighter, but your personnel file reads like an adrenaline junkie's guide to firefighting. Even if none of those sanctions stuck before, your actions today are a clear sign your mindset needs a redirect. McManus is gunning for your job. Now do you want to get your shit together, or do you want to get fired?"

Shit. *Shit.* As much as it ripped at Alex's gut, Westin was right. He needed damage control, no matter how pointless the community service would be. "Okay, okay. How fast can you get me into this . . . whatever. Volunteering thing?"

"I'll call the chief's office to get you into the first placement they have available. But, Donovan? Do me a favor."

Right about now, he'd name his firstborn kid after the man. At least, he would if he were ever going to have one. "Anything."

"I run a tight house with even tighter rules, and your blowback ends up on my desk. Don't make me sorry I went to bat for you." Westin's light brown stare flickered once before turning back to stone, but Alex met it with all the certainty he could muster.

"I won't, Captain. I swear."

Chapter Two

Zoe Westin hustled from her aging Toyota Prius to the even more aging back entrance of the Hope House Shelter and Soup Kitchen with no less than two dozen thoughts marching an orderly line through her head. She had just enough time to make it through prep for today's breakfast service before she'd have to inventory and organize the color-coded produce bins to get ready for their weekly perishables delivery. Then she'd move on to the dry goods inventory, write up next week's volunteer schedule, oversee food preparations for lunch. . . .

Yep. Just another day in paradise, feeding people and making a difference, one meal at a time.

"Okay. Let's warm some bellies," Zoe murmured with a grin, turning the heavy-duty dead bolt with a hard *click*. Returning the building keys to their assigned pocket in her messenger bag, she flipped on the lights to illuminate the back of Hope House's kitchen. Her black and silver kitchen clogs echoed a determined rhythm over the floor tiles as she cut a path toward her office, but reality took a swipe at both her mood and her best-laid plans before she could even shrug all the way out of her jacket.

*Just got the paperwork on a new volunteer. He's
doing four weeks of full-time community service,
and the city says he's all yours, starting in the
morning. Enjoy! T*

Zoe reached for the note that the shelter director, Tina,
had left front and center on her desk, crumpling the oversized purple Post-it with a curse-laden sigh. Her plate was
full enough without having to babysit another one of these
community service yahoos—she'd already been through
three in as many months. They were never serious about
anything other than biding their time by doing the bare
minimum. Damn it, she was never going to get Hope
House's soup kitchen all the way off the ground and make
a difference without good, steady, reliable help.

And failure wasn't an option. Not when this soup
kitchen was the only truth she had left.

Trying to ignore the watermelon-sized chunk of dread
making a new home in her gut, Zoe smoothed out the hem
of her fitted black T-shirt and set her sights on the kitchen,
grabbing an apron from one of the hooks by the deep-
bellied stainless steel sinks. Although they only had the
stock and capability for limited breakfast service on most
mornings, feeding Hope House's residents—along with
anyone else who arrived in need of a meal—was her
number-one priority. She'd have to figure out a way to deal
with her latest risk-taker-slash-rule-breaker later.

Right now, Zoe had food to prepare.

Recalibrating her thoughts back to the task at hand, she
pushed past the twin swinging doors leading from the back
of the kitchen into the bare-bones dining room. Pale, early-
morning daylight filtered in through the oversized windows
at the front of the long, rectangular space, offering just
enough visibility for her to make her way behind the
dinged-up cafeteria-style counter set up along the rear wall.

Not wanting to add injury to the insult she'd already racked up this morning, Zoe hit the panel of light switches by the commercial grade coffeemaker. She turned to grab the filters from the adjacent storage drawer and let the rhythm and the smells and the simplicity of the food soothe her like they always did.

But she wasn't alone in the dining room.

Zoe's heartbeat locked in her throat as she registered the man sitting at one of the tables closest to the counter, although *sitting* was actually pretty generous. His long, jeans-clad legs were kicked out in front of him, crossed one over the other at the ankles of his heavy-soled brown leather work boots. His chin lay tucked against the chest of his navy-blue jacket, just enough for his fashionably tousled blond hair to obscure his face, and the soft sound rising up from his chest doubled the shock pumping through her veins.

Her party crasher was snoring.

"Okay, Sleeping Beauty. Time to rise and shine." Zoe barked the words in her best drill-sergeant voice, although she kept her Danskos planted firmly on the business side of the counter. This guy was pretty horizontal for someone with bad intentions—not to mention far more well-kept than their average residents—but she was still on this side of the shelter all by herself. Looks could be deceptive as hell, and despite the security measures she and Tina had been scraping to put into place, Hope House wasn't exactly in a pristine neighborhood. No way was she taking any chances by sounding too mousy or getting too close. "I don't know how you got in here, but breakfast doesn't start until seven. You'll have to wait back in the residence until then."

He woke up all at once, perfectly upright and focused with just two blinks, and holy cheese on a cracker, he was *gorgeous*. "I'm not here for breakfast. I'm—"

"Alex?" Recognition slammed into her senses, working

on a five-second delay with her mouth. But this had to be a mistake. No way could Alex Donovan, the cockiest and most reckless firefighter in her father's entire house, be standing here in front of her with shoulders twice as broad as the last time she'd seen him and a smile so sexy, the damn thing should come with a sternly worded warning label.

"I'm sorry," he said, his Caribbean blue eyes tapering in confusion as they took a slow trip from her face to her feet and then back up again. "Do I know you?"

Zoe's cheeks went hot, although whether it was from the way Alex was focused on her so intently or the fact that she was forgettable enough to go unrecognized, she couldn't be sure.

"Zoe." She paused, waiting out his continued lack of a lightbulb moment for another few seconds before adding, "Westin."

Alex's eyes went as round and dark as ripe blueberries in August, and *ding, ding, ding*. They had a winner. "Holy *shit*. I mean—" He straightened, tugging a hand through his sun-kissed hair as his grin turned decidedly sheepish. "Your father mentioned you'd moved back to town, but I didn't realize you were . . . jeez, didn't you just graduate from college?"

Zoe's defenses prickled to life. "Five years ago." Two months before the last time she'd seen him, to be exact. Come to think of it, Alex had treated her like a little girl that day, too.

Right. Because just what her blush needed was more fuel.

"Oh. I guess time really flies, huh?" He tried on another smile, this one all sweet talk, and God, some things never changed. "Anyway, you might be able to help me out. I guess I'm looking for your boss."

"My who?"

Alex pointed toward the painted cinder-block wall that the soup kitchen shared with the shelter. "The only door that was open when I got here was the one to the shelter. The lady behind the desk walked me through the security doors and told me to wait here for the director of the soup kitchen. It's kind of a long story, but I got stuck with this stupid community service assignment because of an even more stupid work thing, and this was the first available placement. To be honest, I just want to get it over with." He tipped his head at her, sliding his hands into the pockets of his jeans like no great shakes. "What'd you do to land here, anyway?"

Oh, you've got to be kidding me. Of all the possible community service assignments in the galaxy, this one took the freaking crown. She might not have clapped eyes on Alex Donovan since she'd made a colossal idiot out of herself in front of him at the Fairview Fire Department annual barbecue five years ago, but clearly, he hadn't broken the firefighter mold, and she'd been around Station Eight enough to know his reputation by heart. Alex flew by the seat of his bunker pants twenty-four/seven, taking unnecessary risks the way most people took Motrin.

Not happening in her soup kitchen. She might be understaffed, but she wasn't overstupid.

"The way I landed here was simple, actually," Zoe said, knotting her arms over her chest tight enough to test the seams of her T-shirt. "I interviewed for the position as director and I got the job."

The silence extended between them for a beat, then two, before . . . "Wait. *You're* the director of the soup kitchen? As in, you run the whole program? I thought you went to some five-star culinary school." Alex stared at her over the glass and stainless steel food service counter, and at least she'd found the antidote to his smirk.

"Surprise. But don't worry. You won't be stuck with this stupid community service assignment for long."

Her pulse kicked into motion along with her feet, and she angled herself toward the darkly shadowed hallway leading to the pass-through to the shelter. With any luck, Tina would get to work early and could send his arrogant ass packing before Zoe served her first cup of coffee.

"Zoe, wait." Alex's long legs ate up the space between them before she could even make it halfway to the dining room door. "I think we got off on the wrong foot here."

She gave him a tight smile without breaking stride. "At least being a firefighter has kept your observational skills sharp."

His shoulders snapped into an unyielding knot, his stare flashing cool blue as he kept up with her, step for step. "You want to know what else I picked up with my keen observational skills? You're in here by yourself, Gorgeous. And that tells me that like it or not, you need all the help you can get to run this place."

Zoe's gut took a downhill slide toward her hips, and she froze mid-pace on the threshold of the shadow-lined hallway. "Help from someone who isn't serious about being here isn't going to *help* at all."

"Oh, I'm absolutely serious," Alex said, triggering a borderline unladylike snort from her lips.

"You fell asleep on the job before you even started, then you called your assignment in the program I started from scratch 'stupid.' As far as I'm concerned, that makes you about as serious as a tabloid headline, no matter how short-staffed I happen to be."

One corner of his mouth lifted upward, disappearing briefly beneath his golden-brown stubble before he folded his lips back to neutral-expression territory. "Look, you and I might not see eye to eye on the value of community service, but I can promise you this. I'm as determined to do my job as you are to do yours. The city sent me here for a reason. I can't go back to Station Eight until I do my time, and you need a volunteer. So are we going to help each other out here, or what?"

Zoe opened her mouth, her own personal version of *or what* preloaded and ready to launch from her tongue. But if there was one rule she lived by above everything else, it was not putting what mattered most at risk, and what mattered most was feeding the residents at Hope House. As much as she knew firefighters—*especially* ones like Alex Donovan—were nothing but a great, big recipe for disaster, Zoe needed him.

And that meant she had no choice but to spend the next four weeks with the arrogant, impulsive firefighter in her kitchen and under her skin.

"Fine. But let's get one thing perfectly clear. There's no freelancing on this job. I run a tight kitchen with even tighter rules."

But rather than argue, Alex laughed long and loud, the sound sizzling all the way through her as he said, "Funny. That doesn't surprise me one bit."

"Oh." She swallowed hard, wondering how she'd managed to carve out top honors at one of the most prestigious culinary schools on the East Coast but couldn't come up with anything more intelligent than a single syllable to cover up the heat in her blood or the shock in her chest. "Well, you can hang your jacket in the back. We've got a ton of work to do before the other volunteers get here to serve breakfast, and we're already behind."

Sixty seconds later, Alex pushed his way back through the swinging doors from the kitchen, and the gray T-shirt hugging his every last muscle did nothing to bump her vocabulary out of the range of pure idiocy. God, had she learned nothing at that barbecue five years ago?

"You didn't grab an apron," Zoe managed, gesturing to the swath of white cotton knotted around her waist.

"They're not part of the rules, are they?" Although he kept his expression mostly cool, the challenge edging his deep blue stare was just visible enough to blot out the last of the weird shot of warmth she'd felt at his laugh.

"No." It figured he'd start by pushing his luck. "But the kitchen gets pretty messy. You're probably going to want one."

"I'll take my chances."

"I'll bet." Zoe reached into one of the stainless steel utility drawers behind the counter, unearthing a black three-ring binder and propping it open between them. "This is Hope House's kitchen manual. There's another copy in the back, by the pantry. It's got separate sections for delivery guidelines, kitchen tasks and procedures, and step-by-step directions for breakfast, lunch, and dinner service, with house rules in the front of the book and all the health department regulations in the back."

Alex's brows traveled up his forehead. "This has to be three hundred pages all told."

"Welcome to running a nonprofit. We have a lot of guidelines. I'll walk you through most of the work today, but breakfast starts in"—she flipped her wrist to get a glimpse of her watch, and ugh, this was going to take an act of God wrapped up in a winning lottery ticket and sealed with a get out of jail free card. "Fifty-six minutes, so we're going to need to go fast."

"Now you're speaking my language." His charming smile made its way back home in less than a breath, but Zoe met it with a frown.

"Right, I forgot. You just want to get this over with."

Alex shrugged, following her down the main aisle in the dining room and mirroring her movements as she began to flip the chairs from their upside-down perches on the tabletops. "You're not really surprised that I want to get back to Eight as soon as possible, are you? I mean, no offense, but if I had my heart set on doing community service, I'd volunteer of my own accord."

Well, at least his slick charisma came with a side order of no bullshit. Zoe shook her head. "I guess not. What'd you do to get yourself four full-time weeks of mandatory CS anyway? That's a pretty long assignment." In fact, it was the longest one she'd seen since she'd come back to Fairview.

"I told you, it was stupid. I had a difference of opinion with a captain at another house." He curled his palms over a pair of chairs, one-handing each of them to the time-scuffed floorboards with a *clunk*. The long, lean muscles in his forearms flexed and released as he repeated the process once, then twice, and Lord, she really needed to get out more. Or at the very least, dig up her DVD of *Magic Mike* for a good, long re-watch.

"Sounds like a little more than a difference of opinion," Zoe said, her field-tested caution sensors thankfully dousing her libido with a giant bucket of ice cold *don't be stupid*.

"Well, obviously the department agrees with you, which is why I'm here." Alex finished clearing the table next to hers, his no-bones-about-it shrug making an encore performance. "We were second on scene at an abandoned warehouse fire four days ago. Not far from here, actually."

Recognition tugged at her mind. "The old chemical place over on Roosevelt." According to Tina, the place had been boarded up for at least a year.

"Yeah. Anyway, the captain over at Thirteen was being a dick about us searching ahead of the water lines." He paused, inspecting the floor beneath his boots as he cleared his throat. "Uh, pardon my language."

Zoe huffed out a laugh, although the back of her neck

heated upon its exit. She wasn't in middle school, for God's sake. "I'm familiar with the word *dick*, Alex."

"Right. Of course. So Captain McManus told us we didn't need to sweep the warehouse, but I thought it was a bad call. He and I got into it and I went in anyway, and I guess the rest is history."

Hold on . . . "So you ignored a direct order from a captain in an already dangerous situation." Jesus, that took brass.

Alex's shoulders became a rigid line beneath the thin layer of his T-shirt, but he didn't stop flipping the dining room chairs into place. "It wasn't that big a deal. McManus just blew it out of proportion because he was pissed I knocked him down."

Zoe took it back; brass didn't even begin to cover this. "You knocked him *down*?"

"Not intentionally," he argued. "The situation got heated and I just shoved past him to get to the scene. There could've been squatters in that warehouse. It's my job to get them out, period."

"You didn't find anyone, though, did you." No way she wouldn't have heard about a rescue like that in this part of town, especially one where her father's house had responded, and the tight silence filling the dining room hammered her suspicion home.

Of course, Alex wouldn't stand down in the face of a little thing like common freaking sense. "Making absolutely sure the building was empty was a risk I was willing to take."

"But you were clearly told it was an unnecessary risk. Captain McManus must've felt sure no one was in there if he told you not to go inside, plus, there was obvious danger. The place was on fire." A sudden burst of realization had her chin snapping up. "Did you go on this little recon mission all by your lonesome?"

"Of course not." He turned to look at her, his hard, blue stare narrowed in confusion. "You know the drill. Everything in pairs. Cole went with me."

"So not only did you go all commando against another captain's orders, but you risked Cole's ass, too." The words flew past her lips, brazen and unchecked, but come on. There could've been forty-seven kinds of danger in that warehouse, and Alex had not only barged right into the middle of it against a fire captain's better judgment, but he'd rolled out the red carpet for another man to take the same impetuous gamble.

And Zoe knew all too well how much a risk like that could cost.

"Let me make something perfectly clear, Zoe." Alex set the last chair over the floorboards with an impetuous *clunk*, crossing the room until he was close enough to make her heartbeat hijack her lungs. "I'm in this soup kitchen because I have to be, not because I want to. No amount of rehabilitative community service, including judgment from you, is going to change who I am or how I do my job. So do yourself a favor. Don't try."

With that, he turned and walked through the swinging doors to the kitchen, not even sparing her a backward glance.

Chapter Three

Alex sat back against his bar stool, his mood in the shitter despite the cold beer in his hand and the warm smile of the waitress who'd brought it. But the ten hours he'd spent hitting the bricks in Hope House's kitchen today had done their level best to kill both his stamina and his patience.

The grunt work, however, couldn't even hold a flame-thrower to his new boss.

Alex tilted his bottle to his lips, swallowing a long, smooth sip of pale ale to cover his frown. Yeah, he'd cop to the fact that he hadn't come out of the gate with a stellar first impression, but it wasn't as if he'd meant to drift off to dreamland while he'd waited for Zoe in the dining room. With the circadian rhythms that went hand in hand with Alex's job, five minutes in the dark meant one of two things—either he was falling asleep or getting laid. He had to admit, when he'd first seen Zoe standing there in Hope House's dining room, with those blazing brown eyes and jeans that showcased more curves than a Grand Prix race-track, the option behind door number two had seemed awfully freaking appealing.

Until he'd realized who she was. But how the hell was he supposed to know his captain's only daughter had ditched out on her fancy career as an up-and-coming chef to direct a small-time soup kitchen in Fairview's projects? Or that she seemed to have been living on a steady diet of no-risks, all-rules since he'd last seen her five years ago?

Or that despite the fact that she'd pulled a Judge Judy on his ass over the way he'd landed his community service sentence, then met his cold shoulder with an equally arctic counterpart as she'd worked him into the kitchen tiles, he still found her unbelievably and unequivocally hot as hell.

God, he was screwed. And not even in a way that would leave a smile on his face.

"What's the matter, Donovan? One day of plates and pots enough to send you around the bend?"

Alex blinked himself back to his usual table in Belly-flop's bar area just in time to catch the good-natured glint in the eyes of his former squad mate Nick Brennan. If anyone knew the twists and trials of working in a professional kitchen, it was definitely Brennan. After suffering a career-ending injury two and a half years ago, the guy had spent his time doing exactly that before coming back to Fairview last month to teach at the fire academy.

After all, once a firefighter . . .

"Laugh it up, fry boy," Alex said, giving up half a grin before sliding off his padded leather bar stool to shake his buddy's hand. "I take it you heard about my disagreement with McManus."

"Who hasn't? The story's all over the department." Brennan tipped his darkly stubbled chin at their passing wait-ress, pointing to Alex's beer bottle with one hand while holding up two fingers with the other as he parked himself across the table. "Gotta hand it to you, dude. When it comes to going all-in, you are definitely committed."

Alex shrugged. He'd had the same philosophy for the last twelve years, and while it might've gotten him into a bunch of scrapes, his all-in, all-the-time mindset was definitely better than the alternative. "From where I sit, there's really no other way to be. After all, Cap's not running a knitting circle. We either take risks or people get hurt."

"You're preaching to the choir. Believe me, I remember what goes down on shift." Brennan plucked a specials menu from between the salt-and-pepper shakers on the table to give it a nice, long look-see, and even though his expression didn't vary from its terminally easygoing status, guilt poked holes in Alex's chest all the same. Brennan had been injured the same night they'd lost Mason in that gut-twisting apartment fire. One minute, they'd all been clearing the building, business as usual. The next, part of the third floor had collapsed, Brennan's career had been shattered along with a pair of his vertebrae, and Mason was gone.

And wasn't that one more balls-out reminder that life was short.

"Yeah." He finished the last of his beer, the empty bottle finding the polished wood table with a *thunk*, and Brennan leaned in, his voice notched low against the music spilling down from the overhead speakers.

"Listen, Teflon, I get where your head is, but do you think maybe—"

"Well, well, look who it is! I heard this guy's gonna be the next Martha Stewart." Tom O'Keefe, one of Station Eight's paramedics, arrived at the table, clapping his palm over Alex's with a wry laugh. Cole followed behind him, sending a thread of relief beneath Alex's breastbone. While he'd never disrespect Mason's memory, giving his emotions airtime—especially in the middle of a moderately populated sports bar—wasn't part of Alex's game plan. The past was past. What mattered was the moment you were in, and not a whole hell of a lot more.

After all, if you weren't busy living, you were busy

dying, and no way was he going out with a fizzle instead of a slam-fucking-bang.

"You're hilarious, O'Keefe. Really. Asshole," Alex tacked on, but his buddy just lifted his brows in an exaggerated waggle.

"Oh, now you're just flirting with me." O'Keefe shrugged out of his dark blue quilted FFD jacket as the waitress delivered Alex and Brennan's beers, and he twirled his finger in a tight circle over the table as he put in an order to make the round complete. "So," he said, commandeering the bar stool across from Brennan and next to Cole. "All kidding aside, the house is too quiet without your mouthy ass. What's the word with this community service thing?"

Alex rolled his eyes, suddenly grateful for the fresh beer in his hand. "The word is, the next four weeks are going to be an exercise in futility."

"You're actually going to do the whole four weeks?" Brennan's dark brows winged upward, and as much as it burned, Alex met his buddy's shock with a resigned nod.

"Don't get me wrong. I'm not planning on any circle-of-love transformations while I log my time. But as far as the community service goes, I don't have a choice." Christ, this whole thing was such a waste of time and resources. He should be out there fighting fires, not serving up dry sandwiches in some cafeteria line because that idiot McManus was suffering from a bruised ass and an ego to match. "I've got four weeks before I go in front of the fire chief for my review. Until then, it looks like the department has got me by the short and curlies. I either do this community service as penance, or I lose my job. And I'm *not* losing my job."

"Yeah, but if you do the whole four weeks, you're also not getting paid," O'Keefe said. "That's got to sting."

"I'm good there," Alex replied, the words firing out just a little too fast. Ah, damn it. This situation was sideways enough without having to dig into the truth behind his statement. There were only three people at Eight who were privy to all of his sticky particulars, and Alex wasn't about to bump the number higher, not even by one.

He forced his shoulders into their loosest setting, dialing his expression up to damage control status. "I've got some scratch saved up from my part-time gig. It'll last."

"Right. I forgot about that." O'Keefe propped both forearms on the table, tilting his head as he thankfully switched gears. "Still. You spent all day at this soup kitchen place. You haven't tried to sweet-talk the director into giving you a shorter assignment, maybe moving the whole thing along so you can get back in-house? This is *you,* after all."

An image of Zoe with her hands locked over her lush, denim-wrapped hips as she ran him in circles around Hope House's kitchen ricocheted through Alex's brain, and he barely managed to cough out a humorless laugh with his answer. "Uh, yeah, no. As much as I want to trim some time off my assignment, sweet-talking the director isn't going to be a viable strategy."

Cole's brows slid together, his gaze darkening in confusion under the low light of the bar. "Talking your way out of things is always your strategy. What's so special about this director that makes her a game changer?"

"Well, let's see. For starters, her last name is Westin."

The stunned silence at the table lasted for a breath, then another, before O'Keefe finally broke it with a low whistle. "Ho-ly shit, Teflon. Zoe Westin is the director of Hope House's soup kitchen? *That's* the hush-hush project she came back home to work on?"

Alex's sip of beer went down way more sour than smooth, and he made a face to match. "Unfortunately, yes."

Cole frowned, and hell if it wasn't the sentiment of the day. "Didn't she land an apprenticeship with some high-profile chef or something last year? Why would she come back to Fairview to run a soup kitchen?"

"I didn't ask, and she wasn't exactly forthcoming with her life's details. But not only is she the soup kitchen's first in command, the place is so freaking understaffed, she's the *only* one in command."

"Well, that explains why sweet talk is off the table," Brennan said. "Zoe is Cap's golden child. I know you've got balls of solid steel, but . . ."

"I'm reckless, dude. Not brainless." There were only a handful of hard and fast rules that Alex stood by, but he stood by them hard. Always have another firefighter's back, live every second like it could be your last, don't piss into the wind unless you can handle the mess. . . .

And the captain's daughter is hands down, one hundred percent off-limits. No questions. All the time.

Especially since barely four days ago, Captain Westin had gone to bat to save the career Alex desperately needed, and Alex had sworn above all not to let the man down.

O'Keefe narrowed his eyes in obvious thought, leaning back against his bar stool. "So flirting your way to less time is a no-go, clearly. But Zoe is still Westin's daughter, and even though she hasn't been around much lately, it's not as if she doesn't know all of us from being around the station. You can't get her to throw you a mercy bone for being in-house?"

Alex fought the urge to let loose a rude snort, but just barely. "Despite her heritage, I'm pretty sure Zoe is unfamiliar with the concept of mercy. She's as serious as a sledgehammer, especially when it comes to getting things done at Hope House." Hell if Alex didn't have the screaming muscles and throbbing feet to prove it. Running a kitchen wasn't supposed to be literal, for Chrissake.

"Okay," Cole said, ever the calm, cool strategist. "If you can't catch a break in the soup kitchen with Zoe, how about trying to switch to a different placement?"

Unease took a tour through Alex's gut as he did a mental

revisit of the phone call he'd placed on his fifteen-minute lunch break. "Already ahead of you, brother. But apparently these placements are one and done. You either take what they give you, or you don't take a thing."

The rep from the fire chief's office had been summer-sunrise clear. The only way Alex was getting out of being placed at Hope House was if the director booted him, and if that happened, there would be no parting gifts at the door. As bitter as the community-service pill was on his tongue, his only available option was to grit out his time in the soup kitchen with his head down and his eyes forward.

No matter how curvy Zoe's hips looked beneath that freaking apron.

Alex shook his head in an effort to dislodge the mental picture—and all the heat that went with it—from his frontal lobe. Aside from the fact that, hello, she was his captain's freaking daughter, she was essentially his boss for the next four weeks. Okay, so it was more theory than technical fact. After all, the FFD still signed his paychecks—or at least they would when he got his job back. But Zoe was one hundred percent in charge of Hope House's soup kitchen, and by default, his fate lay smack in the center of her iron fist. Thinking about her curves, or anything other than punching the clock and getting this ridiculous sentence done as fast as humanly possible, was a crap idea of the highest order.

Especially since the last time he'd seen her at the annual barbecue, Alex had damn near obliterated one of the few rules he lived by and kissed Zoe Westin senseless.

"Damn," O'Keefe said, remarshaling Alex back to the crowd noise and clinking glassware at Bellyflop's bar. "That sucks, man. At least maybe the department will let Cole do his community service there with you."

Alex's thoughts screeched to a stop like an old record being yanked from a turntable, his thoughts of Zoe disappearing in a hard snap. "What community service?" He divided his stare between O'Keefe's foot-in-mouth wince and Cole's well-*crap* grimace, his knuckles turning white over the amber bottle in his grasp. "What the hell are you talking about?"

"It's not that big a deal," Cole said, although Alex knew better than to take the qualifier at face value. The guy was levelheaded even in his sleep, and all the unspoken communication flying between him and O'Keefe turned the words into fertilizer anyway.

"Uh-huh. Start talking."

Cole shifted against his bar stool, his palm taking a slow trip over the back of his neck. "Cap gave me the news when we were on shift yesterday. I was assigned fifteen hours of community service for following you into the warehouse fire against McManus's orders."

"Are you shitting me?" Alex asked, the question spiked with both anger and disbelief. "It was my decision to blow off what he said and go in."

"Yeah, but it was my decision to follow you, even after I'd heard him tell you to stand down. You may have led the way, but I didn't think twice about following, and McManus was definitely bent enough to make a point."

Cole's matter-of-fact response glued the rest of Alex's diatribe to his throat. Captain McManus *had* gone all piss and vinegar, to the tune of Alex getting screwed with four whole weeks in Hell's Kitchen. But he'd never thought for a second that Cole would get caught in the crossfire of the guy's posturing.

"I can't believe McManus stooped low enough to drag you into this," Alex said, a shot of unease weaving through the free-flowing aggravation in his chest. "The complaint's not going in your file, is it?"

Another dose of silent eye contact between Brennan, O'Keefe, and Cole was all the answer Alex needed, and damn it, this situation was just turning into more of a train wreck every time he turned around. He and Cole had just been doing their *jobs,* for Chrissake. And while Alex didn't really care if his own personnel file had a few dents and dings, Cole had never made it a secret that he wanted a coveted spot on Fairview's rescue squad.

Damn it. *Damn it!*

"Look, Donovan, while I might not agree with your methods, above all else, we have each other's backs. McManus made a bad call. Someone could've been trapped in that warehouse, and anyway, I heard what he called you, and I know he knows the score." Cole paused, his expression going territorial and tight. "The douche bag deserved to get knocked on his ass."

Alex stuffed the echo of McManus's sneer to the dark hallways in the way back of his brain, because really, he was torqued up hard enough already. "Okay, but this is still on me. You don't deserve any of the fallout."

Cole lifted one plaid-shirted shoulder, his shrug as unvarnished as the rest of his expression. "I made a choice, fallout and all. But seriously, I'm not worried about the fifteen hours. You shouldn't be either."

The conversation drifted to hockey scores and burger orders, and for the most part, Alex went along for the ride. But the news of Cole's sanction just crystallized the certainty that had built all day long in his gut, layer by layer. This latest kick in the teeth was all the more reason for him to keep his head down and get this ridiculous community service over with.

The faster, the better.

Zoe punched in the security code for the interior door connecting Hope House's soup kitchen to the shelter, waiting for the familiar beep and buzz combo to signal her authorized entry before heading down the hallway. Breakfast service was on the downswing, and with her two regular volunteers holding things steady on the service line and Alex on dish duty in the kitchen, she could finally grab a much-needed meeting with Tina. Although Zoe tried to hook up with her codirector daily, yesterday's session had fallen prey to the time she'd spent training Alex—a task made monumentally difficult by the fact that he'd spoken maybe nine words to her in as many hours. He'd been equally tight-lipped this morning, doing the barest of minimums to get through breakfast prep, and although his lack of effort hacked her off to no end, Zoe probably shouldn't be surprised.

After all, Alex wasn't the first firefighter who didn't take her job at this soup kitchen seriously.

She pulled in a stabilizing breath, blanking both the pang in her chest and her thoughts of her father before poking her head past the lavender and yellow door frame of her friend-slash-coworker's office. "Hey, Tina. Do you have a sec?"

"For you, sugar plum? Of course." Tina's half-dozen plastic bangle bracelets clacked out a happy rhythm as she waved Zoe all the way over the threshold. She pushed her reading glasses to the crown of her head, where they promptly got lost in the waves of her dark auburn hair. "I missed you yesterday. I popped into the dining room during lunch, but Millie and Ellen said you were up to your elbows behind the lines."

Zoe sank into the secondhand chair across from Tina's desk, tracing a finger over the bold geometric pattern printed on the fabric armrest. While the room boasted the same dollhouse-sized dimensions as Zoe's office on the other side of the building, between the colors and the clutter, the resemblance definitely stopped there. "Yeah, I'm sorry I didn't get a chance to connect with you. We had perishable and dry goods deliveries back to back, and let's just say things weren't exactly a slice of pie with my new community service volunteer."

"I know you're not talking about Tall, Blond, and Holy Crap in there," Tina said, popping her chin toward the hallway and waggling her brows from behind the mountainous stack of file folders piled high on her desk.

Shock bounced Zoe's ponytail against the shoulders of her loose, white peasant blouse. "Who told you about Alex?"

"Are you kidding? My morning volunteer texted me before I was even halfway here yesterday, wanting to know when we started recruiting from Hot Guys R Us. Then Millie gave me the rest of the scoop when I stopped over." Tina paused, measuring Zoe's expression with open curiosity. "Anyway, he showed up two days in a row, his paperwork is all in order, and he certainly looks able-bodied, if you know what I mean. How bad could the situation really be?"

Zoe's libido pumped out a white-hot reminder of exactly how able-bodied Alex had looked as he'd unloaded yesterday's dry goods delivery, but she cleared her throat in an effort to show it who was boss. There were conservatively a thousand items on her List of Important Things that trumped the way Alex Donovan's flawlessly broken-in jeans pressed over his even more flawless ass.

God, his ass really was perfect.

Zoe snapped her spine as high as it would go, replacing the image in her head with one of a big, bright fire truck, and funny, that killed the sudden shot of heat in her veins, lickety-split. "Well, first off, he's a firefighter."

Tina lowered her red rhinestone-studded pen to the top of her desk, her breath escaping on an audible sigh. "Look, honey, I know you and your dad haven't been on the same page since your parents split up last year, and I definitely know how you feel about his chosen line of work. You've got good reasons to be cautious. But don't you think you're jumping the gun by judging Hot Stuff based on his pedigree alone?"

Oh, if only it were that easy. "Did I mention Alex's home station is the number between seven and nine and that I've known him since I was a sophomore at Fairview College?"

"Whoa," Tina said, her shoulders hitting the back of her creaky pleather desk chair with a *thump.* "I mean, I saw on his paperwork that he's a firefighter, and I figured you might not be in love with the fact given your family history. But I had no idea the guy was from Station Eight, or that you'd know him."

Zoe's frown tasted like day-old coffee and felt just as cold as it crossed her lips. "I know him, all right. Don't let the pretty packaging fool you. He's a firefighter, through and through. Right down to the reckless attitude and the refusal to put the job anywhere other than first, no matter who might get hurt. It's going to be a huge energy suck to rein him in for the next four weeks."

Tina paused, her brown eyes narrowing. "Wait . . . I know these assignments are supposed to be strictly according to need, but your father's worked in the department for twenty-five years, and he's got a hell of a lot of clout. You don't think he got Alex assigned here on purpose, do you?"

Her movements froze at the same time her heart jacked to ninety miles an hour behind her sternum, and she sat momentarily poleaxed to her chair. "No," Zoe finally managed, easing up on the death grip she'd involuntarily locked over the multicolored armrest. "The only reason my father would throw me and Alex together on purpose is if he'd gain something from it. He and I might not agree on much anymore, but I've made it clear how serious I am about making a difference with this soup kitchen, and it's wildly obvious that *serious* isn't anywhere in Alex's operating system. My father has to know that despite Alex's penchant for sweet-talking his way out of things, I'm not going to go easy on him just because he's in-house."

In fact, her father probably wanted Alex back at Station Eight as badly as the cocky Casanova wanted to be there, which meant the last place on earth he'd put the guy was her short-staffed soup kitchen, where he'd have to earn every nanosecond of his community service. This whole thing had to be a coincidence.

"There really aren't a whole lot of places that need community service volunteers more than we do," Tina agreed slowly. "I guess it's not *too* much of a shock that Alex landed in your kitchen."

"Yeah." Zoe huffed out a laugh, because it was that or cry, and she'd never been partial to a whole lot of boo hoo. "Even if it is the mother of all ironies."

"Are you sure there's nothing else between you and Mr. Oooo-La-La?" Tina asked, her obvious spark of curiosity making Zoe clamp down on her lip two seconds too late. "Or do you have something you'd like to share with the class?"

"Of course not," she said, strong-arming her thoughts into submission along with her words. She and Tina worked closely together—they were friends, even—but no way was Zoe copping to the near-miss-kiss that haunted her like the ghost of Christmas Stupid. Her only saving grace was that somewhere over the course of the last five years, Alex seemed to have blanked on the entire incident. Not that being forgettable was a major boost to her pride, but it was definitely better than being remembered for letting your beer become the spokesperson for your girly bits in an uncharacteristically impulsive moment of I'm-going-off-to-college-so-maybe-you-should-kiss-me weakness.

Zoe cleared her throat. "I mean, come on, Tina. It doesn't really get more ironic than the fire captain's daughter getting stuck with the least serious guy in the house for a very serious community service assignment. It's like somewhere out in the universe, my karma totally exploded, and now I've got to deal with the aftermath for four whole weeks."

Tina measured Zoe's answer, taking a sip from a coffee mug broadcasting *There's too much blood in my caffeine system,* before she said, "I don't know, sweet cakes. Maybe once Alex gets used to being here, he'll surprise you."

Please. Zoe was too organized for surprises of any kind, especially ones boasting six feet two inches of nothing but ego. "He's pretty determined to squeak by on as little effort as possible, and he's made it perfectly plain that he doesn't want to be here. Hell, he doesn't even think he did anything to deserve community service in the first place. I highly doubt he'll be shocking me with a change of heart."

"Well, hands are hands, I guess. At least you can use 'em while you've got 'em."

"More like use 'em until they screw up," Zoe countered, her resolve finally snapping back into place in her chest. "I might need help in the kitchen, but I don't have the time or the energy to clean up anyone's messes. If all he wants is to punch the clock, fine. I can't make him love it here."

The admission took a jab at her breastbone, although she didn't hesitate with the rest. "But Hope House is the only thing I can rely on, and this place means everything to me. If Alex Donovan sets so much as one toe out of line, I'll send him packing. You can bet the bank on it."

Chapter Four

Alex auto-piloted his way through the swinging doors connecting Hope House's kitchen and dining room, balancing a slotted tray of coffee mugs between his dishpan hands. He'd spent the last three hours alternating between scrubbing what felt like every last pot in the kitchen and getting the ancient commercial dishwasher to (sort of) run without blowing a gasket. While the tasks weren't exactly neurosurgery, the routine was about as thrilling as watching daisies germinate, and damn it. If he was already counting the minutes on the morning of day two, the next four weeks were going to send him around the bend.

Giving up the bare bones of a smile to the two fifty-something ladies working behind the dented-up food service counter, Alex swapped the clean mugs in his grasp for the dirty counterparts that had amassed since his last trip, hefting the tray back up for yet another round of lather, rinse, repeat. But with T minus four steps to go until he reached the swinging door, he clipped the corner of the unwieldy tray on the metal edge of the coffee station counter. Tightening his stance over the rubber floor mats, Alex managed to keep both his grip and his balance, but there was no helping the slosh of cold, leftover coffee that splashed over his wrist and forearm.

"Shit." He slid the tray to the slim stretch of countertop next to the double-wide bucket sink, giving his hands a quick scrub and quicker pat down on the dish towel he kept terminally slung over his shoulder. Although Zoe had been dead-on accurate about the need for an apron—much to the chagrin of the T-shirt he'd sacrificed during yesterday's shift—he couldn't quite bring himself to do the chugalug with his pride and go grab one from the back. It was a small and fairly ridiculous defiance, but the less of a groove Alex found here, the better. He didn't belong cooped up in a kitchen, wasting his time and energy on some stupid principle.

Christ, he missed the firehouse.

"That's not the right sink for washing your hands." The words arrived barely one notch above the end of the breakfast din, and Alex shook himself back to the dining room with a frown. But the one-two punch of being at Hope House and *not* being at Station Eight took a quick backseat to the stoop-shouldered old man standing on the other side of the counter, peering at Alex through a pair of thick, black-rimmed glasses.

"It's not, huh?" With all the arbitrary rules holding this place together like mortar, it figured there would be some sort of secret code for washing your hands.

"No." The man clutched his coffee mug between both palms, shaking his nearly bald head as if Alex had made some grave infraction. "You gotta use the small one for your hands. See? Over there." He nodded to the separate stainless steel sink a few paces away, next to the door to the kitchen. "Miss Zoe gets mad when people use the wrong one."

"I'm sure she does." Alex lifted one corner of his mouth in the rough measure of a smile, although there was damn little happiness behind the gesture. A hundred bucks said Zoe had never toed the wild side in her life.

"She has a good reason," the man added, and okay. Alex had nothing but time. He'd bite.

"And what's that?"

The man's face brightened, his gaze skimming the tidy work space behind the counter. "The big sink is for consumables. You know, filling the coffeepot or rinsing off vegetables. Haven't you read the book?"

Alex thought of the two solid inches of do-this, do-that collated and clipped into Zoe's kitchen manual, and he covered his grimace with a shake of his head. "Guess I missed that part."

"It's on page one-eighty-six, under the section for the Fairview City Health Code."

Well, that explained a lot. "No wonder the boss loves it."

"It always seemed like kind of a stupid rule to me, too," the old man said, as if he'd periscoped his way into Alex's thoughts. "But then Miss Zoe explained that there are two sinks to keep the germs from people's hands away from anything we might eat or drink. That way no one who eats here gets sick. She even let me borrow the manual so I could read it for myself."

"Huh," Alex said, realization finding his brain in a slow trickle. Come to think of it, keeping the sinks separate to avoid cross contamination wasn't the dumbest idea on the planet. "I'll have to remember that from now on. Thanks for the heads-up . . ."

"Hector." The man brushed a palm over the front of his threadbare button-down shirt before extending it, and Alex's smile took a trip into genuine territory as he reached over the counter to shake the guy's hand.

"Good to meet you, Hector. I'm Alex."

Hector loaded his expression with curiosity that made

his eyes go even wider behind the extra thick lenses of his bifocals. "You're new here."

"I'm working in the kitchen, but it's just temporary," Alex said, and hell if the affirmation wasn't the best thing he'd tasted all day. "Four weeks from now I'll be back at my real job. I'm a firefighter."

"Oh, I see." Hector swung a glance to the end of the counter where the two service volunteers were dishing up oatmeal and cold cereal, but it only lasted a second before rebounding back to the spot where Alex stood. "Listen, you wouldn't happen to be able to give an old man a refill, would you? I promise not to tell Miss Zoe about you using the wrong sink." He lifted his coffee mug just a few inches, but the expression on the guy's face was so hopeful that even though Alex was supposed to be on kitchen patrol rather than the front lines, he didn't even think twice.

"You drive a hard bargain, Hector. But you saved my bacon with that sink there, so I've got your back." He turned to grab the carafe off the burner at the coffee station a few paces away. But rather than zeroing in on the java and getting down to business, he nearly smacked into Zoe instead.

"Whoa!" Alex pulled up about an inch before contact, shock spurting through him at not just her presence, but her proximity. Usually, he was one hundred percent solid on his surroundings, front, back, up and down. Hell, keeping your head on a swivel was pretty much lesson number one at the academy, and God knew it applied in more places than burning buildings.

Of course, Zoe didn't even flinch, and didn't that just throw him even more off-kilter. "What are you doing?" she asked, her arms sliding into what looked like a well-practiced knot over the combo of her apron and her billowy white shirt.

Alex pulled in a deep breath, resetting his pulse to slow and steady. "I'm getting Hector here another cup of coffee."

He shifted to step around her and finish his trip to the coffee station so he could refill Hector's mug and get on with his yawn-worthy day, but Zoe didn't budge from his path.

"Not so fast."

Alex opened his mouth for a verbal push back—she couldn't seriously pick on him for trying to *serve* someone in a soup kitchen—when her hand brushed over his forearm, promptly scrambling his circuitry.

"Hector, I know you know the rules, even if Alex doesn't," Zoe said, her voice gentling even though her palm still curved firmly over his skin. God, her fingers were the oddest combination of softness and strength, and the heat of them kept his brewing protest just out of reach of his mouth.

Hector nodded, his expression flavored with apology. "No refills, no exceptions. I know, Miss Zoe. You can't blame an old man for trying."

"Hmm." One gold-blond eyebrow kicked up, but there was no heat in the gesture to make it stick. "Still, no dice. You're welcome to grab the very first cup of coffee at lunch, though. Okay?" She let go of Alex's arm, and the sudden coolness replacing her fingers jolted him right back into awareness as Hector thanked her and shuffled away.

"Do you have to be so tight with the rules?" Alex murmured, twisting the words from the side of his mouth so only Zoe could hear them.

She returned the favor with a smile as dry as a desert afternoon. "Do you have to hate them so much that you didn't even bother to read them? Or were you just breaking that one on purpose?"

Okay. He had no choice but to go touché on that one. Still . . . "So I didn't know about the no refills thing. But would one extra cup of coffee have killed you?"

Zoe paused, her ponytail swinging in a blond arc over her shoulders as she dropped her chin by just a fraction.

"Why don't you finish up with these dishes and grab the rule book for some extra reading. Clearly, you need to review the food service guidelines again before you'll be ready to work in the dining room."

The heel of her shiny black and silver clogs gave a squeak as she turned back toward the kitchen, but she'd barely gotten past the swinging door before Alex had caught up with her.

"You didn't answer the question." Somewhere, way in the back room of his brain, he knew picking at her probably wasn't the brightest idea he'd ever sprouted. But he'd never been too partial to holding back, and anyway, he couldn't deny his irritation at the extra assignment or his ripping curiosity at how fast she'd been to swerve around the subject.

Zoe had been unapologetic about standing her ground since the minute he'd laid eyes on her yesterday, to the point that she'd marched him around the kitchen like a lieutenant doing stair drills with a squad full of rookies. No way would she scale back over something like a refill rule.

Unless he'd hit a nerve.

"No, I didn't." She crossed the kitchen tiles, propping the dry goods pantry door open with one denim-wrapped hip before sliding a wooden doorstop into place. Alex followed her into the warm, tightly packed space, the residual sounds from the kitchen receding into a distant thrum of background noise as they moved farther into the galley-style storage room.

"That's all you're going to say?"

"A day and a half's worth of zipping your lips and walking around here like you don't care about anything, and you want to break your code of silence over a cup of coffee?" Zoe's hands moved just a fraction too quickly as she searched the open-air metal shelves in front of her, and just like that, Alex left propriety in the dust.

"Obviously," he pointed out, taking another step toward her until he was close enough to feel the vibration of her surprise. Her movements slid to a halt, her fingers halfway over a carton of vegetable stock, and he didn't waste any time taking advantage of the hitch. "So humor me. Are you really so bound and determined to go by the book that you can't give a poor old man a second cup of coffee? I thought the whole point of a soup kitchen was to feed people when they're hungry, not turn them away because of some stupid rule."

In a hot instant, Zoe knocked the surprise directly back to his court. "You really don't get it, do you?" She turned to face him, her chin tipped defiantly so she could meet his gaze despite the seven-inch height differential between them. "It's not that I don't want Hector to have a second cup of coffee. Hell, Alex, I want to give him enough refills to float him to China. But I can't."

Something Alex couldn't label with a name flickered in her caramel-colored stare, replaced by her standard-issue seriousness before he could even be one hundred percent positive he'd seen a change. "Why not? You're the director."

"Exactly," she said, the softness of her voice refusing to match the sternness of her expression. "I'm the director. It's my job to feed as many people as possible so no one goes without. And if Hector gets two cups of coffee, someone else gets none, so yeah. I have to be *that* tight with the rules."

His gut sank in sudden understanding. "Your funding is really that thin?" he asked. The flicker in her eyes made a repeat performance, and Alex was unprepared for the vulnerability in Zoe's answer.

"I treat feeding people the way you treat being a firefighter. Do you really think I'd pull up on doing it for one second unless I didn't have a choice?"

Oh hell. He opened his mouth, but before he could form an answer, her eyebrows tugged into a deep furrow.

"Wait . . . what's that smell?"

Alex blinked, trying to process the question despite all the *whaaaaaat* running rampant in his melon. "Don't look at me," he said, holding up his hands in mock surrender. "I took a shower this morning."

"Not you." Zoe frowned, pressing up to her toes to scan the pantry's top shelf. Rocking back on his heels, Alex mimicked her movements on the other side of the narrow storage space, and come to think of it, now that they were all the way inside, the pantry did seem to be giving off kind of a funky odor.

With their argument seemingly forgotten, Zoe turned toward the deepest stretch of the corridor-like room, where she'd had him unload all those endless cartons of who knows what yesterday. "You double-checked the contents of these boxes before you put them on the shelves, right?"

He swallowed hard, his throat tightening into a knot full of very bad things. "You said to unload them and put them in the pantry, not open them up."

"I said to unload them per the guidelines, which means they should've been checked. Did you not read *any* of the book?"

"Not to move a bunch of boxes," Alex argued. "And anyway, that thing is a doorstop."

"That thing is important!" Zoe's eyes flashed with the color and intensity of double-batch bourbon as she started shushing boxes over the metal wire shelves, popping them open and muttering something unintelligible under her breath. A few seconds later, she jerked back from the ominously stained cardboard carton in her grasp, turning to throw a hard cough into the crook of her elbow.

"Ugh." The pungent smell of something rotten hit Alex

right in the gag reflex, and he squeezed his eyes shut against their involuntary watering. "What is that?"

"*That* appears to be one of the boxes that should have been sorted with the meat delivery and put in the walk-in for today's lunch and dinner service," Zoe bit out, her lips flattening into a hard seal as she swung her gaze from the soggy box to his face.

"But it was on the kitchen counter with all the other stuff during yesterday's dry goods delivery." It had to have been, otherwise he never would've shoved the thing back here with all the others like she'd told him to.

"The individual boxes aren't always marked with what's inside, which is exactly why whoever unloads them is supposed to do an inventory of each one to make sure the items go to the right place, especially on days when we have multiple food deliveries. The procedures are very clearly outlined in the manual."

All of a sudden, the very bad things in the pit of his belly grew into something even worse. "I guess I must have missed this one. I'm sorry." Alex took a few steps toward the kitchen for a trash bag to just suck it up and take care of the mess when the harsh burst of Zoe's exhale stopped him dead in his Red Wings.

"Sorry's not going to cut it," she said, meeting him toe to toe on the dark brown pantry tiles. He could admit to screwing up—hell, he just *had,* and he'd offered a genuine apology to boot. What else could she possibly want?

"Look, I get that you're mad, Zoe, but it was a mistake. I didn't knowingly put that box back here."

"You also didn't *knowingly* do your job like you were supposed to. It's one thing for you to put out minimal effort while you do your community service." A muscle ticked in her jawline, punctuating the absolute certainty of her words as she added, "But I don't have room in my kitchen for blatant screwups, and I certainly can't babysit you every second of the day. Sorry, Alex. But you've got to go."

Alex took a step back, and Zoe had to give him this. The shock on his ridiculously handsome face actually looked genuine. "What do you mean, I've got to go?"

"It's pretty self-explanatory, don't you think? You just cost me money and resources I can't afford to lose. I have no way to feed everyone for the rest of the day, and there's nine kinds of a mess back here where this stuff leaked through the cardboard. Not only is it a clean-up job I don't have time for, but I could probably wallpaper my office with the health code violations I'd rack up if an inspector walked through that door right now. Add all of that together, and it looks like a pink slip to me."

She might need all the man power she could get to run Hope House's kitchen, but she couldn't put up with Alex's ho-hum attitude about community service. Not at the price he'd just cost her, not when it was her job to make a difference. She couldn't feed people with unsafe kitchen conditions and rotten meat. And she *would* feed everyone today, despite the lost food and the mess behind her on the shelves.

Somehow.

"Okay, but you can't just boot me." Alex reached into the back pocket of his jeans, producing a pale yellow slip of paper from his wallet as if it would solve the problems of the universe. "The fire chief's office put in the order, and the city assigned me to you, just like it says right here. My community service is mandatory."

"Maybe." Zoe inhaled long and slow, her decision made as Alex replaced the form he'd clearly thought would change her mind. "But I sure don't have to let you perform it in my soup kitchen."

She angled herself to move past him and head for

daylight, but the pantry space was barely wide enough for both of them to stand side by side. Alex slipped around her with one deft move, stepping directly into her path as he blocked both her forward progress and the door frame with his body.

"Oh!" Her hands flew upward to avoid a complete collision, palms landing smack over the leanly muscled expanse of his chest. Without skipping a beat, Alex reached beneath her elbows, wrapping his fingers over the backs of her arms and pulling her close to keep her steady.

Talk about a plan destined for epic failure.

"Could you just put your machete down for one minute so we can talk about this?" he asked, his exhale moving past her ear in a warm puff as he lowered his chin to look at her. His heart thumped, fast and steady against her fingertips, and the unexpected intimacy of the contact sent a streak of heat all the way down Zoe's spine. Her pulse jumped to match his, and she refused to look away even though her face prickled with what had to be an obvious blush.

"This is simple risk analysis. I need people I can rely on in my kitchen. If you can't take this job seriously enough to get it done right, then we have nothing to talk about." She pushed out a couple of rapid-fire blinks, grounding herself in reality despite the fact that Alex's callused fingers showed no signs of imminent departure from the backs of her arms.

"And what if I can?"

"You can't," Zoe argued, and God, she should've known better than to think that her soup kitchen would mean anything to a firefighter like Alex.

Still, he didn't relent. "If I can fix this mess, will you give me another chance?"

She shook her head. "Alex, I—"

"Zoe, listen." His voice dropped, brittle and tight. "I'll find a way to get it done. But I can't lose my job, which means you can't boot me. *Please.*"

The words took a straight path to her sternum, kicking the air from her lungs without the argument she'd intended to use it for. Alex's eyes glittered, dark blue and determined in the dusky light shining down from the bare bulb over their heads. His normally cocksure demeanor was nowhere to be seen, replaced instead by an expression so oddly intense, Zoe's pulse sped even faster through her veins.

For just a stop-time sliver of a second, Alex Donovan was vulnerable.

And she could either give him one last chance, or she could sign his walking papers out of her kitchen.

Chapter Five

Zoe shifted her weight to the heels of her kitchen clogs, scanning, then rescanning the pantry for even the tiniest hint that merely an hour ago, the place had been a food-borne bacteria factory just waiting to prove the old adage that sharing was caring.

But she couldn't find a single one.

"See?" Alex leaned a sculpted shoulder against the door frame, his cocky smile back in place and even brighter than before. "One hundred percent clean and sanitized, just like I promised."

"Hmm." She ran her fingers over the edge of the shelf in front of her, a ripple of shock working its way through her chest at the freshly scented air and the smooth, scrubbed surfaces. Ruler-straight rows of cartons and canned goods stood organized and ready to go, and as she dropped her gaze, even the buffed brown floor tiles seemed to gleam under her feet. "Well, it certainly looks up to code."

"Wow, Zoe. Don't oversell it." Alex's grin remained perfectly intact as he pushed off the door frame, gesturing grandly through the light shining down from overhead.

"Come on. Don't even try to tell me that the best you've got is 'it looks up to code.'"

"It's pretty clean," she said, and *damn* it, that smile of his was infectious. Zoe knew better than to buy into his boyish charm—after all, sweet talk was Alex's bread and butter, and he was clearly only trying to save his own skin.

Trouble was, he'd saved hers in the process. Her standards might be sky high, but she'd been so lean on man power lately that even before this morning's rotten food debacle, the pantry *had* needed some TLC.

And Alex had given it a complete overhaul, all the way down to the baseboards.

"This pantry is a masterpiece," he corrected, delivering her back to the snug confines of the shelf-lined space. "I bet you'd get perfect marks if the city health inspector walked through that door right this minute. In fact . . ." He broke off, sauntering to the center of the freshly scoured room. "I'd even go so far as to say you could serve a four-course meal, right on this very spot."

Zoe bit back the involuntary laugh tempting the edges of her lips, her curiosity bypassing her caution filter as it made a beeline for her mouth. "Okay, I have to ask. How did you get it so clean in here?"

"Well, the main ingredient was elbow grease, but I wasn't without help. You remember Tom O'Keefe, right?" Alex asked, and she did a quick Station Eight roll call in her head.

"Sure." The paramedic had been with the FFD for the last few years. She didn't know him quite as well as she did Alex and Cole and the other guys, but her father had always spoken highly of him, and in the handful of times she'd seen the guy at softball tournaments and department barbecues, O'Keefe had always seemed to live up to the praise. "But what on earth does he have to do with my pantry?"

Alex laughed in a low, butterscotch-smooth rumble, and the sound took another chip out of Zoe's doubt. "As luck would have it, O'Keefe is really good at sanitizing small spaces. I guess you could call it a product of his occupation, with all those health and safety guidelines on the ambo. Anyway, I told him I needed a deep clean on the fly, so he walked me through a couple of tricks over the phone. And before you ask"—he paused to lift both hands in concession—"yes, I double-checked his advice against the food safety section of your kitchen doorstop, and yes again. Both the methods and the chemicals I used are all legit."

"Oh," Zoe said, the word a lame replacement for the already answered question she'd had preloaded on the tip of her tongue. But the last thing she'd expected was for Alex to come through, let alone hit a grand slam on the last-ditch curveball she'd lobbed in his direction.

"You didn't think you could rely on me to get this cleaned up right, did you?" The question arrived without gloating or accusation, his smile turning wistful as he pushed his hands into the pockets of his broken-in jeans. Zoe tugged at the hem of her apron, smoothing the fabric even though it was already perfectly in place, but screw it. She'd never been a fan of dancing around the truth, and it wasn't as if Alex didn't already know the answer, anyway.

"To be honest, no. I really didn't."

One brow arched up toward his sun-bleached hairline. "I don't believe in wasting time on anything other than honesty," he said. "As for the rest, I'm glad I surprised you."

She pulled in a deep breath to counter the bump in her pulse. Alex might be charming as hell right now, with that aw-shucks expression beneath the sprinkling of rugged stubble on his face, but he'd only helped her to help himself. Plus, she had bigger fish to fry—namely, that she had *no* fish, or protein of any kind for the rest of the day's meal service.

"Well, a deal's a deal. While I don't expect you to repeat your mistakes, or make any new ones because you're un-prepared, this gets you off the hook for this morning's mess." Zoe shifted her weight over the floor tiles, her pony-tail brushing over one shoulder as she tipped her head at the pantry door. "But if you'll excuse me, I've still got to go figure out how to get through the rest of today's meal service without the food we lost."

Rather than taking a step back to let her pass, Alex straightened, keeping himself planted directly in her path. "No, you don't."

"I'm sorry?" She'd been scraping like mad for the last hour to come up with replacement options for the ruined ingredients, to little avail. Did he seriously think her job was so easy that she could work up lunch and dinner for a hundred hungry residents on a wing and a Hail Mary?

"You don't have to worry about coming up with plan B. Not for lunch, anyway. I've got it covered." Alex turned and jerked his chin at the pantry door in a clear request for her to follow, and the shock of his words had her so dumb-founded that she was powerless to do anything other than oblige.

"Okay." She extended the word with the tone of a ques-tion as they crossed back into the brightly lit kitchen, coming to a stop by the stainless steel prep table acting as a make-shift island in the center of the room. "Meal service starts in an hour and a half, and we have nothing to prepare. Do you have access to some sort of magic food genie I don't know about?"

"Something like that, yeah." Alex pulled an iPhone out of the back pocket of his jeans, tapping the screen to life. After a handful of easy moves, he extended the phone in her direction, waiting silently as she took in the Web page he'd opened.

Zoe's jaw unhinged. "You ordered pizza?"

"Look, I'm not even going to pretend I know how to make anything other than a mess in the kitchen, but you needed the food. I go skydiving with one of the guys who owns the pizza place over on Atlantic Boulevard, and he owed me a favor, so—"

"Wait." She held up one palm in a wordless *stop right there,* although the free-for-all of questions flying around in her brain made practicing what she preached a complete and total no-go. She'd known he was slick, but . . . "You got twenty pizzas by cashing in a favor?"

"I got a *deal* on twenty pizzas by cashing in a favor," Alex amended, propping one hip against the prep table and gesturing toward the swinging door. "But yeah. They'll be here at eleven forty-five."

Zoe handed his phone back over, unsure whether she should cry with relief or tread with extreme caution. "You know, if you're not careful, I might actually start to think there's a decent guy underneath all that attitude."

Heat laddered up the back of her neck as she heard the implication of the words, but rather than take offense or trot out said attitude for a test run, Alex just laughed.

"Well. We can't have that, now can we?"

Zoe's smile appeared before she could stop it. "Is there anyone in Fairview you can't fast talk into giving you what you want?"

"You mean besides you?" His blue eyes glinted teasingly, but it lasted for only a second before he said, "Listen, just because I don't want to be here doesn't mean I'm out to torpedo your kitchen, either. This community service thing might not be what either of us wants, but you gave me a second chance. And while I realize delivery pizza isn't the meal you had in mind, I owed you one, and it really is the best I've got."

An odd sensation twisted in her chest, welling up in a soft, involuntary laugh. "Was that supposed to be endearing?"

"That all depends," Alex said, one corner of his mouth lifting into a dark and forbidden version of his all-American smile. "Did it work?"

Did. It. Ever. Zoe's lips parted, and for just a fraction of a second, she wanted nothing more than to rain check everything else around her to find out if his smile tasted as wicked as it looked. But then her eyes dropped to the four-armed crest emblazoned over the top left of his T-shirt, complete with the words *Fairview Fire Department, Station Eight* printed in bold, bright red letters, and the sight yanked her right back to reality.

Alex might've knocked her for a loop by going above and beyond to correct his mistake, and he might be hitting sexy out of the park with that flirty little half grin, but she couldn't lose track of what was important, especially not when she had people to feed.

And double especially not with a risk-happy firefighter who didn't take her seriously anyway.

"It's a good start," she said, giving herself one last mental thump before turning toward the walk-in refrigerator. "According to city nutrition guidelines, we've got to offer at least one serving of fruit or vegetables per meal, though, so we'll have to get a little creative to pull this off entirely."

He followed her to the back of the kitchen, reaching out to hold the oversized stainless steel door she'd just popped open. "I take it the tomato sauce doesn't count."

The cool, manufactured air of the walk-in cemented Zoe's thoughts into marching order, although she couldn't quite keep her smile from resurfacing just a little as she stepped all the way inside the frosty space. "I said creative, Alex.

Not crazy. But if we borrow the garnish from tomorrow night's hamburgers and some of the carrots from Saturday's chicken pot pie, we should have just enough ingredients to make a salad." Naked burgers weren't the most appealing thing on the planet, but at least she had ketchup and mustard packets tucked away in the pantry. She'd certainly made do with worse.

"Looks like you've done this kind of shuffle before." Alex reached out for the carton of lettuce Zoe had slid from the metal shelving, hefting it in front of his chest as she turned back to unearth two oversized bags of carrots from the box next to the now-empty slot.

"Most of the people here won't get fruit or vegetables any other way, so I try to put as many natural ingredients into the meals as I can. Produce is expensive, though, and my budget is pretty slim. I have to get creative to make the ingredients last."

His feet kept time with hers, first over the polished steel of the fridge floor, then the clay-colored ceramic tiles as they moved back into the kitchen and regrouped again at the prep table in the center of the room. "I had no idea running a soup kitchen was so involved."

The muscles in Zoe's shoulders unwound from the spot where her apron looped gently behind her neck. She might not be particularly graceful at tackling personal conversations, or okay, even at polite chitchat, but feeding people in a way that mattered? That, she could talk about.

"Once you get past the menu planning and the set number of meals served almost exclusively buffet style, the mechanics of managing a soup kitchen aren't all that much different from running the back of a restaurant," she said, placing the carrots on the table in front of her. "Good planning and solid prep are half the battle."

She opened one of the storage drawers set beneath the top of the prep-table-slash-island, sliding out the small handful of tools she'd need in order to take the salad from concept to reality. Each movement fell neatly into the foundation of the one that had come before it, all of them smoothing the last jagged edges of her morning.

"You ran the kitchen at that restaurant in Washington, DC?" Alex's shock ghosted over his features, and she met it with some holy crap of her own.

"You know about my apprenticeship at Kismet?"

He nodded. "Your father talked about it for two years straight. He said it was a once-in-a-lifetime kind of thing, but I didn't realize you were in charge of the place."

"Oh, I wasn't," Zoe said, trying as deftly as possible to steer the conversation away from her father. She'd just lost the tension in her shoulders, for God's sake. "But after culinary school, I spent two years there, one on the line and one under the head chef. There's a lot of baptism by fire on the restaurant circuit. You learn how to tame the animals pretty quickly, even if you're not running the zoo."

"Yeah, that sounds familiar, actually."

Although Alex's demeanor remained completely neutral, right down to the detached, one-shouldered shrug he'd been giving ever since he'd arrived in her kitchen yesterday morning, the words arrived with just enough scrape to catch Zoe's attention and hold.

He wasn't detached at all. He was displaced. And hell if she didn't know all the lyrics to that song.

"Well, let's get you started, then." The idea launched itself on a direct route from her chest to her mouth, completely bypassing the blast of *bad plan* pumping from her brain. Working in her kitchen clearly wasn't going to change Alex's stance on how to live his life or do his job. But at the very least, she could teach him *something* of value while they were stuck here together.

And knowing how to feed people was the most valuable thing Zoe had.

"Whoa, whoa, whoa," he said, taking a step back from the prep table as if it had suddenly grown a forked tongue and fangs. "I already told you, I can't cook."

"You can, you just won't." Without waiting for a reply, Zoe bent down low to grab an oversized metal mixing bowl from the shelf beside the storage drawers, and how about that. The king of fast talk was actually speechless.

"You think you can dare me into learning how to cook?" Alex's eyes were the only thing that moved, traveling over her in an impenetrable blue stare, but she refused to give in to the clatter behind her sternum. She scooped up the vegetable peeler from the table in front of her, a strange thread of hope uncurling in her belly as she extended it just out of Alex's reach.

"First of all, it's salad, not advanced biochemistry. Secondly, I don't think you're going to learn good kitchen skills any other way, so yeah. I dare you to learn to cook."

For a second, then ten, then sixty, Zoe simply stood there in front of him, with the white noise hum of the walk-in and the waterlogged groan of the dishwasher serving as the background for her heartbeat in her ears. Finally, just when she was about to open her mouth to renege on the whole stupid, impulsive idea—what had she been thinking, shooting her mouth off like a two-dollar pistol, anyway?— Alex smashed the silence between them into bits.

"Fine. It's your kitchen, Gorgeous. Just do me a favor, and be careful what you wish for."

Chapter Six

How the hell Alex had gone from his rote and remote post at the dishwasher to a red-carpet spot in the heart of the kitchen, he had no freaking clue. But somewhere between the sexy-sweet smile Zoe had let slip in the pantry and the chin-up sizzle she'd dished out along with her cooking dare, Alex had taken his eye off his who-cares kitchen mantra for just a second.

And now he was hanging proper with the carrots and the cutlery. He might have saved his job from imminent doom with a little bit of hard work and a whole lot of quick thinking, but all this domestic goodness was a crash and burn just waiting to go down.

Not that Zoe seemed to notice. "Okay. We've only got a few ingredients here, so this shouldn't be too tough. Like I said before, planning and prep are really the foundation, and we've already got the planning done."

Sliding the box she'd pulled from the walk-in to the neutral zone on the table between them, she popped it open with one hand while unloading the leafy green contents with the other. Alex eyeballed the full heads of lettuce, his trepidation growing to a full squeeze in his gut. He didn't have much experience with roughage to begin with—salad was one of those things that tended to stand in the way of the main event, as far as he was concerned—but this stuff was a far cry from the neat little bags of greens all prettied up and ready to go at the grocery store.

He readjusted the threadbare dish towel over his shoulder, finally giving up as he asked, "So if next up is prep, we just what? Ginsu these into pieces and call it a day?"

Okay, so it had probably been a question straight from the stupid file, especially with her cream-of-the-crop training and experience. But Zoe had made it wildly clear that the ingredients she'd cobbled together to round out this meal were at a premium. While looking clueless wasn't on his list of favorite pastimes, it was better than screwing up what little stuff she had left for lunch. He'd just gotten his ass *out* of that sling, thank you very much.

Zoe tilted her head, the tiny gold hoops in her ears glinting in the bright fluorescent kitchen light, and if she was unimpressed with his simple question, she hid it like a champ. "Well, we've got to core these heads of lettuce and run them through the spinner a couple of times to make sure they're good and clean first, but yeah. That's the idea."

"Core them," he said, certain he'd heard her incorrectly. But then she flipped one of the heads of lettuce between her palms, turning it over to reveal the rough, pale brown disk in the center.

"Mmm-hmm. There's a small part right here in the middle that's too fibrous to eat, so it's gotta go before we can get to chopping."

Huh. Guess that's what he got for dodging his greens. "All right, so how do you do that?"

"Well, most people do it the old-fashioned way by using a paring knife, right here around where the stem used to be. But I'm kind of a fan of the shortcut." Turning the head of lettuce sunny side down, she lifted it over the tabletop, pausing for only the briefest of seconds before slamming it into the stainless steel surface.

"Jeez!" A shocked bark of laughter catapulted past his lips, but it was chased quickly by a ripple of surprise as Zoe crooked her thumb and forefinger to pluck a small, Christmas tree–shaped core from inside the ball of leafy greens.

"See? If you hit it just right, you don't need to bother with the slice and dice." She swapped the head of lettuce for one of its uncored counterparts, passing it off to Alex with a no-nonsense smile. "Go ahead and give it a shot."

He paused, but only for a breath as the effect of her smile slipped away in his bloodstream. If tossing around produce was her idea of cooking, he had this in the bag, no problem. Alex brushed his fingers over the soft, tightly packed leaves, bringing the lettuce down over the flat of the counter with a bang. Rolling it over with a confident *I got this* tacked firmly to his face, he reached out to pop the core free and move on to victim number two.

Cue a whole lot of nothing happening.

"Seriously?" he said, stepping back to lift his brows at the undisturbed cone still nestled tight inside the head of greens. Alex tightened his grip on the base of the lettuce core, a frown taking over his mouth as he went to dig that sucker out come hell or high tide. But then Zoe let loose with a deep-bellied laugh, and the sheer, reckless abandon of the sound jammed his irritation to an abrupt halt.

"Don't worry," she said, the lean muscles in her forearms flexing as she motioned for him to rotate the head of lettuce back to its original position. "Every once in a while a stubborn one pops up. The good news is you can try again without hurting anything."

"I suspect you mean other than my pride." Alex flipped the lettuce back between his palms, determined not to be bested by a head of freaking salad greens. Luckily for both him and the produce, the second time was the charm, or at least mostly. After some awkward and not-gentle coaxing, he managed to maneuver the core free with a soft snap, and okay. This kitchen thing wasn't so bad.

"So, I have a question." Zoe didn't look up from the pile of carrots she'd just amassed next to the scuffed white cutting board in front of her, but despite her obvious concentration on the food, Alex felt certain she had a metaphorical eye on him and an ear on his answer, besides.

"Shoot."

"Why would you jump out of a perfectly functional airplane?"

Oookay. Talk about something he hadn't been expecting. Still, the answer was a total no-brainer, so he said, "Because I can. Life's too short to ask why."

"I'd imagine life becomes drastically shorter if you're prone to doing things as insane as skydiving." She picked up a carrot, sliding the peeler over its surface with a brisk *snick snick snick,* but oh no. No way was he going to let her pin one of his favorite pastimes with the crazy flag just because she had a thing for too much caution.

"I don't go without a parachute, Zoe. Anyway, it's stuff like skydiving that lets you know you're really living."

A soft snort crossed her lips, but the glint of curiosity on her pixie face gave her away. "How does risking imminent death make you feel alive?"

"Because the rush is the best way to live in the moment, and it's a hell of a lot better than walking around saying 'someday,' or worse yet, having regrets when your time runs out. Anyway, skydiving isn't as risky as you think." He held up a hand to quell the not-so-soft counterpart to the snort she'd given a second ago, and to his surprise, she conceded. "Yes, it's an extreme sport, but first of all, you've got a statistically greater chance of being struck by lightning than dying in a skydiving accident. Secondly, it's not as if they just strap a parachute to your back, slap you on the shoulder, and say good luck as they toss you from the plane. There's a lot more to a jump than that."

"Hmph." The rasp of the peeler and the intermittent *bang* of lettuce to countertop filled the quiet between them, and for a minute, Alex thought she might not bite. But then Zoe tilted her head, the thread of bold curiosity making a repeat appearance in her eyes as she said, "Like what?" and ha! He had her.

"Well, the first bunch of times you jump, you have to go tandem with an instructor, who's literally strapped to your back. He's in charge of getting you out of the plane at the right time, pulling the cord for the chute . . . pretty much the only thing you get to do is go along for the ride."

Her brows furrowed into a *V* over her doubtful stare. God, she was going to be a tough nut to crack. "I suppose that would cut back on rookie mistakes somewhat. But you're still jumping out of the airplane at what . . . ?"

He grinned, halfway to a hard-on just thinking about it. "Thirteen thousand feet."

The vegetable peeler hit the countertop with a clatter. "You're serious."

"Sugarcoating isn't my thing," he reminded her, placing the last head of lettuce on the worktable with a shrug. "You have to go up pretty high if you want enough time for the instructor to pull the cord so the parachute works its magic, so yeah. Thirteen K is about average for a good run."

"I don't suppose you can have the guy pull the cord before your feet leave the ground," Zoe said, her tone strongly suggesting she was half joking at best.

"No, but you can have him walk you through about four hours of training before you're allowed on the airplane the first time. In fact, it's required."

"Really?" A different sort of disbelief flickered over her features, lighting her pretty brown eyes with genuine surprise rather than sharp-edged doubt, and the shift triggered a memory, lodged deep and barely touched, from his brain. That same stare, brimming with heat and brash intentions, as they'd bumped into each other on the semi-wooded path connecting Fairview's park pavilion to the open fields where the FFD held their annual barbecue. The way he'd innocently tried to help her untangle an errant strand of hair from one of her dangly gold earrings, and the way she'd not-so-innocently reached up to wrap her fingers around his.

"You know what I think, Alex Donovan? I think you should kiss me."

Christ. He really should fork over a neat one- or two-word answer to be polite and just get on with assembling the rabbit food. Zoe was the walking, talking epitome of off-limits, and anyway, he didn't need any comfort in her kitchen. No, what Alex needed was to shut his cake trap and be on his merry, salad-making, community-service-fulfilling way.

So of course, he didn't.

"Being reckless isn't the same as being stupid," he said, letting the thin thread of curiosity on Zoe's face dare him close enough to watch her lashes fan up into a honey-colored arc. "While I can't lie and say I've ever met an adrenaline high I didn't like, I'm not interested in becoming finger paint, either. So yes, I like to jump out of airplanes. In fact, I like it a lot. But there are guidelines, and I follow them every time I jump."

"Oh." Zoe blinked twice, her breath sliding in on an audible inhale as she opened one of the drawers beneath the island, unearthing a flat, rectangular carrying case. "So, um, the instructor guy has a lot of experience then?"

Alex watched as she freed the zipper rimming the edge of the bright red nylon, revealing a set of flawlessly gleaming kitchen knives. His own curiosity popped like a campfire over dry kindling, but he stuffed it back and stuck to the topic. "Kyle—the instructor I went with before I got my solo certification—he jumps a lot, yeah."

"Okay," she said, handing him a five-gallon bucket with a weird, plastic insert inside that looked like a widely-woven basket. "Define a lot."

He bit back a chuckle. It figured Zoe would want a concrete measurement like a number. "Last time I checked I think he was at nine thousand something."

Her chin jacked upward, hands stilling over the polished black knife handles. "Oh my God, he's not a skydiving instructor. He's a career lunatic," she breathed, realization filtering across her face in slow motion. "Wait . . . how many times have you gone?"

Alex's smile tasted way better than it should, but he let it take control of his mouth all the same. "Twenty-nine."

"You do realize that's deranged."

"And yet still a far cry from nine thousand."

"I think we're going to have to agree to disagree," Zoe said, and although the unyielding line of her spine backed up all the *no way* in her affirmation, her lips curled just enough to put a mostly playful spin on the words. She slid a knife from one of the reinforced pouches sewn into the case she'd propped open over the countertop, and despite the fact that the thing looked menacing enough to belong on the set of a horror movie, she palmed the handle with obvious ease. Sliding over to the cutting board, she sank the blade into the first bunch of lettuce with a *crunch*, her hands becoming a blur of fluid motion as she made quick work of chopping each section into tidy pieces.

The ridge of her shoulders, normally set in firm determination, loosened beneath the softly edged neckline of her shirt, and the wisps of hair that had broken free from her high ponytail did nothing to scale back on the surprisingly wide-open vibe suddenly pouring off her. She repeated the process with each head of lettuce, sending the curiosity in

Alex's gut into comeback mode and the words spilling right out of his mouth.

"Okay, so it's my turn in the question department."

Zoe motioned him forward, scooping the now-chopped lettuce into the plastic container he still held between his palms. "Go for it, although if you're looking for something bold and daring, you're probably not going to find it in my wheelhouse."

"Actually, I beg to differ," Alex said, but before she could translate the shock on her face to an actual, out-loud protest, he asked, "Clearly, this kitchen means a lot to you. If you didn't think I was going to come through with fixing the mess in the pantry, why did you give me a second chance this morning?"

She gripped the lid to the container, her knuckles blanching to match the shiny white plastic. But rather than back down from his straight-up candor the way most people normally did, Zoe lifted her shoulders into a shrug and answered. "I figured you'd either fumble the job and then I'd cut you loose, or you'd manage to pull enough out of your hat to earn the chance to stick around, for now at least. Seemed like kind of a win-win considering the circumstances."

"But it was still a chance you didn't have to take, especially since you're so down on the idea of my being here anyway." Alex put the container full of lettuce on the counter at his hip. He measured Zoe with a sidelong glance, and fuck it. No sense in pretending that decorum was anywhere in his batch files. "Speaking of which, why is that? I mean, I get that I screwed up yesterday's delivery, but you haven't wanted me here from the word go, and it's clear you need the hands. So tell me . . ." He took the lid from her fingers, putting it on the counter and closing the resulting gap until only mere inches stood between them. "Why don't you want me in your kitchen?"

"Because everything about you is a risk," she said, her voice just a notch above a whisper even though her tone was bedrock firm. "Fifty bucks says you're so stuck in the shoot-first-ask-questions-later habits that landed you here that you're not going to be anything other than a huge problem in my kitchen."

Alex's defenses uncurled in his belly, low and hot, like the first few flames of a brush fire jumping to life. "Those habits happen to make me a good firefighter. The kind who saves lives."

But Zoe shook her head, ruffling the loose strands of hair around her face. "Not for the next four weeks they don't."

His molars went on lockdown, with barely enough room for his words to escape. "I don't need a reminder, Gorgeous."

"Don't call me that." Zoe's eyes glittered with high-octane emotion at the same time her cheeks flushed a dark, sexy pink, and Alex would've been shocked if he wasn't so busy being turned on from his brain to his balls.

"Why not?"

"Because." Her ripe-cherry mouth pressed into a thin line. "You're already not taking me or anything else about this placement seriously. I don't need you to make fun of me on top of it."

Alex's gaze traveled the length of her, from the crown of her honey-blond head to the provocative swell of cleavage peeking up from the *V* of her shirt, lowering still to the matching flare of her sweet, sinful hips, and his words grated up from the darkest part of his chest.

"And what if I'm not making fun of you?"

Zoe paused, her pupils dilating enough to darken her stare to a deep, chocolate brown despite the harsh fluorescent lights overhead. For a bare fragment of a second, she tipped her chin toward him, just enough to reveal the wild flutter of the pulse point where her neck sloped into her shoulder. But then she snapped to attention, as if her spine had suddenly discovered it was made of triple-reinforced titanium, and the molten heat in her eyes morphed into cool determination.

"You're not going to flirt your way into my good graces, Donovan. Your reputation and your recklessness are written all over your résumé. Feeding these people is important, and there's no room for your brand of risk-taking in my kitchen, period."

"I'm not completely incapable of following the rules." Hadn't he just proved it by telling her about all those safety regs for skydiving? There had to be dozens of them, for Chrissake, and he followed every one, down to the last syllable.

Zoe scooped up the container holding the lettuce, handing it back to him with the kind of polite smile reserved for your least favorite ex and door-to-door salesmen. "Right. And I'm not completely incapable of taking risks, as you already pointed out."

Alex followed her over to the food prep sink at the back of the kitchen, lettuce in tow. "A little honest to God risk-taking wouldn't hurt you, you know."

He hesitated while an idea took root in his head, his heartbeat kicking against his ribs as the notion grew. He knew—he *knew* this was a bad plan, born of all sorts of self-preserving, fast-talking, bad-plan things. But the image of Zoe's face, caught up in the momentary burst of both curiosity and daring possibility as she'd asked him about skydiving, flashed across his mind's eye, and all of a sudden, Alex was done thinking.

He placed the container on the ledge next to the sink, serving up his cockiest grin. This was either going to be brilliant or it was going to blow up in his face like his own personal Armageddon. But he had nothing to lose except time, and anyway, finding out what Zoe Westin was really made of?

Yeah. Worth every inch of the risk.

"As a matter of fact, let's brass these tacks once and for all," he said, his words carving a hot path out of his mouth. He reached out, slipping the detachable nozzle for the faucet sprayer from Zoe's fingers, and her corresponding laughter popped out on a gasp.

"What are you talking about?"

Alex returned the nozzle to its housing with a *click*, turning to look her right in the eye. "I'm talking about a deal. I'll play by the rules in your kitchen, right down to learning how to cook, for the next four weeks . . . *if* you spend one day doing something risky with me and end up truly hating it."

Zoe's brows slid together, her face marked with more doubt than deep thought. "How do you know I won't just tell you I hate it no matter what?"

"I don't. But you were true to your word this morning when you let me stick around, so if I was a betting man— and it just so happens I am—I'd be willing to take a flyer and say I think you're a pretty honest woman."

For a minute, she said nothing, but then she broke the silence with, "You're willing to risk four entire weeks of following the rules without complaint, all on the microscopic chance that I won't hate whatever risky endeavor you throw in my direction?"

Oh. Hell. Yes. "Absolutely. If you give me your word you'll be honest, I'll give you mine that I'll follow through if you really, truly hate being reckless. All you have to do is trust me—*really* trust me—for just one day."

Her eyes narrowed, and holy shit, she was thinking about it. "And what is it we'll be doing, exactly?"

"Something a little risky," Alex said, his pulse quickening at her obvious shock even though he'd fully expected her reaction.

"You're not going to tell me?"

"That would be the first risk."

Zoe's titanium spine grew a matching facial expression. "I'm not going skydiving, Alex."

Ah hell. He wanted to challenge her, not chase her off. "And based on our earlier conversation, I wouldn't ask you to. No skydiving," he agreed. "But for the rest, you're going to have to trust me."

Alex leaned in, close enough to breathe in the brisk citrus scent of her hair, and the combination of sweet versus tart shot straight to his gut as he said, "So what's it going to be, Gorgeous? Are you in, or are you out?"

Chapter Seven

Zoe traced the bright red Scarlett's Diner logo on the menu in front of her with one finger, her eyes making an obligatory scan of the breakfast options even though she hadn't changed her usual order in over a decade. Clacking the menu shut, she let her gaze wander through the sun-filled window at her elbow, taking in the post rush-hour bustle as she slowly gathered her resolve. These Friday morning breakfast dates with her father, where they exchanged pleasantries and danced artfully around the twin elephants in the room named Divorce and Disapproval, were really bad enough. But today she had to contend with the ridiculous arrangement she'd made with Alex, too, and honestly, all the fortitude in the galaxy might not get her through the double header.

Who the hell had been in charge of her mouth when she'd impulsively blurted "fine" in response to his risk-reward challenge, Zoe had no idea. But the promise of Alex's much needed help sans his reckless, who-cares attitude had been all too appealing, and one eight-hour chunk of her life had seemed like a smart trade-off for four weeks of slow and steady work that she wouldn't have to pry out of him or worry about at every turn.

Even if she was one million percent certain she'd spend all of her day with him regretting it.

"Morning, Zoe. Can I get you some coffee?"

Zoe straightened against the red leather banquette at her back, knocking herself back to the here and now. Sara Martin, who had been waiting tables at Scarlett's since she and Zoe had been in high school together, held up a pot of the diner's city-famous brew, and Zoe's mouth watered in a way that would make Pavlov beam with pride.

"Oh God, yes. Please." Zoe flipped the white ceramic mug in front of her to a right side up position, nudging it across the patterned Formica to put it in Sara's reach. If anything could jump-start her in the right direction, Scarlett's coffee definitely topped the list.

"So how's it going over there at Hope House?" Sara's brown ponytail slid over her shoulder as she leaned in to fill Zoe's cup with just enough room to accommodate the healthy splash of cream Zoe favored. Although they'd spoken more words in the three months Zoe had been back than they had in all four years of high school combined, Zoe worked up an optimistic smile. Sara's steel-toed crowd might've scared her ten years ago, and the woman might still be a little rough around the borders, but Zoe had learned a lot about judging people from the so-called wrong side of Fairview since high school.

"We're getting there," she said. "There's still only enough funding for us to run five days a week, but last month we were able to add hot breakfast on a limited basis, so it's a step in the right direction."

Zoe hated not being able to feed the shelter residents three square meals, seven days a week, but limited five-day service had been her only option since they'd opened the soup kitchen's doors. What wasn't an option, however, was going back-to-back days without offering any kind of food service, especially when the meals at the soup kitchen were often the only thing the residents had to eat. With Friday being payday for most people—as meager as it might be for Hope House's residents—it seemed the best day to close the kitchen in favor of having breakfast and lunch service on Saturdays.

Sara nodded, just a quick tip of her chin. "Well, I think it's cool you're able to feed so many people, although with all that experience you've got, I bet you don't hate the cooking."

"I don't hate the cooking," Zoe agreed, selecting her words with care. Might as well warm up for the dance and defend she was about to have with her father. But, God, even though Fairview wasn't a small city by any means, everybody sure was on a first name basis with what Zoe had left behind in DC.

"Nice to do what you love," Sara murmured, dropping her gaze to the Formica as she gestured to the empty coffee cup across from Zoe. "Let me go ahead and fill that for your dad."

"Oh, but he's not . . ." Zoe shifted her sights from the woman in front of her to the main entrance of the diner, a ribbon of surprise uncurling in her belly at the sight of her father making his way past the brightly stenciled plate glass.

"Wow." Zoe flipped the mug and slid it across the table-top with a soft *shush*. "Your head is on one hell of a swivel."

"Keeps me honest." Sara lifted one shoulder beneath her bright red T-shirt. She filled the empty coffee cup, stepping back from the table at the exact moment Zoe's father appeared at her side.

"Morning, Captain. Can I get you anything else to drink today?"

Zoe's father smiled, the move showcasing a set of wrinkles around his eyes that were a relatively recent acquisition.

"No, thanks, Sara, although you can go ahead and put me down for the usual for breakfast. I'm starving."

"You got it. Zoe, you going for your usual, too?"

No point in knocking a good, reliable meal, and anyway, she needed all the energy she could get today. "Yes, please."

Sara nodded and angled herself back toward the long stretch of counter space that led to the pass-through to Scarlett's kitchen. "One breakfast special, eggs over easy, bacon crisp, hash browns on the side, and one veggie egg white omelet, extra green peppers, no onions, cheddar cheese, coming right up."

"Thanks." The smile Zoe's father gave Sara in parting became decidedly more difficult to decipher as he turned it on Zoe in greeting, gesturing to the booth she'd chosen in the intersection of the L-shaped diner before sitting down across from her. "Still opting for the best seat in the house, I see."

"I never sit with my back to the door. You taught me that when I was twelve." Along with how to catalogue all the exits in a building, how to estimate the number of steps to get to said exits, and how to determine which one was most viable for a safe escape in an emergency. After all, you could take the man out of the firehouse, but taking the firehouse out of the man? Not even Saint Anthony could pull off that miracle.

Her father straightened the cuffs of his dark brown canvas jacket, lifting a brow as he wrapped his hands around the cup of coffee Sara had left on the table. "Well, I suppose it's good to see you haven't lost *all* regard for your safety."

Great. Looked like they were going to bypass well-mannered conversation and jump right in to the disapproval portion of the morning. Not that her father would actually cave and express his emotions directly so they could actually talk about them. God, all this bobbing and weaving was enough to drive a woman bat-shit crazy.

Zoe sighed. "I'm not a little girl anymore, Dad."

"No, you're not," her father said, his voice remaining perfectly level despite the taut line of his jaw that said his molars had just gone tighter than Fort Knox on lockdown. "You're a woman—a pretty woman—who puts in all sorts of odd hours in a terrible neighborhood. You're also my daughter. As much as you might hate it, I'm not going to apologize for not liking your job or worrying about your welfare."

Her hands tightened to fists over the paper napkin in her lap, although she regulated her voice to its calmest setting to match her father's. "And as much as *you* might hate it, I'm not going to apologize for running the kitchen at Hope House. Look, I get that you're disappointed I left Kismet." She stopped, letting the serrated pang of his disapproval stick into her for a second before pulling up her chin to soldier past it. "But feeding people is what I do, and nobody needs it more than the people at the shelter. Anyway, it's not as if I'm putting *my* life on the line every time I go to work just because Hope House is in a poor neighborhood."

Her father didn't flinch at the unspoken implication—not that she'd expected him to. God, this conversation could probably have itself, they'd been through it so many times, which was pretty ironic considering he never actually expressed his feelings in anything other than gruff one-liners and heavy innuendo that reeked of disappointment.

Her father let out a breath, although the ladder of his spine stood firm against the well-cushioned banquette. "I don't want to have another argument with you, Zoe. Can't we just have breakfast together, please?"

She paused. While standing her ground over her work at Hope House was and always had been priority number one, trying to get her father to understand her career change was like shouting into the wind. After three months of her best efforts, all she had was a sore throat and even sorer pride, and she'd sure as hell come by her stubborn streak honestly.

If they weren't going to see eye to eye, the least they could do was share a good, hot meal. Especially since he'd said he was hungry.

"Okay," she said, releasing her breath on a slow exhale. She examined her father more closely across the table, her eyes purposely avoiding the six-inch swath of scar tissue on his neck while taking in his leaner-than-usual frame and the slashes of dark shadow beneath both eyes. "Speaking of having a meal, you look a little worn out. Are you eating enough?"

"I thought it was my job to look out for you. When did we switch roles?" he asked, and although she eked out a barely there smile at the hint of humor in his non-answer, no way was she letting him off the hook.

"At about the same time you started dodging my questions. Seriously, Dad, when was the last time you had a good meal and some decent sleep?"

"I've been a little busy juggling things at work. I know how you feel about the department." Her father held up a hand, probably to stave off the frown fitting itself to Zoe's mouth. "But I'm down a man on Engine for four weeks, and that means I've got to fill a lot of holes in the schedule. It's only temporary, but it's still a pain."

"Boy, don't I know it." Zoe realized a fraction too late that she'd let the words slip out, and damn it, there was no possible scenario involving Alex Donovan that didn't turn her normally unflagging composure into tapioca. But the last thing she wanted was to bring Alex into the mix of an already precarious conversation, so she dove headfirst into a redirect. "Well, even if you're working overtime, you still should eat. And before you argue, those microwave meal-sicle dinners don't count as food. I'm tinkering with some new recipes on Sunday. I'll bring you a few things to keep on hand so you don't go hungry."

"You don't need to take care of me," her father said, clipping out the words just hard enough to make them sharp around the edges. He took a breath, audible and slow, to smooth out the rest. "I'm not a charity case just because your mother and I are no longer married."

An odd emotion Zoe couldn't pin down glinted in his stare like ice cubes in whiskey, and despite the fact that they'd just called a temporary cease-fire, her own emotions came scraping up from where she'd stuffed them behind her breastbone. "I do if you're not going to take care of yourself. And I don't need a reminder that you and Mom are no longer married."

Her father sat completely unmoving even though every muscle in his body went bowstring tight, and Zoe's heart gave a stiff twist as she braced herself to blow past the pleasantries and finally, *finally* air out all the laundry that had been spin-cycling between them ever since her parents had separated last year.

But then Sara arrived with their breakfast plates stacked halfway up her forearms, and by the time she'd delivered the food, whatever reply the captain had intended to launch—along with the strange emotion flashing in his eyes—had cooled right back down to unreadable, impenetrable, and totally silent business as usual.

One hour, two cups of coffee, and three overstarched topics of conversation later, Zoe planted a cool parting kiss on her father's cheek and dropped into the driver's seat of her tried-and-true Prius. While breakfast hadn't exactly been a stroll on the beach, the fact that she'd escaped mostly unscathed gave her hope for the rest of the day.

If only round two wasn't going to be even more difficult to maneuver than a healthy dose of parental disdain.

Making sure her hands-free device was set and ready to go on the polished black dashboard, Zoe popped her iPhone into the waiting dock, tapping her way through the screens to get to her navigation app. She'd only been gone for five years, but downtown Fairview was big enough to make piloting the mostly urban streets a chore, plus the place had seen enough growth spurts in her absence to make her eager for the backup. Alex had stayed true to his promise of remaining completely mum about his plans for their day, to the point that the only advance notice he'd given was that she should wear comfortable clothes she didn't mind sweating in. He hadn't even given her the location for their meet-up until they'd been on their way out of Hope House after last night's dinner shift.

Of course, the address hadn't been immediately familiar. So of course, she'd Googled it.

And of course, other than a grainy aerial photograph of about three city blocks' worth of real estate, she'd come up completely empty.

"Okay. Four-sixty-six Edgewood Avenue," Zoe murmured, forcing the traitorous tremble in her fingers into submission as she hit the green icon marked Go with the pad of her thumb. At least once she got there—wherever there was—she'd know what sort of reckless crash project she was up against. And more importantly, how to manage it.

She recognized the path through scenic downtown Fairview well enough, even after she'd exchanged the familiarity of Scarlett's location on Church Street for about ten minutes of city driving. Confusion combined with the anticipation already pushing a steady course through her veins, thrumming over her skin in a low prickle as she crossed the threshold of one of Fairview's oldest and quietest urban neighborhoods. The automated voice of her

GPS guided her through a maze of neatly kept streets lined with classically understated row homes, and wait . . . this had to be a mistake.

"*You have reached . . . your destination . . . on the right.*"

Zoe pulled over to the curb, alternating her stare between the tidy, brick-faced brownstone outside her passenger window and the GPS display on her phone. The brass numbers on the plate next to the gleaming black door read 466, and she double-, then triple-checked the piece of paper Alex had given her last night at the soup kitchen before quieting the Prius's engine and exiting the car for a better look.

Why the hell did a young, single, impulsive-to-the-teeth firefighter want to meet her for Mission: Adrenaline in one of the most family-oriented neighborhoods in Fairview?

"Hey. I was starting to think you got lost." The masculine rumble of Alex's voice shot through Zoe's blood with twin helpings of mischief and pure sex, and oh, God, she'd seriously miscalculated how much fortitude she was going to need to get through this day.

She unfolded her spine to its full height, turning toward the spot where he'd appeared in the open door frame of the ground-level garage. "Maybe I was thinking of standing you up," she replied, and okay, yeah. Meeting his boldness with some of her own couldn't be that bad a plan.

Except of course, Alex called her bluff. "No you weren't." He lifted a sturdy backpack from a nearby shelf in the garage, the hard contour of his shoulders flexing and pulling beneath the snug material of his compression gear T-shirt.

Zoe's throat worked over a tight swallow. "No?"

"No. You want the chance to get me to follow the rules too badly. Plus, you said you'd be here, and you don't ditch out on your word."

Nothing she could argue there. Unfortunately. "Clearly, I need a better game face," she said, but Alex just laughed.

"I believe in honesty, remember? A game face only covers up what's real. And you're going to need to be up-front with what you're feeling today if you want to get anything out of what we're going to do."

"Speaking of which . . ." Zoe extended one arm in a sweeping gesture to encompass both the brownstone in front of her and the wide ribbon of concrete sidewalk leading up the sun-strewn avenue. "Something tells me you and I aren't going to take a scenic tour of the real estate and call it daring. What are we doing here?"

"We're joining forces." Alex swung the backpack all the way up over one shoulder, and seriously, couldn't he at least have chosen a shirt that didn't showcase *all* of his damn muscles? "I figured if I told you where to meet me directly, it would ruin the surprise. Anyway, we need some equipment for what I've got planned, and it'll be easier to transport it in your car than on the back of my bike. That is, unless you want to go for a ride."

He tipped his head at the single-bay garage behind him, his gaze cutting a path toward the same sleek red and black motorcycle Zoe had seen him ride into the sunset last night, and realization crashed into her like a brick on a one-way trip through plate glass.

"Wait . . . you live here? As in, this is your house?"

He had to be messing with her. There were daffodils and crocuses sprouting from the small rectangular plot by the front doorstep, for God's sake. No way did Alex Donovan, with his predisposition for air travel the hard way and the most lax impulse control in town *live* here. In suburbia.

Was that a lady with a jogging stroller he'd just waved to across the street?

Alex flipped a set of keys over in his palm, the metallic jingle bringing Zoe just far enough out of her shock to catch the nothing-doing expression that went with the gesture.

"That's what the mailbox says. So do you want to drive, or should we take the bike for a spin?"

"Yes. No. I mean . . ." She blew out a breath, praying her idiocy would dissipate along with the carbon dioxide. "I don't mind driving. I'll pass on the motorcycle."

His expression broadcast his complete lack of surprise, although all he said as he grinned and entered the key code to close the garage door was, "Maybe next time."

Zoe bit back the temptation to tell him that today's outing would definitely be a one and done. She didn't doubt the conviction—in fact, with the nerves jangling through her belly right now, she was more certain than ever that today was likely to obliterate her comfort zone to the point that she'd never hit the Repeat button. But Alex was cocky enough all by himself. The last thing she needed was to toss out anything he could construe as a dare. Not unless Zoe wanted him to follow through on the challenge or die trying.

She popped the locks on the Prius, sliding into the driver's seat to refit her iPhone back to the dock on the dashboard. "Okay, so where to?"

"Do you ever go anywhere without a game plan?" Alex asked, placing the backpack firmly behind the driver's seat before situating himself next to her.

Although a smile tilted his mouth as he asked the question, his tone asked for an honest answer, so Zoe said, "Not really, no. I like to be prepared."

"I'll keep that in mind." He pressed himself forward, tapping an address into her GPS app with a few easy flicks of his wrists.

"Do you ever do anything *with* a plan?" She dropped a surreptitious glance at her phone's display before putting the car in gear and starting to drive. At least they were only a handful of minutes from whatever lay beneath the green

End icon. Being in the dark was threatening to send her over the edge.

"Sure. I planned this."

"But not the bet that got you into it."

"No," Alex said, although not before his hesitation told Zoe she'd hit home. "But some of the best things happen when you don't have a road map for them. And anyway, I didn't need much foresight for this bet, since I know I'm not going to lose."

Zoe's laughter popped out despite her efforts to cage it. "You do remember the stipulations of this bet, right? I have to actually enjoy myself in order for you to win."

"Mmm-hmm." He stretched all the way out against the backrest of the passenger seat, the long frame of his body completely relaxed beneath his workout gear. "I remember."

"You seem awfully sure of yourself." God, his body language practically radiated self-assurance from every leanly sculpted, magazine-perfect muscle.

"You say that like there's another way to be." He shifted against the passenger seat, angling both his body and his gaze toward her, and even though Zoe kept her eyes fixed firmly to the road, she felt the weight of his bright blue stare like an unmistakable touch.

Whoa.

She readjusted her grip on the steering wheel along with her mutinous libido. "I'm not saying there's anything wrong with confidence. After all, I never would've made it through five minutes of culinary school without at least a little ego. But when you cross the borders of arrogance, it tends to get you burned, both in the kitchen and out."

Alex let out a huff of surprise. "I never thought of chefs as a ballsy bunch."

"Oh, God. They're even worse than firefighters." She

clamped down on her bottom lip just a fraction too late as a wash of heat crept over her cheeks. "No offense."

"Zoe, please," Alex said, and if he took even the slightest insult from her blip in decorum, it sure didn't ring through in his voice. "You'll have to work up a hell of a lot more than that to offend me, and it's not as if you're wrong about most firefighters being pretty cocky. I just didn't realize chefs were that bad, too."

She guided the Prius through a couple of back-to-back turns, bringing them closer to the portion of Fairview that boasted a lot of restaurants and commercial storefronts, before she answered. "They're not *bad,* per se. Most of the chefs I trained under were unbelievably talented. But they also had a metric ton of hubris, and none of them was afraid to sling it around. All that posturing and tenacity just made it a little tough to concentrate on what's important."

"I don't know. I've seen how you run your kitchen. You seem pretty tenacious to me," he said, and she caught his grin out of the corner of her eye as he added, "No offense."

God, she supposed she'd earned that one. "None taken," Zoe laughed. "But there's a big difference between being confident and taking cocky risks that make you reckless."

"That may be true," Alex said at the same moment her GPS signaled the final turnoff on the navigation screen. "But you might want to trade in a little of one for the other, at least for today. We're here."

Confusion filtered through Zoe's brain. She leaned forward, her seat belt digging into her shoulder as she squinted through the windshield at the row of nondescript buildings beyond.

Quick-Clean Dry Cleaners . . . Milton's Auto Body . . . Miss Marie's Bakery and Sweet Shop . . .

"But there's nothing—"

Zoe's gaze hooked on the red and white sign over the door of the last building in the row, her breath jamming to a hard stop in her lungs.

No way. No. Way. He was out of his freaking *mind*.

Alex pinned her with the full measure of his stop-traffic smile. "Maybe a little bit," he said, and only then did Zoe realize she must've spoken the words out loud. "But a bet's a bet. Which means that if you want to win, you're gonna have to be crazy right along with me."

Chapter Eight

Alex sat back against the passenger seat of Zoe's Prius, watching her expression morph from disbelief to discomfort in about two seconds flat.

"Rock climbing?" She sent a pointed stare at the sign reading FAIRVIEW VERTICAL CLIMB before turning her liquid copper gaze back to his. "You promised my feet would stay on the ground."

He should've figured Zoe would be tough enough to push back a little. After all, climbing certainly couldn't be anywhere near her straight and narrow repertoire. "I promised we wouldn't go skydiving," he corrected, giving her a minute to replay their conversation from the other day in her memory before continuing. "I never said anything about your feet."

She exhaled, crossing her arms over the front of her oversized dark gray hoodie. "Okay, but this isn't going to work. I've never been rock climbing before."

"Lucky for you, I have." Hooking his fingers beneath the car's interior door handle, he made quick work of getting out and retrieving his gear from the backseat. Although Zoe didn't rush to make her feet keep time with his on the pavement, she didn't leave his ass in the dust by running the other way either, so for right now, he'd call it a win.

"How am I supposed to be daring and risky if I don't even know how to get three feet off the ground?" she asked from a few paces away, and he scaled back on his stride until she fell into step next to him. Damn, getting her relaxed enough to enjoy their climb was going to be a tall order with how she was all buttoned up tight enough to bust a seam. But he'd worked with worse, and anyway, there wasn't a whole lot he loved more than a really good challenge.

Alex stopped just shy of Vertical Climb's front door, glancing up at the six-story building before shifting to look Zoe right in the eye. "Oh, you'll be taking plenty of risks. Because not only are you going to learn how to climb," he said. "But you're going to trust me to teach you."

Her lips parted into a pretty, pink *O* before pressing back into a flat line. "I suppose you're some kind of expert."

"You could say that." He pulled his employee badge from the side pocket of his backpack, palming the door handle to usher a shell-shocked Zoe inside the lobby. "Hey, Joss," he said, tipping his chin at the tall, willowy blonde sorting rental equipment behind the counter. "This is Zoe. She and I have a one-on-one. I put it on the schedule a couple of days ago."

Jocelyn pushed back from the counter, her eyes brightening with enough interest to tell him he'd get the full court press over this later. "Hi, Zoe. Kyle's waiting for you two by the north wall." She aimed a catlike smile at Alex before tacking on, "He says to tell you that you owe him."

Alex laughed, the anticipation of both the climb and winning this bet with Zoe starting to hum through his veins. "That might work if he didn't already owe me. That birthday party full of ten-year-olds last weekend was brutal."

"Yeah, you looked like you just hated it, with all the

cheering and high fives you were dishing out." Jocelyn gave her eyes a playful roll before turning her smile back to Zoe. "You're in great hands. Have fun climbing."

"Thanks," Zoe said, waiting until Alex had led her down the hall and out of earshot before turning to look at him. "You're a rock-climbing instructor?"

"Lots of firefighters have second jobs. I spent so much of my downtime here that Jocelyn suggested I get certified as an instructor, so a couple of years ago I did. I fill in whenever I can when I'm not on shift at Eight."

"Yeah, she certainly seemed happy to see you." A wash of pink crept over Zoe's cheeks, and even though Alex knew he shouldn't mess with her, he stopped short to face her anyway.

"Let's just say I'm not Jocelyn's type. Although I'm pretty sure she was happy to see *you*."

Zoe blinked a few times in quick succession, and then bingo. Her blush went for broke. "Oh. *Oh.* I'm sorry. I just assumed you two were . . . um . . ."

Ah, hell. If he didn't let her off the hook, she was liable to start a fire with the flush on her face. "Nah. Even if Joss wasn't gay, she's still my boss. I don't mix business with that kind of pleasure. And speaking of pleasure"—he reached out to open the door leading to the main climbing room, gesturing Zoe inside with a quick jerk of his head—"we should probably get started."

Her cross-trainers shushed over the compact rubber sports matting that covered the subfloor beneath, and she stopped just past the threshold of the large, high-ceilinged space. The climbing room was empty of people, but that wasn't necessarily a huge shock or concern. Kyle was probably in the back, grabbing the gear they'd need to get this party started, and other than the classes they held over the summer and the occasional weekend warrior playing hooky from work a day early, Fridays at Vertical Climb were usually pretty quiet.

Fine by him. More room to spread out and enjoy the top of the boards that way.

Alex watched as Zoe examined the walls, with their black matte background and healthy explosion of rainbow-colored hand and footholds that made the place look like a challenge athlete's Jackson Pollock. The free-standing tower, and Alex's personal favorite as far as bad-ass climbing went, stood off to the south side, where it connected into the ceiling at sharper pitches and angles than the far less advanced northern wall. His pulse jumped in his veins, the familiar tingle of adrenaline heating him up from his blood to his balls at the thought of anchoring in and getting vertical.

"So I guess that's half the risk, isn't it?" Zoe asked, giving the tower one last hard look before turning toward him. "Not just being here with you and doing something risky, but having to rely on you to teach me the ropes."

"Yup," Alex said, and the way her pupils darkened her stare as he fired off his no-bullshit answer felt better than it should. "That's the deal. You get a little reckless and let me teach you how to rock climb. If you don't hate it, I win. But if you do . . ." He paused, watching her eyes glitter darker still as he added, "Then I'm yours in the kitchen, and I'll let you teach me how to cook."

"Fine," Zoe breathed, her voice at odds with the conviction of the word she'd just let out. "Let's get this over with." She pivoted on one heel to head farther into the room, but something dark and forbidden and totally delicious made him snap up her hand just shy of movement.

"Uh-uh, Gorgeous." Alex cupped her knuckles against his palm, shock working through him at the strength in her fingers as she reflexively wrapped them around his in return. "Fair's fair. You don't like it when I don't give your kitchen an honest shake. The least I can ask is that you head into this with an open mind."

Her eyes traveled up the sixty-foot expanse of the main climbing area, fingers tensing even harder as her gaze neared the top of the south wall, with its jutting overhangs and expertly placed, hard to reach and harder to hold on to hand and footholds. "Sure," she said, even though she looked anything but. "Because that's not going to be one hell of a trick."

Alex paused, his brows pulling tight with confusion. Zoe was batting a thousand on both showing up and following through so far, and it wasn't as if she was short on determination. Clearly, she wanted to win this bet. So why would she get right up to the starting line only to balk? Unless . . .

His eyes traveled upward at the same time his gut took a nonstop trip in the opposite direction. Damn it. *Damn it.* He'd been so gung-ho to get to the forest that he hadn't seen the one tree that might hang him.

"You're afraid of heights, aren't you?"

"No." Her mouth cranked shut too hard and too fast for it not to be a lie, and she exhaled in defeat. "Okay, maybe. A little. Or, you know, a lot."

"Jesus, Zoe." He let go of her hand in favor of stepping in toward her. "How come you didn't say anything?"

"Because I didn't think it would matter. You said no sky-diving, and even though I knew you'd still pick something crazy, I figured we'd stay at ground level and I'd be able to manage. Even just now in the parking lot, rock climbing didn't sound so bad; plus, I didn't think I'd get far enough off the ground for it to really matter. But of course you're a raging expert, and I know better than to think you'll settle for anything less than teaching me to climb all the way to the top. Not that I had any clue the top would be—what, five stories up?"

Alex hesitated, but there was no point in scaling back from full disclosure now. "Six."

"Right." She pinched the bridge of her nose between her thumb and forefinger. "So if you want to go ahead and call this a draw and pick some other risky thrill mission, I understand."

"Is that what you want?"

She lifted her chin in surprise, the move loosening a handful of tendrils from the pair of loose, blond braids at her shoulders. "It's only fair. My fear of heights puts you at a total disadvantage for this bet if we rock climb."

God, her affinity for going by the book was really something else. "But that's not what I asked you."

"Why would you teach me how to rock climb even though you know it practically destroys your chances of winning?"

Alex bit down on the urge to laugh, rocking back on the heels of his Nikes instead. "What can I say? I'm a sucker for bad odds. Plus, if you're willing to give rock climbing a shot—" He paused, because as much as he wanted Zoe to make the move, it had to be *her* move. The idea was to appeal to her tough side, not bully the holy hell out of her. "I think you might be surprised."

She made a noise that suggested he had quite a ways to go in the convincing-her department. "Or I might tumble to a slow and painful death."

He closed the space between them to a mere sliver of daylight before his brain fully registered the *move* command pumping up from behind his sternum. "That's not going to happen."

"Oh." Zoe's murmur brushed past his ear on the hot shock of her exhale. "I just meant . . ."

"I know what you meant," he said, the words surging up on a direct path from his chest. "Look, I respect that heights scare you, and if you really don't want to try rock climbing,

I've got to respect that, too. But there's one thing you need to know. If we do this today, nothing bad is going to happen to you."

The fear in her eyes softened for just a second, but it was enough. "How do you know?"

"Because I'm not going to let it, that's how."

Zoe stood perfectly still, gold-colored lashes fanning up into a wide arc as she held on to his stare. The bold curiosity that had flashed through her gaze when she'd first asked him about skydiving resurfaced, and the end of one braid bounced off the gray fleece of her hoodie as she gave a tiny nod. "Okay," she whispered. "I'll give it an honest try."

"All right." Alex's pulse slid faster through his veins, but he tempered it with the same brand of calm he dialed up whenever they rolled out of the fire station, sirens blazing. If he wanted Zoe to stay relaxed enough to enjoy the climb, he'd have to set the bar at practically pulseless to get her to meet him halfway. Although, damn, the flush still covering the apples of her cheeks was going to make keeping cool a job and a half.

"The first thing we need to do is get our gear all set, but we can do that over here where we're going to climb so you can start getting a feel for how everything works." Alex shifted his backpack to keep it in place on his shoulder, kicking his feet into motion across the cavernous climbing room. Zoe stuck pretty close to his side, but she also didn't hesitate to follow him, and yeah. Now they were cooking with gas.

He stopped just shy of the north wall, angling himself toward her while still giving her a clear view of both the space they'd be climbing and the equipment around it. "In most situations, climbing takes two people. One person goes up, and the other person stays on the ground to operate what's called a belay line. That's the rope that gets hooked to the climber's harness, then run through a pulley system that's steel-bolted to the ceiling. The belay operator adjusts the tension on the line as the climber goes up and keeps him from falling if he loses his grip or his footing. Sort of like a backup plan."

"Oh." She examined the length of thick climbing rope clipped into the wall anchor, the impenetrable knot of her shoulders loosening slightly as she said, "So that's what you're going to do then? Be my belay guy so I won't fall?"

"Nope."

Just like that, her shoulders sprang back into loop-the-loop status, and okay, maybe it wouldn't hurt him to think before speaking every once in a while. He said, "If I worked your belay, I'd have to stay on the ground, and I wouldn't be able to climb next to you. But don't worry. Kyle here is going to have your back."

Alex nodded to the spot where his buddy Kyle had reappeared by the door to the equipment room, with a harness slung over one forearm and a smile and "hey" combo on his mouth.

"Wait." Zoe's eyes went wide before tapering to slits. "Kyle, the crazy skydiving guy?"

Of course she'd be able to pull that little chestnut out of thin freaking air. Not that Kyle seemed to mind being called crazy. "That's me," he said with a wave of one heavily tattooed arm.

"You guys rock climb together, too?" Zoe turned her brows-up stare in Alex's direction, but all he could do was shrug.

"We adrenaline hounds tend to stick together across multiple sports. At any rate, Kyle's an experienced climber. He's going to operate your belay line right here from the ground, and I'm going to climb the wall with you, step by step."

"Okay." She ran her fingers over the line running up to the pulley in the ceiling, her delicate brow tucking in nice and tight as she asked, "So if Kyle is in charge of my belay line, who's going to do yours?"

"I am." Alex lowered his backpack from his shoulder to the floor, unzipping the bag to unearth his tried-and-true harness. "Most people, especially beginners, need someone to manage their belay line from the ground. It's a little more comfortable that way. But we've got a self-belay device here, too, and since I'm an experienced climber, I'm going to use that."

He pointed to the separate line running down from the covered circular housing bolted into the top of the wall, and Zoe shook her head. "I didn't realize rock climbing had so many safety regulations."

Ahhh, screwing with her might not be the coolest thing going, but then again, no one had ever accused Alex of being buddy-buddy with the straight and narrow. Plus, maybe a little teasing would loosen her up another notch. "What, you thought I was going to just put you in front of the wall and tell you to hold on tight?"

She chirped out a laugh, and affirmative on getting her to kick some of that tension to the curb. "Well you *are* pretty reckless."

Leave it to Zoe to lead with something he really couldn't argue. Still . . . "It's like skydiving, Zoe. I might want the rush, but I don't want to end up in traction, either. You ready to get geared up?" He gestured to the harness in Kyle's hand nice and easy, and her nod followed in exactly the same manner.

"Okay, sure." She unzipped her hoodie, slipping the slouchy fleece from her shoulders to fold it into a neat square, and in that moment, Alex realized he'd made a huge tactical error.

Not only was Zoe wearing a formfitting tank top that revealed just enough creamy skin to be both disarming and hot as hell, but she'd paired it with black yoga pants. On their own, yoga pants were dangerous enough to a guy's concentration.

On the perfectly curvy hips-to-ass ratio Zoe had just revealed? They were a fucking weapons-grade distraction.

". . . Right, Donovan?" Kyle's voice jerked him back to reality with all the subtlety of an ice bath in August, and how the hell had the guy gotten Zoe into her harness so fast?

"What? Yes! Absolutely," Alex blurted at the same time his brain screamed *Focus, you dick-thinking dummy!*

Kyle buried his smile in the crook of his shoulder, but not before Alex caught it in all its ear-to-ear, asshole-friend glory. "So anyway, like I was saying, before I came out here I was sorting through those new climbing shoes we got from our distributor to use as demos and I'm pretty sure I saw an eight in the box. Since Alex agrees they'll probably give you a better feel for the footholds than your cross-trainers, we can go ahead and get you a pair for your climb if you want."

Zoe turned, propping her chin on her shoulder to look at him. "If you're sure it's okay for me to borrow them."

Alex made a mental note to let Kyle off the hook for the next two birthday parties in exchange for diverting Zoe's attention from his momentary lapse of decency. "Sure. I'll go grab a pair while you guys finish up here," he managed. Thankfully, by the time he'd completed the ninety-second trip to the equipment room, his cock had followed the stand-down issued by his conscience.

Mostly.

"Size eight. Here you go." Alex waited until Zoe's attention was fully engaged in swapping out her footwear before subtly adjusting the last of his hard-on into a more socially acceptable position beneath his loose-fitting climbing pants. Christ, he was a moron for even momentarily forgetting that Zoe was about as hands-off as a woman could get.

Not that he didn't want his hands on her. He might be a moron, but he sure as shit wasn't blind.

Alex stepped into his harness and tightened the straps into place, squelching the heat running through him like a live wire current once and for all. Zoe was Cap's daughter, and anyway, he had a bet to win and a firehouse to get back to, both in short order.

"Okay," he said, the clack of metal on metal sounding off in his palm as he unlocked the carabiner holding Zoe's line from its anchor spot in the wall. Passing it off to Kyle, he let his buddy attach the line to the front of her harness while turning to mimic the process with the self-belay line and his own gear. "As we climb, Kyle will adjust the tension in your belay line by either pulling on it or letting out slack. He'll have a good visual on you the whole time, but just in case the line feels too tight or too loose, all you have to do is twirl your finger like this." He paused to rotate his index finger in a handful of circles. "And he'll adjust it for you. This is a beginner wall, so the hand and footholds are pretty big and easy to use. We shouldn't have too much trouble to start out."

She took in the wall with a methodical sweep of her eyes, calculating every step of the way. "Okay, but there are hundreds of them. How do I know which ones to use?"

Oh, man, she was going to hate this part. But hell if it wasn't half the reason he'd fallen in love with rock climbing to begin with. Not to mention the entire reason he'd wanted to get her on the wall. "No risk, no reward. You're going to have to try them all out to see which ones work best for your frame and your strength."

Zoe muttered under her breath. "Fabulous." Still, the tiny *V* of concentration marking the space between her brows told Alex she hadn't changed her mind about giving this an honest go. Gripping one of the holds at eye level, she edged the ball of one foot to a low-standing foothold, tightening her muscles to pull herself all the way off the climbing room floor.

"Once you start moving, you'll get the hang of what works for you pretty quickly. Just take it one step at a time. Literally." Alex moved a couple of paces up the wall with an easy hand-over-hand, tipping his head at her in a wordless *c'mere,* and Zoe's forehead creased deeper still beneath the slender brim of her helmet.

"Like this?" she asked, readjusting her death grip on the hold in front of her before awkwardly tilting her hips back to search for a place to put her foot.

Okay, yeah, so this was going to be a bigger challenge than Alex had bargained for. But between her fear of heights and her extreme determination to concentrate her face off, Zoe was going to fry her motherboard in about ten seconds unless he scheduled a straight to the point intervention, stat.

"Not exactly," he said, ignoring her *I told you so* glare as he backpedaled to the spot next to her. "First of all, breathe. I promise it won't hurt."

Her glare doubled in intensity, but she sucked in enough of an inhale that he didn't push his luck.

Not too much, anyway. "Okay, we'll call that a work in progress. Next, the wall isn't going to bite you. If you drop your weight backward to look for footholds, you're burning unnecessary energy and risking a fall."

"How am I supposed to move upward then?"

"By bringing your body right up on the wall and leaving it there. Like this." He reached around the back of her rib cage, ushering her torso and hips flush to the wall without warning or force.

Zoe went bowstring taut beneath his arm, turning her chin toward him so they were face-to-face against the profile of the wall. Her parted lips and eyes-wide-open stare put a spotlight on her vulnerability, and even though he had to fight for it, Alex met the tension in both her stare and her body with nothing but calm.

"It's all about balance. You've got to keep your center of gravity nice and tight"—he paused, adding just the slightest pressure against the arc of her rib cage to punctuate the words—"right here while you relax everything else. Then you can move your arms and legs laterally rather than out and back, away from the wall, and you'll stay grounded. Now give it a try."

For a breath, Zoe went completely still, and Alex's gut doubled down to match. But then her body loosened by slow degrees, the rigid line of her torso growing more pliable beneath his grasp as she inhaled, testing her weight on the footholds to nudge her way upward. "That does feel a little more comfortable."

"You need both push and pull to be flexible enough to move. Good, see? You're not going to fall, I promise." He nodded, shifting his arm from a tight hold to the barest press of support on her lower back as she climbed up once, then twice, keeping her motions careful but compact. "There you go."

"Oh." The word curved her lips in its wake, sending a dark thrill all the way through Alex's blood. "Okay, yeah."

Zoe paused to flex the fingers on her free hand a few times, and he took advantage of the moment to show her a couple different types of holds. "Most of the handholds on this wall will accommodate a variety of grips, but I'm not going to lie. You're probably going to feel this tomorrow in some unexpected places. Climbing's a little tough on your fingers and hands."

A quick burst of laughter popped past her lips. "I'm a chef, Alex. Believe me, as far as being tough on my hands, this is nothing."

She furrowed her brow, scanning the selection of multi-colored options in front of her before reaching for the next handhold. Stalwart concentration reset her forehead into a deep crease, drawing her shoulders higher around the column of her neck, and she completed each maneuver as if checking chores off a bottomless to-do list.

Oh, no you don't. "So how come you left that restaurant in DC to run a soup kitchen in the projects?"

Surprise colored Zoe's eyes in a burnished brown flicker, but hell if he hadn't grabbed at her attention just enough to get her to breathe.

"I, uh. Well, it's kind of a long story." She took a second to set her fingers into a pinch hold, the back of her tank top smoothing out over her spine as she relaxed into the move and tugged herself up another step.

While Alex didn't want her to lose focus on what was in front of her, overfocusing, especially when the path to success was to stay loose, was equally problematic. If one thing could not just chill Zoe out, but keep her that way, it was talking about Hope House's kitchen. And as much as he wanted her to find her happy place so he could win this bet, a deeper, darker part of him also wanted to rediscover that reckless-abandon smile she'd let slip the other day in the kitchen.

And Alex wasn't going to stop until he got both.

Chapter Nine

Zoe had been so busy concentrating on how to keep herself balanced and upright that she didn't see Alex's smile until it caught her right in the solar plexus. Although she'd been starting to get the hang of at least some of the climbing movements, being this close to the off-limits firefighter was a completely different ball of wax. Between the utter confidence in Alex's bright blue eyes and the warmth of his lean, hard muscles wrapped tight over her rib cage as he'd guided her against the climbing wall, Zoe was about ready to spontaneously combust.

She didn't even want to get started on the weird pang she'd felt from her chest to her caution meter as he'd sworn to keep her safe.

"A long story, huh?" Alex let go of the climbing wall with one hand, gesturing grandly to the space between them before easily replacing his grip. "As it turns out, I'm a captive audience with nothing but time. So come on, Gorgeous. Wow me."

The laughter that barged past Zoe's lips took her by complete surprise, and judging from Alex's expression, she wasn't the only one. But her reasons for leaving Kismet weren't exactly a secret. Even if they were largely unpopular among both her former colleagues and her family. "Okay, fine. I guess the easiest way to explain it is that working in a professional kitchen just wasn't what I thought it would be."

"Yeah, I remember my first year in the house." Alex slid the toes of his black climbing shoes to a new foothold, pressing his way up the wall with the ease of someone who had done it no less than a billion times. "Jobs with break-neck hours on top of breakneck workloads are a bitch to get used to. I'm guessing that being a chef isn't exactly a nine to five."

She tried—unsuccessfully—to keep her snort in check as she did her best to copy his upward movements. "Definitely not. But I was actually fine with the schedule and the workload. It was the bottom line that ended up driving me crazy."

"I'm not sure I understand."

"I spent three years clawing my way through culinary school because I love food. The smells, tastes, the textures, the way simple ingredients can come together to create something so vital." Zoe paused to let the pure goodness of the thoughts in her head push a smile over her mouth. "God, I even loved the scut work, and believe me when I say, in a professional kitchen, there's plenty."

Alex's laugh was all low, warm rumble. "Like coring lettuce?"

"Please. Talk to me once you've chopped onions for vegetable stock. For like a month straight."

"I don't mean to be a jackass, but that pretty much sounds like hell on earth." He shuddered, although the glint in his eyes made both the gesture and his words more mischievous than malicious. Zoe didn't even think twice as she shrugged and took another tentative step up the climbing wall.

"For someone who's not a chef, I'm sure it does. But it's

just like keeping your equipment in check at the firehouse. You want your irons ready to go when you need them, right?"

"Uh, yeah." Alex tugged his sun-kissed brows into a nonverbal *is that even a question?* and Zoe responded with an equally silent *exactly.*

"So you take good care of your ax and your Halligan bar and you put everything where it belongs even though the inventory you do at the top of every shift is a pain in the ass. When you love your job, even the boring stuff isn't, well, quite so boring."

"I guess that makes sense. But if you didn't mind the grunt work, the long hours, and the weird schedule, what made you want to leave? Wasn't the place pretty upscale?"

She pushed her toes over a new foothold, but struggled to lock in her balance. "Very. I worked in the kitchen at Kismet for two years. Busted my butt to get an apprenticeship under the head chef, actually." Whoa, the peg under her foot was a lot narrower than she'd thought. Damn it. "But despite all that hard work and the thousands of dishes I made in that kitchen, do you know how many people I fed who really needed it?"

"Here. Try using your instep rather than your toes. Like this." Alex shifted his hips back to give her a clear line of sight on his feet as he demonstrated the new maneuver before returning to her question with attention that hadn't even skipped a pulse. "How many?"

"None." Zoe angled the inside curve of her arch across the slim ridge of the foothold, and wow, that sure did the trick on her wobbly balance. "Don't get me wrong. As much as I love being in the kitchen, I understand that restaurants are businesses. They have to make money. But working at Kismet felt so commercial, like the thing I loved most about being a chef was getting lost in the translation of doing as many covers as possible during any given shift. Like despite all my hard work and all the heart I was putting into the food, none of it really mattered."

She hesitated, filling the silence with a reach for the large handhold an arm's length above her. This was right about the point in the conversation where she usually lost everyone. Hell, if she'd had this conversation with *herself* three years ago, she'd have thought she'd lost her crackers.

But Alex just waited, his expression completely unvarnished, from the strong set of his jaw to the tropical-ocean blue of his stare, and it prompted the rest of the story right past Zoe's lips.

"At first I thought I was just restless working the line. While I don't mind doing straight labor and prep, potential chefs aren't exactly taught a lack of initiative in culinary school. Working in a kitchen is extremely competitive."

"Cutting your teeth as a rookie can suck pretty bad," he agreed with a laugh. "For us, at least, a decent chunk of the first year is training and dress rehearsal so you can get used to the work and learn how to manage your adrenaline. It's tough to do the watch-and-learn when you've been eating ambition for breakfast all the way through school, though."

Forget culinary school. Zoe had been lining up goals and knocking them down like bowling pins ever since *middle* school. Her parents had never expected anything less, and she'd never delivered anything but the best, for them and herself. "Exactly. I was sure that if I earned my way off the line and studied under one of the best chefs in DC, I'd make more of a difference as a sous chef and my unease would let up."

"But?" Apparently, patience wasn't one of Alex's virtues. Not that she'd expected it to be.

"But a year later, all I'd done was the same dance with different steps. I know it sounds sappy and idealistic, but I don't just love food for me. I want to nurture people, and

I became a chef so I could make an impact with my cooking. I tried to gut it out at Kismet, I really did, but—"

"You became a chef so you could feed people, and you didn't want to go halfway."

Holy crap. Not only had Alex filled in the blanks of her sentence with freakish accuracy, but his easy nod suggested that he hadn't just taken a lucky stab at what he thought she might say.

For a split second, he looked like he actually *got* it.

Zoe pulled in a fortifying breath, but it got stuck in the vicinity of her windpipe. "You know, most people think I'm crazy when I tell them I left one of *Washingtonian*'s Top 100 Restaurants so I could come back to my hometown to start a soup kitchen in the projects on half a shoestring."

"First of all, I think we've already established that I'm not really the most accurate barometer for deciding what's crazy. Secondly . . . what do you think?"

"Huh?" Great. Now she was confused *and* ineloquent. But even in the face of her verbal bumbling, Alex remained completely even keeled.

"It's not a trick question, Zoe." His eyes glinted in the over-bright fluorescent lights, and sweet baby Jesus, since when did the king of recklessness have an innocent look? "I just want to know what you think about leaving the restaurant circuit to run the kitchen at Hope House."

Something broke free in her chest, letting the words bubble out one over the other like a stockpot left to simmer for too long. "I think that when I went to culinary school, I just wanted the truth of the food, to make a difference by feeding people. The reality of working in a restaurant, with all that focus on the bottom line rather than the big picture never felt like it quite fit me. But working at Hope House does. Even if it isn't upscale or glamorous . . . it's still mine. It's what I love."

Alex froze into place, not moving against the dark sheen of the climbing wall. "Wanting to do what you love doesn't sound crazy to me. It sounds like you're not waiting around to live your life. It sounds honest."

Zoe blurted out her answer before she could lock it down inside her mouth. "You want to know the really crazy part? No one's ever asked me what I thought before. I mean, I've told my former boss and my parents what I felt plenty of times." Not that they'd ever really heard her. "But they were all so lasered in on what I was leaving and what they thought I was throwing away that they missed the part that mattered the most. None of them actually asked me why I wanted to run a soup kitchen."

"Leaving the primrose path is actually a little risky," he said, wrapping his fingers around his belay line and navigating his body around hers just enough to lock her left leg into place with his right. "Want to know what else is risky?"

Zoe blinked, remotely aware of Alex's arm snaking back around her waist. "What?"

"Look down."

For a second, his words didn't register. But then she dropped her gaze from his face to the floor, and a wave of freezing cold fear went skidding through her gut.

They were more than halfway up the wall. Three stories. Thirty feet.

And she hadn't been scared.

No, scratch that. She'd been so at ease, she hadn't even *noticed*.

"Oh my God." Zoe's muscles seized without her permission, her grip going from easy does it to a thermonuclear crush in about two seconds flat. As if he'd anticipated her reaction, Alex firmed his grip on her rib cage, enough to hold her steady but not so much as to alter her position or throw her off balance. He dropped his chin to the spot just above her ear, his slow, easy exhale tickling the back of her neck as his voice threaded past the soundtrack of oh-shit-oh-shit-oh-shit being pumped out by her heart.

"Zoe, take a breath. All the way in."

Miraculously, she did. "We're really high off the ground."

"We're a good ways up," Alex agreed, and his honesty hooked her attention just enough to get her to stop clutching. Okay, mostly. "But you're perfectly fine, just like you were a minute ago. In fact, you're actually doing great."

She chanced a peek over her shoulder. Kyle stood in the exact spot where they'd left him, with her belay line wrapped carefully around both of his hands, and she slid one palm over the smooth nylon of the harness keeping her in check. Her peek became a longer look, and a strange sensation infused her chest before moving outward to her limbs.

"I feel great. Also, a little terrified," Zoe qualified, because hello, they were still dangling above the ground at the equivalent height of a three-story apartment building. "But it's maybe not as horrible as I thought it would be."

"Well, then. I guess that leaves me with just one thing to say."

Although Zoe had regained her balance on the hand and footholds in front of her, Alex didn't scale back on his proximity. The warmth of his murmur coasted over her neck, settling in at her belly as she braced for the gloating that would surely follow.

Only it didn't.

"Up or down?"

"What?" She blinked, certain she'd misunderstood, but Alex just released her with a wide-open grin.

"Do you want to keep climbing up, or should we head back down to the ground?"

Although the cocky gleam in his eyes told her he'd merely tabled his victory dance, right now, in this moment, with her muscles humming from use and her bloodstream soaked with a double dose of bulletproof endorphins, Zoe didn't care.

"A little farther wouldn't hurt. After all, I promised you an honest go, and you're right. I'm a woman of my word."

Chapter Ten

While Alex Donovan had been called a lot of things by a lot of people, patient had never once graced the list. So the fact that he waited to claim his win for nearly five hours while he and Zoe climbed the north wall a half dozen times, took breathers in between to discuss mechanics and practice a few techniques, and had a spirited conversation with both Jocelyn and Kyle about the most intense outdoor climbs they'd ever been on? Hell, that even took him by surprise. But now that they were back in Zoe's car, with her smile bright enough to power a nuclear reactor and the energy to match, the gloves were coming off.

"You look like you enjoyed yourself today," he said, going for the understatement rather than the kill. He *did* have just under four whole weeks to gloat. Anyway, she looked so frigging cute over there, tapping her fingers to a tuneless beat over the steering wheel as she smiled intermittently to herself and followed the backlit path to his house on her phone's GPS. While half of Alex's purpose today had been to win the bet, the other half had been to prove that getting a little reckless wasn't such a heinous infraction. After all, if you weren't busy grabbing life by the hey-nannies, you were pretty much just wasting time.

And time had a way of disappearing with a whole lot of *someday* still left on the table.

"A little. Maybe." Zoe folded her latest smile between her teeth, but even in the dusky evening shadows starting to darken the car, her expression had pure, uncut bliss scrawled all over it.

"You bought a six-month open climb membership before we even went up the wall a fourth time," Alex said, bringing himself all the way back to the moment with a laugh. "I hate to break it to you, but your definition of *maybe* looks pretty tilted from over here."

"Okay, okay!" She broke ranks with her careful ten-and-two-hand positioning on the steering wheel just long enough to nudge him with an elbow. "As much as it pains me to say you were right, I'm not above giving credit where it's due. Even though I have no idea how you pulled it off, I didn't hate rock climbing."

He tamped down the urge to let his inner twelve-year-old break free for an elaborate fist-pump, oh-yeah celebration, opting instead to keep his smile tacked into place. "I didn't think you would. But for the record, I didn't pull anything off. You did."

Zoe crossed the boundary to his neighborhood, squinting hard at the path Alex had known for over half his life. "How's that? You're the one who showed me what to do."

"True," he said, the adrenaline of the day combining with the carefree look on her face to send his blood on a faster circuit through his veins. "But you're the one who took the leap."

"How did you know? That I wouldn't hate it, I mean. Or was that a risk, too?"

"I've got to admit, you threw me for a bit of a rope-a-dope when you said you were afraid of heights." Truly, it had been Alex's only moment of doubt for the entire afternoon. Not that he'd been about to let a little thing like steeper odds stand in his path. Shit. Most of the time, that just gave the risk at hand more of a kick. "But I still had a feeling that if you gave climbing an honest shake, you'd get into it anyway."

She pulled into the narrow stretch of asphalt serving as his driveway, shooting him what she'd probably intended to be a cool stare. Too bad for her, the smile still lifting the corners of her mouth destroyed her game face. "You're a little presumptuous, don't you think?"

"It's not presumptuous if I'm right," he said, releasing his seat belt with a muted *click*. Okay, now he *was* kind of messing with her, but come on. With the holy trinity of a great climb, a winning bet, and the bold look taking up residence on Zoe's pretty face right now? He had enough feel-good endorphins kicking through him to bench press a Sherman tank.

Alex popped the handle on the passenger door of the Prius, retrieving his gear bag from the backseat and waiting for Zoe to slide out from the driver's side before continuing. "Look, I didn't take you rock climbing today to change who you are or how you think, Zoe. You might cover it up most of the time, but under all that by-the-book rule-following and carefully constructed caution, I think you've got a reckless streak. I only took you climbing to prove that letting it out once in a while won't hurt."

Her bright peal of laughter threaded through the cool evening air, tagging Alex right in the chest. "Right. I'm sure the way I nearly called it quits before we even started climbing is a prime example of my wild side."

"Maybe not. But the way you tackled the north wall once you put your mind to it sure was."

"Listen, I'm not trying to renege on our bet," she said, holding up one hand to punctuate the words as she followed him toward the garage. "But believe me, any recklessness you saw from me today was an anomaly."

"And what about five years ago, at the FFD barbecue? Was that an anomaly, too?"

Ah, hell. Alex's unbreakable mood had ushered the question past his lips before he could cage it. But as dangerous as the topic might be, he wasn't about to deny wanting to know what had sparked the by-the-book attitude that hadn't been there five years ago.

Not to mention why she was hiding her boldness beneath it.

Zoe's cheeks pinkened, deep enough for the blush to be visible even in the waning daylight around them. "You remember that?"

Her tanned, muscular legs in the cutoff shorts she'd been wearing, the flush of a couple of beers mixed with the summer heat on her pretty, pixie face . . . Jesus, she had to be completely off her rocker if she thought he'd ever be able to forget.

"Of course I remember it," he said, punching in the garage code and turning to face her as the door trundled up the track with a rhythmic *clack-clack-clack.* "You were wearing a white tank top and that pair of dangly earrings. They kept getting caught in your hair."

"I hated those things." She laughed, soft and self-deprecating. Still, her chin stayed up, and damn, she was the perfect mix of sweet and strong.

"Then why'd you wear them?"

"I wanted to look grown up." Another laugh puffed past her lips, just as enticing as the first. "Fat lot of good it did me."

"You looked pretty grown up when you asked me to kiss you," Alex said, all truth, and although her blush gained intensity, Zoe answered the same way.

"I'd had a few. And by a few, I mean like six. But it doesn't really matter. Just because I was tipsy and voiced my ridiculous crush on you doesn't make me reckless, although I'm sure you got a great laugh out of the whole thing later."

His head jacked up, matching his pulse. "You think I was laughing at you?"

"I don't know." Zoe paused, lifting one fleece-wrapped shoulder before following him all the way into the tidy, shadow-covered space of the garage. "The captain's socially awkward and moderately sloshed daughter who you look at like a kid sister asks you to kiss her, and well . . . yeah. To be honest, once I sobered up, I thought there was no way you *weren't* laughing."

She couldn't be serious. He'd spent the rest of that day alternating between mentally reciting baseball stats to get rid of his hard-on and kicking himself for his sudden and ill-timed attack of scruples.

Alex unshouldered his backpack, lowering it to the narrow wooden workbench nailed along the back wall of the garage. "You're out of your damn mind."

"The concept of a brain to mouth filter is lost on you, isn't it?"

"I don't see much point in trying to pretty things up. Life's too short for bullshit."

Zoe's lips opened just slightly, bold fire combining with unmistakable want in her eyes, and in that instant, the thread snapped.

Pushing off from the workbench to cover the space between them in only a few steps, Alex angled closer, capturing a tendril of hair that had fallen loose from one of her low-slung braids. Without hesitation, he let his fingers glide all the way to the end of the silky length, bringing them to a stop right over her collarbone. "In fact, life's too short for lots of things."

"Like what?" Zoe asked, her voice no more than a husky whisper. She reached up to wrap her fingers around his

hand, and that one small gesture was all the encouragement
Alex needed.

"Like this."

The space between them was gone in a breath, his mouth
covering hers at the same moment she pressed forward to
meet him. The kiss was the polar opposite of the way she'd
claimed to be, fierce and fast and daring, and Alex gave in
to the rush with a groan. Thrusting his fingers through Zoe's
hair, he parted her lips with his tongue, cupping the back of
her neck and swinging her toward the workbench as he
searched and tasted and took. But rather than following his
lead or melting into the intensity of the kiss, she met him
measure for measure. Zoe's hands scooped up to tangle in
his hair, the tug of her grip as she held him close and kissed
him hard sending ripples of pleasure-pain on a straight shot
to his cock.

This wasn't impulse. It was insanity.

And Zoe felt so unbelievably hot, with her tongue sweeping over his bottom lip and her teeth following suit with
just enough pressure to excite without stinging, that Alex
didn't care.

Even though a voice somewhere deep in the basest part
of him growled its displeasure, he broke from Zoe's mouth
to place a string of kisses across her jaw, nudging her chin
up with a rasp of stubble on sweet skin. Not only did Zoe
oblige, but her grasp on him tightened. A heavy, want-
soaked sigh sifted up from her chest and he lowered his
mouth over the soft column of her neck.

Christ. How could this woman taste like sin *and* inno-
cence? And more importantly, why was it driving him so
fucking mad?

Using his hips against hers to guide the way, he walked
Zoe backward to the closed doors of the storage cabinet,
not stopping until her back found the cool, flat surface.
Alex bracketed the space above her shoulders with both

palms, but he left just enough daylight between them that Zoe could choose to either close it or move away.

She didn't move away.

Alex dropped his mouth to hers, coaxing the soft bow of her lips apart. "Open for me, Zoe. Let me taste more of you."

She obliged, sending a spiral of hot, urgent want to the base of his spine. Pressing in closer, he slid his tongue against hers, stroking and searching and lingering in the places that made her sigh in the back of her throat.

"I thought you don't mix business with pleasure," Zoe said, her thick murmur sliding over him like silk and sandpaper and sin as she caught the sensitive spot in the center of his top lip between her teeth, and God *damn,* this woman could turn kissing into a metaphysical event.

He was going to do so much more than kiss her.

"I don't." Alex moved his hands to the front of her hoodie, the zipper hissing softly as he lowered it until the two halves of fleece gave way. "This is going to be all pleasure. Starting with yours."

They didn't so much kiss as crash together, the friction of Zoe's lips and tongue making his cock jump. Without breaking contact with his mouth, she maneuvered her hoodie off her shoulders, shucking it awkwardly to the bench beside them before gliding her fingers under the thin material of his shirt. Christ, he'd thought he was on fire for her, but her hands were warm and cunning on his skin, boldly stroking up his chest, matching him move for move.

Not to be outdone, he hooked his fingers beneath the hem of her tank top to lift the material with one swift tug. Following suit with the bottom edge of her sports bra, Alex freed Zoe's breasts from the cotton, keeping her anchored to the cool metal surface behind them as he skimmed both thumbs over her straining nipples.

"I want to taste you here, too."

She let out a moan of approval, arching high and greedy against his touch. But something dark and wicked flooded through him, slowing his ministrations.

"Do you want that?" Alex circled again, grinning his satisfaction at how Zoe's nipples peaked even further beneath his fingers. "Do you want my mouth on you right here?"

"Alex . . ." Her head dropped to one side, and she canted her hips forward in search of more contact. Ignoring the base demand from his cock to give her exactly what she wanted, he pulled back, stopping only when he'd caught her stare in the depth of the shadows.

"Say it. Tell me what you want."

Alex registered the flash in Zoe's eyes at the same time she slipped her hand into the breath of space he'd created between them, her fingers wrapping around his erection with perfect, delicious intention.

"I want your mouth on me. Right now."

He didn't think. Just moved.

Rounding his back and shoulders, Alex wrapped his arms around her body to cup her bare shoulder blades and hold her close. A slight dip of his chin gave her what she'd asked for, and he drew one nipple past his lips to swirl the hardened tip with a groan.

"Alex." Zoe rocked against him with her fingers and hips, locking their bodies together as the nails on her free hand turned into his shoulders with sweet, sharp pressure. But rather than dissuade or distract, the sensation made him even harder, and he slipped one palm beneath her breast to hold her closer still as he sucked. Her nipple tightened with every pass of his tongue, every taste drawing little moans from her throat and sweet friction from her hand on his cock. Widening his stance, he reached around the lush curve of Zoe's ass, lifting her level with his hips to thrust against the soft, fabric-covered heat between her thighs, refusing to loosen the contact of his mouth even when her moans shaped his name.

"Alex. Take me inside. Please."

Yes. Inside. Oh hell, yes. The pure impulse grated up from the darkest, most reckless piece of his mind. He returned to her mouth to sweep his tongue over hers in one last promise before taking her upstairs and turning his unspoken oath into raw, hot action.

But then the fragments of all the words Zoe had just spoken slid up against what they really meant.

I thought you don't mix business with pleasure . . . business . . . business . . .

Holy *shit*. He was standing in the garage of his childhood home, barely one degree of separation from taking his captain's only daughter into his house and stripping her very, very naked.

And up until this split second, he'd had every intention of letting her return the favor so he could drive her on a straight, hot path from a sigh to a scream.

All night long.

"Zoe . . ." Alex lowered her feet to the concrete floor, his limbs slow and clumsy as if they were weighted and trapped under water. "I can't . . . we can't do this."

"I know. We're in your garage. Why do you think I asked you to take me inside?" Her eyes fluttered open over a slow, sexy smile, but then her gaze narrowed over his face in the scant glow of the streetlight spilling through a side window, and realization covered her features all at once. "Oh." Zoe stiffened, letting go of his shoulders to right her misplaced clothing with a handful of precise tugs. "You don't mean we can't do this here. You mean you don't want this at all."

Shit. Shit, fuck, and damn it to the stars, the hurt slicing across her face sent a pool of guilt to the bottom of his gut. But despite his reputation, as well as the truth that fueled it, he knew the difference between recklessness and a total lack of regard. He'd given Captain Westin his word he'd stay ruler straight and just as narrow, and God knew Alex owed him more than this.

In fact, God alone knew exactly how much he owed the man. Which meant Alex had to make this right, even as much as he wanted to kick his own ass right now—and as much as refusing Zoe would likely launch him right back to square one with her.

The captain's daughter was always, always off-limits.

He pressed his lips together, ignoring the way they still tingled and tasted like want. "We did a lot of climbing today, and the adrenaline must've gotten to me. I guess I just got carried away."

"I thought you believed in being reckless. Life's too short, and all that?" A tinge of something Alex couldn't place flickered through Zoe's voice—there, then gone in the same breath. Still, his answer was absolute.

"I do, but . . . not like this. Not with you."

"I see," she said, stabbing her arms through the sleeves of her hoodie before turning to stare at the expanse of the garage door in front of her. "Well. At any rate, you won your bet. I guess I'll see you Monday."

For a split second, Alex nearly backpedaled. But better for her to think him a jerk than for her to know the whole, harsh truth.

It wasn't that he didn't want her. But he sure as shit couldn't have her, and he double sure could never tell her the whole reason why. So Alex took the only option left on the table.

He said, "Good night, Zoe."

When she squared her shoulders and walked a straight path to her car, he didn't turn to watch her go.

Chapter Eleven

Zoe propped her elbows over the gray-flecked Formica tabletop in her favorite booth at Scarlett's, staring into her mostly full cup of coffee while mentally banging her head against the closest solid surface. Alex's community service dictated that he serve four ten-hour shifts Monday through Thursday, which meant she'd had Hope House's kitchen to herself today for both breakfast and lunch. Considering the code red embarrassment of their parting last night, Zoe had thought not having the outlandishly gorgeous firefighter right there in front of her as she nursed her battered pride back to working order would be a relief.

But every time she'd tried to squelch the memory of Alex's lips, so strong and bold and undeniably good on hers, she couldn't get around one simple fact. She'd thrown herself at him not once, but twice now. And even though twice, he'd gone for the old *thanks but no thanks*, the bald-faced rejection still couldn't stamp out how recklessly hot she'd felt with his hands on her body. How hot—even now—she still felt at the memory.

Turned out they didn't have to be actually sharing the same airspace in order for Alex Donovan to make her pride feel like it had been run through a high-speed wood chipper.

"Come on, girl," Zoe whispered, brushing a hand over the fresh prickle of warmth on her cheeks. "Time to get back on the reality horse."

So Alex had blamed their kisses on the heat of the moment, not the heat of the attraction she'd felt sure had been building between them all day. But Zoe was already highly acquainted with how being risky and impulsive only led to errors in judgment. While in this case, the only thing that had been torched by Alex's hot and heavy risk-taking had been Zoe's pride, she knew all too well that the stakes of not playing it safe could be so much higher. Family relationships. Marriages.

A person's life.

Taking risks, even with something as seemingly small time as rock climbing or a heat-of-the-moment hookup, just wasn't worth it. After all, if Zoe slept with hornets, at some point she should sure as hell expect to wake up stung.

Nope. Not happening. Not now. Not again. What she needed was to forget the rush she'd felt while rock climbing, the pure electricity of Alex's kisses on her skin, so she could nail her caution sensors right back into place.

"You've been working on that coffee for a while," Sara said, hooking Zoe's thoughts back to the diner in short order. Which was just as well, since Zoe was really just throwing confetti at her own pity party. "Can I get you a fresh cup? I brewed a pot of French roast not even five minutes ago."

"Oh, no, I'm good." Zoe lifted her mug to her lips in an effort to prove the fib, but karma bit her square on the butt when she got a mouthful of coffee that had long since gone cold. "Ugh. Okay, maybe I'm not that good."

"Change your mind about a pick-me-up?" Sara tipped her chin toward the wait station behind the front counter, but Zoe shook her head.

"No thanks. I think in order to really pick me up, you'd

need to put something a hell of a lot stronger than coffee in my cup."

"Whoa. Not to put my nose where it doesn't belong, but that sounds like man problems."

Zoe shrugged, and what the hell. Her pride had already taken the hit, and as much as it smarted, she was still standing. Maybe copping to her schoolgirl syndrome would let her put the whole stupid kiss behind her so she could get back to normal, once and for all. "If by 'problems' you mean I got all jacked up on rock climbing endorphins and tried to twist myself around my community service volunteer like a bag full of pretzels, only to have him friend-zone me without the friendship, then yup. That's exactly what I've got going on right now."

Sara's brows disappeared beneath the thick fringe of her dark brown bangs. "Ouch. If it's any consolation, the guy kind of sounds like he graduated with high honors from the asshole academy."

Zoe couldn't help it. She laughed. "Maybe a little. But to be honest, it's really just as well. Heat of the moment hookups with the wrong guy never end in happily-ever-after, and anyway, I've got way more important things to focus on right now."

"You're probably right about getting down and dirty with the wrong guy, but it still sounds like you've earned something stronger than coffee in your cup." Sara slid a glance at the watch strapped to her wrist. "My shift at Bellyflop starts in half an hour. Not to brag, but I make a pretty kick-ass martini. If you feel like downloading your crappy day, first one's on me."

The coffee cup still in Zoe's grasp found the table with a *clunk*. "You work at Bellyflop, too?"

"Working two jobs pays the bills," Sara said with a nonchalant lift of one shoulder. "Plus, staying busy keeps me honest, and I don't mind the restaurant scene. Anyway, the offer stands if you feel like chucking your worries."

Zoe paused. Not that she didn't feel like chucking her troubles far and wide, but . . . "I'm kind of gross from spending the day at Hope House," she said, running a hand over her sauce-splattered T-shirt. Of course she had to have served spaghetti for lunch, of all things.

But Sara just gave up a grin. "Sing me a song with a tune I don't know. I've got a bag in the back with an extra top and some trial-size toiletries. You'll be fresh as field greens in no time."

"Wow." A smile tugged at the corners of Zoe's mouth, the knot of tension that had lodged itself right between her shoulder blades unraveling by just a fraction. "I guess I don't have much of a choice, then."

"Oh, you've always got a choice. You just might not always like your options."

God, wasn't *that* the truth. But while it wasn't as routine as going home to flip through cookbooks and sink up to her chin in a bubble bath, heading to Bellyflop for one impromptu drink was hardly wild and crazy. Sara's offer certainly sounded more fun than Zoe's standard go-to; plus, even though it was a step outside her norm, breaking bad with her usual Saturday night schedule paled in comparison to rock climbing and sizzling hot firefighter kisses and all the other things she wanted to put in her rearview.

After all, how much damage could one martini and an hour at the local sports bar really do?

Zoe stood, her mind made up. "Well, right now, my choice is to take you up on that drink. Just give me ten minutes and your bag of tricks, and I'll be good to go."

Zoe smoothed a hand over the hem of the formfitting black and white striped top she'd borrowed from Sara, unable to dampen her smile as she looked up at the blue neon sign boasting *BELLYFLOP SPORTS BAR, HOME OF THE HOTTEST TEAMS AND THE HOTTEST WINGS IN FAIRVIEW!* Okay, so she'd had to get a little creative with her kitchen-frazzled hair and her eau de pasta sauce scent, but it hadn't been anything a fistful of bobby pins, a couple of Purell hand wipes, and some body spray couldn't fix—at least, temporarily. In fact, between the tube of mascara Zoe had found lurking at the bottom of her messenger bag, the swipe of merlot-colored lipstick she'd borrowed from Sara, and the deep scoop that rendered the new-to-her top practically backless, she felt pretty darn good.

Thank God for getting back to normal. Even if she was taking the scenic route.

"I haven't been here since I've been back in Fairview," Zoe said, meeting Sara halfway between their cars in the partially full parking lot. In fact, since she'd left for culinary school at the ripe old age of twenty-two, she could pretty much count the total number of times she'd been to Bellyflop on the fingers of one hand.

"It's still a little early, but the Saturday crowd is usually fun." Sara's black leather boots clacked over the pavement as she led the way toward the bar. "There are a bunch of regulars who like to come in to watch whatever game is on, maybe play some pool while they have a couple of beers. Just hang with me at the bar and I'll introduce you to anyone you don't already know. You'll be totally fine."

"Okay, sure." Zoe eyed the low, darkly bricked but warmly lit building, the last of her residual unease disappearing from her veins. Two pairs of oversized picture windows graced the bar's facade, one on either side of the massive glass and mahogany double doors. The bright blue awning that ran the length of the upper ledge of the window casings fluttered gently in the spring evening breeze, and the light from the brass fixtures flanking the windows combined with the glow from the interior of the bar itself, cutting through the shadows to unfurl like a slightly raucous but still cheery welcome mat.

As Sara swung the front door in a wide arc of invitation, the earthy aroma of beer fresh from the tap and the tangy-spice scent of hot wings hit Zoe's senses like a culinary frat party. Small clusters of people gathered either in booths or tables dotted throughout the dining room or tall, communal tables by the bar in the back of the wide, airy space. Every ounce of all four walls was covered in team pennants and memorabilia from every sport Zoe could think of, and even a few she hadn't. Bright neon mingled with the soft gold light overhead, illuminating the place with a festive glow that put her instantly at ease even though she didn't know a home run from a hat trick. A couple of pool tables were barely visible in a smaller alcove to the right of the bar, and yeah. Forgetting her troubles in a place like this was going to be a piece of cake without the calories.

Except for the fact that Alex Donovan was sitting at a table full of firefighters, right smack in the center of the bar.

"You cannot be serious," Zoe breathed, her heartbeat doing the hey-now in her chest despite her best-dressed effort to keep it level. But from what she'd been able to glean, there wasn't anybody in Fairview who Alex didn't work, skydive, or swap favors with. It figured he'd spend his Saturday night at the hottest bar in town.

"What's the matter?" Sara asked, but she was too perceptive for her own good. She followed Zoe's stare—which she'd dropped just a second too late—to the table across the dining room. "I'm sorry, I just figured you knew that the guys from Eight sometimes hang out here, what with it being your dad's house and all." Sara gestured to Alex with a subtle nod. "I take it you know Mr. Congeniality."

"Oh, I know him, all right." The words were out before Zoe could capture them for a do-over, and Sara connected the look on her face with the reason she was making it in about three seconds flat.

"Wait . . . *that's* your Wrong Guy? The one you, ah . . . you know. Tried to pretzel?"

Zoe's laugh was a three to one ratio of irony to actual humor. "Yeah. That would be him."

Thankfully, the steadily growing crowd gave them just enough cover to go unnoticed as she and Sara made their way to the stretch of oak and brass lining the back wall of the dining room. She slid onto an out-of-the-way stool by the break in the bar that served as the waitstaff's pass-through, bracing for impact as Sara settled in behind the wood with a catlike smile.

"Girl. I'll give you this. When you jump into the pool, you sure do aim to make a splash. Alex might be a little all-American for my taste, but there's no denying he's not hard to look at."

A ripple of heat dashed down Zoe's spine as if to second Sara's observation, but Zoe sat up as tall as she could to snuff it out. Alex might be off the roster at Station Eight for the next three weeks, but he was still a firefighter, all the way from his helmet to his hell-yes attitude. She might've had a momentary lapse of sanity yesterday with all that risk-taking, but it couldn't—*wouldn't*—happen again.

"Yeah, well, easy on the eyes or no, firefighters and I don't mix. What happened between me and Alex was an impulsive mistake. I came here to have a drink and put it far behind me, and that's exactly what I intend to do."

Sara grabbed a stainless steel drink shaker from the tray of clean barware on the counter behind her, filling it with a hefty scoop of ice before following suit with an even heftier portion of Grey Goose. "You sure about that?"

"Yes." Zoe cleared her throat once, then twice to make sure the words held conviction. "Absolutely. I'm sure."

"Well, good, because he looks about as serious as I've

ever seen him," Sara said, although if her eyes had strayed from the drink ingredients under her hands, Zoe hadn't caught the sneak peek. "Also, he's about five paces behind you and coming in hot at four o'clock. Heads up."

Zoe sucked in a breath, hoping like hell that the *huh?!* flooding her central nervous system didn't translate to the expression on her face. "Thanks," she murmured, and Sara had barely winked in reply before Alex arrived at the bar.

"Zoe? What are you doing here?" he asked, and damn it, those wide-open baby blues were just freaking unfair. But they were going to have to do this face-to-face soon enough, and anyway, they were both adults. She had a kitchen to run, and he had community service to fulfill. There was no reason they couldn't both do precisely that.

"I know I take my job seriously, Donovan, but I am human. Plus, I heard these were the best in town, so . . ." She gestured to the martini glass that had magically appeared on the stretch of glossy oak at her elbow, softening the edges of her expression just enough to take any heat out of the words.

"Okay, okay. Fair enough. I guess that was kind of a dumb question." He tipped his head in concession, his smile lasting for less than a second before pressing into a flat line. "Listen, I'm not really a beat-around-the-bush kind of guy, so I'm just going to say this. I owe you an apology for last night."

Zoe's belly did the knot-and-squeeze beneath the thin cotton of her shirt. "You don't owe me anything," she said, but the sudden flash of determination darkening his stare locked the rest of her protest in her throat.

"Yeah, I do. Kissing you like that was out of bounds. I won't cross the line again."

Her pride prickled at the conviction tightening the angle of Alex's lightly stubbled jaw, but she stuffed the feeling aside. This was their chance to get back to business, and she'd be a fool to let her blistered ego keep her from making the smart play. "I'm sure you won't. Fresh start on Monday?" Zoe held out her hand, and after a pause so scant she'd have missed it if she'd blinked, Alex met it with a firm shake.

"Sure." He let go of her fingers, pushing both hands into the pockets of his jeans before nodding at her untouched drink. "Anyway, I don't want to keep you. Have a good night."

He turned back toward the dining room, but before Zoe could even swivel halfway around on her bar stool, he'd retraced his steps back to her side. "I know you think I don't take you seriously, but you're wrong."

Too surprised at his about-face to speak, Zoe sat glued to her bar stool, staring at Alex as he continued.

"The reason I didn't kiss you at the picnic, and the reason I didn't take you inside last night isn't because I look at you like you're my kid sister."

"It isn't?" she managed, lifting a brow to broadcast her doubt, but Alex stepped in to meet her mistrust head-on. With his hip angled against the bar and her still-seated position, the shift brought them perfectly face-to-face, both his expression and his stance unwavering as he caught her gaze and held it.

"No. It isn't."

Wait. He was serious. "Then what is the reason?"

The edges of Alex's mouth twitched into an irony-laden smile, but he answered with no hesitation. "The reason I didn't take you inside last night is because I *don't* look at you like that. I see exactly what's in front of me, Zoe. But you and I aren't the only people in this equation, and that's why I was out of line. That's why it can't happen again."

Zoe's brows tightened in confusion before a bolt of understanding sent them flying high. "You turned me down because my father is your captain?"

"Yeah, Gorgeous," Alex said, shooting just as straight as ever. "I turned you down because your father is my captain."

Just when Zoe had thought this whole thing couldn't get any more embarrassing, she'd gone and gotten cock-blocked by her father.

She was going to need more than one drink to relax her way past this.

"That's one hell of a code of ethics you've got there," Zoe said, the lemony tartness of her martini shrinking her tongue as she took a much-needed sip, and now Alex's smile came more easily.

"Don't sound so shocked. Anyway, you've got some pretty ironclad principles of your own."

She held up her hands, signaling *guilty as charged*. "I guess I shouldn't be surprised. After all, that's the deal at Eight, right? Band of brothers. All you firefighters have each other's backs no matter what."

"We do." Alex's answer was slow but didn't lack certainty. "Somehow, though, I get the feeling your father has your back even above that."

Zoe's inhale sent a slice of pain between her ribs, jagged and unexpectedly deep. "I used to think so."

"But not anymore." Although it wasn't a question, the words hung in the air between them, wanting an answer, and Zoe took another sip from the thin rim of her glass.

"It's complicated."

But rather than giving in to the deflection, Alex leaned one elbow on the bar, the muscles in his forearm flexing just slightly beneath the pushed-up sleeve of his gray Henley as he got good and comfortable. "Uncomplicate it for me."

Zoe knew—she *knew*—she should let the subject drop, thank Sara for the drink, and head home to her cookbooks and her bubble bath. What's more, she knew that when the rubber met the raceway, Alex would let her take the out if she dodged the conversation with a little more gusto. But something way down deep in her belly sparked to life at the bold yet simple way he stood there in front of her, calmly waiting, as if spilling her feelings about the recent strain on her relationship with her father was just as no-big-deal as talking about Monday's lunch menu at Hope House.

And Zoe had been dying to spill her feelings for months.

Chapter Twelve

One of these days, Alex was going to remember to be careful what he wished for *before* he got to hankering, but today? So not that day. He hadn't meant to ask Zoe about her father; hell, he hadn't meant to say a single word beyond the apology he knew he owed her. After he'd gotten over the two-sided shock of her being in his local hangout and the down-to-*there* back of the top she'd chosen for her night on the town, Alex had walked himself over to Zoe's spot at the bar to deliver the "I'm sorry" and leave her in peace. But the hurt on her face combined with the vulnerability beneath it had his words flying out before he could temper them.

The best laid plans had nothing on this woman.

"My father and I haven't really seen eye to eye for a while," Zoe started, picking at the edge of her cocktail napkin with her fingernail. "I guess it all started a couple of years ago when he got hurt."

Alex's breath went tight in his lungs. "That was a hard time for all of us."

It was an understatement, of course. Mason had died and Brennan had fallen off the grid in the wake of his career-ending injury only six months before Captain Westin had been hurt, too. The scene had been hairy when they'd arrived, with a storefront already heavily involved and multiple reports of entrapment. Another engine had been on scene, and Westin had relinquished his second-in-command post to run point, going inside to lead one of Eight's squad guys and a woman who had been trapped to safety. Part of the ceiling had come down just before their exit, burning through Westin's safety gear and knocking him unconscious. Although he'd proved his salt by making a full recovery, the second-degree burn scars on his neck and shoulder were a constant reminder that life could pirouette on a dime.

Zoe nodded, a tendril of hair spilling free from the loose knot at her crown. "It was always my mother's worst nightmare, that something would happen to him on a call. When you guys lost Mason, and Brennan was hurt badly enough to end his career, she nearly lost her mind with worry. My father swore up and down that he was careful and he'd be fine, but even as a captain, he's always been so hands on."

"He has," Alex agreed. Shit, Cap had run the obstacle course with them at FFD's training facility not even two weeks ago, and that thing was grueling enough to make Alex want to tap out on most days. "We prepare for the job the best we know how, but at the end of the day, risk still goes with the territory."

"Maybe, but for him it didn't have to. When he got hurt, my mother and I begged him to apply for a promotion to battalion chief." Her voice went low, and Alex's gut took a downward trip to meet it.

"You're serious." No way. The house could deal with a lot of things, but losing their captain wasn't one of them. Westin was more of a cornerstone at Station Eight than the bricks and mortar, for Chrissake. Every firefighter in the place saw him not just as their commanding officer, but as a father figure.

Some of them more than others.

Zoe's expression didn't budge. "Of course I'm serious. He's been with the department for twenty-five years, Alex. He could've made chief ages ago. He just never wanted to."

Alex proceeded, albeit with care. "I take it he still doesn't."

"No. My parents went rounds over it for months. The risks of the job scared the hell out of my mother, and they still scare the hell out of me. After he got hurt, my mom just couldn't take it anymore. But he is who he is. Ultimately, she left."

Damn. Alex—just like everyone else at Eight—had been shocked to hear about Westin's divorce, although the man had mentioned the split once and once only. The job put a strain on even the best marriages, and probably kept countless relationships from even getting to that stage. Alex had always taken it as a given that marriage was off the table for him anyway. But still, no wonder she was so anti-risk. "Zoe, I'm really sorry."

"I am too." Her lashes swept downward, guarding her gaze in the low, soft light of the bar. "Their divorce took me completely by surprise. I know it's kind of corny and clichéd, but for my whole life, our family was perfect. Like, Christmas card, backyard barbecue, Sunday dinner every weekend perfect."

"That's not corny," Alex said, and damn it, the words came too fast and too loud. "What I mean is, it sounds like you were happy."

Zoe froze against her bar stool, her shoulders becoming a long, rigid line. "That's just the point. We *were* happy. I mean, my parents had expectations of me and they set the bar pretty high, but that was okay. Even though my dad was a little ambitious on my behalf, what he wanted from me was mostly fair, and he and my mom always did all that they could to help me reach my goals. The three of us were a team, and we supported each other. Right up until my father didn't."

"He's a damn good firefighter, Zoe." Alex reached out, wrapping his fingers around her forearm to quell the *but* he could see already forming on her lips. "I get that it ended your parents' marriage, and that their divorce hurt you. But just because he's devoted to a risky job doesn't mean he doesn't still have your back."

She dropped her chin, her brown gaze flashing to the spot where his hand curved just above her wrist, but she didn't pull away. "It's not just their divorce and my fear for his safety, although that's certainly not either of our favorite topics."

"Okay. So what else is there?"

Zoe laughed softly, the sound taking him by surprise. "You really are no holds barred, aren't you?"

"'Fraid so," he said, but she shook her head, the dark red of her lipstick outlining her wistful smile.

"Don't be. I don't really have anyone I can air this out with, and to be honest, it's kind of nice. In a weird, spill-my-guts kind of way."

Her pulse beat a strong, steady pattern against Alex's thumb, and he let his grasp linger for a long, sweet second before letting go like he damn well knew he needed to. "I'm glad, I think. But you haven't answered the question."

Zoe paused, but she didn't dodge the topic. "Let's just say my father is rather disappointed in my career move."

"He said that?" Shock pulled Alex's head back to look at her full-on. Cap had practically made a full-time job of bragging about her accomplishments, from college to culinary school to the fancy restaurant in DC. He'd been pretty tight-lipped about her coming back to Fairview, but Alex hadn't thought anything of it.

Until right this second, anyway.

"Pretty much, although he's so tight with what he really

feels, part of me is just guessing. I mean, I get it. I gave up a sure thing—a successful thing—in order to scrape my way through a very unglamorous uphill battle of a job. He says he doesn't like me working at Hope House because it's in a dangerous part of town, but come on. Where else is a soup kitchen going to be?"

"The neighborhood's a little tough," Alex ventured slowly, not wanting to admit out loud that he'd specifically timed his departure from Hope House on Thursday to match up with hers for that very reason. While he hadn't seen anything this week that qualified as an obvious danger, Alex had lived in Fairview long enough to be smart about certain sections of the inner city. Plus, he'd responded to enough calls in the warehouse district to know the neighborhood could dish up some bite to go with its bark.

But Zoe wasn't having it. "I'm tough, too, and my father knows it because that's how he raised me. I know he thinks I'm wasting my time and my talent, and he's right that the pay and the stability at Hope House are a lot less solid than what I'd have on the restaurant circuit. But of all people, I expected him to get my being dedicated to my job. After all, he's so dedicated to his that he chose it over his family."

A curl of something Alex couldn't quite name unwound low in his belly, launching his words out without thought. "Being in-house doesn't quite work that way," he said, and shit, he was veering into dangerous territory. But for eight years, he'd lived by the words Zoe's father had said to him on his first day at Station Eight, and those words had quite literally saved Alex's life.

"Really?" Zoe asked, half stubborn argument and half genuine question. "Then how does it work?"

"Being a firefighter isn't something you choose. When you're really meant for it, the job chooses you." He took a sip of the beer that had mystically appeared at his elbow, making a mental note to double Sara's tip, both for being so observant and for not interrupting his conversation with Zoe. "You can't phone it in, and you can't fake your way through it. You're either a firefighter, right here." Alex paused, just for a second to brush a palm over the center of his Henley. "Or you're not. If you're not, you eventually move on to something else. But if you are, then it's not just your job. It's who you are."

After a minute of clear and quiet thought, Zoe said, "I don't know. I guess I just thought . . ." Her words faltered, but the warm-whiskey fire in her eyes didn't dim. "I thought he'd always have my back, and that we'd always be a family, but now he and I can't even have a conversation without fighting, even though we never really *talk* about a thing. Between my career implosion and my parents' divorce, I feel like everything I thought I knew just got yanked out from under me. One minute I had things I could rely on, and the next, I just . . . didn't."

"Yeah." Alex had his hand over hers before his brain could kill the move. "Sometimes life slaps you with a whole lot more than you bargained for."

Zoe's brows tucked into a gold-blond *V* of concern and curiosity. "Sounds like firsthand knowledge."

Annnnnnd he'd officially pushed the boundaries of this conversation. Jesus, since when had spouting platitudes become part of his blueprint? He needed to button his goddamn yap before this little chat needed a tourniquet.

So what if Zoe was dead-on accurate.

"It's a long story," Alex drawled, digging deep for his most charming smile. "And anyway, we're talking about you, remember? Do you feel any better? You know, in a weird, spill-your-guts kind of way."

Her laugh loosened the screws on both the conversation and the tension pulling tight behind his sternum, and hell, with those little wisps of hair that had fallen loose to frame her face and the sudden burst of genuine ease in her smile, she really was beautiful.

"Yeah, actually. I do. Thanks for listening."

Alex tipped his beer at her, although for the first time he could remember, his cocky default felt just the least bit ill-fitting. "Not a problem, Gorgeous. Just remember this next time you want to put me on trash duty in the kitchen, okay?"

The conversation turned to polite but pleasant enough chat about her apartment (not terribly far from the fire-house), hockey play-offs (she was a Flyers fan, which had to piss her Pittsburgh-loving father off something fierce), and whether or not the hot wings at Bellyflop truly earned their "atomic" moniker. (They did, but Alex wasn't above watching Zoe find out for herself. Sadly, she took Sara's word for it.) Finally, after her drink was gone and the conversation coasted to a natural stop, he walked her to her car, forcing himself to zero in on the pavement in front of him rather than risk getting another eyeful of the barely there back of her shirt. The damn thing was cut so decadently low, chances were slim to none that she was wearing anything other than body lotion underneath it.

How a mere swath of cotton could turn even the most in-control guy into a knuckle-dragging Neanderthal, Alex really had no clue. But holy hell, he wanted to slide that shirt off her shoulders to explore the hot, bare expanse of skin underneath. With his eyes. His hands.

His mouth.

Off-limits, you jackass! No matter how seductively sweet she sounded when she begged you to take her to bed last night.

"Well, *that* was interesting."

Alex hadn't even made it back to his regular table in the middle of Bellyflop's still semi-crowded bar area before Cole had lasered in on him as if he'd suddenly sprouted a two-foot bull's-eye in the middle of his chest.

"What was interesting?" Alex asked, even though he heard exactly how lame the question sounded before he'd finished asking. But the last thing he needed was for Cole to make a big deal where there wasn't one, so he sank a thumb into the belt loop of his jeans and leaned against the touch-screen jukebox on the far wall of the bar, pretending to peruse his options while he worked up the most bored expression he could muster.

Cole shot an obvious glance to the now empty spot at the bar where Alex had just spent the better part of ninety minutes listening to Zoe give her frustrations some airtime. "Seriously, Teflon? You're not really going to try and no-big-deal me on this. She's Westin's daughter, for Chrissake. And she's a hell of a lot more grown up than the last time we saw her."

"Come on, Everett. She had a rough day," Alex said, modulating his voice to its easiest setting despite Cole's implication. His main reason for going over and talking to Zoe in the first place had been because he'd owed her an apology, not that he could tell Cole that. Even so, letting her sit there all by herself would've been rude. "She just felt like blowing off steam and she doesn't really know anyone else in Fairview. We were only talking. That's all."

"That's all," Cole repeated, and the words weren't a question.

Alex's fingers curled tight at his sides, his molars locking together with a soft *clack*. "If you've got something to say, get to saying it."

One light brown brow lifted, and damn it. What was it about Zoe Westin that threw Alex so roundly out of whack?

"Look," Cole said, taking a step back like the peace-keeper he was. "I'm not trying to jump in your shit, and I don't make a habit of telling people what to do. Least of all, you. But I wouldn't be doing my job as your best friend or your fellow firefighter if I didn't point out that you're heading toward dangerous waters. I know you like to tempt fate, and I also get why. But one of these days, if you're not careful, karma is going to knock you clean on your ass."

"My tempting fate has nothing to do with Zoe, and that's exactly how it's going to stay." As much as Alex wanted to find a way around the words, he also knew he couldn't. "Look, I'm not stupid, man. I know the score. But I'm also not going to turn a blind eye if she needs a good vent. Really. What's going on between me and Zoe is nothing personal."

"You sure about that?" Cole asked, and this time there was leeway in his voice.

Alex took it without thinking twice. "After everything the old man did for me? Absolutely."

He belonged at the firehouse, and the firehouse alone. No matter how much a wicked little part of him still wanted her—and wanted her badly—Alex knew beyond the shadow of a doubt that his karma couldn't have anything to do with Zoe Westin.

Chapter Thirteen

Zoe slung the thick strap of her messenger bag over one shoulder, the keys to Hope House's back door jingling against her palm as she made her way to the entrance and put them to work first on the dead bolt, then on the bottom lock. She had to admit, getting breakfast together was a whole lot easier with Alex on the schedule, and even though he'd probably put in the bare minimum because she'd lost their bet, it was still more help than she had on most days.

Better company, too.

Zoe's normally confident stride faltered into a stutter-step as she crossed the back threshold to the kitchen. Okay, so she'd let loose with way more personal information than she'd meant to two nights ago at Bellyflop, and Alex had shocked the hell out of her not just by being a good listener, but by actually seeming to get how she felt even though he'd offered up a different viewpoint. But he was still a fire-fighter, one of her father's to boot, and that meant Alex took risks for a living in addition to taking them for fun. She simply couldn't put herself on the line by getting involved with a guy like him. No matter how good she'd felt when he'd put his hand over hers and listened like he knew exactly how she felt.

No matter how badly she wanted his hands in other places, too.

"Good morning," came the rumble of a very smooth, very male voice, and Zoe let out a graceless yelp and flail combo while cranking her fists in a knee-jerk defensive maneuver.

"Whoa, whoa, whoa! Hold on there, slugger." Alex stepped directly into her line of vision, holding up both hands in surrender. "It's just me, your kitchen jockey."

A moderately unladylike curse chased the shock from Zoe's veins. "Jeez, Alex! What are you doing here so early?" It was barely six A.M., for God's sake.

"I'm broadening my horizons," he said, the obvious gleam in his bright blue eyes heating her cheeks along with a couple of places due south despite the unease she knew his words should trigger.

"That sounds dangerous." She released her death grip on her keys, slipping them into her bag before covering the handful of steps toward her office. Alex's boots kept time with her Danskos on the kitchen tiles, but he waited until she'd stowed her belongings and started moving toward the kitchen proper before coming out with an answer.

"It is, but I promise you'll like this kind of danger."

"The last time you said that, I lost a bet," Zoe reminded him, snagging a clean apron from one of the hooks by the dishwasher, realizing only belatedly that it matched the one molded over Alex's FFD T-shirt.

"Yeah, about that. Since you need the help, and I've got nothing but time for three more weeks, I was thinking we could call it a draw and you could teach me how to cook, after all."

"I'm sorry. What?" She froze into place, one hundred percent certain she'd mis-heard him, but Alex gestured to the copy of the weekly menu posted on the wall outside the pantry, and holy shit, he was serious.

"Today's breakfast is bacon and scrambled eggs with vegetables, right? That sounds pretty good, and I figure it wouldn't hurt me to know how to make a decent hot breakfast. If you're still willing to teach me, that is."

Zoe closed her mouth. Opened it again. Closed it once more before forcing herself to say, "I am, but what's the catch?"

Alex laughed, long and loud, and she heard the less-than-polite implication only after the question had popped out.

"You know what, I'm sorry. That was—"

"Honest," he supplied, flipping a dish towel over one shoulder. "And also well deserved, because as it just so happens, I'm not entirely without motive. I came early to help in the kitchen, but I also wanted to ask you about something."

She moved toward the small sink at the back of the prep space, giving her hands a good scrub down before waiting for Alex to do the same. "Okay. I'll play. What's got your attention so much that you're willing to make breakfast for it?"

"Have you ever heard of the Collingsworth Grant?"

Just when Zoe thought he couldn't say anything that would shock her. "I run a nonprofit, Alex. Of course I've heard of the Collingsworth Grant. A better question might be how on earth you've heard of it, though."

"Let's just say I have a black belt in Google-fu and I don't sleep very much by habit. What do you know about the Collingsworths?"

Zoe shrugged. Albeit a bit strange, it wasn't the worst topic they could've chosen for discussion. "They're the richest and most influential family in Fairview. Marcus and Emily Collingsworth both do a ton of philanthropic work at Fairview Medical Center, along with a handful of select local charities." The grant was a whopper—or twenty-five thousand whoppers, if you wanted to get technical about things—and the application process was about as rigorous as the bar exam with Navy SEAL training sprinkled on top. "What does their grant have to do with anything?"

Alex followed her past the door of the walk-in, his breath coming out in wispy white puffs around his face as he said, "Hope House could use that money about a thousand different ways, right? So why don't you get a little ballsy and apply?"

"Because I'd never get it." She didn't skip a beat, reaching for the carton of green peppers on the metal-wire shelving in front of her, but of course she should've known Alex would take the word *never* as a personal challenge rather than a concrete impossibility.

"What makes you so sure?" He slid the box of peppers from her grasp, balancing it solidly over one forearm, and Zoe added two containers of mushrooms to the pile as she picked the most obvious answer out of the ten she could've offered.

"Most nonprofits have to be up and running for years before an organization will seriously consider them for a grant."

"Great. So you'd be a pioneer," Alex said, his half smile loaded with full confidence, but she just huffed out a laugh and continued.

"Even then, for every available endowment, there are usually dozens of applicants. In cases like the Collingsworth Grant, it's probably more like a hundred, each one equally deserving and in need." Zoe pulled a tray of eggs off an adjacent shelf, bracing it between both palms as she bumped her hip against the push-bar on the walk-in to pop it open. She'd done a boatload of research on available grants about six seconds after she'd seen the soup kitchen's proposed budget. Finding one she actually had a Hail Mary of getting right out of the gate? Definitely more fantasy than reality. She had no track record, no time to take from the kitchen to apply.

No prayer of getting the grant, no matter how much Hope House might need it.

Alex tipped his head, watching for a minute as she assembled the handful of necessary utensils to get them started on breakfast prep. "I'm still not seeing a good reason not to at least give it a shot. The deadline for the Collingsworth Grant isn't for almost a month."

"It would take three of me to get that application done in time, and I can barely run this place as it is. Look, I get where you're coming from." Zoe paused, meeting his stare with a soft smile that said she meant it. "But realistically, my chances of getting a grant like that for Hope House are negligible. I've got to put what little energy and resources I have into less risky endeavors. Spending all that time on an application for a grant I won't get just isn't a shot worth taking—not when I could be using that time to do things I know will make a difference, for sure."

Alex paused, and for a second, Zoe thought he might actually argue. "Okay," he finally said, dropping his eyes to the stainless steel countertop on the worktable in front of them. "So what's first for breakfast?"

She let out the breath she'd been unknowingly holding, angling her body to face the prep table. "Well, the bacon's pretty self-explanatory, but if you want to get started on the veggies, I'll get the egg mixture together and we can meet in the middle." She pressed a vegetable brush into his hand, and he promptly looked at the thing as if it had sprouted wings and asked to be cleared for takeoff.

"You say 'get started on the veggies' like I have a clue what that entails," he said, holding up the brush in one hand and a cardboard container of mushrooms with the other. "I take it I should scrub these first?"

Zoe nodded, cradling an egg in each palm and popping

the shells apart with a gentle slide of her fingers. "Yes, but not with water. Just give them a gentle dry brush to loosen any dirt on the undersides. Easy."

"Looks like you got the fun job." Alex flicked a glance at the oversized bowl propped beneath Zoe's wrist, and she couldn't resist the curiosity tickling at the back of her mind.

"You forget, being in the kitchen is all varying degrees of fun for me. You, on the other hand, seem to have had a change of heart." The quiet stretched out between them, made no less comfortable by the steady hum of the walk-in and the soft *crack* and *pop* of eggs going into Zoe's bowl, and finally Alex lifted one shoulder in a nonchalant half shrug.

"I'm not going to lie. The only place I want to be is the firehouse. But I don't get to pick that right now, and I *do* see that this place matters to you. I'm stuck here anyway. Seems kind of stupid not to help."

She creased her brow in thought, reaching for the last two eggs in the row. "You were pretty anti-cooking last week."

His shoulders hitched, the increase in tension so slight that Zoe would've missed it if she hadn't looked up at just that second. "You were pretty anti-rock climbing, and you still did it."

She opened her mouth, the fact that he hadn't answered the question burning on her tongue. But the look that crossed his features, there for barely a blink before it was gone, made her capture the words back at the last second.

He hadn't balked at learning how to cook because he thought it was stupid. He'd pushed back for the same reason she'd wanted to resist rock climbing.

The kitchen was outside the perimeter of Alex Donovan's wide, vast comfort zone. And for some unexplained reason, even though he was willing to brave learning how to cook, he didn't want her to know it.

Zoe moved without thinking. "What do you say we get

these vegetables diced together? Then we can get to the good part and you can scramble some eggs." She pulled her padded knife roll from the utility drawer beneath the prep table, sliding both of her multipurpose chef's knives from their reinforced resting spots. Placing one on the counter in front of Alex, she paused to give him a tiny smile before reaching for one of the green peppers in the carton in front of them.

"Are you sure you don't want to just give me the grunt work? I know you've got a limited amount of food, and I don't want to screw up breakfast." His words arrived on nothing more than honesty, which was exactly how Zoe answered them.

"You won't." She held up the pepper, admiring its smooth, jewel-green skin beneath her fingers for just a second before placing it on the cutting board between them. "This part is a lot like coring lettuce. All you have to do is remove the parts that aren't edible, and then cut the rest into pieces. Like this." Purposely slowing her movements, she went through the process, removing first the stem, then the ribs and seeds before treating the pepper to a neat, efficient dice. Then she nudged the box in his direction, turning most of her attention to assembling the first batch of egg mixture.

Alex fumbled the pepper he'd unearthed across the cutting board, chasing it with a swift grab and a low swear. "You make it look easy."

Zoe laughed, although without heat or disdain. "Well, for me, it kind of is, but I've had a little practice, remember? Try cutting off the bottom, too. The flat surface makes it easier to remove the seeds and get to slicing, see?"

She guided him through the motions one more time before turning the cutting board back over. Although his effort lacked finesse, all extended elbows and tight, hunched shoulders, the motions were functional enough, and Alex muddled through without destroying the bell pepper. For the most part. "Okay. That's not so bad." A smile lifted the corner of his mouth, pure mischief, and he slid the fruits—or in this case, the vegetables—of his labor into the bowl waiting on the counter. "What's next, Gorgeous? I could do this all day."

Whether it was his sexy smile or the *really* sexy confidence that fueled the gesture, Zoe couldn't be sure. But rather than giving in to the blush begging to take over her cheeks, she looked Alex right in the baby blues with some confidence of her own.

"Good, because I just got started with you, pretty boy. The rest of these peppers aren't going to dice themselves, and we're going to have a dining room full of hungry people in an hour. So are you going to get to work on your meal prep, or are you just going to talk about it?"

Alex's jaw unhinged, but the shock quickly fell prey to his deep-bellied laughter. "Far be it for me to turn down a challenge." He reached into the carton for another pepper, but just when Zoe was about to let herself enjoy an internal *gotcha!* he tacked on, "So you think I'm pretty, do you?"

He delivered the words with just enough suggestion to catch her unaware, and the blush she'd held at bay roared over her face without remorse.

"It's a figure of speech, Alex. The same as you calling me 'Gorgeous.'" Her blade flew over the mushrooms on her cutting board with a quick-fire *tat-tat-tat,* but despite her flashy knife skills, Alex refused to be distracted.

"That's not a no," he drawled, and all at once, whatever it was that had made her toe the line with him in the first place came charging back to dare her right over the edge. Even though Zoe knew he was a firefighter—one with unflagging loyalties to both the job and her father—something dark and forbidden and utterly magnetic made her put down her chef's knife and move right into Alex's personal space.

"No," she said, hearing the traces of velvet in her voice, watching his eyes darken to a near navy blue as he heard it, too. "That's not a no."

He froze into place, so close Zoe could see his pupils flare, and there was no softening the keen edge of the thrill in her blood at the desire banked behind his stare. "Zoe."

"Alex. I wish you would—"

His fingers were on her lips, quelling the rest with a single stroke. "You should be careful what you wish for."

But the connection of Alex's fingers, still hot on the center of her mouth, took her from bold to brazen in the span of a breath. "Is that what you want?" she asked, catching his hand in hers. "For me to be careful?"

"No. It's not."

The answer vibrated through her, and despite the caution sensors clanging full-bore in the back of her mind, Zoe wanted him to say it again.

Because careful was the furthest thing from what she wanted.

But then a familiar set of footsteps echoed, first on the floorboards of the dining room, then on the kitchen tiles at the pass-through door, and Alex and Zoe flew apart like smoke in a stiff wind.

"Hey, you two." Tina stopped just past the threshold, clasping a manila file folder over the front of her purple blouse with a smile that didn't come close to reaching her eyes. "I'm sorry to interrupt. I know you're in the middle of breakfast prep."

"You're not interrupting," Zoe chirped, just a beat too fast and a shade too bright. But then she registered the look on Tina's face, and her friend's troubled expression hijacked the heat from Zoe's veins to replace it with concern. "Tina? What's the matter?"

"We've got two new residents, Rochelle and Kenny. They're mother and son, but there are some extenuating circumstances about their stay. Social services brought them both in about an hour ago."

Alex's brows winged upward, his attention clearly as focused on Tina as Zoe's was. "Isn't five in the morning a little unusual for that kind of thing?"

Tina nodded, the half-moon shadows beneath her eyes growing more pronounced with her frown, and Zoe's pulse did double time as her codirector turned toward her, all business. "Everything about this one is unusual. Look, I know there's a staunch rule against food leaving the kitchen and the dining area. I also know there are good reasons for those rules."

"There are," Zoe said, calling up the city's code in her mind. It was strict for any number of reasons, not the least of which was proper sanitation and to keep residents from hoarding food. "The health department regs are pretty cut and dried, Tina. We'd have to have a damned good reason to violate food service rules and risk getting written up, or worse."

"Well, we might have one. Kenny's father, Damien, beat Rochelle senseless two days ago, and she's terrified he's going to come here and find her."

Zoe's stomach pitched at the same time Alex went triple-knot tight at her side. "Jesus," Zoe breathed. "Did she file a report?" If social services was involved, chances were good that the police were, too, but domestic cases were dicey. Zoe had heard of way too many women refusing to file out of fear, or worse.

"The doctors at the clinic called in the FPD. Apparently this wasn't the first time they'd seen her, and her injuries were . . . more significant this time," Tina said, pausing to dip her chin in agreement at Alex's muttered curse before she continued. "Of course, Damien made bail after spending twenty-four hours in the tank. Social services is trying to place Rochelle and the little boy with some family in Grand Rapids. But for right now, we're the only bed they've got."

"And how old is the kid? Kenny?" Alex asked.

Tina slipped her thumb and forefinger over the bridge of her nose. "Five."

Zoe reached out for the counter in front of her, gripping the stainless steel in an effort to steady the emotions flinging themselves around in her chest. "Okay. Millie and Ellen will be here in a few minutes, and I'll get them on food prep for breakfast service. Alex, I need you to get the dining room set up."

He nodded, no hesitation. "I can tell Millie and Ellen what's going on when they get here, too."

"Thanks. I'm going to make two hot meals and bring them over right now, Tina. Then you and I can connect after breakfast to get a longer-term plan in place for how to handle the rest of their meals while they're here. Let's get this woman and her son taken care of."

"Thanks, sweetie." Relief washed over Tina's face, loosening her shoulders. "Normally, I wouldn't ask you to break the rules, but this woman is terrified to leave her bed."

Zoe turned toward the pantry, her resolve already tacked firmly into place as she said, "Sometimes you've got to chuck the rules in order to make a difference."

Chapter Fourteen

Alex made his way through the swinging door between Hope House's kitchen and dining room, his body in the here-and-now even though his mind was still squarely stuck two hours in the past. Everything about this morning had taken a whack at his comfort zone, from his impulsive offer to let Zoe teach him to cook to the gut-twisting news Tina had brought about the shelter's new residents. The only thing that had kept Alex grounded this morning was the way Zoe had moved through the kitchen as she'd shown him the basics, so fluid and easy and completely at home in her space that despite his reservations, he couldn't help but feel that way, too. The teasing confidence she'd shown before Tina had arrived had made it all too easy for him to slide into the cocky demeanor he wore like a set of broken-in turnout gear, and her fiery determination to hang the rules to help the young mother and her son had made it all too obvious that Zoe's bold side lived closer to the surface than she'd like to let on.

Trouble was, when Zoe Westin got reckless, Alex wanted to hang the rules, too. And the more he let his attraction to her smolder and burn, the less he'd be able to resist giving in to the heat growing between them.

"Oh, Alex. Great timing." Ellen's warm smile unstuck his thoughts, and he slapped together a return gesture that hopefully covered up any traces of where his impetuous brain had taken him.

"Hey, Ellen. What's up? Do you two need another round of clean coffee mugs out here?" He turned to check the shelf behind the food service counter where Ellen and Millie usually spent their volunteer shifts, but Ellen cut off the movement with a laugh.

"No, no. Nothing like that. We've got plenty of plates and mugs. It's just that breakfast is winding down a bit, and, well . . ." The gray-haired woman dropped her gaze past the serving tray of scrambled eggs in front of her, focusing on her plain white tennis shoes as she pressed a hand to her lower back. "My sciatica is acting up, and quite frankly, I'd love a break."

He blinked. "Oh. Okay. I'll go get Zoe for you, then."

"Sweetheart, please," Ellen said, lifting an eyebrow as she waved him into the spot she'd vacated at the counter. "She slipped next door a little while ago to check on that poor girl who arrived this morning, and I wouldn't dream of pulling her away so I can take a breather. Zoe said you're part of the crew. That's more than good enough for me."

"She said that?" Alex tried—and failed—to keep his shock in check. But come on. Only a week ago, Zoe had done her Sunday best to boot his ass out the door. Not that he hadn't given her good reason, but at the time, he'd have rather had a fistful of root canals than spend a minute more than necessary in her kitchen.

Damn. Had that really only been last week?

"She said it this morning when you were getting things set up out here," Millie offered, gesturing to the dining room and adding her nod along with Ellen's. "You've been a big help, especially today."

"I'm just trying to do my job," Alex said, sending his

gaze on a quick tour around the halfway-full dining room. "Listen, all of these residents have already been served, and breakfast really is winding down. Why don't you two both go take a breather? If we get an unexpected last-minute crowd, I'll holler."

Both women's faces creased in concern, but Alex amped up his smile. "Ten minutes, girls. You can time it if it makes you feel better."

"You're quite the charmer, aren't you?" Millie asked, but it didn't escape his notice that she hadn't said no.

"That's the rumor. Go on, you two. I promise not to sneak any bacon."

He shooed both ladies through the swinging door leading to the kitchen, taking a closer look at the dining room. Most of the people were seated and already eating, with only a few milling about the clearing station to return their trays and dishes to the kitchen. Alex had to admit, Zoe really had come up with an efficient system, with designated bins for trash and recycling, plus bus bins for dirty utensils and dishes requiring a run-through with the geriatric dishwasher in the back. Even understaffed and understocked, Hope House ran like a precision instrument, from the regulations to the routines.

And every last one of the people who came in hungry and in need would leave with a full stomach. All because Zoe cared enough to make it happen.

"I see we haven't run you off just yet," came a familiar voice from the other side of the service counter, and despite the gravity of his morning, Alex's grin was inevitable.

"I'm hanging in there, Hector. Have you had your cup of coffee this morning?" He gestured toward the carafe at the back of his workstation, but the old man waved him off with a lift of his weathered hand.

"I was first in line, fireman. But don't worry, Miss Millie filled my cup to the top."

"Good to know she's taking care of you," Alex said, pausing for a second to do the same for the woman who had stepped up next to Hector with an empty coffee cup on her tray. "So how's life in the fast lane? Are you behaving yourself?"

Hector's laugh welled up, rusty and deep. "I'm trying. The windows over by my bed let in a draft something awful, but it's not so bad now that the weather's turning warmer."

Alex's eyes skimmed the painted cinder-block walls, landing on the windows at the far end of the dining room by the double doors leading to the street. "Yeah, this building is probably twenty years old, at least. I had the same problem with the windows at my place a couple of years ago."

"I wanted to put something around the windowsill— I have an extra sweater I could stuff in the cracks—but Miss Tina says it's against the rules."

"Take it from an expert, you definitely want all possible exits unimpeded. Just in case you need them," Alex said, his mind tumbling back for only a second before he added, "You know, I ended up being able to fix a bunch of the windows at my place with new weather stripping. It's not a permanent solution, but it helped for a while before I could get the windows replaced. If Zoe can spare me for a few minutes between now and lunch, I'll come take a look, see if I can't get you fixed up over there." He remembered those drafts all too well, and the weather stripping hadn't been too tough of a fix. With a handful of materials and just as many hours, he could probably hook Tina up pretty quick.

"Oh." Hector blinked, his surprise magnified by the thick lenses of his glasses. "You're kind of handy for a fireman, aren't you?"

Alex's gut squeezed behind the thin white cotton of his apron, but he covered the sensation with a half shrug.

"Gotta be prepared, Hector. You never know what life's going to throw at you."

The hard-edged *bang* of the door leading in from the street stole whatever response Hector had planned to give, and Alex's pulse did a lightning fast zero-to-sixty even though he moved nothing but his eyes. A man he'd never seen before appeared in the door frame, wild-eyed and radiating anger. His shoulders were drawn up tight around his neck, his movements broken and rough as he crossed over the threshold, and every last internal alarm bell in Alex's arsenal went ballistic.

"I'm going to guess this guy's not a regular." Alex kept his tone low and purposely neutral despite the increasing worry lining Hector's face, and the older man's barely there head shake was all he needed in response. Although the stranger hadn't spoken or moved from the front of the dining room since bullying his way through the door, he was clearly agitated and *very* clearly searching the room for something he couldn't find.

This guy had thirty-one flavors of *not right in the head* written all over him.

"He looks like trouble. Do you want me to go get Miss Zoe?" Hector asked, and Alex's head jacked around on a fresh push of adrenaline.

"No." He forced an inhale past his vocal cords, long and deep. Channeling every last ounce of his waning nonchalance into the move, Alex took his cell phone from the back pocket of his jeans and slid it nice and easy over the food service counter. "I want you to take this and be ready to call nine-one-one. Don't get Zoe or Tina. Do you understand?"

Hector had barely closed his fingers over the phone before Alex rounded the food service counter to the back of the dining room. He'd memorized the layout after his third hour at Hope House, complete with all possible entry and exit points, only some of which were doors. Blocking out the extraneous variables like averted glances, hushed murmurs, and clattering silverware, Alex shrank his focus down to one, single pinpoint, assessing, collecting, calculating.

Six feet tall. Linebacker frame. Worn flannel shirt and even more worn out work boots.

A face full of rage and dark, flat eyes that promised nothing short of murder.

Zero percent chance this wasn't Damien, doing exactly what Rochelle had feared.

"Rochelle!" The man's shout echoed through the room like cannon fire, kicking Alex's breath through his lungs. "This is the only damn shelter on this side of the city and I know you ain't got the cash to get far. Where the hell are you?"

Damien stomped up the aisle bisecting the two sides of the dining room, slanting nasty, narrow-eyed glares at all the residents who had been effectively shocked into their seats, and Alex was moving across the floorboards before his brain got the oh-hell-no message all the way to his feet. Damn it, there had to be fifty people in here, all of them in close enough proximity that this scenario could go pear-shaped in less than a second. As twitchy as he was to act first and ask questions later, his most viable option was to chill this shit-bag out. At least until he could boot his ass back outside the shelter.

"Can I help you?" Alex asked, scraping up the words as he laced his arms over his chest.

Damien turned to flatten Alex with a beady-eyed stare, and hell. He looked rabid-dog mean, and just as remorseless. "Who the fuck are you?"

Alex's jaw cranked as tight as his fists, and he scratched together every last fragment of his willpower. "I'm serving breakfast. And you need to watch your mouth."

"What I *need* is to find my kid." Damien raked him with

a gaze, slithering a step closer, then another. "You in charge of this shit hole? Because I ain't leaving without my boy, and I know he's gotta be hiding in here someplace with his little bitch of a momma."

Pure anger climbed the back of Alex's throat, turning his response barbed-wire sharp. "Oh, you're leaving, and you're leaving right now. There are a lot of different ways this can go down. Only one of them has a happy ending for you. Now get out before I haul you out."

"I told you." Damien stabbed his boots into the floor-boards, growling along with a stare made of pure malice. "I want my boy. And if you're in charge, I'll go through you to get him."

Alex's decision took less than a second. He lurched forward, every last intention of dragging this miscreant out of Hope House burning fast and hot in his blood. But a very familiar, very furious voice stopped him clean in his tracks.

"If you want the person in charge, then you're looking for me. But I can promise you, you're still not going to get what you came here for."

Zoe's heartbeat slammed behind her breastbone, the white noise *whoosh* of blood pumping so hard against her eardrums that she was almost dizzy. Okay, so mouthing off to Damien might've been a little impulsive, but she'd had to do *something* to keep Alex away from the guy. She'd called nine-one-one the second she'd passed through the side door from the shelter and heard Damien slam his way through the dining room.

Please, God. Let me be able to talk this animal down until the cops get here.

"You run this fucking place?" Damien turned on his heel to fasten her with an unrelenting stare at the same time

Alex froze over the floorboards to look at her in disbelief, but she blocked out one in favor of the other.

"I do. And you need to leave." She pulled in a shaky breath, sticking it with all her resolve. "Now."

Damien's smile was all teeth, the tread on his boots calling out a hard *thump* as he took a step toward her, then another. "That's not how this works, little girl. You got something that belongs to me, and I *will* get it."

Zoe jammed her hands over her hips, mostly to stop them from trembling. The fresh memory of Kenny, curled up against the side of his mother's body not encumbered by the sling holding her dislocated shoulder, flashed through her mind, strengthening her words to steel. "Unless you've got a court order I'm not aware of, no. You won't."

For just a breath, everything in the dining room stood stop-motion still, the hum of the overhead fluorescents the only thing cutting through the palpable tension in the room.

And then everyone moved at once.

Damien sprang toward her, creating a shock wave of startled shouts and scraping chairs in his wake. Zoe's lungs constricted in spite of her burning need to inhale, her pulse tearing through her veins on a flood of high-octane adrenaline. From the corner of her eye, she caught flickers of motion in the center of the dining room, scraps of speed and undeniable intention. But by the time she registered the blond hair, the blue eyes turned dark with fear and ferocity, Damien's fingers had wrapped around her upper arms, digging in without quarter.

"Give me my boy." The stale-whiskey stink of his exhale hit Zoe full force with the bite of every word, and oh God oh God oh God oh God, she couldn't get out of his grasp.

"No." Her voice betrayed her with a wobble, and Damien's hands cranked down over her thinly covered arms, sending twin spears of pain all the way to her fingertips.

"Bitch, you are going to regret this."

Zoe's muscles locked down for a single second before her survival instinct ripped into gear, and she thrust one foot out in a swift kick. The front of her steel-toed kitchen clog connected with Damien's shin, the force of the contact reverberating back up her leg. He reared back in pain at the same time Alex reached him from behind, and relief flooded through every last part of her.

A half second too early.

By the time Zoe registered the increased pressure on her arms, it was gone, along with her balance as Damien shoved her backward with what had to be all his strength. Her feet left the floorboards, arms wheeling in a hard arc as she scrabbled for purchase. Vaguely, she heard clips of sound, pounding feet and voices, gruff and full of panic.

And then her shoulder slammed into the door frame, forcing every last shred of oxygen from her chest with a hard *whump*.

"Zoe!" After she made a series of foggy attempts to nail her focus all the way into place, Tina's voice broke through the chaos in Zoe's ears, quickly followed by a white-hot streak of pain lighting down her shoulder and into her fingertips as she tested out both her lungs and her limbs.

"Ow." Zoe sucked a breath through her teeth, flattening her free palm against the floorboards in an awkward attempt to find her feet, but both the heavy tingling in her other hand and the gentle pressure of Tina's grasp halted her before she could get more than halfway upright.

"Rochelle," Zoe spit out, a brand-new stream of panic uncurling through her rib cage. God, there were so many people jostling around and making an unholy racket that locking in on one specific target was impossible. "We have to keep Damien away from her."

"Oh, I wouldn't worry about Damien," Tina said, catching the question in Zoe's confused blinks before adding,

"Alex just knocked him clean out, and the police are outside. The only place Damien's going is back to the precinct."

Zoe sagged in relief, although the sensation didn't last. "What about the other residents? Is anyone hurt?" Her second attempt got her to her feet, although, whoa, her legs were none too thrilled at the prospect of holding her upright.

"Just you," Tina said at the exact moment Alex appeared at her side.

"Jesus Christ, Zoe. Sit down and let me look at you." He snatched up a nearby chair, guiding her off her feet without leeway for an argument.

Of course, she still gave one. "Alex, I need to—"

"Do you feel any pain?" He knelt between her knees, sweeping her with a critical head-to-toe gaze, and she belatedly noticed the angry bruise blooming over the knuckles on his right hand.

"I could ask you the same thing." Zoe reached for his hand, but the thudding protest of her shoulder cut the move short.

Alex caught her wince, and although his eyes flared, the rest of his demeanor remained perfectly calm. "Did you hit your head when you fell? Lose consciousness, or anything like that?"

"What? No." She shook her head, but the gesture felt oddly sloppy. "Just my shoulder."

"Can you rate the pain on a scale of one to ten?"

"I'm fine, I just—ouch!" The ache along the back of her arm went full throttle under Alex's touch, and he pulled his hands back as if her involuntary protest had burned him.

"Rate it, Zoe."

"It's a bump, Alex." It might be a nasty one, but still . . . "Really, barely even a four. Can I please stand up? This is my soup kitchen, and I need to make sure everyone's okay. I don't want Rochelle and Kenny to hear the commotion in here and get frightened." The poor woman and her son had been through enough.

Tina and Alex exchanged a look loaded with unspoken communication. She said, "I'll have Millie and Ellen go check on them, but, honey, you need to let someone check on *you*."

As if conjured by the words alone, a uniformed police officer arrived beside Alex, taking careful visual inventory of all three of them before politely interrupting.

"Hey, Donovan. Your perp seems like a gem according to the two witnesses my partner just got a brief statement from, but we've got him in custody. The rest of the scene is secure."

Alex nodded. "Thanks, O'Halloran. You and Macklemore got here damn fast."

"We were only about six blocks up," the officer said, tipping his dark head at the dining room windows facing the street. "I know I don't have to tell you the neighborhood can get a little tough." He swung his gaze toward Zoe, indicating the badge pinned to the front of the black Kevlar vest strapped over his uniform shirt. "I'm Brett O'Halloran, Fairview PD."

"Zoe Westin," she said, lifting a brow in Alex's direction. "Let me guess. You guys skydive together. Or is it rock climbing?"

The officer's lips twitched in the suggestion of a smile as he shot a glance at Alex. "No, ma'am, just softball. How are you feeling, Ms. Westin?"

"Oh, just Zoe, and I'm fine, thanks. I'll be even better if you tell me that asshole is going back to jail, though." She trapped her tongue between her teeth too late, but if Officer O'Halloran was shocked or offended by her brassy statement, his expression sure didn't betray him.

"If you're up to telling me what happened, we might be able to work on that for you."

"I'd be happy to." Zoe gave the officer a succinct rundown of events, with Tina peppering in some of the details that happened after Zoe had been knocked down. After a handful of follow-up questions, Officer O'Halloran flipped his notebook closed.

"With all three of your corroborating statements and a room full of eyewitnesses, this looks pretty cut and dried, especially if this guy's record checks out. Did you want to pursue assault charges?"

Zoe rolled her shoulder, the move hurting like hell. "Yes. Absolutely."

The officer dipped his chin in a nod. "Okay. We've got paramedics on the way to give him the all-clear before we take him downtown to process him, just in case." He paused, splitting his dark brown gaze between Alex and Zoe. "I can roll another ambo out here if you want. It might not be the worst idea to go to Fairview Hospital and get that shoulder looked at."

"No!" Zoe's mouth went dry at the same time her palms turned damp, and Alex, Tina, and Officer O'Halloran narrowed their eyes over her in unison. "What I mean is, I feel fine, and I'd really like to stay here and make sure the residents are okay." Plus, the last thing Zoe needed was the chance that Station Eight's paramedics would catch the call. If her father heard so much as a peep about this, he wouldn't ease up on her until she was ninety.

"Zoe, I really think . . ." Tina started, but Alex stepped in, his most charming smile taking over his handsome features.

"Why don't I just take her to the outpatient clinic over on Broadmoor? It won't be nearly as crowded as the Emergency Department, and the docs can give her the all-clear just the same."

"I'm sitting right here, you know." Zoe scowled, but somehow, she couldn't put much force into it.

Tina, on the other hand, had enough high-test for both of them right now. "Yes, but Alex is right. You *should* be sitting in front of a doctor."

Zoe got halfway to crossing her arms over the front of her gray button-down top before her shoulder gave up a definitive *not today, sweetheart.* But she was quickly running out of steam to fight, and letting Alex take her to urgent care was definitely the lesser of two evils. Between him and Tina, she knew better than to think she'd skate by on her own recognizance. "Fine. But only after I get lunch squared away."

"I've got lunch squared away. You go, and don't come back without a doctor's note," Tina said, her tone brooking no argument. "Officer, I'd like to take care of the residents if you don't need anything else right now . . . ?"

"No, ma'am. We'll be in touch."

Tina turned, giving Alex's forearm a squeeze. "Thank you." She added one last promise that she would make sure Rochelle and her son were well taken care of before quickly stepping off to take charge of the crowd, leaving Zoe with Alex.

"Thank you for not calling the paramedics." With the easy-does-it way he'd suggested the outpatient clinic over the hospital, Alex had to realize that a couple of bruises were really no big deal. Hell, he'd probably sustained worse in any given sports junkie session.

Which was why it shocked Zoe right down to her Danskos when he looped his arm around her, leading her out of her chair and toward the door with nothing but dead-serious intention in his eyes.

"I might've gotten you off the hot seat with Tina, but you *will* get every inch of yourself checked out by a doctor. And you're not leaving my sight until you do."

Chapter Fifteen

Alex sat back against the hospital-grade chair in the exam room, trying like hell to ignore both the bruises peeking out from beneath the sleeves of Zoe's gown and the brows-up I-told-you-so taking over her pretty face.

At least her moxie was easier to handle.

"Are you happy now?" she asked, holding up the doctor's release form and the disk containing her X-rays. "I'm one hundred percent fine and cleared for work."

"Tomorrow," he corrected. "The doctor said you should take it easy for the rest of today."

Zoe smiled. "Right. I should've known you'd have an in at urgent care, too."

"I know a couple of people on staff here, yes. . . ." He was a firefighter with adrenaline issues. Of course he was on a first-name basis with a doc or two. "And I might have particularly strong people skills. But come on, Zoe. As good as I am, I can't finesse a medical diagnosis."

"Fine," she sighed, her shoulders rounding beneath the loose blue cotton of her gown. "But first thing tomorrow, we're back in the kitchen."

Alex's gut shifted with unease, but he put it on hold. Arguing with Zoe right now wouldn't get him farther than frustration, and anyway, she looked about as worn out as he felt. "Yeah, about that. If it's okay with you, I can make up for my lost community service by coming in on Saturday."

Her forehead creased into a delicate *V*. "You haven't lost any time, Alex. Not only did you bring me here to get checked out, but you stayed for two hours while I got the all-clear. I know I fought you a little, but you still didn't have to do any of that."

A smile tempted Alex's lips, and he gave in to it, if only halfway. "You fought me more than a little, Gorgeous. But you let me stay to make sure you were okay, even during your exam, and you definitely didn't have to do that, either." He'd made it clear that while personally walking her through the door was nonnegotiable, he'd wait in the reception area while she talked to the doctor, but she'd shocked him by turning him down.

"It didn't bother me to have you stay; plus, I knew you probably wouldn't take my word for it when I turned out to be fine. And"—Zoe broke off, twisting the floppy sleeve of her gown between the thumb and forefinger on her opposite hand—"I guess it was nice not to be alone."

"Oh." *Eloquent, Donovan. Real suave.* So much for his freaking people skills. "Well, in that case, I'm glad I was a pain in the ass."

"Me too." Her soft laugh loosened the tension on her face, and the sound prompted his thoughts into words without pause.

"Since I'm batting a thousand at being bossy today, what do you say I aim for the fence and insist on driving you home?"

"Won't that leave you stranded in my neighborhood?" Zoe asked. But it didn't escape his notice that she hadn't said no, and screw it. He'd never been good at dancing around the truth.

"Yeah, but you live pretty close to the fire station, which

means I can either hitch a ride home or hop on the subway. I know you can take care of yourself." Alex pushed up from his chair, impulse and endorphins and something he had no name for moving him in front of her with mere inches to spare. "It's just that right now, I don't want you to, okay?"

Zoe's eyes went warm and wide, but she didn't pull back. "Okay."

He slipped past the curtain hanging down from the ceiling, making sure the door was shut all the way so she'd have enough privacy to get dressed before going to wait for her in the lobby. She joined him a few minutes later, and although they didn't say much as they traded the building for the parking lot, then the parking lot for her car, the silence wasn't uncomfortable. In fact, by the time Zoe had guided him through the fifteen-minute drive uptown, Alex had gained back most of his easygoing calm.

And as long as he replaced his thoughts of Zoe's bruises with the satisfaction of having knocked the man who had given them to her into next week, he just might keep it, too.

Zoe reached into her messenger bag, her keys ringing softly as she pulled them from the dark blue canvas. With a quick turn and click, she led the way past a pair of sturdy oak and glass doors, then through a brightly lit lobby lined with metal mailboxes and bulletin boards. A few dozen steps had them in the elevator, and a few dozen after that, she slid the key into the lock on a glossy black door marked 4B.

"I can't guarantee that there aren't any dust rhinos or unfolded laundry lurking about, but this is me."

Alex's curiosity jumped, but he covered it with a half shrug as he followed her past her tiny foyer and into a cozy, sun-filled living room. The last thing he wanted was for her to feel anything other than relaxed right now. Shit, she'd probably burned through her monthly allotment of adrenaline the minute she'd barked out Damien's name from the door frame of the shelter.

Don't think about it. Do. Not. Think about it.

"Dust rhinos, huh? Sounds pretty ferocious."

Zoe lowered her bag from her unhurt shoulder, and bingo. Her smile slipped out. "Occupational hazard, I guess. Hope House keeps me pretty busy, and in the off hours that I am here, I'm either in the kitchen or asleep."

"Didn't anyone ever have that whole all work and no play conversation with you?" he teased, but even off her game, she was still razor-wire sharp.

"What, you mean the same way someone should probably have the whole pot, kettle, look who's talking conversation with you? Come on, Alex. I think it's pretty clear we're both devoted to our jobs."

"Yeah, you definitely proved that point this morning," Alex said, the words crowding out before he could stop them. Zoe tensed, halfway across the carpet, and ah, fuck. Even though he meant every inch of what he'd said, calling her out after the morning she'd had was a pretty sizable dick move. He opened his mouth with every intention of telling her to forget it, but she spoke first, beating him to the punch.

"Before you read me the riot act, I know."

Wait . . . "You what?"

She knotted her arms over the front of her gray button-down, which had to hurt under the circumstances, but still, she didn't flinch. "I avoid being reckless the way most people avoid sinkholes and hand grenades. Believe me, I get that baiting Damien wasn't the most well-thought-out plan."

"No," Alex agreed, slow and deliberate. "It wasn't."

Zoe's chin lifted, just enough to broadcast the flash of determination in her amber-colored eyes. "But what was I supposed to do? That's my kitchen, and when the residents are there, I'm responsible for taking care of them. No matter what."

He crossed the floor, lowering his gaze to put her in his direct line of sight. "I'm not saying you shouldn't have stood up for your residents, Zoe, or that you shouldn't have taken a risk in order to do it. Hell, I'd have done the same exact thing."

"You would?" she whispered, confusion sliding over her features. "But I thought you were mad that I tried to stop Damien."

"I'm mad that you got hurt," Alex qualified, inhaling past the tightness in his jaw. "But to answer your question, instead of trying to take on the world all by yourself, what you were supposed to do was let me help you."

"Oh." The word collapsed past her lips, a thin wisp of hair fluttering forward as she dropped her eyes. "I'm sorry. I guess I'm not used to having anyone in my corner like that. Not at Hope House, anyway."

Alex paused, taking in the sweep of her lashes as she blinked, the barely there sigh behind her exhale. He'd thought Zoe's brazen side was beautiful, but her mettle was really just the flip side of her tenderness.

God help him, he wanted her. *All* of her.

And if he couldn't have her, the least he could do was have her back.

"Well, get used to it. It might only be for the next three weeks, but for as long as I'm at Hope House, you're not going it alone."

Zoe stood utterly still, her feet glued to the living room carpet and her heart doing a bang-up job of trying to break free from her chest. Her emotions had been through the blender today, she knew, but with Alex standing here in front of her with those impossibly blue eyes and even more impossibly enticing words on his lips, she didn't just feel comforted.

She believed him.

"Thank you," Zoe whispered. She tilted her face up, so close to Alex's lightly stubbled jaw that one forward move from either of them would erase the space entirely. Her breath threaded through her lungs, shallow and hot. But at the last second, Alex squeezed his eyes shut and took a step back.

"You're welcome. I really should go so you can get some rest."

"No, please don't." The protest tripped out without her consent, but hell. Too late to pull it back now. "I mean, um. You're not keeping me from anything. After all the drama of this morning, I doubt I'd be able to relax enough to take a nap. So, you know. You don't have to go. Unless you want to." Sweet God in heaven, she was botching this. But honesty was Alex's number-one policy, and screw it. He'd already said he had her back. "I guess what I'm trying to say is that I don't want to be alone, and I'd really like it if you'd stay for a little while."

"Oh." Alex's brows slid upward. "Okay, sure. Are you hungry? I mean, our cooking lesson got cut short earlier, so I'm still not much good in the kitchen unless you want coffee or something microwaveable. But I can order something."

"You know what, coffee sounds great, actually." She motioned toward the kitchen, turning to lead the way with only a handful of steps. Crossing the threshold, she settled in at the stretch of slate countertop next to the fridge, tugging open the cabinet over the coffeepot to unearth a stack of tissue-thin filters from the shelf.

Alex cupped her elbow with one palm, capturing her attention and sending a bolt of warmth on a direct path between her hips. "You're supposed to be letting me do that."

"Ah. Right." Zoe let out a soft laugh before handing over the filters. "Habit. But I really do feel fine."

As if sensing her need to be more than an innocent by-stander, he said, "Why don't we split it? I'll get the coffee started, and you get the mugs. Fair?"

"Fair."

The rush of the water from the faucet became the rich, earthy scent of perfectly brewed coffee in less than five minutes, and Zoe handed over one cheery red mug while pouring healthy doses of both milk and sugar into the bottom of her own.

The muscles in Alex's forearm twitched right along with the corners of his mouth as he filled her cup the rest of the way with coffee. "Not to be flip, but I hope you don't like your men like you like your coffee. Nobody should be that sweet and blond."

She opened her mouth to make a smart comeback—with that cocky look on his face, he had to know she would—but she trapped the words between her lips just shy of delivery.

Alex hadn't stepped away from her a minute ago be-cause he'd wanted to, just like he hadn't turned her down the other night for lack of desire. He'd walked away because he thought he *needed* to.

And if they were going to get reckless, she'd have to make the first move.

Zoe sat down at the tiny breakfast table by the window, waiting for Alex to get comfortable in the chair across from her before meeting his eyes with a wide-open gaze. "Actu-ally," she said, purposely taking her time as she ran one finger around the rim of her mug, and oh hell, yes. His stare dropped to her hands and darkened. "While the blond part appeals well enough, I'm not really a fan of sweet men."

He lifted his eyes, his focus lingering on her mouth for a long, hot second before returning to her gaze. "You're not?"

Zoe sipped her coffee without breaking their eye contact. She knew she shouldn't want him, with his rough edges and hot risks. But no matter how hard she tried to fight it, she couldn't get past the truth.

Alex Donovan made her want to break all her rules. And oh, how she didn't hate it.

"No," she murmured. "See, I might've been raised as a bit of a golden child, but I was also taught to be tough. To go out and get what I want."

"Zoe—"

She cut off his words with a lift of her hand, and oh God, the dark, wicked glint in his stare shot thrilling heat right between her legs. "I might not take many risks, but I don't believe in sitting on the sidelines, either. I believe in doing things that matter. Things I want."

"It's been a crazy day." Alex's voice was all gravel, and she met it with the softest whisper as she stood.

"It has."

He exhaled a hard breath as she moved right next to him, until he had no choice but to turn in his chair to bring them knee to knee. "Your emotions are all over the place, Zoe. It's a natural reaction to the adrenaline."

She pushed his shoulders against the backrest of his chair, tightening her palms and widening her stance to slide first one leg, then the other over his lap. "You keep telling me that."

Alex groaned, his hands finding her hips and turning to fists over the denim there. "You're hurt. I should go."

"I'm perfectly fine." Zoe pressed forward against his unmistakable erection, her nipples tightening at the hot, decadent friction. "You should stay."

"We can't do this," he said, even as he thrust against

the cradle of her hips, and Zoe cupped his face, her heart locked in her throat.

"Are you saying you don't want to?"

"No." Alex's answer arrived tipped in steel, matching his stare. "Jesus, Zoe. I've wanted this all goddamn week."

"Then take it, because I want you, too. Just me and you. Right now."

He reached up, knotting his hands in her hair to pull her close, and Zoe gave in to the move without hesitation. With the higher vantage point of being seated in his lap, she slanted her mouth over his, brushing the soft skin of his lips with a featherlight kiss. Alex arched beneath her, pressing up to increase their contact without deepening the connection of their mouths. He looped his arms around her shoulders, taking care to avoid the back of her bruised arms as he held her fast to trace the outline of her lips with his own. Teasing her mouth open with a slow sweep of his tongue, he explored the curve of her lower lip, sucking and testing and making her breathless as he took in every nuance. Her mouth parted wide on a gasp, and Alex slid his fingers to the back of her neck, loosening her hair from the knot at her nape until the waves spilled over her shoulders to cover them both.

"Do you know what I see in my mind's eye when I call you Gorgeous?" he asked, putting just enough gentle pressure against the column of her neck to tilt her head to one side.

"No." The word trembled out of her, her breath going even tighter in her lungs as Alex skimmed a touch from her ear to the divot of her throat, then followed the path with his tongue.

"I see you like this. Hot." His fingers found the tiny buttons on the front of her shirt, slipping the top one open with a muted rustle. "Sweet." Another button fell loose, her nipples pearling harder in anticipation. "Brash." His gold-blond lashes arced lower, and he thumbed one more button free from between the swell of her aching breasts. "Wide open and honest."

Zoe dropped her chin, her pulse pushing faster and faster as she watched Alex undo the rest of the buttons to reveal her black lace bra. "God damn," he whispered, his breath spilling into the hot expanse of her skin. "You really are gorgeous."

"Then touch me." The request flushed her cheeks. But something about Alex, about the way he was looking at her with both reverence and pure, wicked intention, had drawn the words right past her lips, and sweet God, she'd never felt want like this in her life.

Alex's hands shaped her waist and tightened. "Be sure."

"I am," Zoe said, dropping her mouth to his in promise. "I want this, Alex. I want you."

His fingers glided up to splay wide around the back of her rib cage, and she arched into his touch. Cupping the bottom edge of her bra with his thumbs, he lowered his mouth to her breastbone, slowly kissing his way down the *V* of her cleavage. Zoe's head tipped back, the ache in her nipples bordering on sweet pain as Alex freed the clasp nestled in the center of the black lace. He trailed a line of soft kisses down the midline of her body, pausing to show the curve of her breasts the attention of both his lips and his tongue. The rasp of his stubble sent tiny shock waves straight to her core, and Zoe thrust against him, wanting even more.

But Alex wouldn't be hurried. "Look at you. Look how pretty you are in the sunlight." He pulled back from her body, but only enough to let the natural light pouring in through the curtains spill over her breasts and his hands. He grazed one flushed pink nipple with the pad of his thumb, and she bit down on her keening sigh, too late.

Alex's eyes glittered. "You blush everywhere, don't you?"

Zoe writhed beneath his touch, so agonizingly close to

where she needed it. But then something unraveled, deep in her chest, and it welled up on a seductive smile. She pushed him against the ladder back of his chair, relishing the flash of surprise that parted his lips. Emboldened by his expression, Zoe slid her shoulder blades together, letting the edges of her shirt fall open over the tops of her arms, exposing her body all the way to the low rise of her jeans.

"If you want to see all the places I blush, go ahead and find them."

His mouth was on her in an instant, hard and unyielding as he pulled her nipple past the heat of his lips. The friction sent a tug to the center of Zoe's thighs, and Alex swirled his tongue even harder, as if he felt her need by mere contact. Unable to hold back, she rocked against his hips, the damp center of her body pressing tight to his cock despite the layers of clothing between them. Every thrust sent sparks to her core, every pass of his lips urging the sparks into flame, until finally, Zoe's breath became short, honeyed moans.

"Watch." Alex ran his tongue along the very tip of her nipple, moving away just far enough to growl the word against her breast.

She blinked, still caught in the haze of want building low in her belly. "What?"

"You're gorgeous," he said, repeating the openmouthed kiss on her other side. Slowly, his hands traveled up, cupping her face and tilting her line of sight to her breasts, then lower to the spot where her jeans slid over his visibly hard cock. "I want you to watch me make you come."

Locking one hand over her hip, he guided her back into rhythm at the same time he returned to her nipple, a slow, dark smile edging the corners of his mouth as he met her eyes and held. The sight of his intensity tripled the sensation pulsing through her, the sunlight illuminating the sinful ministrations of his lips and teeth and tongue making it that much more forbidden, and oh God, oh *God,* if he stopped, Zoe was sure she'd die.

"Alex." Release uncoiled, low and hot between her hips, but he didn't pull back.

"Gorgeous."

Reaching down low, Alex hooked his palm beneath her thigh, opening her further as he pushed against her heat through the layers of denim. The change in angle coupled with the sweet pressure from both his mouth and his cock, and together they sent her right over the edge.

"*Oh.*" Zoe's orgasm crashed over her in wave after wave, the pleasure of it enough to draw laughter from her chest. She threw her head back as she arched the rest of herself forward, not willing or able to lose the connection Alex had given her from hips to breast. He scaled back his touches in slow sweeps, bringing her back down to earth gently, but the only thing Zoe could get past her lust-drenched mind was that she wanted more.

This time, she wanted to watch *him*.

"Follow me." She shifted off Alex's lap, mourning the loss of their connection for only a second before she pulled him from his chair. Moving down the hallway, she led him to her bedroom, not stopping until they'd crossed the threshold and reached the foot of her bed.

Alex paused, pressing a soft kiss to her mouth before drawing back to look at her. "You know we can't undo this."

Zoe nodded, reaching down to lift the hem of his T-shirt over his chest, then his shoulders, before guiding it all the way off. "I do."

Her fingers traced the top edge of her jeans, a bright ribbon of desire uncurling in her core at the way he watched her slide the denim over her thighs.

"And you're still sure," he said, hissing out a low oath as Zoe turned her focus to his button fly. She ran her palm over the length of him, stroking his cock with one hand while undoing the buttons with the other.

"I am."

In a tangle of hurried movements, they undressed each other to the bare essentials, although Zoe kept her open shirt loose around her shoulders. Still standing in front of her bed, she lowered Alex's boxer briefs, kneeling down in front of him to trail her fingertips over his hips. She wrapped her fingers around his cock, pumping once, then twice before following her fingers with her tongue. Alex threaded a hand through her hair, tension thrumming beneath his skin as Zoe parted her lips over his crown to draw him into her mouth.

"Zoe." Her name was a prayer even as he grated it out. His exhales turned fast and heavy, and she adjusted the glide of her mouth to meet each one. Letting her gaze drift upward, she caught Alex's stare, his eyes glinting with so much intensity and raw want that they were practically molten. But his pleasure just made her own longing rebuild, fast and unrelenting between her legs, and she continued to stroke him with her hands and mouth, all the way from root to tip.

"Come here," he finally said, interrupting her motions with a swift yet gentle grab. Bending low to hook his arms beneath hers, Alex lifted her to her feet, holding her there for only a second before pressing her back against the middle of her bed. Pausing for the scant moment it took to search his discarded clothes and take a condom from his wallet, he returned to her side, sheathing himself and dividing the cradle of her hips with his frame. Her panties disappeared from her hips with a quick slide, and Alex leaned forward to bracket her shoulders with both palms.

"Alex." Zoe lifted her hips, searching. Her aching core brushed along his cock, her nipples re-hardening to tight points as she let her knees fall wide in encouragement. "Please."

He reached between them, sliding a finger along her seam before testing her heat with a moan.

"Don't wait," she whispered, her muscles clenching, begging for more.

Alex shifted forward, filling her with a long, slow thrust, and Zoe's breath flew out on a gasp. She stilled, her body adjusting to the tight fit of his cock inside her and the flood of sensuality that went with it. He drew back just slightly, creating the perfect combination of pressure and friction inside her core. The second push grew deeper, guiding them into a cadence of thrusts and retreats that heated Zoe's blood. With every motion, Zoe crested higher, thrust faster, wanted more. Her fingers curled around Alex's hips, and he shifted to balance the bulk of his weight on one forearm, dipping a hand between their bodies to slip the pad of his forefinger deep into the folds at the top of her sex.

"That's it. Christ, you're so hot like this." His murmurs kept time with her moans, and God, even his voice made her want to come. He circled the slick bundle of nerves above while thrusting hard into her body below, and with one last press forward, Zoe flew apart. For a minute, she was weightless, wrapped in pure pleasure and calling out Alex's name. He lessened his movements, but despite the riot of sensations still pumping all the way through her, Zoe wrapped her hands around his lower back to keep him deep inside her.

"I like you right here," she said, tipping her hips until there was no space at all between their bodies. Alex tensed, biting down on his bottom lip as she lifted to meet him again. But then he covered her chest with his, angling forward to kiss her as their rhythm grew stronger, and Zoe couldn't hold back. Opening her knees as wide as they would go, she knotted her legs around his corded waist, matching him thrust for thrust until it was impossible to tell who gave and who took.

"Ah, God." For a second, he slowed, shifting his body almost to the point of withdrawing completely, but Zoe reached up to cup his face.

"Alex, watch." She tilted her hips, the movement sliding his cock deeper into her aching center, and his eyes glittered, nearly midnight blue with lust and want. Sliding her palms over the strong line of his cheekbones, she guided his gaze to the spot where their bodies joined. "Watch me make you come. And don't hold back."

Zoe rocked against him, her hips canting off the bed in a heated rhythm that sent spirals of pleasure from her belly to the deepest part of her core. Alex moaned, framing her shoulders with both hands as he thrust back once, then again, filling her completely. His ministrations became faster, more purposeful, until the tension in his muscles broke loose, signaling his climax with one last shuddering push.

For a second, a minute, an hour—Zoe had no concept of passing time—they lay in a twist of limbs and heated breath, until finally, Alex slipped from the bed to clean up. He returned just as quietly, and she braced herself for the awkward aftermath that surely had to follow.

Only it never did.

"You okay?" Alex asked, skinning back into his low-slung jeans before pulling aside her rumpled bedcovers, guiding her under the quilt with a gentle nudge.

"Yeah, absolutely." The answer defaulted out of Zoe's mouth, fundamentally true and yet also inaccurate. Things like store-bought cookies and B-grade movies were okay. The mind-altering, pulse-scrambling, multiple-orgasm sex they'd just had?

So far past okay that the two syllables seemed pretty much ridiculous.

"Good." He righted her shirt all the way around her frame, redoing the buttons and pulling her close. The afternoon sun slanted in past the blinds, scattering just enough golden light around them to be cozy but not blinding. Alex's body was warm and strong on hers, with his arms wrapped around her and his breath spilling over the crown of her head in long, drawn-out exhales. Zoe meant to say something, to get up, to move in some way, but with each rise and fall of her chest, her body unwound, her mind starting to drift.

You're supposed to let me help you.

It was the last thing she thought before falling asleep.

Chapter Sixteen

Alex woke the way he usually did, all at once and on full alert. He pulled in a deep breath of sweet orange citrus, and despite the cozy quiet and dusky twilight filling the space around him, a sudden chill stole down the length of his spine.

Holy shit. He'd totally, completely, irrevocably slept with Zoe Westin. And rather than feeling the remorse he damn well knew was proper, all Alex could think about was sleeping with her again.

And again.

As if the thought had been sent south from his brain in a direct memo, his cock stirred to life, no doubt encouraged by the fact that his arms were still full of the very enticing blonde in question. Alex forced himself to take a deep breath and recite quarterback ratings, but then Zoe gave a hazy, half-asleep sigh, shifting her ass right up against his hips in a perfect, excruciating fit, and oh hell. Not even a force of nature could make him want to let go of her.

"Mmm." She burrowed deeper beneath the warmth of the quilt, her body loose and languid and damn near perfect in Alex's grasp. But then both her body and her breath went stiff, sending a slice of worry through his gut.

"Hey," he said, the whisper spilling into the fall of her hair. She smelled so good, all sweet and citrusy, and he tightened his arm around her waist out of pure reflex.

"Hey." Without breaking his hold on her, Zoe turned to face him, but before she could get all the way around, she yelped in pain.

Everything about Alex froze but his pulse. "Your shoulder." God, he was such an *ass*. How could he have slept with her when he'd known full well she was hurt? "Here, let me look."

"It's really . . . oh. Okay then." Zoe's protest faded as he levered them both to a sitting position in her bed. Reaching through the shadows, he clicked on her bedside lamp, not even pausing to blink before returning his fingers to the buttons on her shirt.

"Alex," she started, her voice still thick with residual sleep. "I'm just a little sore. The doctor at urgent care said I probably would be, remember?"

"I remember." He scooped up the hem of the quilt, tucking it over her chest to keep her covered and warm before sliding the shirt from her arms.

It took every last ounce of his willpower not to swear out loud.

Alex forced a deep breath through his windpipe. The finger-shaped smudges on Zoe's upper arms were bad enough. But the purple bruise blooming like an angry, soft-ball-sized starburst across the back of her shoulder made him want to find the guy who had muscled his way through Hope House and beat the snot out of him.

Not wanting to freak her out, he dialed back his expression even though his chest felt like it was chock-full of thumbtacks. "I'm going to get some ice from your freezer. That should help the swelling."

"If you give me just a second, I'll come with you." Zoe reached for her discarded jeans, and instinct had Alex in motion before he could fully register his hand on her quilt-covered knee.

"You need to rest, Zoe."

She shifted from beneath the covers, putting on first her panties, then her jeans before grabbing a tank top from the nearby dresser. "What I need is to eat something, and you probably do, too." A smile flitted over her face, but her slow, clumsy movements as she worked the tank top over her head canceled the humor right out. "So can you please do me a favor and stop going all Cro-Magnon man for just a couple of minutes so I can finish getting dressed and make that happen?"

Good *Lord,* this woman was certifiable. "You're not cooking," Alex said, but the lightning-fast lift of Zoe's brows had him rephrasing just as quickly. "What I mean is, if you're sore, you should take it easy. Especially if you want to make it through your day at Hope House tomorrow without that shoulder locking up."

Zoe paused, a frown unbending on her lips, and he took the ball and ran like hell. "Why don't I help you get dressed, and then we can order something for dinner? In the meantime, you can ice that bruise. Fair?"

She reached for the hoodie draped over the chair at her bedside, her frown intensifying as Alex slid out of the bed to guide it over her hurt shoulder before letting her do the rest. "Hmph. You're lucky you know how to talk your way into getting what you want."

"And you suck at letting me have your back." Okay, so he hadn't really meant to tease her—it had just slipped out. But Zoe laughed, and the sound scattered the tension pulling tight at Alex's muscles.

"All right, all right. Chinese or pizza?"

He followed her out of her bedroom and down the narrow

hallway, shouldering his way back into his own T-shirt as he went. "Pizza. I can call my buddy and have it here in twenty minutes, tops."

Zoe laughed again. "Of course you can."

Five minutes later, he'd put the call in to his friend who owned the pizza place and filled a bag with ice from Zoe's freezer. Turning toward the spot where she stood on the threshold, he nodded her into a kitchen chair. "You know your father's probably going to hear about what happened today." He met her partly panicked *you wouldn't dare* expression with raised palms. "The paramedics who responded to check Damien out were from Station Four. Your father is pretty tight with Captain Lewis. There's no way the dots won't connect if your name got mentioned somewhere down the line."

"Lovely. Just what my father needs is another reason to hate my job." Zoe slumped, the bag of ice she'd propped between her shoulder and the back of her chair crinkling.

Alex's gut dipped, but not enough to keep his words at bay. "You can't really blame him for wanting you to be safe."

"I can when his desire for that safety is a double standard," she said, her light brown eyes flashing beneath the glow of the kitchen lights. But her fire didn't last. "Ugh, I'm sorry. I'm not trying to be difficult. I know he wants me safe, and I get that—after all, part of why I'm so mad at him is because I don't think he's being smart about his own self-preservation. But I'm not a kid anymore. We should be able to at least talk about it without fighting, but every time I try to explain that Hope House isn't some death trap, and that he risks his safety at every shift, too, he just argues and then clams up. Keeping all this tension inside makes me so . . . *frustrated*."

"I'm not sure I'm an unbiased ear," Alex admitted, dragging a rough hand through his hair. As much potential as this conversation had to turn sticky, that didn't mean they shouldn't have it. "Look, Zoe, I have a zero-tolerance policy for bullshit, so I'm going to be honest. I didn't intend for this to happen between me and you. I'm not saying I didn't want it," he qualified, straightening his spine against the back of his chair. "Because I did. I do. It's just—"

"I'm still my father's daughter."

Her words stopped the rest of his in his throat. Damn it. The him-and-her part of the conversation, Alex could have, no sweat. The chunk that involved the history between him and her father? Not so freaking much.

Not that his silence stopped Zoe from pushing back. "Alex, you and I are adults. We mutually agreed to have sex. Together. The two of us."

A muscle pulled tight across his jaw. "There's more to it than that."

"But there isn't," she countered. "Look, I understand your sense of loyalty. But I'm twenty-seven years old. At a certain point, that's got to factor in."

"Of course it does. But your father has been my captain for eight years, Zoe. That makes things complicated."

Zoe paused, and for a minute, he thought she'd let the topic drop. Part of him was relieved—he might not tolerate a whole lot of runaround, but there was a difference between saying what needed to be said and airing out too much. The past was the past, over and done. Nothing could be said or done to change it.

So why were the events he'd tried so hard to leave behind still burning to come out?

"Okay," she said. Only instead of changing the subject, or lapsing into silence, or doing any of the other things she could've done to let Alex off the hook, Zoe slid into the chair next to him to scoop up his hand.

"So uncomplicate it for me."

Alex pulled back, staring at her through the soft overhead light and the softer evening shadows beyond. The fact that she'd blown his goddamn mind in bed had been reason enough to give him pause. But now that he sat next to her, in her kitchen of all places, not just ready but willing to green-light all the things he usually kept on emotional lock-down?

Yeah. This couldn't fucking end well.

He opened his mouth anyway.

"You were surprised the other day, when you picked me up at my house." He'd seen it on her face as soon as she'd gotten out of her car, and she certainly hadn't been the first person to go brows-up over his zip code. "Probably wondering why I live in suburbia, right?"

Zoe's forehead furrowed in confusion, although the blush that said Alex was spot-on with his assessment didn't get by him, either. "Well, yeah. Most young, single guys live a lot closer to the city."

He nodded, his rib cage going tight as he thought of where Brennan lived, and Cole and O'Keefe and even Crews, who had a family. "They do. But I live in my neighborhood because that house belonged to my parents."

Her confusion turned to clear surprise. "You bought your parents' house?"

"No." The truth crowded up, shoving its way out of his mouth despite the rust on the words. "I inherited it."

"You . . . oh." Zoe froze, her copper stare going wide. "Oh my God, Alex. I'm so sorry. I didn't know."

"It happened a long time ago, so not a lot of people do. My parents both died in a car accident, coming back from a long weekend on Sapphire Island." He took a deep breath, waiting for the rest of the story to logjam in his throat. But instead, the words spilled out. "It was late, but they decided to come home at night rather than get up early the next morning to make the three-hour trip. A guy driving a tractor trailer fell asleep behind the wheel and crossed the center line on Route Seventeen to hit their SUV head-on. All three of them were killed instantly."

Zoe's breath released on an audible exhale, and Alex steeled himself for the inevitable pity party that always accompanied the story on the rare occasion that he actually told it. But Zoe didn't offer one, and hell if that didn't make him want to talk even more.

"How old were you?" she asked, and his gut twisted hard before dropping toward his knees.

"The accident happened two months after my eighteenth birthday."

She paused, her fingers tightening over his on the dark wood of her kitchen table. "Oh, Alex. I don't know what to say. That must have been really hard for you."

"It was," Alex replied with honesty instead of heat. "Our family was just the three of us, aside from my great-aunt and uncle who I'd seen maybe six times in my life. Even though I was legally an adult, my parents left everything to me in a trust. For all intents and purposes, I was pretty much an orphan."

He shifted, his chair scraping softly over the ceramic tile. As if she'd grasped his need to do anything other than be still, Zoe let go of his hand, tilting her head slightly toward the center of the kitchen in a nonverbal *c'mon.*

Alex followed her to the counter, a thread of relief spreading out in his chest as he continued. "College was really important to my old man, and he and I were close. Although he had a good job with the city, he'd never gone to college, and he always regretted it. My parents left me everything they had, with the one stipulation that I had to earn my degree. So I started at UVA that fall."

"That must have been difficult, going to college so soon after they passed away." Zoe reached into the fridge for a pair of beers, handing one over. The simple act of uncapping the bottle, then trading it for the other to repeat the process, chilled him out, and he rolled his shoulder in a shrug.

"Actually, it saved my ass in the long run. I'd already been accepted, and I landed a decent baseball scholarship. My parents had thankfully planned for a lot of the rest. In truth, without that stipulation in their will, I probably wouldn't have gone to college after their accident, and I damn sure wouldn't have stuck through it for all four years to get my degree like my dad wanted me to." God, those first few years after his parents had been killed had been a blur, just motions to get from one step to the next. College had been the last freaking thing on his mind.

Alex took a sip of his beer, letting the smooth flavor linger for just a second before continuing. "Even though I knew enough people from baseball and stuff like that, I never really fit in. All they cared about was getting through exams and hanging out and drinking. Meanwhile, I was going home over Christmas break to fix leaky pipes in the bathroom and sort through personal property taxes. Looking back, I probably could've tried harder to find a place to belong. But at the time, I just didn't want to."

"You felt like friends would replace your family," Zoe said, and although her tone didn't make it a question, he answered anyway.

"I didn't realize it then, but yeah. Going to college got me thinking about all the things my parents never got to do. Part of me was so angry that my dad would never be able to go back and get a degree like he'd wanted, or see me get mine."

She bit her lip, but didn't shield her suddenly tear-bright gaze. "All things considered, that anger seems justified."

"Yeah, but I didn't even have anybody to be mad *at,* you know? And after a while, spending all that time angry just seemed like a waste. No matter how hard I tried, or how pissed I got, I couldn't change what had happened. I couldn't rewind, make my parents come home earlier, get sick so they couldn't go at all—I couldn't do anything. So instead, I decided I was going to do everything."

"Oh." Realization wrapped around Zoe's single syllable, her beer bottle finding the counter with a muffled *clunk*. "That's why you take so many risks."

He nodded. "Once I graduated, I was determined to experience every single thing I possibly could, the wilder, the better. I enrolled at the fire academy about fifteen minutes after graduation."

"Not a whole lot of places with more opportunity for an adrenaline high," she admitted, and Alex didn't even bother biting back the ironic laugh welling up from his chest.

"Or with so many rules." He may not have been short on the balls to do active fire drills or haul himself a hundred feet in the air on nothing more than a ladder and a Hail Mary. But scraping up the patience to follow the regs while he did it had damn near killed him. Figuratively and literally. "Even though I nailed both the physical stuff and the written exams, I still didn't want to fit in or fall in line, and my attitude made that wildly clear. I found plenty of trouble at the academy, and I nearly got tossed out twice. Even though I was at the top of my class, by the time I graduated, none of the captains in Fairview wanted to take a flyer on me. Except for one."

Zoe leaned against the counter, a tiny smile of irony playing on her lips. "My father."

"Your father," he agreed. "I graduated from the academy in a pretty good-sized class, and Eight is one of the bigger houses in the city. Although having two candidates is pretty unusual, your father agreed to take me and Cole together."

"I remember that," Zoe said, her eyes sparking as she took an obvious tour down memory lane. "It was the same year the Perfect Church caught on fire. God, that place has been around forever."

Alex's shoulders went tight at her mention of the Fairview landmark that had given Church Street its name, and the fire that had ironically saved his life. "That was the first big fire call I ever went on."

"Really?" She pulled back in surprise, and even though his defenses took one last potshot at his gut, Alex still kept talking.

"Yeah. I'd only been in-house for about three weeks. After a year of training for the real deal, I was completely jacked up. The church is so close to the firehouse, we could practically smell the smoke from the engine bay." In fact, with her apartment only a handful of streets away, he'd put even money on being able to see the church's spires from her east-facing window. "We were obviously first on scene. The electrical was ancient, and the old wiring sparked a fire inside the walls and part of the roof. The place was pretty heavily involved even though we got there in minutes."

Zoe tipped her beer to her lips before nodding. "I remember the damage being really extensive. With all the wood in the original construction, it's not too surprising that the fire spread quickly."

"I'd never imagined anything like it," Alex admitted. "Even with what I know now, that fire moved unbelievably fast. Your father was cool as could be, though. Handing out orders like Halloween candy."

"That sounds like him," she said, her smile small and wistful. "I cracked my head on a coffee table once when I was eight and ended up needing fifteen stitches. My mother damn near lost her mind. My dad took one look and said, 'Guess we're going to the emergency room, kiddo.'"

Alex nodded, and Christ, he could still hear Westin's calm, clear voice telling everyone what to do, as if the fire had gone down yesterday. "Of course, I didn't want any part of playing it safe. Your father paired me up with Oz for search and rescue."

"Jeez. That's a hell of a first run."

"Tell me about it." Dennis Osborne was about as old school and salty as firefighters came. He'd been Station Eight's squad lieutenant since before Alex had even arrived in-house, and the guy had been a firefighter for nearly as long as Westin himself. "Oz definitely lives by the whole my-way-or-the-highway mantra. Needless to say, he pretty much told me to stay on his hip and not to so much as burp unless he said so."

"And knowing you, I'm sure that didn't go over well." Her gently raised brows told Alex she knew exactly how the next part of the story played out, and he didn't disappoint her by watering down the truth.

"Oh, it was a pissing contest from the word go. Between the gables and the church spires, squad had their hands full venting the roof, so we had to split up water lines and search and rescue until another engine could respond. I knew Oz and I would cover more ground if we broke off for search and rescue, but he wasn't having it. I was so antsy to get my hands dirty that I told him to go screw."

Zoe's eyes went round and wide as she pulled back against the counter to pin him with a stare full of shock. "You broke ranks in the middle of that huge fire? On your first fire call?"

God, the stupidity of it still rang in his ears, even if the feelings that had motivated his actions still ran bone deep. "I thought that if someone was trapped in there, splitting up to find them was smarter." He hadn't realized at the time how fast fire could spread, or that Westin was so adamant about his men pairing up for damn good reasons. "But I got turned around in one of the storage rooms in the back of the church and couldn't find my exit path. I ended up making it out before the fire flashed over, but just barely."

"Oh my God," she whispered. "Alex, you could've been killed."

He washed down the bitter tang of irony with a long sip of his beer. Funny how scraping elbows with death had ended up saving his life. "Yeah, well, after Oz went up one side of me and down the other—in front of the entire house, which was a real treat—a part of me was wishing for it. And all that time, your father didn't say a single word."

Alex broke off, his stomach doing somersaults. But he'd come this far, and telling Zoe the rest even though he hadn't admitted it to anyone in ages just felt right, like somehow, weirdly, she was meant to know. "Finally, after the paramedics on scene checked me out and gave me a little oxygen for my trouble, we went back to the station and your father pulled me into his office. I thought he'd yell, or write me up, or even boot me. But instead he just looked at me and said, 'Do you know why I took you on, Donovan?'"

Zoe's expression outlined her surprise, but she didn't interrupt, so Alex kept going. "Of course, I told him I didn't. But then he said something I won't ever forget, even if I live to be a hundred."

Alex took a breath, the deep swirl of long-hidden emotions pulling him back, until he heard Westin's voice, soft yet dead serious in his ears.

"*I took you on because I think you could be a damn good firefighter, but damn good firefighters are never a party of one. There's a big difference between recklessness and bravery, and you can't afford to learn it the hard way. You're either going to be a firefighter and save lives, or you're going to get yourself killed, and the second one doesn't happen on my watch. So you'd better decide right now, son. Are you going to be part of this house, or aren't you?'*"

"Alex." Zoe's voice brought him back to the present, and

only then did he realize he'd actually spoken the words from his memory out loud.

"The risk of putting my life on the line never scared me, Zoe. Living out loud is the only way I know how to be. But the part of becoming a firefighter that scared the shit out of me was trusting that if I belonged to a family, that family would always be there, and they'd always have my back. Your father was the only person willing to prove that to me. And I owe him everything for it."

"Being with me doesn't betray that," Zoe said, closing the space between them to fold her arms around his shoulders, and Christ. How could something so off-limits feel so purely right? "Look, I don't know what will happen tomorrow, or next week, or next year, and there are parts of this that scare me, too. But I'm not going to lie to you. Right now, in this moment, I want to be with you."

Alex wrapped his hands around her denim-clad hips, want rebuilding all the way through him to cancel out his hesitation. "I want to be with you, too. As far as I'm concerned, you're either moving forward or you're moving back. And back isn't an option for me. Not now. Not ever. But I can't lose what I have at Eight, Zoe. I belong there. It's the only family I've got."

She pressed up to kiss him, and Christ, despite all the old memories churning through him, Alex didn't think twice about kissing her back.

"Okay," Zoe said. "So let's just move forward, one minute at a time."

Chapter Seventeen

Zoe looked down at the color-coded and tightly ordered page in the day planner spread over her desk, and damn, she'd never been so happy to see a workweek hit the past tense. In the plus column, Damien had been booked up to his eye teeth on assault charges, Rochelle and Kenny had boarded a bus to Michigan, and—miraculously—Zoe's father hadn't caught wind of the commotion that had rattled through Hope House like a five o'clock freight train. On the negative side, things in the soup kitchen had slid right back to business as usual, with too few ingredients for meal prep, too many tasks for the man power at hand, and monthly budgets that were tighter than a snare drum on game day.

And somewhere smack in the middle was her personal life, which had gone from zero to oh-my-God in the span of the same week, and as much as it scared the hell out of her, Zoe couldn't deny one simple fact.

Between their last five days in the kitchen and their corresponding nights in the bedroom, reckless, impulsive, all-in Alex Donovan totally bent her spoon.

Zoe pushed up from her over-the-hill chair, bypassing the stack of notes on her desk for the greener pastures of the kitchen. Yes, she and Alex had found a comfortable groove of balancing work and play this week, and more yes, the seamlessness of both felt down-to-her-marrow delicious. But no matter how enticingly good their last week together had been, Alex wouldn't stay in her kitchen forever. In a measly two weeks, he'd return to a job chock full of frightening risks—a job where he belonged—and that job still scared the hell out of her. Keeping things casual and temporary was the only way to avoid complications for both of them. Plus, she had way bigger things on her plate right now than blowing her supremely hot sex life out of proportion with Serious Thoughts.

Like keeping the soup kitchen she loved afloat despite stormy waters.

After a quick round trip to the walk-in, Zoe unloaded an armful of carrots and celery to the stainless steel worktable in the center of the kitchen, letting the familiar motions do their best to calm her. Her knife roll joined the vegetables, along with a cutting board and oversized bowls, until finally, she released a slow exhale. As challenging as it was going to be to get Hope House right side up and running smoothly once and for all, Zoe was going to dig in and get the job done.

Or die trying.

"Hey," came a sexy rumble from over her shoulder, and Lord, the tool belt slung over Alex's faded blue jeans was enough to make her want to break something on principle alone. "Tina was looking for you about an hour ago. Did you find her?"

"Yeah," Zoe said, reluctantly shelving her Mr. Fix-It fantasy. At least for now. "She wanted to go over some ideas for tightening up security. We hooked up just after breakfast."

While Tina had finally stopped clucking over Zoe like a mother hen on overdrive, she'd been adamant that Hope

House needed better security measures in case of another code-red emergency.

Zoe agreed wholeheartedly. Even if after three extended sessions of brainstorming ways to make the leap from should-happen to would-happen, their budget didn't.

"Added security might not be the worst plan ever." Alex leaned in the door frame between the kitchen and the empty dining room, running a nonchalant hand over his chin, but Zoe called his bluff before he could cap the whole thing off with that perfectly easygoing shrug of his.

"You don't have to sweet talk your way into convincing me, Alex. I know this is a rough neighborhood, and as tough as I am, I also didn't just fall off the turnip truck. Hope House could clearly use better safety measures to keep everyone protected."

Relief washed over his features, and Zoe nearly laughed. "Thank God. I know psychos like Damien are the exception, not the rule, but seriously. The thought of what could've gone down the other day still gives me the goddamn shakes."

"Yeah, well, unfortunately, making big changes to things like security isn't as easy as bribing your volunteer to come in on a Saturday to install new weather stripping on the windows. Which, by the way, was very nice of you to agree to."

Alex dropped his gaze to the tool belt around his waist, and now his easygoing shrug did make an appearance. "Ah. It was a fair trade. You made me dinner last night, remember? Anyway, I already knew how to do the windows, and the whole project only took me a couple of hours. No sweat."

Zoe had her suspicions that his morning hadn't been the piece of cake he was claiming, especially since he'd managed to do the repairs *and* help her get the dining room ready for breakfast service, but she trapped the observation between her teeth. "Well. The fact still remains that Tina and I are going to hit a dead end for security upgrades pretty fast unless we win the lottery. Or we stumble across about ten volunteers the size of linebackers." Or both, but really, she didn't want to get greedy.

"That's a tall order," Alex admitted, unhooking his tool belt to swap it for one of the aprons hanging on the far side of the kitchen. "I'm guessing security services aren't cheap."

"Definitely not." Zoe's breath pulled tight in her lungs. She'd wracked her brains trying to think of ways to ensure tighter security without hiring an outside company, but the truth was, half the time she couldn't even get Hope House's kitchen properly staffed for meal service. Every potential solution she'd come up with to steer the place into smoother, safer waters required either more money or more man power, and in some cases both. All except for one.

God, this idea was crazy. Check that—it was downright insane.

And it was also her only hope.

"I've been thinking about what you said the other day." Zoe reached for one of the bunches of celery she'd laid on the counter, desperate for the food to comfort her like it always did.

But Alex's laugh did the job instead. "For the love of all that's holy, please tell me you've decided that curly fries should count as a vegetable. They're freaking *potatoes.*"

"First of all, they're tubers, and fried ones at that," she said over a laugh of her own. "No dice on nutritional value. Secondly . . ." She looked up to meet the playful glint in his eyes, the last remaining twinge of tension in her chest taking a hike. "That's not what I've been thinking about."

Alex gave his hands a quick scrub before sliding in next to her at the worktable. "All right, Gorgeous. I'll bite. What's on your mind?"

Now or never, now or never, now . . . "The Collingsworth Grant."

"Are you serious?" Alex pulled back to look at her, his blond brows climbing high over his forehead, but hell, it was too late to stuff the words back in now. Plus, she really was out of options, and asking for his help just felt right. Even if the idea itself still felt crazy.

"Yes," Zoe said. "Don't get me wrong. My chances of actually winning the grant are still pretty much microscopic, and it's going to take every last ounce of my time and resources just to go through the application process. Hope House is my kitchen, and ultimately I'm responsible for making smart decisions to feed and take care of the people who live here, but . . ." She trailed off for only a second before delivering the rest with quiet resolve. "I've been swimming upstream for three months, trying to play it safe and do everything in this soup kitchen alone. I need to take a risk in order to make a difference, and I was hoping maybe you could help me."

"Okay. Sure."

"Really?" She clamped down on her bottom lip as her blush took a tour from her temples to her throat, but Alex just reached for the peeler sitting in front of them on the worktable.

"Yeah, really." Grabbing a couple of carrots from the tidy pile by the cutting board, he set his sights on the vegetable in his palm even though Zoe felt his attention still firmly on the topic at hand. "What, did you think I was going to say no? I am kind of a captive audience, being your volunteer and all."

Zoe paused, but screw it. He'd had her back all week at Hope House, and if she was going to trust him with something as important as her kitchen, half measures weren't going to cut it. "I thought you might, yeah. The deadline is less than three weeks away, and it's going to take a lot more than unloading inventory and prepping meal service to make this work. Applying for this grant is going to be a huge undertaking."

"Applying for this grant is a great idea," he corrected.

"Anyway, I told you. While I'm here, I've got your back. Hard work or not, I meant it."

"Does anything rattle you?" The question slipped right past her brain-to-mouth filter, but if Alex minded her sudden burst of candor, his expression didn't give him away.

"I'm a little upset about the curly fries thing. I don't think you're giving them a fair shake, honestly—*oof!*" He held up his hands, fielding off her nudge to his rib cage with a laugh. "Okay, okay. Of course I get rattled. I am human, you know."

The image of him standing in her bathroom five hours ago wearing nothing but a towel and a good-morning-to-*you* smile flashed through her brain, and oh yeah. Zoe knew exactly how human he was.

"Right." She slid a bunch of celery to the cutting board on the counter, praying like hell that her face didn't betray the sexed-up slide show she'd just pushed from her mind's eye. "But you dive into everything without so much as blinking. I get why you're audacious." The story of his parents' horrible accident sent a quick jab at her breastbone, but it didn't stop her from asking, "But how do you take all those risks without being scared?"

"Are you kidding? Half the time, I'm scared as hell." He didn't break stride with the peeler in his hand, even though his movements were slow and unpracticed. "But I can't let fear cloud my judgment. You want to know what happens if I don't take those risks, even the ones that shake me up?"

"What?" Zoe's pulse sped up at the look of sheer honesty on Alex's face, and it double-timed when he put down the peeler in favor of stepping in close to hook a finger under her chin.

"Nothing. And while sometimes that nothing isn't a huge deal, other times, letting nothing happen is more dangerous than taking the risk."

She closed her eyes, letting go of the breath holding

tight to her lungs. "Hope House needs help, and I know my best chance of making a difference right now is to take a leap of faith. But throwing all my time and energy into trying to get the Collingsworth Grant is a huge risk, especially now that this place needs man power and resources for stability more than ever. I'm just afraid to put so much on the line."

"Do you know why I dared you to go rock climbing with me?"

Zoe blinked, and talk about a question with origins in left freaking field. "What?"

"I know it's a weird question. Just go with me here."

"Okay," she said, her answer automatic. "Why did you dare me to go rock climbing with you?"

"For the same reason I brought up the Collingsworth Grant in the first place. I don't want you to be reckless on principle, Zoe. Hell, I treat adrenaline like it's the biggest food group in the pyramid, but even I'm not impulsive for shits and grins alone. There's a difference between recklessness and bravery. I'm just asking you to take a risk and show it to me."

Possibility prickled through her, enticing and sweet. Still . . . "The people who live here depend on me to feed them, and to help keep them safe. What if I risk it and fail?"

Alex met her eyes for a split second, his gaze piercing all the way through her before he dropped a soft kiss over her mouth. "Isn't the more important question, what if you don't?"

Her stunned silence filled the sliver of space between them, but Alex refused to pull up or scale back. "Look, I understand that the risk scares you, and that you've got your reasons for being cautious. But after spending the last two weeks in this kitchen, I also know that Hope House is a whole lot more than your job. You want this grant? Be bold and go get it. For the next few weeks, I've got you."

Zoe pressed her kitchen clogs into the tile to stand up as tall as her frame would allow. Alex was right. The prospect of channeling the efforts she knew Hope House needed into a long shot that damn well might fail *did* scare the hell out of her.

But not doing all that she possibly could—even if it included a giant risk and some even bigger trust—scared her even more.

"Well. With backup like that, how can I refuse?"

Alex grinned, giving his blond brows a cocky waggle and brushing her lips with one last quick kiss before turning back toward the vegetables on the cutting board. "Speaking of backup, we're going to need all the help we can get while you work on this proposal. As awesome as I am, I'm only one man."

"So modest." Zoe laughed, her muscles flexing and releasing in a familiar cadence as she started chopping the celery in front of her. "But, as it turns out, you're also not wrong. I can barely get through meal service with the staff I've got in place right now, and that's with me working a minimum of fifty hours a week in the kitchen. If I'm going to give this grant proposal enough attention for Hope House to be a contender, we absolutely need more hands in here. I can talk to Tina, see if we can't shake a few more trees with the city." Not that they didn't already do that on a fairly regular basis, but at least it might garner something more than the next-to-nothing she currently had.

"You know," Alex said slowly, his expression as unreadable as his voice. "There is a way you can get a lot of people in here to help on the fly, and I guarantee it's something you've never done before."

Zoe's fingers went tight over the knife handle in her grasp. "What's the catch?"

"The catch is, in order for the plan to work, you're going to have to take this risk outside of the kitchen."

Zoe sat in the corner booth at Scarlett's Diner, her eyes on the cup of coffee in front of her even though her mind was a million miles away and her heart was stuck somewhere in the vicinity of her windpipe. Caught in the sweet spot between Saturday's long-gone lunch crowd and the not-yet-started dinner rush, she had the cozy diner all to herself.

Until her father walked through the door two minutes later.

"Hi, Dad. Thanks for coming out to meet me on such short notice." Zoe stood to give him a hug, the cinnamon and cedarwood scent of Old Spice filling her with a nostalgic pang.

"You said it was important," he said, pulling back to scan her carefully from head to toe before sliding into the booth across from her. "What's going on? Is everything okay?"

Leave it to her father to go gruff on the pleasantries when there was an issue at hand. Not that she wasn't the same way, she supposed. "Yes. No. Sort of."

Zoe's gut spiraled downward, and she grabbed the carafe of coffee the waitress had left on the table, pouring her father a full cup before topping off her own. His already serious expression sharpened around the corners of his eyes and mouth, but damn it, this needed to be said, and not just for Hope House. "Something happened this week at the shelter. I didn't tell you when we had breakfast yesterday because I didn't want you to worry. But we've been fighting about my job and yours ever since I came back to Fairview. You deserve to know the truth, starting with this."

Her father listened, the flat line of his mouth growing thinner and thinner as she boiled down the events surrounding Rochelle and Kenny's arrival at Hope House. She didn't get any further than Damien's appearance in the soup kitchen and the shoving match that ensued before her father slapped a palm onto the Formica tabletop, hard enough to send a slosh of coffee over the rim of his cup and into the saucer beneath it.

"God damn it, Zoe! I told you that place isn't safe."

Although she didn't argue outright, Zoe still stood her ground. "I get it, Dad, and I know the shelter isn't in the best neighborhood, but—"

"But nothing," he interrupted, his brown eyes going dark in a flash. "Even with a seasoned firefighter right there in the building, this thug still made his way inside."

Her shoulder blades met the red leather banquette behind her with a shock-induced *thump*. "You know Alex is doing his community service at Hope House?"

For a split second, her father paused. "Of course I know Alex is doing his community service at Hope House. I'm his captain. All of his paperwork ends up on my desk."

Oh *hell*. Aside from the obvious reminder that he was Alex's boss, her father had always been invested in his firefighters, both personally and professionally. Of course he'd be privy to Alex's placement for community service.

Still, she frowned. "Why didn't you say anything?"

"Because you didn't bring it up." Her father took a long draw from his coffee cup before placing it back in its saucer. "Anyway, I assumed the placement was going as expected. Unless he's a problem?"

"Oh, uh." Shit. *Shit.* She really needed to rock one boat at a time here. "No. I mean, he'd obviously rather be at Eight, fighting fires. But he's okay in the kitchen, and he did play a big part in helping to handle the situation the other day."

Her father's expression returned to watchdog status, and he slashed a hand through his hair with renewed aggravation. "A dirtbag shoving his way through a soup kitchen and assaulting its occupants is more serious than a 'situation,' Zoe. I mean it. Working in that part of town is dangerous, no matter how noble the cause. You have to be smarter about your safety."

But rather than turning the tables and digging in with the same argument that had stalemated them since she'd come home to Fairview, Zoe said, "I know."

Confusion narrowed her father's stare beneath the bright glow of the diner's overhead lights. "You know," he repeated, half question, half caution, but damn it, Zoe was so tired of butting heads with him that even though she knew the truth would leave her vulnerable, she let the rest of it spill out anyway.

"I know. I know you had high expectations for me when I went to culinary school, and that running a soup kitchen in the roughest part of Fairview wasn't part of them. I know you're disappointed in my choices." She sucked in a breath. "And I know you're disappointed in me."

Her father's eyes flared, but Zoe barreled on. If she didn't get this all out now, she wasn't going to. "You're right. There *are* parts of my job that are more hazardous than I realized they'd be. But making a difference at Hope House is important to me regardless of the risks, and I think you understand what that's like. I didn't ask you to meet me here to pick another fight with you about either of our jobs. I did it because I need your help."

For a minute, nothing broke the silence between them except the strains of the catchy pop song filtering down from the speakers in the ceiling and the muted clatter of kitchenware being prepped for the impending dinner service, and oh God, she'd miscalculated this risk. The rift between them was too big, too irreparable to bridge by asking him to back her up at the job he'd hated since she took it. Zoe scrambled for a quick *never mind* to erase her impetuous request, but before she could fumble the words past her lips, her father spoke.

"You think I'm disappointed in you?"

The question screeched her thoughts to a halt, bringing forth a graceless, "Huh?"

Now it was her father's turn not to budge. "Do you think I'm disappointed in you because you chose to work at Hope House?"

Zoe blinked. "Well, um. Yeah. You've made it pretty clear that you're not a fan."

"Of you being threatened by some deranged lunatic?" The muscle pulling into a hard line over his jaw suggested that his molars were just shy of their breaking point. "No. But I'm concerned for your well-being, not disappointed in what you do or who you are."

After a full five seconds of shock, she finally managed, "But you've hated the idea of my working at Hope House since the second I resigned from Kismet."

Her father tugged at the cuff of his plaid button-down shirt even though it was already perfectly straight. "That's because your personal safety isn't the only part of your well-being that I worry about."

"What else is there?"

"When your mother and I got divorced, you took it harder than either of us expected you would," her father said, his gaze softening over hers. "I know you weren't entirely happy in Washington, DC. But you quit your job at Kismet pretty abruptly, and you've been angry with me over my decision to stay at the firehouse since well before that." He broke off, and for the first time, Zoe saw a flicker of genuine worry hiding deep beneath his stoic expression. "It's not exactly a secret that you're stubborn, or that you come by it honestly. I've been worried that maybe you came back to run Hope House to prove a point, rather than to do the best thing for your career. And as stubborn as I am, too, I only want the best for you. I want you to be happy."

"Why didn't you tell me any of this before now?" she whispered, and her father's wry smile tugged her heart in four different directions at once.

"You and I haven't exactly been on the best of terms lately. Plus, I'm your old man, kiddo. I might not think twice about fighting fires, but when it comes to airing out things like emotions . . . let's just say I'm not a pro."

"Me neither, I guess." As much as Zoe hated the dissonance that had lingered between them, she couldn't deny that half of it belonged to her.

"Even so, there's something you need to know. Despite all the arguing we've done since you came back to Fairview, I've never been disappointed in you, Zoe. Worried, frustrated, maybe even a little overprotective." He paused just long enough to lift one shoulder in a self-deprecating shrug before his voice grew raw with honesty. "But you're my daughter. I've never been anything less than proud to be your father."

Tears pricked at Zoe's eyes, but she held them back in favor of her answer. "I'm not angry with you," she said, but her father's arched brow had her scrambling to rephrase. "Okay, I *was* angry with you at first, and a small part of my motivation for taking the job at Hope House was to prove that you don't have to put your life on the line in order to help people."

Her father opened his mouth, clearly to protest, but she lifted a hand and continued. "That wasn't the main reason I left DC to run a soup kitchen, though. I came back here to feed the people who need it most. To make a difference."

After a minute, her father said, "I can relate to wanting to help people. But you've still got to be smart about it. Just because you're tough doesn't mean you're indestructible."

Zoe dropped her chin into a slow nod. "Clearly, even though Tina and I have some security measures in place, there are still dangers at Hope House that I didn't bargain for. No matter how much I want to feed the people who live there, and make the soup kitchen as safe as possible while I'm at it, I can't do either of those things alone."

"The hard jobs are never solo endeavors," her father agreed, wrapping his fingers around his coffee cup as he looked at her. "What did you have in mind?"

"Well, I guess that depends."

"On?"

Zoe's heart knocked against her rib cage, her breath trembling with uncertainty.

But still, she took the leap of faith.

"On whether or not you've got my back . . . and Hope House's."

Chapter Eighteen

Alex sat back against the passenger seat of Zoe's Prius, watching the neon glow of Bellyflop's overhead sign illuminate her pretty features as she put the car in Park and let loose a deep-bellied laugh.

"Wait. You're seriously telling me you've Geronimoed your way out of an airplane twenty-nine times, skied three different black diamond trails, and gone white water rafting in class four rapids, but you've never tried sushi? Not even once?"

Alex shuddered, but mostly just to mess with her. God, that no-holds-barred smile was a fucking stunner. "I might like adventure, but even I have a threshold. Eating raw fish is crazy."

"It's not *all* uncooked. Plus, you've never even tried it," Zoe argued, albeit without heat. "For all you know, it could be the best thing you've ever tasted."

He leaned across the console, cupping the back of her neck to pull her in close. "Doubt it, Gorgeous."

"You are so bad." The accusation coalesced into a breathy sigh as Alex parted her lips with a greedy stroke of his own. Sliding his tongue over hers, he captured her smile with his mouth, and damn. He'd rather taste her than anything that could be dished up in a kitchen.

"Guilty as charged," he murmured. Zoe arched up to press her lips back to his, and for a fleeting second, Alex considered telling her to put the car back into gear and break every traffic law imaginable to get back to his place so he could savor more than just her mouth. But finally, his conscience—freaking killjoy that it was—made him pull back against the well-cushioned seat.

"We should probably go inside." He nodded toward the brightly lit sports bar across the parking lot, which already appeared to be more than reasonably populated for eight o'clock on a Saturday night. After the handful of texts he'd placed earlier that afternoon, he knew essentially everyone from the firehouse would be here, and a quick survey of the lot told him at least half of them were more punctual than he and Zoe. Not that he felt an ounce of guilt over making the two of them late.

"Yeah, you're right," Zoe said, smiling as she smoothed a hand over her bright pink top. "After all, I already talked to my dad about this. We might as well make it official."

Alex went from cocky to cock-blocked in about six seconds flat. "I'm sorry . . . what?"

Zoe got out of the car, the heels on her shoes echoing out a *tap-tap-tap* that kept time with the sudden riot of his pulse. "I met my dad at Scarlett's after I left Hope House today. I didn't want him to hear about what happened this week from anyone else, and anyway, asking everyone at Station Eight for help means starting from the top down. Getting my father on board first just made sense."

"You told him about Damien?" Shock pushed the question out of Alex's mouth, and Zoe answered it with a no-nonsense nod.

"Yeah. He took it about as well as you'd expect. But in the end, we had a good talk. Although he's still not thrilled with me working at Hope House, he did agree to help with the paperwork end of the grant proposal. He runs things meticulously at Station Eight, so that'll go a really long way."

Alex's urge to bend down and kiss his ass—and his job— good-bye ebbed just a little. "So you two just talked about your plans to apply for the Collingsworth Grant?"

"Yeah. What else would we talk about?"

They made it a few more steps across the parking lot before his silence filled in the blanks, and Zoe's head sprang upward. "Oh. Oh God, no. I mean, my father has been cc'd on all your paperwork, so he knows you're doing your community service at Hope House, and that you were there last week when the whole Damien thing went down. But I didn't tell him . . . you know. About this." She drew an imaginary circle between them with one hand before returning her arm to her side. "My dad and I have always gone *don't ask, don't tell* on my dating particulars, and anyway, what you and I do in our personal time is nobody's business but ours."

"Right." Alex gave himself a swift mental kick to dislodge his unease. "Yeah, right. Of course."

The captain ran a tight house from process to paperwork, so his knowledge of Alex's placement pretty much fell into the *duh* category even though they hadn't shared any face time in weeks. And considering how heavily the plan Alex had helped Zoe strategize earlier today relied on the guys at Eight pitching in, asking her father's help in trying to land the Collingsworth Grant made sense. Even if the mention of their father-daughter get-together had just pushed Alex's panic button six ways to Sunday.

"Well, I'm glad your father is on board."

His nod capped off the conversation, the cool press of the brass door handle in his palm grounding him back in the moment as he ushered Zoe inside the busy bar and grill. They'd managed to stick to the whole each-day-as-it-comes thing pretty easily so far, and without any weirdness or drama to boot. What he really needed to do was file the whole thing under *if it ain't broke* and move the hell on.

Starting right now.

Alex pushed a smile over his mouth, relieved when his mood went along for the ride. "So, you'll probably remember most of the guys, although there are a few new faces, not all of which belong to guys."

"Really?" Zoe's eyes lit with obvious curiosity as they crossed the dark, scuffed hardwood in Bellyflop's lobby. "When did you guys get a female firefighter at Station Eight?"

"Zoe, please. I know you and your father have kind of avoided talking about the firehouse lately, but don't you think you'd have heard about a whopper like us getting a female candidate?"

She arched a brow, all warning. "And why exactly is having a female firefighter on the roster such a whopper?"

"Don't get me wrong," Alex qualified, bypassing the smiling hostess in favor of heading toward the open area by the bar. "I'm all for anyone who can hold their own on Engine, period, and most of the guys I know feel the same way. But being a firefighter is a backbreaker even on the light days, and right or wrong, there are still some pretty old-school guys out there who disagree that a woman can handle the physical rigor. I mean, could you imagine the dust Oz would kick up at the idea of a female candidate? Or that he wouldn't turn it into a huge deal?"

"I guess you're right," Zoe said slowly. "I don't suppose there are a whole lot of female recruits at the academy, and although I'm sure they're all perfectly capable, it *would* be pretty monumental if a woman landed at Eight."

"Monumental is a good word for it." Keeping up on Engine or Squad was tough for most guys. Plus, adding a new person to the house always messed with their dynamic, at least for a while. As good as Cole was at keeping things on the level at the firehouse, not even he would be able to balance out the chaos if they ended up with a female rookie.

Alex shrugged off a sudden pang of missing the firehouse. "Anyway, let's get the roll call out of the way. I'm sure everyone who knows you will want to say hi." He tipped his head toward the tall bar tables where he could already see Cole, Brennan, and O'Keefe jawing about who-knew-what, but rather than keeping time with him as she had all the way through the parking lot, Zoe's steps slowed.

"Okay," she said, biting her lip as she dragged her feet to follow him past the maze of softly lit booths and tables scattered throughout the front of the sports bar. The hard, sudden flicker of hesitation in Zoe's eyes caught him square in the chest.

"You really aren't used to anyone having your back in the kitchen, are you?"

She paused, then admitted, "That obvious, huh?"

Alex had never dressed things up, and he wasn't about to start now. "Pretty much. But you don't have to worry. These guys have my six all the time. I bet once you tell them what you've got going on at Hope House, they'll have yours, too."

In a handful of strides, they covered the rest of the floorboards leading up to the long bar table where half of Station Eight's C-shift sat in various states of drinking and joking. Alex's gut gave one last squeeze of self-preservation, but he stuffed it back as he dialed his expression all the way down on the big-deal meter. Zoe was right. What they did on their own time was up to them, and anyway, they'd come to ask everyone for help at Hope House, not have a relationship reveal-all with his squad mates.

"Someone please tell me who let you animals out of the zoo." Alex kicked one corner of his mouth up into a tried-and-true smirk as he leaned in to clap his palm against Brennan's, the expression becoming a full-scale grin at O'Keefe's chuff of laughter from across the table.

"Right." The paramedic tipped his time-creased FFD baseball hat at Alex after he and Brennan and Cole had exchanged the requisite hey-how-are-yas. "Because you're a regular saint. You dick," O'Keefe added without pulling up on his smile.

"Aw. You miss me. That's so cute." Alex lifted a brow before spreading a palm over the front of his T-shirt in mock hurt. "And I'll have you know, I'm a pussycat."

"Yeah, you're a real pu—whoa!" O'Keefe's words screeched to a halt as Cole's elbow landed in his rib cage and his eyes landed on the spot where Zoe stood just behind Alex, and not a nanosecond too soon. "Holy crap. Look what the pussycat dragged in. Zoe, is that you?"

Alex took a side step to usher her closer to the table. She lifted her hand in a small wave, but the laughter shaping her lips was unmistakable. "Hey, Tom. It's good to see you again. Nice save, by the way."

"Thanks," he said, his cheeks flushing slightly as he tacked on, "Sorry about that."

"Don't be. I learned how to swear from the best of them." Zoe split her easy smile between O'Keefe, Brennan, and Cole. "How have you guys been? Staying out of trouble?"

Cole pointed to the pitcher of beer in front of him in an unspoken question, quickly filling one of the plastic cups on the table at Zoe's nod. "Trouble is kind of relative when you're dealing with this group."

Although Alex had busied himself with pouring a beer of his own, he felt Zoe's pointed glance as if she'd reached out and touched him. "Funny, I don't doubt that for a second," she said, turning toward Brennan and continuing smoothly. "So how's it going, Nick? I heard you're training recruits now. That must be pretty exciting."

"The academy's keeping me busy. I can't complain."

It was about as wordy as the guy ever got about his return trip to Fairview and his career change, but after what Brennan had gone through in the two and a half years following his injury, Alex couldn't blame him for being tight-lipped.

Zoe didn't even skip a beat, though. "Well, I'm glad I'm not the only one who couldn't stay away."

"Yeah." Brennan reached out to slide his arm around the woman sitting next to him, who'd just finished chatting with Station Eight's other paramedic, Rachel Harrison, and damn. The guy's entire demeanor changed as he looked at the pretty brunette. "I even brought reinforcements. Ava, this is Zoe Westin. Zoe, my girlfriend, Ava Mancuso."

"Hi, Zoe. It's nice to meet you," Ava said, her warm smile dipping in obvious thought. "Wait . . . Westin. Any relation to the captain?"

Zoe's nod knocked a few wisps of gold-blond hair from the low, tousled braid slung over one shoulder. "He's my father."

Ava darted a lightning-fast *oh really* glance in Alex's direction, which—knowing her everything-on-the-table attitude—he probably should've seen coming. But thankfully, before Ava could put her curiosity to words, Rachel leaned in from the bar stool next to Ava's.

"Ohhhh, you're the chef, right?"

Cue up Zoe's comfort zone. She said, "I am, but how did you know?"

"Cap brags. A *lot*." The redhead pushed all the way forward, a grin on her face. "I'm Rachel. I'm on the ambo with the wordsmith over there."

"Nice to meet you, Rachel." Zoe laughed, dodging the crumpled-up bar napkin O'Keefe winged in the other paramedic's direction. Alex grabbed the opportunity to run the length of the table, finishing the introductions with Crews and Jones.

"Hey," Alex said, swiveling an assessing gaze from the jukebox on the wood-paneled wall to his left to the outward curve of the bar at the back of the place before settling on the far alcove housing a pair of pool tables and the bathroom on the right. "Are any of the squad guys here?"

Crews took a sip of his beer before shaking his head. "Oz said he already had plans. You know how he is. And Andersen is at home with his twins, but he told me to tell you 'hey.'"

"Wrangling a set of five-year-old twins is definitely fair game in the good excuse department," Alex joked.

Rachel nodded, leaning toward Zoe with obvious interest. "So, Zoe, you're a chef. That must be a pretty cool job."

Zoe smiled, her ease clearly growing. "It is, although it's a lot different than I thought it would be."

Ava gave a knowing nod. "My brother is a pastry chef. He runs his own bakery out in the Blue Ridge with his wife. Makes the most ridiculous Linzer cookies you've ever tasted," she said, running an appreciative hand over the spot where her dark red shirt covered her stomach. "What restaurant are you working at now that you're back in Fairview?"

"Ah," Zoe started, her brown eyes going wide over the verbal stutter-step. She pressed her lips together, and Alex's hand found her shoulder of its own free will, offering up a quick squeeze.

"Zoe's running the new soup kitchen down at the Hope House transitional shelter. I've been doing my community service there."

The words brought looks of curiosity to everyone's faces, and both the gentle nudge and the interest seemed to bolster her resolve. "We opened the soup kitchen three months ago, just after Christmas, although the shelter has been there for just about two years now. Hope House has about seventy-five beds on the residential side of the shelter, although we do our best to feed everyone who comes in hungry and in need."

"Damn." Cole slipped out of his seat to grab an empty nearby bar stool, making room for Zoe in the middle of the long, communal table. "That sounds like a hell of an undertaking."

Smiling her thanks, she sat down between him and O'Keefe. "Truthfully, it is. I only have enough of a budget to pay two part-timers, although they volunteer a lot of their own time to make up for the holes in the schedule. Between only being able to afford a skeleton crew and trying to scrape up enough food to go around, we've really been having a lot of trouble covering all the bases."

"Great cause, though," Jonesey said, and Rachel nodded in agreement.

"Tom and I go on a lot of med calls down in that part of the city. The living conditions are pretty scary, and the crime level doesn't help."

Zoe shot a tentative look in Alex's direction, but his nod of encouragement was a total no-brainer. "There's a lot of potential danger in the area around Hope House. I want to apply for a pretty substantial grant that will help us feed and take care of everyone more easily, along with putting some security into place to keep them safe, but with the shortage of hands, well . . ." She paused, her deep breath straightening her spine with determination that Alex was fast becoming addicted to. "I need help if I'm going to have any prayer of getting it."

Cole sat back against his bar stool, his perma-relaxed expression tacked firmly to his face. "You know, I've got some community service coming up," he said, and even though his words were completely no-big-deal, they still peppered Alex's gut with unease at the way his friend had landed the hours in the first place. "I bet I can ask to do my hours at Hope House, if you think it'll help."

"Anyone volunteering at this point would be a huge help," Zoe said, and Brennan tipped his chin at Cole, chiming in.

"I'm game to volunteer. I kind of miss working in a kitchen, and anyway, you don't want these chuckleheads in charge of anything culinary unless they're heavily supervised."

"Trust me." Alex laughed, toasting Brennan with the frosty cup in his hand. "She knows."

Zoe lifted her cup to meet both of theirs, her eyes brightening with amusement as she admitted, "While you definitely don't need a lot of experience with food in order to volunteer, if you've got some, it does help."

She launched into a basic explanation of Hope House's meal schedule and volunteer services, with everyone at the table offering to pitch in and help with either food service, kitchen work, or a bit of both. Their waitress brought a jumbo-sized plate of hot wings to the table, and Zoe kept track of the growing list of volunteers as they all ate, putting everyone's contact information into her phone.

"You know," Ava said, tapping a finger against her bottom lip. "It sounds like you've got the man power end covered with these guys for the next few weeks. But have you ever considered different avenues for gathering resources?"

Alex's curiosity perked, and he wasn't the only one.

"Like a food drive?" Zoe asked, the edges of her lips twisting downward at Ava's nod. "I tried one right when I first started out. But my reach only extends to the people who need the food, and I've had my hands so full with the basics of getting everyone fed that I simply haven't had the time or the man power to effectively spread the word about a food drive, much less coordinate drop-off points and pickup schedules."

"You do now." Ava flipped her cell phone into her palm, tapping it to life with a few quick touches. "I'm a reporter with the *Fairview Sentinel*. If you'd be willing, I'd love to run a personal interest piece on both the shelter and the soup kitchen. We could spotlight the services Hope House provides and talk up a food drive while we're at it."

"You would do that?" Zoe's lips parted in surprise, but Ava's fingers didn't even slow as she answered.

"Nope. I *did* do that." She lifted the phone, the backlit glow flashing across the dimmer lighting in the bar. "My editor should get back to me first thing Monday morning on this, but I'm sure he'll be game. I don't mind helping co-ordinate the food drive in conjunction with writing the story. If you want, that is."

Shock prickled all the way up Alex's spine. He'd known everyone would be willing to help, but . . . "A newspaper story is a brilliant idea, Ava."

"I helped my friends in Pine Mountain run a really suc-cessful fund-raiser for their bar and grill last year," Bren-nan added, running a hand over the neatly trimmed goatee covering his chin. "I can reach out to them, see if they've got any suggestions you might find useful for getting the word out without spending a lot of cash."

Before Zoe could agree with anything more than a wide-eyed nod, Rachel said, "My parents own the hardware store over on Atlantic Boulevard. I bet they'd let you use their place as a drop-off point for nonperishable donations."

"Don't forget all the local firehouses," Crews interjected, and Alex leaned in toward Zoe with a grin he couldn't help.

"You know Joss would let you use Vertical Climb as a drop-off point if we ask. Kyle even has a pickup truck. If I agree to take another birthday party full of ten-year-olds, he just might help with transporting donations."

"Wow," Zoe finally managed, sending her gaze over

everyone sitting at the pine bar table. "I don't know what to say. I mean, I know I came asking for help, but this is—"

"What we do," Alex said as her eyes finally settled on his. Zoe's gaze brimmed with gratitude and something else, something deeper that Alex couldn't quite pin, and all of a sudden everyone else in the bar—hell, in the universe—felt really far away.

"Teflon's right." Cole's voice, coupled with the reminder of his nickname and its deep roots at the firehouse, knocked Alex back to the buzz and chatter of Bellyflop's busy bar area. "Zoe, your father has had each of our backs since we arrived at Station Eight. If you need our help at Hope House, we've got yours."

"You have no idea how much this means to me," she said. "Thank you."

"Are you kidding?" Rachel grinned, reaching for Zoe's cup to top it off with a healthy splash from the pitcher at her elbow. "You're Cap's daughter, and Hope House sounds like a great place. Besides, those of us with XX chromosomes are totally outnumbered in this group. Lord knows we need another woman around here to help offset all these knuckle draggers."

"Hey!" Jones and Crews protested in unison, but Rachel gave a snort that belied both her delicate features and her slender frame.

"Please. The last time we were all here, you guys had an arm-wrestling tournament to settle the bar tab. Don't even get me started on the beer-pong-is-a-legitimate-sport argument, either."

Alex cocked a brow at Rachel, looping his fingers through the handle on the pitcher to tilt the last of the beer into his cup. "Beer pong takes skill, Harrison. You're just cranky because you lost last time and had to karaoke that Britney Spears song."

"Keep talking, Teflon," Rachel said over a genuine

laugh. "We'll just quietly add to Team Estrogen over here as we help Zoe plan this food drive."

"That's my cue." Zoe held up her hands as a smile took over every inch of her face. "Let me grab a pen, and we can start getting a few of these details hammered out. Then I want to hear this karaoke story, with all the gory details."

Someone produced a ballpoint pen from the bar, and Zoe didn't waste a second getting started. She came up with a volunteer schedule that managed to accommodate everyone's work and personal commitments, then shared some of the ideas she'd come up with for the grant application, patiently listening to everyone's questions and suggestions of ways to help. The more Zoe talked about her plans for Hope House, the more her face lit up, as if she couldn't possibly be meant to work anywhere else. Her eyes glimmered, whiskey gold with excitement as her notes overflowed from the back of one bar napkin to the next, then to a third, and damn, Alex had never seen anyone so fierce or beautiful in his life.

"Hey," Cole said, interrupting his thoughts by holding up an empty pitcher to match the one just outside Alex's reach on the table. "Looks like we're all out over here. You want to head over to the bar for refills?"

"Sure." Alex kicked his boots into motion, angling his way through Bellyflop's now-bustling crowd. Nearly every seat at the mahogany bar was occupied, and he and Cole parked themselves by two of the last remaining spaces next to the pass-through.

"You slept with her."

The empty pitcher in Alex's grasp hit the top of the bar with a sharp *clunk* at Cole's straight-to-the-point statement, but there was no fast-talking his way out of this. Anyway, as highly sensitive as the topic was, lying about it—or, okay, lying about anything—just wasn't Alex's speed. "You really should take that mind-reading show on the road. You could make a freaking fortune."

Cole's normally laid-back expression turned graveyard serious. "Jesus, Teflon. Have you lost your faculties?"

"No." The word fired from his mouth, low and sharp around the edges, and Alex took a deep breath to smooth out his redirect. "I'm helping Zoe with this grant project, yes. . . ." He broke off, dropping his voice. "And yes, she and I are spending time together after hours. But we agreed to keep things casual. It's not a big deal."

Cole ran a hand over the back of his neck, shaking his head in obvious disbelief. "Not a big deal. You do remember Zoe is Westin's daughter, right? The one he brags about every time her name comes up in conversation. And also when it doesn't."

"Believe me, I remember," Alex said, replacing any heat the words might carry with straight-up honesty. "But she's an adult, and so am I."

Cole leaned one forearm against the bar, finally nodding. "Okay, family tree aside, I thought you wanted to do this community service as painlessly as possible. Don't get me wrong, it sounds like Zoe helps a lot of people at Hope House, and that's admirable as hell. But you seem awfully invested for a guy aiming for nothing more than a volunteer drive-by."

Unease filled Alex's chest instead of air, but he tamped the emotion down. "I don't have any choice but to do this community service, and phoning it in when Hope House is so short staffed is a dick move, no matter where I'd rather be. Just because I'm helping Zoe for a few weeks doesn't mean I don't know the score, though, and Zoe knows it, too. I'm a firefighter. I belong at Eight, and Cap is more than just my boss. When I come back to the house in a couple of weeks, things will go back to normal."

They had to. Alex's livelihood—his life—depended on it.

He met his best friend's eyes without hesitation. "Trust me, Cole. I know exactly what I'm doing."

But Cole's stare didn't waver, either. "That, my friend, is exactly what I'm afraid of."

Chapter Nineteen

Alex woke slowly for the first time in a dog's age, sleep clinging to him like a lover as he rolled over beneath the warmth of the comforter. Not a terrible analogy, considering how the rest of the night before had shaken out. Zoe's high-velocity excitement from their gathering at Bellyflop had been contagious, to the point that after they had gotten to his house, they'd barely made it to his bedroom before the last of their clothes had hit the carpet. And that had been after he'd made her come in the hallway.

Twice.

Huh. No wonder he'd slept like a baby.

His cock stirred at the sleep-edged memory of Zoe, with her panties in a pool of lace on the shadowy hallway floorboards as he'd knelt between her thighs, teasing and tasting her until she'd screamed. With her throaty, honey-covered moans and her blond hair wild around her face, she'd been the picture of lust-blown sexiness, and Alex blinked his eyes open, wanting to match the image in his mind's eye with the sight of the woman who had fallen asleep next to him.

But his bed was empty.

Letting his eyes adjust to the sunlight spiraling in past

the blinds, Alex scanned his room. The navy-blue sheets and matching comforter were appropriately rumpled, albeit unoccupied. The pink top and faded jeans Zoe had worn to Bellyflop lay neatly folded on top of his dresser, in the exact spot she'd put them after retrieving them from the hallway last night. Soft, indistinct sounds filtered in through the doorless entryway to the alcove on the far wall of his bedroom, past the small, sunlit sitting area. Alex slipped from the bedcovers and into a pair of basketball shorts, shaking off the last of his sleep as he padded toward the short pass-through leading to the master bath. The bathroom door was ajar just enough for him to catch the sound of running water and the strains of a crooked song being hummed by a familiar, velvety voice.

Alex knew propriety dictated that even though Zoe had left the door cracked open, he should knock. But with the toilet itself set off to the side of the en suite behind a separate door, chances were pretty high he wouldn't catch Zoe terribly indisposed. Even though Alex knew he was skirting the boundaries of propriety, he nudged the door just far enough from the frame to take a quick peek inside.

Zoe stood in front of the far-side vanity, a toothbrush in one hand and a wide-open expression on her face. The L-shaped room gave him a good enough vantage point to see her without being noticed, and he used the opportunity to take her in from head to heels. The hair that had tangled around her shoulders last night in provocative waves now sat in a tidy knot at her crown. Her face had been scrubbed free of any makeup she'd had on, leaving behind a trail of light freckles over her nose and a pair of bow-shaped, pale pink lips. The dark blue tank top reading *Do Not Disturb* and the pair of matching, ruffled short-shorts she'd slipped into offered Alex a flawless view of her decadent curves as she leaned in toward the mirror to brush her teeth.

A minute later, she paused in her humming to wipe a

smudge of toothpaste from her lip with a washcloth, her eyes finally connecting with his in the mirror as he stepped farther into the room. Rather than jumping out of her skin or becoming self-conscious at his watching, though, Zoe's face broke into a smile that took over her whole face, and all of his chest along with it.

Holy hell. He'd thought she'd been gorgeous last night, with her sexy moans and barely there lace panties. But standing here in her silly pajamas, smiling over at him through the honest, bright light of morning, Zoe Westin was the most stunning woman Alex had ever seen.

"Hey. You're up." She lowered the washcloth to the vanity, her bare heel squeaking softly against the ceramic tile as she turned to look at him.

If the current state of affairs in his shorts was any indication, her words could headline the understatement of the month club. "Mmm-hmm."

"I didn't mean to go poking through your stuff," Zoe said, biting her lip and dropping her gaze to the toothbrush still in her hand. "But I left my toiletry bag at home by accident. You had an extra toothbrush in the medicine cabinet, so . . ."

Alex cut her off gently with a shake of his head. "It's fine. That's what the extra is for."

"You keep an extra toothbrush for all the women you seduce in your hallway?" Her retort arrived with a saucy tip of her lips, but Alex had already seen the sweet side tucked deep beneath her moxie.

He'd already had one. Now he wanted the other.

"Nope." The tiles were cool against his feet as he took the handful of steps necessary to reach her. Plucking the toothbrush out of her hand, he turned toward the sink on the other end of the counter, placing it in the holder next to his before saying, "I bought it three days ago."

Her lashes fanned upward in a honey-colored arc. "You did?"

"Sure." Running his own toothbrush under a steady stream of water, he lifted one shoulder in a half shrug. They'd spent all of their nights together at Zoe's apartment, but ending up here at some point had only been a matter of time. "I figured we'd stay here sooner or later."

"The house is beautiful." Zoe gestured to the ivory-tiled space around them, and Alex completed a quick but thorough scrub-down of his teeth before answering.

"I had the master bedroom and the bath in here completely redone a couple of years after I graduated from college. I wish I could take credit for how the job turned out, but I kind of just let the contractor do his thing."

Her expression softened, but she didn't pull back from the subject. "Wanting to make the space your own makes sense."

Alex nodded, his words coming easily enough to surprise the hell out of him. "My parents left me the house, and even though it was a tough choice, I decided to stay rather than sell. After that, it seemed disrespectful not to really live in the place."

As if Zoe could sense that he didn't want poor-baby sympathy, her lips curved into an honest smile. "So does really living involve nice, long soaks over there? Because I have to tell you, that bathtub looks like heaven."

"Ah, there's another thing I let the contractor take charge of." He followed her gaze to the oversized multi-jet tub on the wall to his right. "I've used it a few times after a really hard shift or a long day of rock climbing. But I'm not here enough to take full advantage on a regular basis."

"That's a travesty," she said, a soft puff of laughter crossing her lips. "And here I thought you were all about seizing the moment."

The earlier bolt of want in Alex's blood charged back to

life, running the length of his spine in a hard ripple before settling low and deep between his hips. He eliminated the space between him and Zoe in the span of time it took her to suck in an audible breath, pressing his palms to the granite vanity top to cage her tight against his body. Where last night had been fast, full of the thrill of the moment, right now he wanted to slow down, to explore every inch of the flip side of Zoe's sexiness.

To draw out that sweet, hidden part of her, only so he could rediscover it again and again.

"So tell me." Alex dropped his mouth to the sliver of space just above Zoe's ear, close enough to feel the heat radiating off her in a thousand places although he touched her in none. "Do you want to seize this moment?"

She pulled back just far enough to meet his eyes, the small of her back pressing flush against the vanity. "Yes."

"And do you trust me?" He tightened his grip on the counter behind her, keeping his hands anchored in place even though every instinct he had screamed at him to touch her.

"Of course," she said, the words wrapped in husky desire. Alex's lips hovered over the sweet, pale expanse of her neck, his cock growing instantly hard at the rasp of her shaky breath and the brisk citrus scent of her hot, mostly bare skin. But when Zoe shifted forward to link her arms around his shoulders, he dodged back to capture her wrists, one in each hand.

"If you want to take this moment and really live, then let me show you how."

Swinging Zoe around, Alex lowered her hands to the vanity top, pressing her palms against the cool granite before covering her fingers with his own. The good half foot he had on her in height gave him the perfect vantage point to see over her shoulder. The contact of their hands was their only connection until Zoe's eyes met his in the mirror, and fuck, this was going to take every last ounce of his already questionable restraint.

He didn't hesitate.

"Leave your hands where they are," Alex murmured, squeezing once for emphasis before letting go of her fingers. Although her palms didn't budge, her gaze widened in confusion, and he leaned in to answer her unspoken question with a dark smile.

"One sensation at a time. All of them are yours. Which means I do all the touching."

Zoe's stare glinted in the mirror's reflection, his pulse burning faster in his veins when she complied with a tiny nod. Alex lowered his attention to the column of her neck, sliding the edge of his tongue over her skin while keeping his distance from the rest of her body.

"Alex." The sigh that spilled out of her vibrated beneath his lips, but he refused to give in to the want screaming through him. With only the very slightest pressure, he strung a path of kisses from Zoe's neck to her shoulder, following his movements with an equally featherlight glide of his fingertips. He hooked the edge of one finger under the strap of her tank top, her hips arching toward his as he lowered the ribbon of fabric just enough to run his teeth across the spot where her neck met the curve of her shoulder. But rather than giving Zoe the added contact she sought, he shifted back.

"Uh-uh, Gorgeous. No touching unless I say so." Alex buried his smile deep in her shoulder. Christ, the blush on her skin was enough to undo him right here on the damn tiles.

"We're supposed to be seizing." Zoe's tone toed the line between sensuality and sweetness, both daring him to take her hard and fast and right freaking now, but he didn't give in.

"If you want to really live in this moment," he said,

swirling his tongue against the pulse point in her neck before lifting his head to lock eyes with her in the mirror, "then feel each touch all by itself. Let me give you the experience. Bit"—he broke off to dust his fingers over the indent above her collarbone, skimming over her sternum and down the midline of her belly before falling away from the flare of her hip—"by bit."

Zoe's answer came by way of a want-soaked sigh that was far from an argument. Alex returned his gaze to the reflection in front of him, her parted lips and shuttered, warm honey gaze testing his resolve while hitting every one of his *fuck yes* triggers. Zoe's face flushed dark pink with desire, and his cock grew even harder as he raked his gaze lower over her body. Her shallow breaths lifted her chest in quick rhythm, her nipples beaded into tight points against the loose cotton covering them, and Alex pressed his mouth to the shell of her ear.

"Close your eyes."

Her lashes fluttered before settling, sending a shot of heat to the base of his spine. Reaching beneath the arm Zoe still had extended toward the vanity, he spread his palm over the front of her tank top at the top of her chest, her heart answering the pressure with a wild thrum against his skin. He centered himself behind her, lowering his hand to the slope of her belly before moving back up to the valley between the curve of her breasts. Zoe's rapid breaths became heady moans, and each one pushed Alex to repeat the circuit with slow, soft strokes.

"Are you with me, right here?" He let his fingers play in the spot right over her breastbone, dipping to the underside of one cotton-covered breast to tease her delicate skin through the fabric. Zoe's shoulder blades squeezed together on another moan, her knuckles going white over the granite ledge in front of her hips as her nipples peaked into hard points, begging to be touched.

"Yes. Oh, God. Yes."

The wicked thrill of her voice sent his hands over the hem of her top. "Where do you want me now?"

Zoe's eyes flashed open, her expression so sensual and wanting at the same time that it stole Alex's breath.

"Everywhere, Alex. I want you everywhere."

Forcing himself into slowness that shook his hands, he lifted her tank top over her head, guiding her hands back to the counter as the garment fell to the floor. He stepped in behind her, bringing his chest as close to her back as possible without making a connection before brushing his lips over her neck. Zoe gasped at the contact, her body tightening even further as he kissed his way down the ridge of her spine. Every response to his touch, no matter how subtle, made Alex crave the next one all the more, and he kissed a path over her neck, her shoulders, her back, until he'd shown every inch of the skin in front of him the attention of his fingers and tongue. But between the overt sexiness of the rest of her mostly bare body and the sheer desire on her face as she stood there trusting him to pleasure her, Alex couldn't wait any longer. Keeping one hand steady around Zoe's rib cage, he linked his other arm beneath hers, sweeping the pad of his thumb slowly over her nipple.

"*Ohhhhh.*" Her breath kicked out on a sharp cry, his cock jerking hard as she arched all the way into his touch.

"See? Just feel my hands on you. Right here." Alex circled again with his thumb. From over her shoulder, he sent his stare back to their entwined reflection, watching her nipple tighten and flush dark pink under his touch. "I'm with you, baby." He rolled the tip of her nipple between his thumb and the callused edge of his forefinger, picking up speed and pressure. "Right here. I've got you."

Zoe nodded, the strands of sun-kissed hair that had come loose from their twist tickling over Alex's skin, and even that slight suggestion of her closeness pushed him harder. The curve of her spine bowed upward with each pass of his fingers, her breath sawing out in ragged sighs. Alex watched in the mirror as Zoe arched against the friction, her eyes shut tight and her expression lost in sensation as he worked her nipple in faster strokes.

"Please. You're driving me crazy," she moaned, pressing up on the balls of her feet to fit her breast into more of his touch. The shift brought her head back against his shoulder, and while he wanted to give her a slideshow of sensations one at a time, he wasn't about to deny her, either.

"Then go crazy."

Alex lowered his hand from her nipple to the swell of her hip. Her shorts were little more than a blue and white scrap, with a deceptively sweet ruffle at the bottom hem, and he dragged a finger along the line where her leg tapered into the lush curve of her ass.

"These are so fucking hot." He let his finger follow the flutter of fabric back and forth, sliding beneath the cotton to find soft, bare skin. "No panties?" Jesus, now they were both going crazy.

"They seemed . . ." Zoe stopped, her breath hitching as he added another finger to skim her inner thigh. "Kind of pointless. Oh God, don't stop."

Alex slipped his hand between her thighs to cup her sex, and damn, her heat was an addiction. Wicked satisfaction speared all the way through him at the eager way she opened to his touch, but still, he kept his movements whisper soft. Trailing two fingers over her fabric-covered center, he wrapped his other arm around the front of her hips with firm intention. He anchored Zoe's body in place, pressing against the indent at the seam of her body one more time before pushing aside the damp fabric to finally touch her skin on skin.

"Right here," he grated, channeling every last shred of his willpower into not saying screw the experience and sinking his cock all the way inside her right goddamn now. She met his touch with a tilt of her hips, the fabric of her shorts riding up just enough to give him a sultry glimpse of her sex beneath, and Alex stroked her again just to hear her moan.

"There. Don't stop touching me there."

The words quivered past Zoe's lips, her eyes squeezing shut even tighter as she rocked against his fingers. Sliding his free hand past the waistband riding her hips, he pushed lower, over the rise where her hip bones came together to land at the apex of her smooth, bare sex. Zoe widened her stance, leaning forward against the vanity in invitation, and fuck if he was refusing her, no matter how hard his impulse screamed.

His cock could wait. Right now, he was going to give this woman the most earth-ripping orgasm of her life.

Alex dipped a finger into Zoe's core from behind, drawing a sharp cry from her chest. Her slick inner muscles clenched around him, begging for movement.

But he didn't give it.

"I'm still with you," he whispered, hot and dark in her ear. Without moving the finger buried inside her, he parted her folds with his opposite hand, bracing his palm over the lowest part of her belly while he tested and teased. Alex circled the swell of her clit, letting another finger join the first one inside her. Holding her still and steady, he cupped his palm against her sex, crooking his fingers as he withdrew in a sinful slide. Her sighs turned to moans in an instant, each one daring him to pleasure her more, and he didn't wait. His thrusts grew harder, blooming into a faster-paced rhythm as he sank his opposite fingers deeper against the swollen bud at the top of her sex. Alex stroked and pressed and caressed, until finally, Zoe started to tremble from the inside out.

"I've got you, Gorgeous," Alex said with one last punishing thrust inside her. "Take the moment. Come for me."

She climaxed in a hard wave, clutching the counter in front of her and screaming out his name. He watched her in the mirror, increasing the contact of their bodies as he slowed the motions of his hands. Shifting the arm he'd wrapped around the front of her body, Alex curled his hand over the thin waistband of Zoe's shorts, lowering first hers, then his before turning her around to face him.

"Are you still here?" he asked, dropping a kiss over each of her eyes as they fluttered open. But rather than utter a sweet murmur to match the blush on her face or the loose, golden curls that had fallen to frame her shoulders, Zoe shocked the hell out of him by throwing her head back to laugh.

"Oh, I'm here all right." Her tenderness made way for a saucy smile, and his pulse ratcheted higher as she dropped a hand to the slice of space between them. She slid her nimble fingers up the length of his thigh, with just enough friction to make his balls draw up tight against his body. Knowing the demand from his dick was going to become time sensitive in about T-minus zero seconds, Alex palmed Zoe's shoulders, turning toward his bedroom.

She didn't budge. "Where do you think you're going?"

"I'm taking you to bed."

"No, you're not."

His confusion had to have shown on his face, because Zoe continued before he could speak.

"Make no mistake," she said, her hand gliding over the flat of his abs, destination: lower. "I want you." Her fingertips brushed the head of his cock, and Alex's groan was involuntary as she kept talking, kept stroking. "But if we're going to really seize this moment, we're going to do it together."

Zoe reached the base of his shaft, but instead of sliding her touch back upward, she dropped her fingers to tease the sensitive skin beneath.

His breath slapped to a stop in his lungs. "We are?" he choked out, doing his best to find his resolve. Yeah, he wanted her with desire that bordered on insanity right now, and yeah again, he had every intention of staying very, very naked with her until that desire was satisfied. But no matter how badly he wanted her, no matter how sexy their foreplay had been in other places, the least Zoe deserved was to end up in a bed.

Alex darted a glance toward the door, renewing his efforts to get her to the comfort of his sheets and pillows, but she wrapped her fingers around his cock for a slow, delicious pump that damn near laid waste to his restraint.

"We are. Which means I want you to fuck me. Right. Here."

In a blur of motion and white hot want, Alex's hands shot around her hips to pull her off the floor. Their mouths crashed together in a tangle of urgent lust, and he pushed his way inside her mouth with a greedy sweep of his tongue. She tasted like peppermint and sin, her arms hot around his shoulders as he carried her to the small, sturdy niche where the two sections of countertop intersected.

"Wait," he demanded, putting Zoe down just shy of the L-shaped space. Backtracking to the soft fall of pima cotton hanging on the wall by the shower, he returned with the towel to drape it over the cold granite. He guided Zoe back, scooping her up to the counter while parting her knees with the frame of his body.

"Alex." She slid her silky inner thighs over his hips, bracketing them and beckoning him closer. Alex sent up a silent prayer of thanks that he kept his stash of condoms in the bathroom drawer, and he slid one out as Zoe reached down low to stroke him with growing speed. Between his hands and her ministrations, he was sheathed in seconds, and he moved in to cut the space between them to barely more than a breath.

"You want this moment." He angled himself against her body, sliding his cock over her folds, and it took all he had not to press into the wet, waiting heat between her legs.

Zoe's head dropped back, but the rest of her arched forward in reply. "Yes. I want this moment."

"Then take it, Zoe. It's yours."

Alex plunged into her sex with one long, hard thrust, his pulse going haywire while time slowed way the hell down. Sensations hurled themselves at him—the rasp of Zoe's voice, calling his name, the heat and squeeze of her body where they were so provocatively joined—and he exhaled hard as he gathered his bearings. He pulled back, only to rock home again, and Christ, even if he filled her all day, he'd still want to do it again as soon as the sun set.

"Gorgeous. God, you are . . ." Alex trailed off, his words shorted out by the sexy-sweet tilt of her hips. He reached around the flare of her hips, palming her ass to pull her flush against him as he thrust once, then twice, then quickly found a rhythm that made him want to shout even as he held her close.

"Yours."

The single word from Zoe's lips halted him, mid-stroke, and he met her eyes with a burning stare.

"I'm yours, Alex." She answered his unspoken question with a smile split between passion and vulnerability. "So take me. Give me the moment. Give me whatever you want."

His fingers tightened over her skin, digging in harder to the firm curve of her ass. Their bodies molded together from shoulder to belly to hips, and Alex anchored her in place as he filled her, again and again. Zoe wrapped her arms around his shoulders, pressing toward him even though there was no space to close. The friction of her nipples on his chest and her core gripping his cock dared him closer to the edge, and he ran toward his climax, full speed. Zoe's hand knotted in his hair, tugging hard as she shuddered and moaned, and the bolt of pleasure-pain sent his orgasm slamming up from the base of his spine.

Alex came so hard he forgot his name, even as he called out Zoe's over and over. Keeping their bodies locked together, he rode out every wave, every breath, every mind-blowing sensation before cupping her face to brush his lips over hers.

"Stay right here," he whispered, punctuating the words with one last kiss as he slipped past the door leading to the lavatory. After quickly dealing with the condom, Alex returned to the en suite, grabbing another towel from the bar on the wall and wrapping it around Zoe's shoulders.

"What are you doing?" she asked, her pretty, kiss-plumped smile sliding into confusion.

But he led her over to the bathtub without hesitation. "You still want the moment, right?"

"Yes." Her amber-colored eyes gleamed, going wider when he reached down to twist the oiled bronze faucet handles in front of him. Alex waited until the water was a perfect hot-but-not-too-hot before pushing the stopper and guiding her into the tub, pulling her close on pure impulse.

"Good. Because I just got started with you, Gorgeous. And I've got all damn day to finish."

Chapter Twenty

Zoe clicked Save on the last document on her to-do list for the morning, pushing back against her desk chair with a weary grin. Her eyes burned from a combination of near-constant focus on the Collingsworth Grant proposal and an equally steady lack of sleep. But the last four days had been worth every ounce of effort she'd put into them. Between the abundance of able bodies in Hope House's kitchen and the one-two punch of her planning and her father's proficiency with paperwork, Zoe had been able to make more strides than she'd even thought possible. And the more she detailed the soup kitchen's worthiness and strategized a bid outlining the ways she'd put that grant money to work, the more her hesitation turned into hope.

Hope she wouldn't have without Alex Donovan in her kitchen.

A hard prickle spread over Zoe's cheeks, and she swallowed the thought. Alex's hearing with the battalion chief was a week and a half away, and he'd put in more than enough time and effort for his community service to be considered a success. Although he'd worked just as many hours at Hope House as she had this week—all without complaint—Zoe hadn't missed the way Alex interacted so easily with everyone from Station Eight while they were here volunteering, or the levity that lit up his bright blue eyes whenever they were around. No matter how purely good she felt with him in her kitchen, he belonged at the firehouse, doing a job that meant taking risks on a daily basis.

But what if really living means taking risks? What if all you have to do is trust?

"Knock, knock."

Rachel's voice whipped Zoe back to her office by way of a good, hard reality check, and she sucked in a breath to counterbalance her slamming heartbeat and the yes-yes-yes pumping hot and heavy through her veins.

"Crap. I'm sorry," Rachel said, shifting a telephone-book-sized stack of folders to her jeans-clad hip as she gestured to the door frame around her. "Your door was open, but I should've known you'd be up to your elbows in work. Didn't mean to take you by surprise."

"No, no, you didn't," Zoe replied, and okay, fine. So the words were only true because her inner voice had tiptoed up and startled the crap out of her first. Good God in heaven, she needed a break. "Is everything okay out there? Do you need any help in the kitchen?"

Rachel's lips twitched into a smile. "Breakfast service went without a hitch, and I just walked by Alex, Cole, and Brennan unloading the produce delivery in nothing but their shirtsleeves and smiles. Everything's coming up roses. Speaking of which . . ." She paused for a minute, flipping through her armload of file folders before plucking one from the pile to hand over. "Tina asked me to give this to you."

"Thanks." Zoe held the folder, unopened, as she slid a glance at Rachel. "You know, Tina's never had an assistant before. Your volunteering to be a liaison between me and her has helped a lot this week."

Rachel lifted one shoulder of her black T-shirt into a

demi-shrug, but the warmth in her eyes totally called her no-big-deal bluff. "You're right side up in the kitchen with all the guys helping, so I figured this was a good way to pitch in." She pointed at the file she'd passed to Zoe. "Anyway, that's the finalized list of organizations willing to act as drop-off points for the food drive. Tina said you'd want it ASAP."

"Oooh, not wrong," Zoe said, flipping the folder open over her desk. She gave the list a quick visual, but wait. This couldn't be right. "There are sixty-seven locations listed here."

"Ah." Rachel reached out, motioning for Zoe to pass the list back over. "I forgot to add the bookstore over on Church Street. The owner owes me a big one for all the romance novels I buy in that place."

No way. "Are you serious?" Zoe breathed.

Rachel just huffed out a laugh. "Have you seen the covers on some of those babies? Of course I'm serious. Anyway, not everyone can have a firefighter-slash-underwear-model-lookalike sending stares at her like she's good enough to eat."

"Rachel!" Zoe's cheeks went thermonuclear, but damn it, Rachel's cat-in-cream smile was more contagious than the flu in a freshman dorm. Still, Zoe had to aim for a *little* dignity. "First of all, I meant are there seriously sixty-eight drop-off points for this food drive. Secondly, no one's looking at me with quite that much enthusiasm."

"First of all," Rachel said, playfully mimicking Zoe's tone along with her words, "underneath her pretty exterior, Ava is a barracuda. Of course there are that many drop-off locations. Secondly"—she clucked her tongue, although her smile didn't budge a millimeter—"I may have been born at night, but it wasn't last night. You can play Cleopatra, Queen of Denial, all you want, but I'm here to tell you, Donovan looks at you like you are all that."

"Really?" Zoe's mouth formed the question without

consulting her brain or her sense of self-preservation, and she shook her head in an effort to negate it. "I'm sure it's just the sex."

Rachel's brows disappeared beneath her auburn bangs. "So you and Donovan are more than just work partners, huh?"

Well, shit. "Okay, yeah," Zoe admitted, knowing when she'd been beat. Plus, the words felt unbelievably good coming out of her mouth. "I guess we are."

Rachel slipped past the threshold, shutting the office door behind her before perching herself in the spare kitchen chair across from Zoe's desk. "Lord, girl. Look at that great-sex glow on your face. If I didn't like you so much, I'd hate your guts."

"Sorry," Zoe said, although yep. It was pretty much a giant freaking lie.

"Ah, don't be. It's not your fault I haven't gotten laid since Thanksgiving. Anyway, Alex is a pretty cool guy. He's clearly into you. Better living through orgasms, I say."

Zoe's laugh took a swipe at her nerves. "Yeah, well, I wish it was that cut and dried. It's no raging secret that Alex's motto is 'risk first, ask questions later,' and let's just say I'm not usually on speaking terms with recklessness. Plus, when you add the whole my-overprotective-dad-is-totally-his-boss land mine . . . the odds of this not getting complicated are pretty anorexic."

"I don't know," Rachel said, although the certainty in her voice belied the words. "You seem pretty fierce for someone who's anti-risk. I'm not trying to overstep my bounds or piss you off, but the whole proceed-with-caution thing doesn't exactly suit. Professionally or personally."

"Playing it safe is the smartest call when it comes to protecting the things that are most important." But as soon as the default statement fell from Zoe's lips, she heard how lame it sounded. After all, she'd never have a shot at the

Collingsworth Grant if she stuck solely to the sidewalk, and she sure as hell wouldn't have spent any time with Alex without a risk or two. "Most of the time. Usually. Ugh, old habits die hard."

Rachel nodded. "Now that, I hear loud and flipping clear. I work in a firehouse. We're all about protecting what's important. But for what it's worth, Alex really does seem to want to help you." She paused to waggle her brows. "In both the kitchen and the bedroom."

"He is, um . . . pretty helpful," Zoe conceded, unable to cage her idiot grin.

"I see. And how helpful would that be, exactly?"

"Let's just say his quick tongue isn't limited to fast-talking, and as far as his enthusiasm is concerned, there are no hard limits."

Whether it was the unfettered goodness welling up in her chest or the look of pure oh-no-you-didn't shock dominating Rachel's face, Zoe couldn't be certain. But she let out a rare giggle, another one following on its heels, and pretty soon, she and Rachel were lost in a fit of laughter. Pressing her lips together so hard that they tingled, Zoe tried her best to take a deep breath and smooth herself back into seriousness, but then Rachel's attempt to inhale became a snort, and another wave of giggles had them both clutching at their sides and gasping for air.

Which was exactly how Alex found them when he knocked on the door to Zoe's office thirty seconds later.

"I hope I'm not interrupting," he said, peering past the door frame with a look caught halfway between awe and primal fear.

"Not at all," Zoe sputtered. A fresh peal of laughter tickled behind her breastbone, but thankfully Rachel stepped in to save her bacon.

"I should be going anyway. Let me know if you need any help coordinating the first round of pickups for the food

drive. I'm happy to pitch in. Especially at the bookstore."
She gave Zoe a covert wink before squeezing past Alex to
saunter from the office, and it took all of Zoe's effort to
keep a (mostly) straight face.

"Do I even want to know what that was all about?" Alex
asked, his blue eyes going for the full-on crinkle factor as
he leaned against the door frame to smile at her.

"Probably not." Better to stick to the truths she could
tell. Without blushing, anyway. "So what's up in the kitchen?
I heard you guys were on delivery duty."

Alex nodded, tipping his chin over one shoulder toward
the kitchen. "Yeah, Cole and Brennan and I just inventoried
and stored the last couple cartons of produce. We were
going to head out to start delivering collection boxes for the
food drive, but I didn't see any volunteers on the schedule
for lunch prep. Did you want us to stick around instead?"

Zoe pushed up from her chair. "Nah. I'm glad to be
making headway on this grant proposal, but if I don't take
a break from Paperwork Mountain, I'm going to lose my
cookies." The thought of getting hands-on with the food,
even for something as simple and seamless as lunch prep,
made her smile, and Zoe smoothed the hem of her red T-shirt
into place over her jeans as she aimed herself at the door.

Alex caught her by the elbow, the grab seemingly innocent even though she felt the tingle all the way up her
arm. "Are you sure you don't want me to stick around?" he
asked, but she just laughed in reply.

"Of course. That's not to say I won't miss you in the
kitchen." The corners of her mouth lifted along with her
brows. "But I'm pretty sure I can handle lunch service on
my own."

"Believe me," Alex said, sending a ribbon of *ooohhhhh
yeah* through her chest as his fingers glided up her arm to
play softly at her shoulder. "I'm not asking because I think
you can't manage. I know how tough you are."

Zoe melted into his touch. "Then why are you asking?" she asked, chasing the question with way more sigh than sass. But his hands felt so good, suddenly holding her tight and cupping her face, that she blew past every last one of her caution sensors to let him pull her in.

"Because." He dropped his forehead to hers, his lips enticingly close. "I've got your back. That's why."

"I know."

Alex's eyes went wide, but Zoe erased his surprise with a slant of her mouth. Letting someone care for her was risky, she knew.

But with the heat of his arms and the promise of his smile around her, trusting Alex to guard her kitchen felt too damn good for her to do anything other than let him.

"I know," Zoe repeated, pressing up to the toes of her kitchen clogs to kiss him one more time before turning toward the kitchen.

Zoe leaned over the two deep-bellied pots perched over the front burners on the stove, stirring the vegetable stock in first one, then the other, before seasoning them both with her secret mix of dried herbs and spices. After spending the last few weeks with Alex right next to her at Hope House, the kitchen felt eerily quiet as she moved through the steps of prepping lunch all by herself. But he'd promised to be back by the end of the meal service, and Millie and Ellen would be arriving in less than an hour. Once she got new funding in place, Zoe would be able to hire a few more part-timers to help balance out the schedule, and they'd be able to fill the dining room to the rafters, seven days a week. Then quiet like this would probably become a hot commodity, she thought with a laugh. She should probably take advantage of the peace while she could.

The more Zoe chopped and tasted and stirred, the more the food calmed her, smoothing out the exhaustion of the last week—hell, the last few months, really—and replacing it with something brighter. Something she'd not only been missing since she'd moved back to Fairview, but something she'd needed fundamentally for even longer than that.

Hope.

"Hey, sugar plum." Tina's voice tipped Zoe from her reverie, snagging her attention as her codirector pushed through the double doors leading in from the dining room. "I found this handsome gentleman out by the front desk, and thought you might be able to put him to work."

"Dad?" Shock wheeled through her from belly to breast-bone. "What are you doing here?"

Her father's eyes took a split-second tour of the kitchen before landing on hers. "I'm not on shift today, and I know you've got a lot of work to do in only a little time. So I thought"—he paused, gesturing to the twin stockpots on the cooktop at her hip—"maybe you could use some help."

Zoe dropped her wooden spoon to the worktable with a clatter. "You came out here to help me cook?"

While she and her father had hooked up at Scarlett's this week for several marathon sessions to chip away at her proposal for the Collingsworth Grant, he'd stayed notice-ably absent from Hope House itself. On one hand, his avoidance—especially when nearly every firefighter from Station Eight had showed up to help in the kitchen for at least a few hours this week—had stung. But on the other, Zoe wasn't about to deny that she still feared for her father's safety every time he strapped on his helmet. She couldn't exactly fault the man for wanting her to be safe, or disap-proving of the job that he felt kept her from being that way.

"Ah, well . . ." Her father ran a hand over his military-precise gray-blond hair in a move Zoe had long since recognized as a nervous tell, and her gut tightened out of habit. This crossroads between emotion and denial had been the sticking point for every one of their conversations since she'd come back home to Fairview.

But rather than clamming up or stuffing his emotions away like he had for the last few months, her father shocked the hell out of her by saying, "The first thing I teach my firefighters when they walk through the door to Station Eight is to look out for one another, above all else. I know I'm just your old man." His shoulders lifted on a shrug that was far from indifferent. "But if my firefighters are going to have your back, then the least I can do is come in here and show them how it's done."

"Oh," Zoe breathed, her smile welling up and taking over her face completely of its own accord. "Well, in that case, I guess you'll need an apron."

"Thanks, kiddo." A rare shot of raw emotion whisked through her father's eyes, landing right in the center of Zoe's chest.

But she was his daughter, through and through. "Don't thank me yet," she said, lifting an apron from one of the nearby hooks and handing it over with a squeeze. "You weren't wrong about there being a lot of work to do around here. If you want to help, we need to get cracking."

"Well, then, by all means. Put me to work, ma'am."

Their laughter lasted for just a minute before being interrupted by a loud sniffle, and Zoe pivoted on her heel toward the sound. Tina stood by the swinging doors, one hand pressed over the front of her blouse and the other swiping at her cheeks. With the sheer surprise of her father's arrival in the kitchen, Zoe had totally forgotten Tina had escorted him in.

Realizing that both Zoe and her father had turned their attention in her direction, Tina lifted her chin, waving one hand in pure *nothing to see here* fashion, and Zoe couldn't help it. She cracked a grin.

"You okay, Tina?"

"What? I have something in my eye, okay?" Tina let out another sniffle before heading to the door in defeat. "Just . . . make lunch, you two!"

Zoe's father met her chuckle with one of his own. "So what's on the menu today?" he asked, cocking a finger at the stockpots simmering away on the stove. She split her attention between the cooktop and the kitchen island, treating the vegetable stock to one last stir before aiming herself at the ingredients piled high on the worktable.

"Unfortunately, our budget doesn't let us get too fancy over here, so I try to stick with healthy versions of comfort food. Today it's vegetable soup and good, old-fashioned grilled cheese. The soup is nearly done, but we'll have to make a lot of sandwiches. Think you can manage that?"

"Manage it? Please." Her father rolled up the sleeves of his light blue button-down shirt, meticulously turning the cuffs over each forearm once, then again, before donning his apron. "Grilled cheese sandwiches were the only thing you let past your lips the entire year you were four. I could probably still make them in my sleep."

Zoe's laughter escaped in a sharp pop. "Really?"

"You don't remember?" Her father gestured toward the butter, and Zoe answered the wordless question with a nod.

"I don't think so." Biting her lip in concentration, she sifted through her memories, but came up empty.

Her father picked up a butter knife, sliding one of the sheet pans Zoe had filled with bread slices in front of his workstation and setting his hands to purposeful motion. "God, I remember it like it was last week. The first time you asked your mother to make you one, you strung the words together. We spent three days trying to figure out what on earth a 'grouchy sammich' was."

Zoe tucked her smile between her lips, reaching toward the other end of the cooktop to snap the griddle to life. "How did you finally figure it out?"

Her father wasn't so cautious with his smile. "After three days of us making you peanut butter and jelly and serving it with frowns on our faces, you marched right on over to the refrigerator and took out the ingredients."

"I did not!" As soon as the laughter-laced protest fell from her lips, Zoe knew it wouldn't stick. Although she couldn't remember the incident, going the practical route *did* sound like something she'd do. Maybe even at four.

"Oh yes, you did," her father replied, emphasizing the words with a lift of his butter-smudged knife. "You handed over the cheese and the bread, no muss, no fuss, and you and I ate grilled cheese sandwiches that very night in front of the hockey game."

An image, time-fogged and fragmented, bubbled up from deep in her memory, and her hands froze into place over the slices of cheese she'd been separating on the counter. "Oh my God, I *do* remember that! We had that awful chair in the rec room. The really ugly one, with the plaid cushions."

Her father lifted a brow. "I'll have you know those Barcaloungers are timeless pieces of high-quality craftsmanship."

"Daddy, that thing was a monstrosity." Zoe laughed, sliding in next to him to start assembling the bread and cheese into sandwiches for the griddle.

"That thing was a classic," he argued, completely without heat. "There's nothing quite as good as the tried-and-true things in life."

Zoe's heart thumped against her sternum. But her father had taken a leap of faith by coming to Hope House. The least she could do was leap back to meet him square in the middle.

"Kind of like sharing a grouchy sandwich with someone you love?"

"Yeah, kiddo." Her father's eyes crinkled at the edges, the warmth of his stare melting all the way through Zoe's chest as he nodded. "Exactly like that."

Chapter Twenty-One

"I've got to be honest with you, Gorgeous. Your meat loaf is flying onto plates so fast out here, I'm thinking all you need is a food truck and a fast route to every firehouse in the city, and you could make a mint for Hope House all on your own."

Zoe's fingers squeezed over the fresh tray of green beans she'd just walked from the kitchen to the dining room. The corners of her mouth twitched as Alex capped off his words with a sexy little wink, begging her to let her lips bloom into a full-fledged smile. The urge doubled as she scanned Hope House's service line and saw that Alex wasn't really exaggerating, but still, she refused to respond with anything more than a lift of her brows.

"Are you deliberately messing with me, Mr. Donovan?"

Alex clapped a palm over the front of his apron, feigning insult. "Of course not." At Zoe's and Cole's twin looks of are-you-kidding-me, though, he recanted. "Okay, maybe a little. But come on. Just look at all these happy people."

Zoe followed his gesture over the dining room, where the Thursday night dinner service was in full swing. All eight of the long, communal tables were more than halfway full, with the two closest to the service line being completely occupied. The quiet buzz of conversation was peppered with clinking cutlery and the shush of sturdy plastic trays being pushed down the resident side of the service counter. At the end of the line, Hector and two of his cronies picked up their post-dinner oatmeal cookies and coffee with wide smiles. Brennan stood by the clearing station just waiting to whisk the dirty dishes back to the kitchen, laughing and joking with Ava, and okay, Zoe had to admit it. Everyone really did look happy.

"All right," she said, passing the green beans to Cole so he could take them to the front of the service line. After pausing for a quick this-is-all-we-have-left-so-please-make-it-last reminder before sending him off, she turned back toward Alex. "You win. The meat loaf is a success."

He dropped his tone a register, ensuring that their conversation stayed private even in the bustle of the dining room. "You're taking care of these people one meal at a time. The food might be good, but face it, Zoe. Anyone else in your position would've thrown in the towel ages ago. Only you didn't. Instead, you made a difference in these people's lives. *You're* the success."

Her cheeks warmed for a brief second before her gaze landed on the large, twilight-shadowed windows at the front of the dining room, and the unguarded door adjacent to them. "Feeding everyone who came in tonight is a success, yes. But for every hungry person in this room, there are at least three more out there who qualify for assistance that I still have to turn away because we don't have enough food to go around, and I still can't even think about the most bare-bones security yet. Guys like Damien are still out there. As much as I want to, I have no way of *keeping* them out there."

She reached out, squeezing his forearm to quell the protest clearly tightening the line of his jaw beneath his gold-blond stubble. "Don't get me wrong. I'm grateful for what

I can do right now, but I've still got a long way to go, and I know you guys can't volunteer forever. When I land the Collingsworth Grant, then we'll talk success."

Slowly, the tension in Alex's jaw slid back into his trademark cocky smirk. "I guess I shouldn't be shocked," he said, turning toward the stainless steel counter behind them for a stack of clean plates. "After all, you told me on my first day that feeding everyone at Hope House was your number-one priority. I should've known you'd do anything to make it happen."

"Including boss you around, pretty boy." Zoe grinned, grabbing the dish towel draped over her shoulder to give Alex's denim-covered leg a playful snap. "We still have thirty minutes left in this dinner service, and sitting around isn't on the menu."

"You know you're going to pay for that later, don't you?" His eyes glinted, the color of an ocean at sunset, and even though none of the tenants or other volunteers were within earshot of their conversation, Zoe leaned in closer anyway.

"Why do you think I did it in the first place?" she asked, connecting her gaze with his for just a beat longer before turning to saunter toward the pass-through to the dining room. A quick tour around the space wouldn't hurt for security's sake, and anyway, as excited as she was getting over this grant proposal, she'd missed being in the dining room with the residents.

Zoe stopped at the first table by the service line, greeting some of the longer-term residents and chatting with a few newcomers before repeating the process at the next table. She got a third of the way through her circuit around the dining room when Rachel slipped through the door leading in from the shelter, putting her barely two steps to Zoe's left.

"Oh hey, just the person I was looking for," Rachel said,

tucking a strand of red hair behind one ear. "Do you have a sec?"

Zoe tilted her head toward a small dish-return alcove, and they took the handful of steps to reach the out-of-the-way space. "Sure. What's up?"

Rachel tugged some papers from the stack on her hip. "I coordinated an early pickup schedule for the food drive. I know we were going to wait until next week to start, but Ava's article on the shelter made huge waves. Half of the businesses are calling to tell us their boxes are already over-flowing, so I drafted this up on the fly."

"Oh my God." Zoe's brows lifted as her jaw dropped in the opposite direction. She flipped through page after page of the detailed list, her surprise doubling. "This is incredible."

"I told you this food drive would be awesome. Plus, I'm happy to help," Rachel said over a playful smile. "I know Hope House is important to you, but your job can't be the only thing going on in your life."

"You have a life, too," Zoe argued, but Rachel just winked.

"One with zero romantic prospects. Come on, Zoe. It's one thing to throw in extra hours when you've got nothing personal on the horizon. But I wasn't kidding about the way Alex looks at you. He might be doing his damnedest to fight it, but this isn't my first rodeo. I've worked with him for years, and I know what I know. That guy has it bad for you."

Zoe's blush served as a quick chaser to the chirp of laughter pushing past her lips. "I told you, it's just the sex."

Rachel put on her very toughest don't-fuck-with-me face, and whoa. Girlfriend meant business. "It's not. He likes you. And I think you like him, too. So do yourself a favor, please. Stop being afraid to risk it and give the guy a real chance."

"I want to," Zoe admitted, the words startling her and yet feeling perfect at the same time. "But this thing between me and Alex was never meant to be long-term. My parents' marriage fell apart because my mother couldn't handle the risks of firefighting, and I can't lie, Rachel. Between Mason Watts being killed a few years ago and my dad's injury after that, the danger scares the ever-loving hell out of me, too. Being with Alex while we've worked here at Hope House is one thing. But . . ."

"You don't know if you can handle that fear when he goes back to fighting fires," Rachel finished.

Zoe shook her head. "Old habits, remember?"

She let out a breath even though it did nothing to ease the indecision squeezing her rib cage. Yes, she knew Alex had her back in the kitchen, and yes again, Hope House had enough volunteers to give her a bit of a reprieve right now. But in little more than a week, her grant application would be finished and turned in. The firefighters would go back to Eight, she'd go back to running the soup kitchen solo . . .

And Alex would go back to jumping into things feet first, risking his life every minute of every day.

Rachel shifted toward Zoe, her stare serious in the shadows of the alcove. "Old habits aren't always a bad thing. In fact, sometimes, those instincts to keep yourself protected are the only things that save your ass."

Zoe waited, sensing the forthcoming *but*, and she wasn't disappointed.

"But sometimes, old habits can hurt you." Rachel's voice softened to one step above a whisper, although she didn't scale back on her delivery. "I'm not trying to get all kittens and rainbows on you. You wouldn't buy that, anyway. All

I'm saying is that from the outside, you and Alex look like you could have something that works. When you're listening to your gut, don't forget to ask your heart's opinion, too, okay?"

Zoe looked across the dining room, the pressure in her chest tightening as she watched Alex lean in toward Cole, listening to something the other firefighter said for just a brief second before throwing his head back in pure, carefree laughter.

"I won't," she said, but even so, Zoe knew her gut was too headstrong not to win out.

Alex sat all the way back against his kitchen chair, ninety percent certain he was going to explode. Then Zoe pulled another tray of oatmeal raisin cookies from the oven, ushering the scents of brown sugar and warm cinnamon through the space between them, and yup. That just about sealed the deal.

"We have got to figure out another way for you to channel your nervous energy; otherwise I'm going to gain about a thousand pounds." Not that it stopped him from grabbing one more cookie off the plate she'd put in front of him twenty minutes ago. Damn, these things were addicting.

Zoe slid the cookie sheet over the cooling rack on the counter, folding her bottom lip firmly between her teeth. "Sorry. But I only have three days before I turn this grant proposal in, and . . . well, have you ever had that nightmare where you stand up in front of a huge group of people only to discover you're naked?"

He nodded, pushing back from the table to close the space between them while she continued. "Multiply that by about four million, and it's kind of where I stand right now."

"Sorry, what? You lost me at naked."

"Alex," she warned, although her laughter puffed past his cheek as he pulled her in close.

"Okay, okay." He dropped a quick kiss over her mouth, mostly because he couldn't help himself. But that little crease of worry that had set up camp between her eyebrows was honestly killing him. "I know you're nervous. But you spent all day today on the last section of the proposal." He kissed her again, just a brush of his lips. "We've got a full house with volunteers tomorrow, which means you've got all weekend to put the finishing touches on the thing. Not that it needs any," he added, punctuating the affirmation with another, slower slide of his mouth, and bingo. Zoe melted into his touch. "You brought your A-game, Gorgeous. We've got this."

"You're always this sure of yourself when you take risks, aren't you?"

Her question arrived on nothing more than an honest whisper, so that's exactly how Alex answered it. "I'm always confident when I put my mind to something, yeah. But in this case, it's not me who I'm sure of. It's you."

"What?" She blinked up at him, her body tightening in surprise beneath his grasp.

But no way was he letting her go. For three weeks, he'd watched her uncover the fierceness he'd seen beneath her caution all along. It was high time she took some credit.

Alex smiled. "You made the whole thing happen. From start to finish, you're grabbing the moment to give Hope House all you've got. You might not want to admit it, but trust me. If there's anything I'm sure of, it's you."

"I did a lot of the work," Zoe said slowly, her body fitting further against his with every word. "But I never would've taken the leap if you hadn't shown me how to be a little reckless. So really, it's us."

Alex took a deep breath, but still, his pulse picked up

speed in his veins. He'd been totally committed to living every inch of his life big and bold and right out loud for the last twelve years. He'd jumped from one thing to the next, letting each moment burn bright before it burned out, one hundred percent cocksure that he'd been living his life to the fullest.

But somewhere between that first morning at Hope House and this moment, with Zoe's arms around his shoulders and that vulnerable expression that hit him right in the heart, Alex had changed. He didn't just want to live in the moment in front of him. He wanted to live in *all* the moments, and he wanted to do it with Zoe.

Beginning with this one.

"I want to be with you," he said, cupping her face to capture both her gaze and the surprise shaping her expression.

"You're with me right now."

"I want more than now." Alex skimmed his thumb over the curve of her lower lip, and hell. He'd never felt so reckless or so right in his life. "I want to wake up next to you tomorrow and see your face, just like this, and then I want to fall asleep next to you so we can do the same damn thing all over again. I want you, Zoe, and I don't want to stop wanting you. I want to take the risk. I want to be with you."

He dropped his mouth to hers in nothing more than the hint of a touch, but he felt the kiss everywhere, from his bones to his breath to his balls. Fitting the rise of her cheekbones against each of his palms, Alex held Zoe close, placing soft kisses on every part of her mouth until she pulled back on a gasp.

"Your hearing is first thing Monday morning, and after that, you're going back to Eight. You belong there," she whispered, her eyes roiling with emotion as she stared up at him through the glow of the kitchen lights.

"I do belong there," he agreed. "But working with you

at Hope House showed me I can belong in more than one place."

Zoe's lips parted, if only for a second. "And what about my father?"

Alex's heart pounded a rhythmic warning against his sternum, but he pushed past his clanging sense of self-preservation. Westin might be an old-school firefighter with an honor code to match, but he was still a fair man, and the closest thing Alex had to a father.

And he wanted Zoe enough to put it all on the line.

"It's going to take a delicate conversation, and we'll have to figure out the best way to have it. I'm not saying it won't be . . ." *Awkward. Brutal. A carte-blanche invitation for the man to kick my ass.* "Difficult at first," he managed past his tightening vocal cords. "But like you said, we're adults. This isn't just some one-night stand."

Zoe's hair slid over her shoulders as she nodded in agreement, and Christ almighty, she was stunning, standing there in his kitchen with flour smudged on her face and his name spilling past her lips. "I know, and I want this, too."

The words bolted all the way through him with uncut goodness, until she followed them with, "But I'm scared. I know that being a firefighter isn't just what you are, it's who you are. I do. It's just . . . God, Alex. What if you get hurt?" The unspoken *or worse* hung in her tone, and even though he wanted to reassure her, his no-bullshit demeanor didn't take a sabbatical just because the topic of conversation got a little dicey.

"I might," he said, dropping his chin to bring his gaze completely level with hers. "My job is an all or nothing proposition, and I can't promise you I'll never get hurt doing it. But you can't sink yourself in *what if*. At some point, you've got to trust. You've got to take the leap."

Alex leaned all the way in, so close that he could feel Zoe's breath hitch beneath the tissue-thin cotton of her shirt. But he was all-in, all the time, and as reckless as it was, he couldn't think of a stronger, sweeter thing to put everything on the line for than this woman.

"So tell me, Zoe. Do you trust me enough to take the risk?"

Chapter Twenty-Two

"Yes."

The word collapsed past Zoe's lips in a whisper, although it rattled her pulse as if she'd launched it on a scream. The thought of Alex going back to the firehouse—and all the risks that went with it—still scared her to death. But when he looked at her with that Caribbean blue stare and told her in his own wide-open, utterly confident way that he wanted to be with her, she couldn't ignore the truth.

He'd had her back, and he'd never faltered. Alex had been there every step of the way, making her believe in not only mending the fences of her past and really living the moments right in front of her, but in wanting more. In wanting him.

Zoe didn't just trust Alex with her past and her kitchen. She trusted him with her heart. And she wanted him enough to take the ultimate risk.

"Yes," she whispered again, pressing up to her toes to taste the surprise on Alex's mouth. "I trust you. I want this, Alex. I want *you*."

His shock turned to a look of pure desire, and he wrapped his arms around her, cradling her tight against the frame of his body. "If you want me, I've got you, baby. C'mere."

He dipped his mouth to meet hers, returning her quick

kiss with one that lingered. Cupping the back of her neck with hot fingers, he coaxed her lips apart with a sweep of his tongue. Alex explored her mouth with slow, lazy strokes, tasting and sucking and nibbling. Sparks flared, low and dangerous in Zoe's belly, as one palm slid to the back of her head to knot in her hair, while the other found the curve of her chin. Focusing the attention of his mouth on her upper lip, he swept the pad of his finger over the sensitive center of its counterpart, working her skin back and forth with just the hint of a touch.

"*Oh.*" The moan was all Zoe could manage past the tingling heat of Alex's movements. Oh God, she'd never known such a tiny spot on her lower lip could be such an absolute turn-on. She parted her mouth further to allow him better access, but he kept his finger where it was, stroking her slowly.

"You like that." The rumble of his voice raked over her, turning her nipples to hard, achy peaks behind the soft satin cups of her bra. She darted her tongue over his finger in reply, and the rumble became a growl.

"I'm going to touch you here until you scream," he said, nipping at her upper lip with just enough pressure to make her cry out with want before soothing the pleasure/pain with a soft, openmouthed kiss. "Then I'm going to find all the other places that make you hot." Alex swept his finger harder against her lower lip, the friction sending sparks of wet heat between her thighs.

The sparks nearly combusted when he pulled back to pin her with a glittering blue stare full of promise.

"And then I'm going to touch every one of them until you scream all over again."

Shifting his weight over the ceramic kitchen tiles, Alex guided Zoe away from the counter, the distance creating just enough space for the leverage he needed to drop his hands over her hips and lift her feet off the floor. His shoulders flexed and squeezed beneath her fingertips, and she wrapped her legs around the corded muscles of his waist. The move put the seam of her body in perfect contact with his rock-hard erection, pulling a moan from her chest as she canted her hips over his in a fast, demanding thrust.

"Jesus, woman." Alex's steps became less steady as he crossed the threshold to the main living space. "Are you trying to wreck me?"

"Maybe," Zoe countered, her grin getting lost somewhere between his neck and his shoulder as she strung a line of kisses between the two.

But Alex stuttered to a halt halfway across the living room. "I mean it, you know."

"Mean what?" Confusion ribboned past the want pulsing through her veins.

He gently lowered her to the carpet, his glittering blue stare never leaving hers. "Everything about you just unravels me." He paused to kiss her, both punishing and sweet. "Your hot little sighs when I touch you. The way you look so fierce one minute, then so open and honest in the next. You're just so . . . beautiful."

Zoe had heard the word countless times in her life—had even heard people say it about her on occasion. But never, ever, in her twenty-seven years, had *beautiful* sounded brand-new, like a word that belonged only to her and one other person.

Until now.

"Alex," she whispered, arching against him to fuse their bodies from hips to chest. Her heart pounded so hard she knew he had to feel it, too, but Zoe didn't care. He lowered his lips to hers, but he didn't increase his tempo, didn't push into her with fast, greedy hunger. He simply kissed her, testing her mouth with the perfect balance of give and take, and sweet God in heaven, she was going to die right here in this spot, in his arms.

"Please," she begged on a need-soaked groan. Despite all the sensations flying through her body, Zoe pulled back far enough to keep their gazes connected. "I know how much you want me, because I feel it, too. Take me to bed, Alex. Please. Take me."

In a flash of fast movements and faster intentions, they moved up the stairs, kissing and touching and building anticipation. When they reached the threshold of Alex's bedroom, he stopped, pulling her close for a long, slow kiss.

"No rushing," he said, running his teeth over the still tender spot on her lower lip. Heat pulsed in her core, begging to be stoked, but he held back. "You deserve every second of this, and I plan to give them to you. Nice"—he drew her lip between his own, sucking for a brief second before letting go—"and slow."

Alex led her into his room, the carpet soft under her bare feet. Scant strains of golden streetlight slanted in past the blinds, illuminating the space only enough to cut through the nighttime shadows, and Alex stopped just shy of his bed. Reaching down low, he crossed his arms in front of him, pulling off his shirt with one quick tug.

Zoe's eyes followed the trail of hard muscle and lean lines, and holy *shit*, he was gorgeous.

His gravelly chuckle told Zoe that she'd spoken the words out loud. "Your turn." He treated her to the same motions, lifting her T-shirt over her head. Her nipples hardened, aching from the slide of the satin still covering them despite the fabric's softness. Alex skimmed his hands over her rib cage, pausing with a hard exhale before letting his palms fall away. Zoe nearly whimpered in protest—God, she wanted his hands on her with desire that bordered on mind-blowing—but then he reached for the top button on his jeans, and the sound jammed in her throat.

Alex freed each button, then lowered his jeans with a muted rasp of denim on skin. He stood in front of her in nothing but his boxer briefs, letting her take in the crisp trail of gold-blond hair leading down to the outline of his fully erect cock beneath the black cotton. She squeezed her thighs together, the seam of her jeans brushing against her already hypersensitive clit, and this time the whimper tumbled past her lips. Alex answered it with a slow, promise-filled smile. His fingers found the edge of her jeans, sliding from hip to hip before loosening the button and zipper to reveal her white satin panties.

"So hot." The murmur melted between his mouth and her skin as Alex leaned in to guide her jeans all the way off. Turning toward the bed, he slid over the sheets, still rumpled from the night before, situating himself with his shoulders against the pillows as he beckoned for her to join him.

Zoe complied, her body thrumming with anticipation. The sparks between her thighs reignited at his touch, threatening to combust completely when he pulled her over him, parting her knees with his frame. Her core rested over the flat plane of Alex's belly, the thin, damp fabric of her panties the only barrier between them, and Zoe canted her hips over his heated skin. His fingers curled seductively around the flare of her ass, gripping firmly.

But rather than pushing her lower to cover his cock, he pulled her toward him with just enough force to guide her knees into the bedsheets and her sex mere inches from his sudden, wicked smile.

"You like this, too," Alex said, with just enough question in the words that she nodded in reply. He locked his arms around the small of her back, holding her snugly in place as he flicked a glance to the sturdy expanse of wood behind him.

"Hold on to the headboard, Zoe." With a look that shot right through her, he added, "Tight."

She shifted forward, her palms finding the cool wood. Ripples of want pulsed through her in a steady wave, and even though she knew she should feel vulnerable at the lack of control of her current position, she didn't.

She trusted him.

"You're so fucking sweet. I could taste you forever." He backed up the affirmation with a slow slide of his tongue along the line where her panties met her inner thigh, and Zoe widened her legs, desperate for contact.

Alex didn't disappoint. Darting his tongue past his lips, he treated her core to the same glide. He worked the fabric over her folds, the soft satin combining with the harder motions of his tongue until she dug her fingers into the headboard hard enough to make her knuckles throb.

"Do you want more?"

She clenched her inner muscles, but oh God, release only built harder between her thighs. "Please, yes."

Alex spread his fingers wide around the small of her back, tipping her hips against his mouth for another exquisite thrust of his tongue. "I'm going to make you come hard and fast," he said, hooking his fingertips over the waistband of her panties before licking her over the satin one last time. "But only so I can take my time with you when I make you come again."

He shifted her just far enough to lower the satin from her body, pulling her back into place in less than a breath. Zoe's hands trembled as she braced them back on the headboard for balance. Her knees pressed into the soft sheets by his shoulders, and when Alex bracketed her hips with both palms, she angled her body forward, closing the space between them.

"Oh . . . oh my *God*." Heat ricocheted under her skin,

forcing her breath from her chest in a gasp. Alex didn't waste any time making good on his promise, parting her folds with his mouth and thrusting into her with clear intent. His tongue slid in and out of her body, his hands driving her hips into a rhythm to match, both combining to coax her maddeningly close to the brink of release. With every part of her screaming for more, Zoe slid one hand from the headboard to the apex of her folds, her fingers making a brazen sweep over her swollen clit.

Alex's eyes flashed up at her, his moan of approval vibrating against her core, and her last thread of control snapped. Her orgasm broke free from the deepest part of her belly, shock-waving through her from the inside out. Alex stayed with her, only slowing his motions when he'd wrung every last *yes* from her throat. Shaping her waist with both hands, he rolled her to one side, propping himself on one arm so they lay face-to-face.

"Alex." Zoe reached out, her hands itching to touch him, to return the favor, to get his cock inside her in very short order.

He stopped her with one quick grab of her wrist. "Sorry, Gorgeous," he said, although his smirk said he was anything but. "But by now you should know that I mean what I say."

"What?"

"I made you come fast and hard." He placed her arm back at her side, dusting his fingertips from her shoulder to the rise of her hip. "And now I'm taking my time."

Her skin tingled beneath his touch, dotting goose bumps in the wake of his hand as Alex skimmed the pad of one finger up to the center closure of her bra. He stilled for just a moment, with his hand resting between her breasts, and Zoe's nipples hardened even further at his touch.

But instead of freeing the clasp and touching her, his

hand traveled up, over her breastbone to the hammering pulse point in her neck. Zoe bit down on her bottom lip. Alex caught the motion with his mouth, cupping her face to kiss her until he'd freed her lip from between her teeth.

"You don't have to hold back."

She arched a brow through the barely there light. "I'm not the one holding back," she murmured brashly, a tendril of surprise working through her when Alex didn't offer up a cocky comeback.

"I'm not holding back either, sweetheart." He pressed his forehead to hers. Squeezing his eyes shut, he whispered, "I don't want just a night in bed with you. I want to give you everything. I want all of you, and I don't want to rush through having you."

He followed the words with just a soft brush of his mouth, and Zoe was lost. She wrapped her arms around his shoulders, letting him press her gently to her back in the covers as he kissed her with languid strokes of his lips and tongue. Alex tunneled his hands through her hair, sliding his kisses from her mouth to her jaw. He explored the stretch of skin behind her ear, down the back of her neck, uncovering sensitive spots she hadn't even known existed. He teased and tasted and touched, moving over every inch of her body with growing intensity. Heat rebuilt between Zoe's legs, but rather than treating it like a now-right-now demand, she took each moment in slow, sexy progression.

And Alex gave her every single one.

"Beautiful," he said, finally parting her legs with a press of his palms against her inner thighs. She chased the affirmation with a lift of her hips, and he gave in with an audible exhale. He took off his boxer briefs in a quick move, grabbing a condom from his bedside table drawer. Zoe reached out, pushing to her knees in the middle of the bed as her fingers curled around his.

"Wait."

Alex stilled, his body going bowstring tight in front of her. "What's the matter?"

"Nothing." Laughter whispered past her lips for emphasis. God, she'd never felt so perfect in her life. "But this is you and me, together, right?"

"Of course."

Zoe kissed him, taking the condom from him before running her fingers down the flat plane of his abs. "Then I want to give you everything, too. Please, Alex. Don't just take me. Let me in. Let me have you right back."

He didn't protest, and Zoe didn't wait. Letting her hand travel lower, she wrapped her fingers around his cock, a thrill sparking through her blood at the groan grating up from his throat. She pumped slowly, pressing her body into Alex's side as they knelt face-to-face on the mattress. He tilted his hips into the movement of her hand, letting his head fall to the side as she kissed her way from his shoulder down to the fold of muscle just above his heart.

But stopping was the last thing on her mind, and Zoe slid her tongue even lower, using her free hand to push Alex's knees farther apart. The sharp lines of muscle wrapped around each of his hips pointed her to exactly what she wanted. Bending lower at the waist, she kissed her way between his legs, replacing the fingers on his cock with her mouth.

"Holy . . ." Alex finished the sentence with a hiss, and Zoe's lips curled into a smile before parting to take him in again. She added her hand back into play, circling her fingers to stroke the base of his cock while she tasted the rest of him with her lips and tongue. His palms turned to fists at his sides, one falling open over her shoulder as her ministrations picked up speed. Alex's exhales gave way to moans, each one daring her into the next glide of her mouth. But Zoe had meant what she'd said. She didn't just want to give herself up to him, as exquisitely good as he made her feel. It was the give coupled with the take that made Zoe burn for Alex hotter than she'd ever thought possible. She'd never wanted anyone with so much pure, sweet intensity.

And she wanted this forever.

"Zoe," he ground out, his fingertips turning into the heated skin of her shoulder. "This night is going to have a different ending than you're expecting if you keep that up."

She pulled back to look at him, caught between an honest question and a grin. "Is that what you want?"

Alex bit out a curse, but he guided her back to the bedsheets anyway. "Not this time." He knelt between her parted legs, reaching for the condom she'd placed on the sheets. Seconds later, he divided the cradle of her hips with his body. All the longing banked in Zoe's blood came charging back as the hot length of his cock slipped over her entrance, and she canted her hips upward for more contact.

"Don't hold back," she whispered. Alex angled himself over her, spreading his hands wide on either side of her shoulders and closing the space between both their bodies and faces to mere inches.

"You either," he said, his voice going as soft as his stare. "You and me, remember?"

Zoe's breath caught in her lungs. "Together."

Alex filled her with a slow thrust, and she was helpless against the cry spilling past her lips. For a minute, he stayed perfectly still, their bodies joined together and their breath twining between them.

Then he started to move, and Zoe nearly lost her mind.

Steadying his weight between his hands, Alex drew back, the friction of his cock sending bursts of sensation through her oversensitive core. Her muscles squeezed to accommodate the movement, her body growing slicker with need as he pushed back into her heat. Zoe rocked up to meet each thrust, wrapping her hands around the hard curve of his ass to keep him locked against her as she moved. She dug her heels into the mattress, her hips bucking into the slide of his body as he plunged into her sex. Release unraveled from deep between her legs in a hot curl, daring her to break apart in Alex's arms.

"Together, baby," he said, the promise raking over her skin as he dipped his mouth forward to kiss her. "And I've got you. I swear."

Zoe arched up to meet him in one last thrust of her hips before she climaxed hard, her pulse racing through her veins while pleasure rolled through her in one surge after another. Alex never stopped making love to her—not when she screamed his name, not when her fingernails curved into the small of his back to keep him close, and not even when she was so filled with bright, beautiful sensation that she couldn't do anything but gasp for breath. He pushed up to his knees, gripping her hips to keep her flush against his cock as he rocked into her over and again, until finally, his hands trembled at her sides.

"*Christ,* Zoe, I . . ."

She grabbed his wrists, dug in tight. "I've got you, too, Alex. Don't hold back."

He came on a harsh moan, thrusting inside her to the hilt. Zoe blinked up at him, a ribbon of shock spiraling through her at the vulnerability in his release, and the way that even caught up in his pleasure, he was looking right back at her. After one last exhale, Alex lowered his chest to hers, the rapid thump of his heart beating a pattern against her breastbone.

"Together," he whispered. "Just like this."

And as they lay there, surrounded by shadow and caught up in nothing but each other, Zoe knew with undeniable certainty that she was one hundred percent, completely over the line, insanely in love with Alex Donovan.

Chapter Twenty-Three

Alex stood outside the battalion chief's office, fiddling with the buttons on his uniform shirt and trying to convince himself not to puke. He didn't get nervous often, but like everything else in his wheelhouse, when it happened, it was an all-in type of affair. Considering his freaking job was on the line, he'd give himself some leeway in the feeling-a-little-tense department.

Provided he got reinstated and not shit-canned.

"Donovan." Captain Westin's voice slipped through Alex's gut-clenching thoughts, delivering a fresh batch of *other* gut-clenching thoughts, and Jesus Christ, Alex wasn't going to make it through this day.

But it wasn't his fault he'd gone and fallen for his captain's daughter. Or that the thought of her was the only thing keeping him from losing his fucking marbles right now.

Breathe in, you idiot. One career-trashing thing at a time.

"Hey, Cap." Alex tried on a smile, reaching out to shake Westin's hand. "Thanks for asking the chief to schedule this hearing as soon as possible." The first Monday morning slot must've cost Westin a few withdrawals from the favor bank, and hell if the realization didn't pang through Alex's gut with renewed vigor.

One corner of Westin's mouth kicked up. "I've been down a man on Engine for four weeks, Alex. I know you think highly of yourself, but I assure you, my motivations aren't entirely selfless."

Alex coughed out a laugh, his nerves scattering. "Fair enough." He opened his mouth to tack on a joke to lighten the mood even further, but a figure down at the end of the hallway caught his attention. "We've got a second, right?" he asked, jutting his chin at the door with the chief's name emblazoned across the glass in gold lettering.

"Yes, but . . ." Westin's gaze narrowed in confusion before going momentarily wide as he followed Alex's stare. "Donovan, this isn't a good idea."

Of course Westin was balls-on accurate. Not that it changed Alex's mind.

He turned toward the spot where Captain McManus stood at the end of the wide expanse of linoleum and office doorways. "I'll be right back."

Alex's boots thumped out a steady rhythm, his heartbeat kicking in to match it as he made his way down the hall. McManus's normally shifty stare hardened a few degrees at the sight of Alex approaching, but the man stood firm, arms crossed into a menacing knot over his navy-blue uniform shirt.

"What do you want, Donovan?"

Alex inhaled on a five-count before saying, "I want to offer you an apology."

The thin line of McManus's lips fell open. "I'm sorry?"

"No, sir. I'm sorry," Alex said, drawing his shoulders tight around his spine. This was going to sting, but the words were still due. Even if it had taken him a while to realize it. "I know you and I had differing opinions on how to run that warehouse fire. While I stand by my reasoning, my actions were out of line, and for that, I apologize."

"You apologize," McManus said, disdain darkening the word like a heavy layer of soot. "That's rich, coming from you. But it's going to take more than just slick talk to get you out of this."

Alex shook his head in a clipped back and forth, his response all truth. "I'm not trying to get out of anything."

"Well, good, because I'm still going to recommend that you get sanctioned up to your ass." McManus glared, and although Alex's molars came together hard enough to test their fortitude, he refused to give in to the impulsive urge to tell the guy to get bent.

"That's your prerogative, sir. I stand by my apology either way."

After a minute of silence on Alex's part and a whole lot of nasty scowling on McManus's, Alex stepped back to break the stalemate. He turned on his heel, retracing his steps back to the spot where Captain Westin had moved closer to listen in.

"Well. I have to admit, that's not what I was expecting from you," Westin said quietly, his eyes showing his surprise.

Alex straightened the front of his shirt, smoothing his fingers over the FFD crest stitched over the pocket by his heart. "It was the truth. There *is* a difference between recklessness and bravery. Even though McManus and I have our differences, and God knows he pisses me off to no end, I still needed a wake-up call to remember where the line is."

"It takes a hell of a man to admit something like that," Westin said, but Alex wasn't about to ditch all his personality traits just yet.

"It's cool. I might've screwed up by knocking McManus down, but we're still going to beat his ass in this year's softball tourney." Christ, he was practically salivating just thinking about it.

Westin's laugh only lasted for a minute before his expression slid back into seriousness. "You might've done a stupid thing, but you're a good man, Donovan. What you did for Zoe at Hope House this month . . ." He trailed off, and Alex's mouth went Sahara Desert dry.

"It was all part of community service," he croaked, and okay, yeah, the lie tasted like a mouthful of ashes with a battery acid chaser.

"You had her back out there at that soup kitchen, even when you didn't want to be there." Westin extended his hand, the pure gratitude in his expression sending Alex's gut into a free fall toward his knees. "I'm grateful, son."

Oh God, he was on the bullet train straight to hell. He and Zoe had agreed to come clean to her father together, in private, where he'd be able to get used to the idea of them as a couple on his own terms, but damn it, holding back now in the face of the man's sincerity just felt like a lie. Alex opened his mouth, the truth tearing a path toward his lips.

And then the door to the battalion chief's office swung open, killing his confession before it could even fully form.

"Alex Donovan?" the chief's assistant asked, and Alex nodded mutely over his slamming pulse. "Chief Williams will see you now."

He auto-piloted his way into the chief's office, his spine at full attention. Captains Westin and McManus filed in after him, leaving Chief Williams's assistant to close the glass-paned door with a heavy *thunk*.

"Gentlemen." The chief addressed all three of them with his trademark steely stare. "This is familiar territory for us, so I think we can skip the pleasantries."

"Yes, Chief," Alex said, revisiting his compulsion to throw up. But Chief Williams hadn't earned his reputation as a hard-ass by selling Girl Scout cookies, and in truth, he wasn't wrong about how many times Alex's file had turned up on his desk. They went through a brief recounting of the events of the warehouse fire, both via the official report and McManus's overblown account. Captain Westin filled in a few blanks, bringing the overall story to a way more unbiased level, and McManus countered by blustering on about Alex's shortcomings. Finally—thankfully—Chief Williams cut the whole bitch fest short with a lift of his hand.

"Donovan, you've been unexpectedly quiet over there. Do you have anything you'd like to say?"

Alex paused, pulling a deep breath into his overtight lungs. "I can't argue the events of the warehouse fire in question," he admitted. "They pretty much speak for themselves per the report. In the same way that Captain McManus didn't appreciate my challenging his orders, I didn't appreciate him putting his hands on me."

McManus opened his mouth with the clear intent of protesting, but Chief Williams killed the move with a brows-up stare. "Captain, please don't insult my intelligence with an argument here. You've made your thoughts more than plain, and the report contains several statements corroborating a mutual shoving match between you two."

A crimson flush crept over the captain's face, but he had the wherewithal to keep his trap shut, so Alex continued. "It was my goal at that warehouse fire to do what I thought would keep people safe. I don't set out to be reckless on purpose, but I don't shy away from my job, either. I regret the way this incident played out," he said, the truth of the statement ringing in his ears. "But I assure you, Chief. I'm prepared to return to Station Eight and do my job to the best of my ability. All I want to do is fight fires and serve the community of Fairview."

Chief Williams paused for only a second before tapping the manila file folder on top of his desk. "I'm going to be blunt, Donovan. Your track record doesn't speak well for you, and your behavior at this warehouse fire is the crown jewel of your bad choices. Fires are dangerous enough, even when everyone involved in fighting them respects the chain of command."

Alex's palms went instantly damp, his *yes, sir* wedging in his throat. There had to be some way to make Chief Williams understand how desperately he needed this job, and he scrambled to come up with something—Christ, *anything*—to plead his case.

But the man beat him to the punch. "However . . . both Captain Westin and your peers speak very highly of your skills as a firefighter, as well as your dedication. You've had an entire month to cool off, during which time you've gone above and beyond to complete your community service assignment. All things considered, I believe we can call this one a draw. I'm reinstating you to active duty, effective immediately."

Relief took the slingshot route through Alex's chest at the same moment McManus blurted out a heated "*What?*"

The chief turned his gaze on McManus. "Donovan might not have been in the right in this situation, but neither were you, Captain. I'd like to advise you to think twice next time you're tempted to put your hands on another firefighter. You're a superior officer in this department. I expect you to act like one. Am I clear?"

McManus paused before finally mumbling, "Yes, sir."

Chief Williams shifted, splitting his scissor-sharp stare between Alex and Captain Westin. "As for you, Donovan. The next time I see you in this office, I'd better be awarding you a commendation. If you so much as put your uniform on crooked, I will show you the door permanently, and I won't lose a second's sleep over it."

Alex nodded past the slamming *whoosh* of his pulse in his ears. Holy shit. His job was safe. *He* was safe. "Thank you, sir."

But the chief just raised one gray brow, his expression going steel-tipped and serious. "Don't thank me yet. You're the one who has to stay in line. Now get out of my office, would you? You've got a shift to prepare for."

* * *

Zoe stood on the neatly kept threshold of Station Eight, the warmth of the late-April sunshine nothing in comparison to the all-out burn spreading through her shoulders. She balanced the two oversized food trays full of mac and cheese more firmly between her palms, wondering if maybe she'd overdone it just a little in the kitchen today. But with the grant proposal having been turned in for a whole workweek and the food drive being complete, Zoe had found herself at loose ends on her Friday off. Alex was on shift, and she'd needed some way to burn all of her nervous energy while she waited for news on the Collingsworth Grant. She'd heard rumblings that the committee had already culled the front-runners from the rest of the applicants, which meant in theory, Hope House could be that much closer to getting the money it so desperately needed.

On second thought, maybe Zoe hadn't cooked enough.

The muscles in her shoulders burned with a fresh wave of exertion, and she snapped back to attention on Station Eight's threshold. The trio of overstuffed grocery bags looped over her wrists gave up a loud crinkle as she shifted her weight, extending her elbow in an awkward attempt to ring the buzzer.

"Whoa! Hey, let me help you with that." Jones slipped in from behind her to trade the broom in his grasp for both trays.

Zoe's shoulders sang with relief. "Whew, thanks, Mike."

"No sweat," Jones said, lifting the trays full of mac and cheese with a slight smile. "Did you cook all of this?"

She bit her bottom lip and gave a well-yeah half shrug, but she'd needed the outlet, and cooking for everyone at Station Eight had calmed her. At least, as much as anything could right now. "If there's one thing I learned ages ago, it's to never come to a firehouse unless you plan to knock with your elbows."

As if the presence of food had somehow stirred the energy in the building, Cole and Crews stuck their heads down the hallway from the junction into the main common area. "Zoe!" they called out in near unison, and she burst into a smile.

"Hey, you guys. I thought you might like a little dinner."

"Rookie." Crews met them halfway down the hall, delivering a hearty nudge to Jones's shoulder. "You just totally got sprung from KP. Thank freaking God."

"Ah, don't mess with him," Cole argued. Zoe's heart melted a little bit—Cole always was kind of the peacekeeper, but it was nice to see that his even keel extended to their rookie, who usually got the lion's share of ribbing and crappy station chores by virtue of his newbie status. Of course, then Cole added, "Let him hand over dinner first," and yeah. So much for his sweeter side.

"Did someone say dinner?" O'Keefe appeared at the end of the hallway with Rachel at his side. "Oooh, look. It's my very favorite chef."

Zoe's laugh bubbled up from her chest as she made her way into the common room. "Aren't I the only chef you know?"

"Details, sweetheart. Details," O'Keefe said with an exaggerated wave. "So what's on the menu, Chef?"

"Well, I couldn't help but notice how you guys all hovered around the soup kitchen like vultures last week when I made macaroni and cheese, so . . ."

"Stop." Rachel's eyes flashed with oh-yes goodness. "Did you use that super-secret recipe you were telling me and Ava about? With the spicy chorizo and bell peppers?"

She kept her smile as coy as possible, but holy crap, it was a ten-foot-tall order. "Possibly."

"Brennan is going to be bent out of shape that he missed

out," O'Keefe said, his tone implying that he'd be more than happy to describe the meal to his buddy in borderline-bragging detail.

But Zoe had his number. "I thought you might say that," she flipped back, sending a playful wink in the paramedic's direction. "Which is exactly why I dropped off a tray for him and Ava just before coming out here."

Rachel's laughter met O'Keefe's groan head-on, and she hip-checked her partner with a gentle bump. "Serves you right."

"Okay, okay!" O'Keefe returned the gesture with an enthusiastic nudge. "Anyway, you have great timing, Zoe. We all just got back from a pretty hairy fire call."

Just like that, her heart stuttered hard against her rib cage, her throat turning instantly dry. "Is everything okay?" She swung her gaze around the common area as subtly as possible, but caught no sign of either Alex or her father.

Crews stepped in beside her to take the grocery bags from her fingers, the bitter-burnt scent of smoke still clinging to his uniform. "Some brainiac didn't want to miss a single second of the baseball game on TV. So he fired up his humongous gas grill inside his garage to keep him closer to the house."

"Really?" That didn't sound *so* bad.

"Yup." O'Keefe shook his head, unfolding his frame in one of the chairs surrounding the long communal dining table. "We got there just in time to keep the damn propane tank from blowing a crater into Oak Street. Too bad for the guy his garage didn't fare quite so well."

"Oh," Zoe managed weakly, and God, she wasn't cut out for this. "Did anyone get hurt?"

"Nah. Just a few scrapes and a hell of a lot of property damage," Cole said, his smile small but reassuring. He leaned in, his voice flawlessly nonchalant even though she was certain he knew the score. "Alex is in the engine bay, rechecking all the equipment."

She ran her clammy palms over the front of her jeans, but at least now she could breathe. Mostly. "Thanks."

Zoe knew she should take a few minutes to get the mac and cheese in the oven and start preparing the green beans she'd brought as a side before rushing out to the engine bay. After all, she and Alex hadn't told her father about their relationship yet, and dropping everything to make a bee-line for the guy would probably raise every eyebrow in the room.

But the knee-jerk urge to lay eyes on him won out. Zoe headed for the double doors on the opposite side of the common room, her hand hitting the handle on the door leading to the dormitories on one side and the engine bay on the other at the same time its counterpart swung on its hinges.

"Oh! Hi, Lieutenant Osborne." Zoe smiled at the veteran firefighter who had been at Station Eight since she'd worn knee socks and pigtails, and whoa, time had added some hard edges to his face.

Oz ran a hand over his graying stubble before recognition settled over his stare. "Hey, little girl. Look at you, all grown up now."

"That's me," she agreed, taking in his gaunt frame with a pinch of concern. "How's it going?"

"It's going," he said, tough as ever. "What brings you out here to visit a bunch of graceless firemen?"

Zoe slipped her smile back over her face. "I brought dinner."

"Hell, girl." Oz's return smile brightened his face just enough to remind her of how he'd looked last time she'd seen him, and maybe he'd just had a couple of long shifts. "You sure know how to take care of us, now don't you?"

"I do my best. I threw in a bunch of brownies for dessert, so make sure you save room."

"Will do. Good to see you."

He continued toward the common room with a wave, leaving Zoe to complete her trip to the engine bay. Rescue squad's vehicle stood directly in front of her, nose out and doors wide, with Station Eight's blue and white ambulance directly adjacent and equally ready to go. Her feet shushed over the concrete floor, anticipation thrumming through her veins as she rounded the ambo's back bumper to make her way to Engine Eight. Alex stood about ten feet away in front of one of the large storage compartments, his blond brows creased in concentration even though his movements were completely fluid, and oh God, Zoe was so in love with him it hurt.

Her feet moved faster, completely of their own accord. "Hey," she said, the word arriving about two seconds before she threw her arms around him, and Alex grunted in surprise.

"Hey." He pulled back just far enough to swing a gaze around the engine bay. But Zoe pressed up to slide a kiss over his mouth.

"Between the engine and the ambulance, we're pretty well hidden, and anyway, no one else is in here. I checked."

The hard ridge of his shoulders relaxed under her touch. "Well, in that case, c'mere, Gorgeous." Alex threaded his fingers through her hair, his kiss making up in ferocity what it lacked in slowness.

After a few seconds that heated Zoe from head to toe—with layovers in all the best places—he pulled back. "So did you come all the way out here just to give me a hard-on while I work? Because I've got to tell you, mission complete."

"Thank God for bunker pants," she said, her body tingling at the sight of the turnout gear slung over his frame before she tamped it down for the sake of propriety. "Actually, I came out here to bring everyone dinner. I figured you guys wouldn't turn down a home-cooked meal." She tipped her head toward the doors leading back to the firehouse, and Alex raked her with a slow gaze before hauling her close for one last kiss.

"When you come in here wearing those jeans *and* bearing food, you make it really freaking hard for me to keep my hands off you. We need to tell your father what's going on, otherwise I'm liable to lose the cool for which I'm so popularly known around here."

Zoe wanted to roll her eyes, but her laugh tumbled out instead. "I know, but we need to tell him in private, and between your shifts and my schedule at Hope House, this week was kind of crazy."

"We're all here right now," Alex said, and oh hell, he was serious.

"Alex, think about it. You're on shift with my dad for the next fourteen hours. Telling him now would be insane." Not that she didn't want to come clean. But she also didn't want her highly overprotective father to smother her boyfriend in his sleep.

The realization seemed to hit Alex after another moment. He tugged a hand through his hair, hard enough to leave the blond locks tousled. "You're right. I just hate not saying anything. I feel like I'm lying to him, and that bugs the crap out of me."

"How about Sunday?" she asked. "It's only two days from now, and we can meet for breakfast, first thing."

"Sounds perfect." He stepped back, shifting his focus. "I take it you haven't heard anything from the Collingsworth Foundation today."

Zoe's gut squeezed. "No." She shook her head, pulling her screamingly silent cell phone from the back pocket of her jeans as proof. "I know the foundation offices don't close for another half hour, but it's looking like we won't hear anything about the next round of decisions until at least Monday."

"That might be a good sign." Alex leaned back against the engine, running a thumb beneath the suspenders keeping his dark gray bunker pants in place.

Zoe hedged, not wanting to jinx her chances with an out-loud admission of what she'd been thinking for the last two hours. No news was good news, and all that. "Maybe," she allowed. "I'll be honest, though. I wish they'd just call. The waiting is making me crazy."

"Let me guess." He leveled her with a smile so charming, it made his bright blue eyes crinkle at the edges. "You made seven pounds of lasagna today, didn't you?"

"Mac and cheese," she admitted, huffing out a laugh. "But I'm nervous as hell. Plus . . ." She trailed off, but they'd never been anything but honest with each other, so there was no point in holding back. "You're back on shift, and that scares me."

Alex's relaxed demeanor didn't even budge by a fraction. "I was on shift Tuesday, too. A-okay, as promised." He gestured to himself with one hand as he reached for her with the other, and she melted into his side with a sigh.

"I know, and I know that your job is as important to you as mine is to me. But the guys were telling me about a fire call you went on just now, and how it could've been so much worse, and . . . I guess the worry is just going to take some getting used to for me, that's all."

He straightened, kissing the crown of her head before turning to shut the storage compartment on the engine with a metallic *bang*. "I know something that might make that a little easier. Come on."

She followed him through the engine bay and back inside the firehouse. But rather than moving toward the happy sounds of pre-dinner chatter coming out of the common room, Alex turned down a different, more secluded hallway, one lined on either side with photograph after photograph.

Nostalgia rippled outward from the center of Zoe's chest. "The hall of pictures. God, some of these have been here since I was a kid."

"Yup," Alex said, his gaze extending down the line of the sunlit hallway. "Pretty much any and every big deal that's gone down in Station Eight over the last two decades is up here on these walls. You name it, and chances are, we've got the photographic evidence."

"Mmm." She ran her fingers along the edges of the plain black frames, leaning in closer to scan the images with care. Some depicted firefighters doing drills, others were shots of active fires. Commendation letters were peppered into the mix, along with a healthy handful of photographs of Station Eight's firefighters in more casual settings like Fairview's legendary softball tournament.

Zoe stopped in front of one of the frames about halfway down the wall. "Oh, that's a great picture of you and Brennan and Cole. Although . . ." She squinted in confusion before arching a brow at him. "Why are your hands bright purple?"

"Because Brennan is a dick," Alex said with way more affection than ire. "He put Kool-Aid powder in my gloves one shift as a practical joke."

Her laugh escaped in a quick burst. "I'm sure you were just minding your own business and did nothing to earn that."

"I'm a saint. Anything he tells you about me waking him up by testing our chain saw ten feet away from his bunk is pure myth."

"Uh-huh." Reminding herself to congratulate Brennan on his creativity the next time she saw him, she continued down the row. She took in picture after picture, each one an obvious testament to the paramedics' and firefighters' skill and camaraderie.

"I remember this fire," she said, pausing in front of a series of eight-by-ten photos of a two-story house, engulfed in smoke and flames. "I was home from college on a break when it happened. The house wasn't too far from where my parents used to live."

Alex leaned in, tapping the glass with one finger. "I remember it, too. There's Oz and Andersen, up on the roof." He traced a line down to the ground level, pointing to two firefighters running water lines into the smoke-filled house. "And that's me and Cole. Ah, and Brennan's right there, too."

"How can you tell who's who?" she asked. She was lucky she could make out how many figures there were in all the flashing lights and chaos.

"Partly by what we're doing. We've all got really specific things we're responsible for on a fire call. It keeps us organized, focused." He moved his gaze from the photo to Zoe's face, his expression completely pared down in its honesty. "But mostly, I know who's who in all of these pictures because we always have each other's backs. I know where my fellow firefighters are, just like they know where I am on any given call, and none of us do the job halfway. We go into every fire as a team, and that's how we come out."

Understanding dawned, bright and sweet. "Is that why you wanted me to see this? So I'd know how much backup you have?"

"It's part of it, yes. You already know this job is dangerous, and that goes with the territory. But I wanted to show you that there *are* precautions, and I don't do it alone. You've seen how dedicated these guys are outside the house. I'm here to tell you, they're ten times as intense when things go pear-shaped. Fighting fires might be risky, but I've got the best team on the planet with me. I'll be all right."

"Promise?" she asked, and even though the question was a shaky whisper, Alex answered it with clear, complete confidence.

"I promise."

Zoe nodded, but before she could back the gesture up with anything further, her cell phone let loose with a loud buzz from her back pocket. "Oh, hang on. Let me see . . ."

Her words screeched to a halt just as her heartbeat catapulted to Mach 2 in her chest.

"Zoe?" Worry colored Alex's expression, his boots echoing on the linoleum as he closed what little space stood between them. "What's the matter? Who is it?"

Excitement collided with the hard prickle of fear in her veins, but finally, somewhere amid the ocean of adrenaline coursing through her, she found her voice.

"It's Sharon Gleeson. She's the director of the committee that awards the Collingsworth Grant."

Chapter Twenty-Four

A mile-wide smile tore over Alex's face, even though Zoe's had gone completely blank and just as pale.

"This is awesome," he said, not even bothering to keep his enthusiasm in check. But come on—what better place for her to get her kick-ass good news than here at the firehouse, where they could all help her celebrate in style?

"Go on, Gorgeous. Pick it up." He encouraged her with a wave, guiding her to the end of the hallway in a few hurried steps. The location wasn't ideal for privacy, but the only other thing down this way was Cap's office, and he knew better than to slip in there without permission. At least the out-of-the-way corner was better than nothing.

Finally, Zoe nodded, her hands noticeably shaking as she tapped the icon on her phone to take the call. "Zoe Westin."

Although it damn near killed him, Alex moved a handful of paces to give her a little breathing room. Not that it seemed to matter. Zoe's face remained totally unreadable, other than the marked seriousness creasing her honey-colored brows and pressing her bow-shaped mouth into a flat line. But this was Zoe, cautious to a fault. Of course she wouldn't get excited until she hung up. Damn, he couldn't wait to see the sheer happiness break over her face.

"Right. Yes, I see," she murmured. The woman on the other end of the phone must be giving all sorts of details, because that was all Zoe said. She nodded a few times, her blond hair tumbling forward to shield her eyes from Alex's view.

"Of course. Thank you so much. I really appreciate your letting me know tonight." Finally, she lowered the phone from her ear, and not a second too soon as far as the adrenaline in Alex's veins was concerned.

"Well?" He looked at Zoe's face, the sight of the tears brimming in her eyes sending a pang to his gut even though they were surely the happy kind.

One breached her eyelid, then another. "I, um . . . I didn't get the grant."

What. The. Ever-loving. Fuck?

"Are you kidding me?" Alex blurted, disbelief ricocheting through him only to be followed by a hard spurt of anger. "You worked your ass off for that grant. Nobody deserves that money more than you."

Zoe shook her head, clearly in a fog, and Alex's heart nearly imploded. "They had a record number of applications, and she said ours was very impressive. It just . . . wasn't enough for them to consider Hope House for the final round."

He moved toward her, thumbing the tears from the apples of both cheeks even as they killed him. "Okay. It's okay."

"It's not okay," she choked out, collapsing into his touch. "Everything I had was riding on this, Alex. I don't . . . I can't . . ."

"You *can*," he interrupted, sticking the words with all his mettle. "Look, this is a setback, but we'll get around it. We'll figure something out."

Her face broadcasted her doubt loud and crystal clear, but she let him pull her close. As soon as he wrapped his arms around her, the tension holding her together unraveled. Every sob tore a hole in his chest, but he rode out the pain of each one, right there with her. Finally, Zoe quieted, and he cupped her face to place a soft kiss on her mouth like a promise.

"We'll find a way," he said, and she looked up at him, her lashes still spiky with tears.

"Can you just not let me go right now? Please?" She arched into the connection, clutching the sleeves of his T-shirt as she pressed her lips to his. Need deepened the kiss in less than a breath, making Zoe's chest quake against his as he held her tight, and Alex didn't even think about denying her. He parted her lips, pouring every shred of feeling he could muster into the kiss, sweeping her tongue and diving in deeper until—

"Just what in the hell do you think you're doing to my daughter?"

Dread skidded through Alex's limbs at the same time Zoe jumped, both of them turning toward the adjacent doorway to face her father.

Holy shit, Alex had never seen the man look so irrevocably furious.

"Captain—"

"Dad, I—"

Their words crashed together, arriving simultaneously, but Westin silenced them both in an instant.

"Don't." He flashed a stare full of warning at Zoe, which only threw Alex's protective instincts onto the huge pile of emotions hurtling through his gut.

But Zoe didn't stop. "This isn't what you think."

"Believe me," Westin grated, his eyes drilling Alex chock-full of holes. "You don't want to know what I think."

She pinched the bridge of her nose between her thumb

and her forefinger, taking a step toward her father. "Okay, look. Let's just talk about this like adults, please."

"I just came out of my office to find my only daughter spontaneously lip-locked with one of my firefighters. That's not going to happen," he grated, the deep breath that followed visibly lifting his chest beneath the dark blue shirt of his uniform.

"This isn't some spontaneous thing," Zoe argued, and oh shit, Westin's face flushed dark red with anger.

"Really. And just how long has it been *not* spontaneous?"

Zoe bit her lip, clearly realizing the catch-22 of her words. "I—"

"A month," Alex said, quietly straightening.

A muscle in Westin's jaw twitched once. Twice. "I'll deal with you later, Zoe. Donovan, get in my office. *Now*."

Alex hesitated. He didn't mind taking the brunt of her father's anger, and yeah, considering the way he'd stumbled upon them, the man had every reason to be righteously indignant. But Zoe was an equal part of the equation. She didn't deserve to be brushed off and not heard. "Captain, with all due respect, Zoe—"

Westin took a swift step forward, jamming Alex's words to a sloppy stop. "Don't—*do not*—talk to me about respect. You've been sneaking around with my daughter for a goddamn month while I went to bat for you with the chief! Now get in my office, before I haul your ass out the door."

Alex exhaled, the full measure of his dread replacing the air in his lungs. "Yes, sir."

He turned to look at Zoe, to somehow grab one last burst of calm at the sight of her before he walked into Westin's office for what might be the last time, but she threw her hands in the air, decimating the very notion of the word.

"Do you really want to talk about respect?" Her hands lowered, only to lock into place over her hips as her eyes glittered with built-up frustration and anger, and hell, she was fraying at the seams. "I'm twenty-seven years old. I get that I'm your daughter and that you want to look out for me, but damn it, I'm right *here*. I'm not a little girl anymore, and I don't need protecting. You said you had my back, and that you believed in me. For once, can't you just trust me?"

"No. I can't." The words sliced from Westin's mouth with all the sharp and nasty of a six-inch switchblade, cutting Alex to the bone as he added, "In fact, I don't trust either one of you. Now walk out of this fire station, Zoe. For your own good."

Zoe's shoulders folded inward, a fresh round of tears tracking over her weary face. But before Alex could launch the reply swirling up from the part of him shrieking to leap to her defense, the electronic signal for an all-call pierced through the firehouse speakers.

"*Squad Eight, Engine Eight, Ambulance Eight. Structure fire, reported entrapment. One-nine-seven Windsor Avenue. Requesting immediate response.*"

"We're not done here, Donovan. This changes nothing," Westin said, leveling him with one last frown before sprinting down the hallway.

But Alex had a feeling that was as far from the truth as any man could get.

"Look sharp, boys, because this shit is not a drill." Crews's voice cut through the crush of engine noise, blaring sirens, and controlled chaos flying around in the back step of Engine Eight, signaling a neon-colored *shut up and listen* through the headphones each of them wore. "Dispatch has multiple nine-one-one callers reporting active fire in a block of row homes on Windsor."

Cole took Alex's inward groan and gave it a voice. "Those

row homes are three stories up and six units across. Not to mention they're goddamn ancient."

Translation: fire fucking loved them. Firefighters? Not so much.

"Affirmative on both. There's reported entrapment in at least one unit, but no details on location or how many people, which means we're going to have to keep our eyes wide the hell open. Looks like we'll be first on scene, so be ready to run some lines and get this place wet while squad hits the roof for a vent. Cap's behind us, and he's going to call the ball. Copy?"

"Copy," came the string of responses, but Alex barely heard them as he tugged his headphones off and hung them on the hook above his seat.

"You good?" Cole asked, turning sideways to get geared up. The move let him not only peg Alex with a critical stare, but it effectively blocked Jones from hearing any strains of the conversation from his spot on the other end of the step. "And don't even think about fracturing the truth just because we're on the way to a fire and you want me to keep my head straight."

Well, shit. So much for that. Might as well come out with it, because once they got back to the house after this call, everybody and their mother was going to hear the sonic boom coming from the captain's office. "Westin caught me kissing Zoe."

Cole's expression triple-timed into *son of a bitch* territory. "When?"

"About twelve minutes ago."

"You're freaking kidding me," Cole said, and Alex plastered his expression with as much *I wish* as he could work up. Cole pulled on his hood, then his gloves, waiting for Alex to do the same before asking the inevitable. "Did he lose his shit?"

"Scale of one to ten?" Alex's stomach twisted, his unease

multiplying at the scent of bitter-black smoke filtering in through the window. Cole nodded, and Alex let himself linger on the acidic aftertaste of the confrontation for one last second before mashing his dread all the way down to the bottom of his rib cage.

"It was about a forty."

Engine Eight jolted to a stop with an overloud groan of the brakes, and Alex forced himself to switch gears and focus. Popping the door handle at his hip, he jumped down to the pavement, scanning from left to right, then back again as he methodically took in the scene from the middle of the narrow street.

Stretches of white clapboard-covered row homes lined the asphalt on either side, most of them six units long with barely a ten-foot break in between buildings. Steady rolls of smoke funneled from the windows of the three attached units in front of them, although between the quickly growing haze and the limited visibility from the tight confines of the street, pinpointing actual flames was essentially a million to one. But with the walls and attics these homes always shared, it was a solid bet that if the flames had reached the roofline of one of them, they'd all be on fire in a matter of minutes, not hours. *If* they weren't all burning already.

Talk about getting tossed out of the frying pan. But after five solid weeks of not fighting fires, Alex was so ready to shake the rust off, it was damn near painful. The radio on his shoulder crackled to life, and he stood between Cole and Jones, his adrenaline taking a potshot at his pulse as he waited for the directive to put his pent-up energy to good use.

"Osborne, you and Andersen get up on that roof for a vent and get the rest of squad inside for search and rescue. Two residents made their way out of the far right unit on their own, but let's not waste any time in case any others are occupied." Westin clipped out orders from his spot on the street between the engine and the ambo, dividing up the remaining members of the rescue squad for search and rescue before turning his attention to Engine. "Everett, you're on the nozzle. Donovan, put Jones on your hip and back him up. I want water in this building starting yesterday. Go."

Alex sucked in a breath, turning toward Jones as everyone fell into action with precise yet urgent movements. "You catch any fires like this while I was gone?" he asked, and the recruit shook his head.

"Not in a row home, no."

Alex's shoulders burned with exertion as they readied the heavy lengths of hose from the engine, and damn, he needed to keep himself on the level. "It's the same deal you learned in the tower at the academy," he said to Jones, slowing the tempo of his inhale-exhale so his freaking pulse might get the memo. "Nozzle man goes up with the officer to start running water. But these places have tight, pain in the ass stairwells, kind of like a high-rise. Because of that, the nozzle man usually has a hell of a time advancing the line, so someone always backs him up to keep it from getting tangled or caught on corners. Today that someone is me and you. You got it?"

Jones nodded, his brows bent in concentration beneath the brim of his helmet. "I think so."

"Don't think so, rookie. *Know* so, because there's no dress rehearsal and we're up."

Cole cut a path across the swath of grass serving as the row home's collective front yard, and Alex fell into step behind him with Jones at his six. He had to give the kid credit—he'd been a quick study in finding the right distance at which to follow along, and Alex wasn't about to sneeze at the extra assistance with the hose, since his muscles were already halfway to Jell-O and the damn thing felt like it weighed a metric ton. But someone could still be trapped inside one of these houses, so Alex didn't give a shit if the line weighed six metric tons and he had to haul it solo. He had a job to do, and after a month of not going on a single fire call, he was damn well going to get to doing it.

The group moved forward toward the center of the row home, but their boots had no sooner hit the bottom porch board than one of the guys on squad shouldered his way out of the unit directly to their left, yanking his mask from his face.

"Search is clear in here, and neighbors are reporting they haven't seen the guy who lives in that one since he left for work this morning," he barked over the rush of flames and the steady roll of heat. "From what Oz can see from up top, he said the Charlie side of the third floor is pretty heavily involved, and if these units are all alike, you've got your fucking work cut out for you with that line. The stairs over here were a bitch and a half."

Anything else he might've added was cut off by the radio request for an immediate search in the end unit, and Cole jerked his chin at the unit in front of them with nobody home.

"Go. We've got this." He nodded as the guy fell out with the rest of squad to search the end unit. He paused at the front door just long enough to force the wood from the hinges with his Halligan bar, angling past the threshold with steely purpose. Smoke clung to the air in a curtainlike haze, and Alex reached up to pull his mask over his face, motioning for Jones to do the same before they elbowed their way after Cole.

"I'm going up to floor three. We've got to keep this fire from walking," Cole hollered from just inside the entryway, motioning toward the set of thinly carpeted stairs in front of them. "I'll knock this thing down before it spreads any further and work my way down to you."

They maneuvered their way up the first set of steps single

file, waves of soot and ash clogging the visibility in the windowless space and hampering any quick progress Alex had hoped to make. The second-floor landing was little more than a series of boxy angles and tight turns leading up or down, all with potential roadblocks and range of motion that amounted to Alex's new best friend, Jack Shit.

"God damn it." Cole surveyed the situation, his frown evident even behind his mask. "There have to be seventy different recipes for disaster with a layout like this."

But Alex motioned his best friend upward with a brisk back-and-forth of one hand, while giving Jones the signal to hold steady where he stood with the other. "Go," he said to Cole. "Jones and I will keep this from becoming a cluster fuck." His kept his *maybe* to himself as Everett hauled ass toward the third floor; at least they could radio if things got hairy.

Alex swiveled a calculating gaze in a quick three-sixty, turning on one booted heel to scan as much of the second floor as he could. Strains of daylight did their damnedest to poke in from the trio of open-doored bedrooms just off the stretch of the hallway leading toward the rear of the house, and Alex measured three—no four sites of active fire in his line of sight alone.

"Okay, Jones. Stay right there between floors one and two. Make sure you—"

Out of the corner of his eye, Alex caught the barely there outline of a figure hunched in the doorway of the far bedroom.

"Jesus!" His pulse went ballistic, and he cursed fluently as he whipped his hand up toward the radio on his shoulder. "Donovan to command. We need a search on the second floor, like *now*."

"That's a negative, Donovan." Westin's voice crackled over the two-way. "Everett is reporting that the third floor is a goddamn train wreck. I need those lines clear."

"Yeah, well I've got . . ." Alex squinted back down the hallway, sweat dripping into his eyes and fogging his mask.

No one was there.

"Did you see that?" he asked, swinging toward Jones. "I swear I saw someone in that back room."

Jones gave his head one tight shake. "I was concentrating on the line."

Shit. Of course he was. It's what Alex had told him to do.

"Not the time to stop being chatty, Donovan," Westin grated through the radio, and Alex arrowed his stare back to the bedroom, nearly engulfed by smoke and shadows.

"I saw . . . something in the rear bedroom, east side. I swear." His legs itched to bolt down the hall, but he settled for a lung-burning shout. "Fire department! Call out!"

The only answer was the incessant rush of flames and Alex's breath sawing in and out of his own ears.

"Neighbors say there's nobody home," Westin radioed, yanking Alex's attention back to the landing. "I can't green light a search on a maybe. Not with a fire like this."

Alex assessed the line, a sharp curl of relief spiraling through his gut as he saw it advancing, albeit slowly. "We're straight down here on the landing. I'm telling you, Cap." He turned again, taking a few steps toward the mouth of the long, tightrope-thin corridor. "I had eyes on somebody."

"Is that an affirmative?"

Alex paused. "Not entirely, but—"

"Can't do it, Donovan." Westin's growl was all bite, and for a minute, Alex froze. He hadn't run a fire call in over five weeks, and his screaming muscles and overeager adrenaline were living proof. While they were able to advance the water line right this second, Alex knew shit could go south on a dime—hell, he'd seen worse consequences from more stable situations. His brain cautioned him to stay put, to stand down on the search and work with Jones to back up Everett so they could all put this fire out as fast as possible.

But then the figure reappeared, and Alex lunged down the hallway.

"Fire department!" he bellowed, sweat streaming between his shoulder blades as his heart pumped his blood on a lightning-fast circuit through his veins. Blocking out the shouts from behind him—presumably Jones's—as well as the abundant stream of curse words coming in from the radio that were definitely Westin's, Alex barreled toward the bedroom.

A man, thin and frail and wrapped in a bathrobe, stood bent over by the bed, his face pale white and panic-stricken as his chest heaved with weak coughs, and holy hell, he looked barely a step away from keeling over.

"Tried . . . to call out, but . . . I came home sick, and . . . I think I passed out. . . ."

"Don't worry," Alex said with a shake of his head. "I'm going to get you out of here."

He crossed the threshold to grab the guy and haul ass out of there, but he only got three steps inside the bedroom before his gut plummeted all the way to his feet. More than half of the Charlie side wall was on fire. Bright streamers of flame hovered over the doorway, reaching up to the ceiling in a malicious orange arc, and hell. No wonder the man hadn't come running out to the safety of the hallway beyond.

Alex reached for his radio with one hand while guiding the man away from the door with the other. "Donovan to command, I've got a man trapped on the second floor, Charlie side. Needs medical attention. Our exit is compromised." Big. Fucking. Understatement. More than half the damn door frame had gone up in flames in the fifteen seconds Alex had been inside the room. "I need a ladder to this window, and I need it now."

"This fire's burning like a sonofabitch. We're trying to get to you, but it's going to take a couple of minutes."

The man swayed in place, his coughs rattling all the way through him as he gasped for air, and Alex turned to yank the window as far as it would go against the sash. Ah hell, there wasn't even so much as a tree or a porch roof within range of the twenty-five-foot drop, and a straight jump would be upper-level dangerous. "I don't have a couple of minutes," he said. "*Hurry.*"

Alex stabbed his boots into the floor, looking around the room for something—anything—he could use to get them either out the window or past the deteriorating door frame. But there was nothing usable in the tiny room, and the odds of surmounting either obstacle were growing more shitastic by the second.

The man collapsed into a heap on the floor.

"Whoa!" All of Alex's air abandoned his lungs on the shout. He hit his knees, the jolt running up his legs even through his heavily padded turnout gear. But the man was unresponsive, his breathing thready and irregular as Alex checked his vitals. He craned his neck to look at the window over his shoulder, and cold fingers of dread slithered up his spine at the realization that no matter how fast squad appeared with that ladder, he didn't even have ten seconds to wait.

"Okay, buddy." Alex choked back the harsh tang of fear before scooping him from the carpet. "Let's get you out of here."

The man's frail body was an easy lift, even for Alex's wailing muscles. The left side of the door frame was completely swallowed up by flames, so he swung the man's body over his right shoulder. Locking his molars together with a determined *clack*, he aimed himself at the burning exit, not even giving himself a chance to second-guess as he burst past the falling ash and flames.

And slammed right into Cole and Jones on the other side.

"Christ, Teflon!" Everett shouted, and Jones reached out, sliding the unconscious man from Alex's shoulder in a quick grab.

"He's barely breathing. Get him to Rachel. Go," Alex barked. Relief blasted through the unchecked adrenaline, making his vision shaky and his mouth tilt upward into a holy-shit-that-was-close smile. He jerked his chin at Cole, signaling for his best friend to follow Jones down the hall so they could get the hell out of Dodge.

But before Alex could take a single step, the door frame he'd just charged past came crashing down over the left side of his body, and then everything went black.

Chapter Twenty-Five

Zoe stood in the eerily silent hallway at Station Eight for what could've been a minute or an hour. Hell, it might've been a day, except that no firefighters or paramedics had come back through the door.

Not that there was any sort of guarantee that they would.

Something twisted in her chest, dangerously close to her heart. Between the blow of not getting the Collingsworth Grant and the showdown with her father, this night had already destroyed both her confidence and her faith. The numb shock of losing the grant had quickly worn away after the phone call with the director, leaving raw streaks of pain in its wake. Hope House was so in need, its residents so deserving of the money to make their temporary home a better, safer place, with warm food and a chance for more. Zoe had worked for months on end to make it happen, throwing not only her heart and soul into the effort, but asking everyone around her for a piece of theirs as well.

She'd believed beyond the shadow of a doubt that she would get that money so she could finally make a real difference at Hope House. To the point that she'd risked everything.

And *lost*.

With her nerves feeling like they'd been scorched over high heat and left to stick to the bottom of a frying pan, Zoe blinked herself back to the firehouse, where fresh waves of dread stuck into her like needles. Her breath trembled in her lungs, her chest rising and falling in shaky bursts. The black-framed photos marching down the wall in front of her slid back into focus, and tears re-formed in her eyes as she looked at them again. Oz and Andersen, their faces creased in concentration as they hung from harnesses off the side of the practice tower, a dizzying four stories above the ground. O'Keefe at the back of the ambulance, arms outstretched as he helped a woman huddled helplessly on the gurney in front of him. Alex and her father, arms slung over each other's shoulders with smiles they might not ever wear around each other again. And Brennan and Mason Watts, hamming it up for the camera in the engine bay, both of them blissfully unaware of the tragic consequences that would wreck the career of one and take the life of the other.

Alex had promised her he'd be okay, that *everything* would be okay. But clearly, risks failed. Hell, she hadn't even made it to the final selection round for the Collingsworth Grant before her leap of faith had fallen spectacularly flat. How the hell could he make a promise so enormous and expect to keep it when every single time he went to work, his life was literally on the line?

Like right now.

Choking back the sob squeezing the back of her throat, Zoe forced herself down the hallway. She needed to focus, to breathe, to take the panic rising in her chest and get rid of it.

She headed for the kitchen.

The grocery bags she'd handed off when she'd arrived stood in a precise row on the stainless steel counter next to the refrigerator, and she emptied them one by one. Jones had put the trays of mac and cheese in the fridge, but pulling them out to get them in the oven seemed kind of pointless since she didn't know when everyone would be back.

Or if.

"Stop it," she chided, and fabulous, now she was talking to herself. She turned toward the pantry—there had to be something in there she could chop, mix, or bake—when the flash of the muted TV caught her eye from across the common room.

Everyone had hauled out to respond to that fire call so fast, they must've forgotten to turn the thing off. Zoe crossed over to the pair of couches arranged in an L shape in front of the television, where a quick pat-through of the cushions yielded the remote.

But the image on the screen turned her blood to ice water, and instead of hitting the power button to turn the television off, she jammed her finger over the volume, cranking it loud enough to vibrate in her ears.

"*. . . Breaking news at the scene of a fire in the one hundred block of Windsor Avenue, where firefighters have made dramatic attempts to put out the massive blaze now taking over four units of a row home. Moments ago, our very own KTV crew witnessed a breathtaking rescue that left at least one person critically injured. . . .*"

"No, no, no, no, no," Zoe gasped, fear slamming through her with enough force to knock the air from her rib cage with a cry.

In the background, over the reporter's shoulder, O'Keefe and Rachel scrambled to take care of the lifeless figure strapped to the gurney, their faces as ash white and serious as she'd ever seen them. The man stretched out between them, prone and unmoving, was fully decked out in turnout gear, with one exception.

His helmet was missing, and Zoe would know that sun-kissed blond head anywhere on the planet.

The remote had barely hit the floor before she tore out

of the fire station with her keys in her hand and her heart shattering into a million pieces in her chest.

By the time Zoe had made the ten-minute drive to Fairview Hospital, her panic had grown six rows of razor-wire teeth and sunk them all the way into her bones. Barging past the hiss of the automatic double doors, she flung herself over the linoleum toward the information desk. Her breath hitched at an unnatural pace, tumbling her words together in a rushed mess.

"The man . . . the firefighter hurt at the fire on Windsor. Please. I need . . . I need . . ." Absolute terror clotted the rest of her request, and the woman behind the desk leaned forward with obvious concern.

"Are you a family member?" she asked, and Zoe froze. "I, uh . . . I . . ."

"She's with us," came a familiar voice from her left. Her heart vaulted into her windpipe as she swung around to see Cole walking toward the desk, his face streaked with sweat and soot and seriousness as he came to a stop beside her.

"Oh my God, Cole." Zoe threw her arms around him, choking on the pervasive stench of smoke clinging to his turnout gear. "What's going on? I saw the fire on the news and they said—"

"Come on. Let me take you to the waiting room down the hall, okay?"

A wave of nausea roiled in the pit of her belly. "Please just tell me," she whispered, wiping away the tears wobbling on her lashes.

Cole motioned her toward a quiet corner of the hospital's lobby. "We just got here five minutes ago. Alex was injured during a rescue. They're assessing him in one of the trauma rooms right now."

Zoe locked her knees to keep herself upright. "Injured,"

she repeated, and God, if she didn't get a straight answer, she was going to lose her ever-loving mind. "How bad? Come on, Cole, talk to me here. I need to know."

The firefighter hesitated, only for a second, but with Cole, it might as well have been a screaming admission of things gone wrong. "Part of a ceiling beam collapsed across his back and shoulder. He lost consciousness, and Jones and I dragged him to the ambo. Rachel said he woke up just briefly on the way here, but . . ."

"But?" Zoe rasped.

"The docs have to check him out, Zoe," Cole said, his voice canting lower with concern and the sharp undercurrent of fear. "He's hurt pretty bad, but I don't know any more than that."

Every ounce of despair that she'd stuffed into her chest in the last few hours came surging up in a hot rush, the absolute irony of Alex's voice echoing through her head.

"Fighting fires might be risky, but I've got the best team on the planet with me. I'll be all right. . . . I promise. . . . I promise. . . ."

Except the promise had been a lie. Just like all the other ones that had come crashing down on her today.

Zoe exhaled, and her fingertips and toes tingled with numbness that started working its way inward. "Is everyone else in the waiting room?"

Cole nodded, just one lift of his cleft chin. "Everyone except for your father. He said he needed some space. Last I saw he was by the ambulance bay." He paused. "Do you want to try to talk to him?"

"No," Zoe said, her arms heavy with the prickle of nonfeeling. "I'd like to sit in the waiting room with you guys, if that's all right."

"Of course," Cole said, ushering her toward the double doors marked EMERGENCY DEPARTMENT.

By the time she'd reached the tiny room filled with

stony-faced firefighters, her heart had gone as numb as the rest of her.

Alex swallowed past the steady stream of fire ants in his throat, and God *damn*, whoever was playing the samba in his skull needed to lay off the fucking percussion.

"Mr. Donovan. Nice to see you made it back." The voice was just as unfamiliar as Alex's surroundings, and wait . . . where the hell was he?

"Thanks," he croaked, shocked to hear that his own voice vaguely resembled forty-grit sandpaper. "Where . . . ?"

"Take it easy." The voice was joined by the face of a gray-haired man in a white coat. "My name is Dr. Ward, and I'm the attending physician here in the Emergency Department at Fairview Hospital. Do you remember being brought in?"

Alex squinted, which proved to be a stupid move because now there were two guys in front of him, and he was pretty sure the doc didn't have a twin. Clips of memory swirled in his mind's eye, surging and then slipping away. Narrow stairs, a smoke-filled hallway, backing up Everett on the nozzle . . .

"There was a man in that bedroom." Alex froze in realization for only a second before bolting upright against the mattress where he lay. The move sent a shock wave of pain on a nasty route from his left shoulder to his fingers and back, and what was with the sling on his arm?

"Take it easy, Mr. Donovan." Dr. Ward's voice tacked on an unspoken *or I'll restrain you*, but Alex didn't really give a shit. "You've sustained a few injuries. You need to be still so you don't make them worse."

Yeah, yeah. Alex shook his head even though the move made throwing up a distinct probability. "I pulled a man out of that fire. Where is he?"

"He's here at the hospital, too." Dr. Ward's expression stayed completely neutral, but he moved forward to look Alex in the eye. "Let's start at the beginning, shall we? Are you feeling any pain right now?"

Even though he wanted to barrel past the Q & A, it was clear from the look of things that getting chippy wouldn't take Alex very far. "The back of my shoulder hurts a little." Okay, so by *a little*, he really meant *a butt ton*. But still. "And my head feels kind of weird, but otherwise, I'm fine."

"I see." Dr. Ward took a hard look at the monitor by Alex's bedside, following up with the whole stethoscope-flashlight thing. "Well, you were brought in by ambulance with injuries to your head, your upper back, and your shoulder."

"Really?" Shock prickled a path up his spine. How did he not remember being in the ambo?

"You sustained a moderate concussion. It's not unusual for people to have memory gaps immediately following a traumatic brain injury," Dr. Ward assured him, as if he'd sensed Alex's concern. "Fortunately your gear kept you from sustaining any burn damage, and your colleagues got you here very quickly, but you did lose consciousness at the scene, and you've been in and out during your assessment."

"Good to know," Alex said, the joke falling flat. Holy shit, how much time had he lost?

The doc continued. "We've cleared you of any immediate spinal injuries, although you sustained some blunt force trauma to the back of your shoulder and neck, apparently from a falling ceiling beam. X-rays don't show any significant damage to the bone in your upper arm or shoulder."

"So I'm fine," Alex said. His arm throbbed in protest, so he tacked on, "Mostly."

"What you are is lucky. And I imagine, what you will be in the coming days is very sore."

Alex matched Dr. Ward's raised brow, shifting against

the overstarched sheet on the gurney beneath him. "That's not a no."

The corners of the doc's mouth tipped upward in a touché-like smile. "We'll have to monitor you overnight per concussion protocol, and I'd like to run a CT scan and a few more tests just to hedge our bets. But yes. Your prognosis is for a full recovery eventually, provided that you follow your standards of care."

"What about the man from the fire?" Concern peppered Alex's gut. The guy had barely been breathing, and God, he'd been so limp when Alex had picked him up to get him out of that room.

Dr. Ward shifted his weight, his internal debate raging clearly on his face. "Hospital policy dictates that I can't share patient information with nonfamily members. However, I can tell you that every patient brought to Fairview Hospital's ED gets the very best care we can offer."

God *damn* it, why had Alex hesitated when he'd first seen the guy in that doorway? "So he's in pretty bad shape."

"He's being extremely well attended," Dr. Ward said, the subtext of his nonanswer screaming through loud and freaking clear. "At any rate, you've got a room full of fire-fighters outside who are champing at the bit to see you. I'll need to restrict visits to one at a time, and only for a few minutes each, but I can apprise them of your condition if you'd like."

Oh hell. The last time any of them had been hauled off in an ambo, their captain had been critically burned, and the time before that, they'd lost a man. Knowing everyone at Eight, they were probably flipping out. "Please. Make sure you tell them the prognosis part first."

He sat back against the gurney, his head and neck duking it out for the title of I Hate You More. Everett had needed backup on the nozzle—there was no denying those stairs had been ridiculous, and not in the good way. But Jones had been there, too, and just because he was a rookie didn't mean he was an idiot. If Alex had gone down that hallway earlier, even by a minute or two, he might've gotten the guy to safety.

But he hadn't. He'd hesitated, and that caution could've cost a man his life.

Movement in the door frame by the foot of his gurney captured Alex's attention, his surprise quickly becoming a bolt of pure goodness as the sight of Zoe registered in his fog-filled brain. Even if she did look like she'd been through the wringer.

"Hey, Gorgeous." He lifted his arms to reach for her, but between the sling on his left side and the IV tubes snaking up from his right, it was pretty much a no-go. "Don't take this the wrong way, but you kind of look terrible."

"After everything that's happened, you're going to joke with me?" she asked, her lips pressing into a pale, practically nonexistent line, and shit. *Shit.* Her news about the grant—along with the argument they'd had with her father— came crashing back into focus.

"Zoe, I'm sorry. I know today's been rough, but we'll find a way to help Hope House. And to patch things up with your father." *Eventually. Maybe.* Damn, Cap had been so angry. But at some point, Alex would convince him that what was going on with Zoe wasn't fast and furious.

He was in love with her. And he didn't even care if Westin, or everyone at the station, or everyone in the whole goddamn galaxy knew it.

"That's not what I mean." Zoe wrapped her arms around her body as if she were holding on for dear life, but she didn't move past the three steps she'd taken into the trauma room. "I saw the fire on the news, and then Cole told me what happened, how that ceiling beam just came down right on top of you, and I thought . . . I thought . . . God, Alex, I thought you were dead."

The shell-shocked look on her face took a slap at his sternum, and he gestured to himself with his right arm in an effort to reassure her. "But I'm not, see? Totally fine."

Disbelief bled into her expression, taking over her tear-stained face. "You suffered a traumatic brain injury and blunt force trauma to your shoulder."

Ah, she sort of had him there. "Okay, I guess you're right. I did get a little banged up. But my shoulder's not even broken." He didn't voice his *probably*, because really, she looked frightened and furious enough.

"Do you honestly think this is no big deal?"

Alex paused, his gut going tight. "I think getting hurt is part of the risk involved in my job, but I promise, Zoe. I'm no worse for wear."

"You promise," she whispered, her eyes flashing with a sharp flare of anger before the emotion dulled into sadness. "You promised me you'd be fine to begin with. Just like you promised that sinking all my time and resources into applying for the Collingsworth Grant would be worth the risk."

"I didn't try to get hurt at this fire, Zoe. And we both know you deserved the hell out of that grant." There was only so much of life you could control. Fuck, he'd learned that lesson at the ultimate cost when he'd lost his parents twelve years ago, then again when Mason had been killed in that apartment fire.

Still, she shook her head. "I understand that you made those promises to me in good faith, Alex. I really do. But it doesn't change the fact that they turned out to be wrong."

His chin snapped up, and even though it scrambled his vision a little, his determination didn't budge. "Have I ever been wrong when I said I had your back?"

"No, but—"

Even though he knew it would likely piss Zoe off to no end, Alex interrupted her anyway. "And have I ever been wrong when I told you I'd be fine?"

"You're not fine now!" The fiery glint returned to her stare, and yup. Pissed.

But again, Alex pressed. "This will heal. Have I?"

"It doesn't matter." Zoe's voice wavered, her arms curling even tighter around her body. "You can't promise me you'll always be okay."

A dark ripple of frustration pulsed through his blood. "I'm a firefighter, Zoe. There are no absolute guarantees. You know that's not how it works."

"And I also know I can't live like this."

The words were no more than a feather-soft whisper, but they ripped through every part of Alex as if she'd screamed, and impulse had him answering, hard and fast and with everything in his heart.

"Yes, you can," he said, leaning forward in the bed just to bring himself closer to her. "You just have to take the risk and believe in me. In us."

"I can't take any more risks!" Zoe cried, stabbing her feet into the floor as her face hardened with determination Alex knew all too well. "Don't you see? They all *fail*. I wasted all that time and energy that could've gone toward feeding people who depend on me. I put something that mattered on the line and I lost. I risked my relationship with my father, who won't even speak to me right now. And I . . ." She broke off, her chest shuddering on a swallowed cry. "You let me believe that all of this would be okay. That the risks were worth taking. But they're not. You could've died today, Alex, just like you could die every time you're on shift. And I can't take risks when all they do is fail."

Just like that, Alex's last thread of control snapped. "They *don't* always fail. Sometimes, risks save lives. If I'd taken one today, the man I pulled out of that fire wouldn't be in the shape he's in now. But I hesitated, and it cost valuable time."

Zoe blinked in surprise, but she didn't say anything, and

hell if he was stopping before he'd unloaded his piece. "I get that you're raw right now, and I know taking risks scares you. But the flip side scares me. Every day that we have is a gift—a goddamn treasure. Not living my life because of what-if is the one risk I'm not willing to take. If you want to go live in a bubble, I can't stop you. But I can't go with you either. Please, Zoe. Stay with me. Take the risk."

Alex looked at her, willing her with all he had to take a step toward him, or even to make the slightest move that said she'd trust him enough to stay.

But instead, she said, "I'm sorry."

And then she turned and walked out the door.

Chapter Twenty-Six

Zoe made it all the way through the Emergency Department, past the double doors and over the stretch of asphalt in the parking lot before the tears she'd been fighting told her stubborn pride to kiss their ass. Wiping her face with the back of one hand, she used the other to get into her Prius, shutting the door so she could cry in peace.

Peace. On second thought, just crying would have to cut it for now.

She started the car, cutting a careful path over the handful of streets between Fairview Hospital and her apartment. Even though the drive wasn't terribly taxing or terribly long, by the time she'd parked her car and reached her threshold, her throat burned as much as her eyes.

Neither one of them came within a trillion miles of the hole in her chest.

Dropping her keys to the kitchen counter with a lackluster *clank*, she surveyed her favorite room. The kitchen had always been the cure-all for her frustrations, for her anger and her sadness and her doubt.

But now when she looked around, all she saw was the box of Lucky Charms Alex had conned her into buying, the skillet he'd washed and put in the dish drainer just that morning before he'd left for his shift, and the dish towel he'd snapped at her legs as they'd cooked together last week. In just one short month, he'd left an indelible mark in her space, her kitchen.

Her heart.

Another wave of fresh tears rimmed Zoe's eyes, and she didn't even bother swatting them away. Yes, she felt as if she'd been dragged across an emotional battlefield today, but the alternative was simply a non-option.

The fear of loving a firefighter had torn her parents' marriage apart after two and a half decades, proving that it never went away, and if anything, it only got worse over time. If Zoe had been this terrified at Alex's near miss, she couldn't even imagine how much worse *really* losing him would be. And between the profession that defined him and the lifestyle that was just as woven into the fabric of his being, the risk was too great.

She wasn't cut out for taking chances. All it did was leave her burned.

Zoe took a deep breath, trying to stuff her sadness down along with it. She wasn't hungry by any stretch, even though she couldn't remember for the life of her when, or even what, she'd eaten last. Deciding to forgo food, she slid a bottle of pinot noir off the shelf over the counter, uncorking it and filling her glass ridiculously high. She padded into the living room with both her glass and the bottle, putting them side by side on the slender coffee table in front of her as she plopped to the sofa, pulling a throw pillow across her chest.

The masculine scent of Alex's shampoo drifted up to greet her, and God, she was going to lose her mind.

Placing the pillow in the armchair across the room with the mental note to do laundry first thing in the morning, she flipped on the TV to scroll through the channels. She avoided anything vaguely hinting at local news, finally landing on a hockey documentary on the sports network. But after an hour of sitting there and not seeing a damn thing other than the level of liquid in her glass go all the way down to empty, Zoe finally decided that if she didn't at least eat something, she was going to be drunk as well as heartbroken.

She was halfway to the kitchen when a businesslike knock sounded at her front door, grabbing her attention and making her pulse rattle. She'd made a passable enough excuse to everyone at the hospital as she'd left, citing exhaustion as she'd slipped away. Rachel didn't know where she lived, and Tina would've certainly called before coming over. Could be a misguided pizza man. But it also could be a misguided serial killer, so Zoe deepened her voice with as much authority as possible before asking, "Who is it?"

"It's me, kiddo."

Zoe pressed herself flush to the door to look through the peephole, her confusion warring with shock. Sure enough, her father stood in the hallway, looking right at her through the tiny lens.

She unlocked the dead bolt with a heavy *click*, swinging the door wide. "What are you doing here?"

"Chief Williams called in Captain Lewis from Station Four to finish the shift with the rest of the house so I could make sure things were taken care of at the hospital."

"Okay," she said, her tone labeling the word as a question. "But you're here instead."

Her father nodded. "Everett elected to stay behind for a while to attend to any immediate needs, and Alex is resting comfortably, probably asleep for the night. But in order for me to handle this, I needed to talk to you first."

Zoe's heartbeat picked up speed in her chest, and she ushered her father inside. "I can probably save you the conversation. Alex and I have decided to stop, um, seeing each other."

He paused, his eyes falling on the empty wineglass and the half-empty bottle beside it. "I see," he replied slowly. "I thought it was a little strange that you'd decided to leave the hospital, but I can't say I was expecting that."

"That makes two of us. But we definitely broke up, so . . ." The ache in her chest kicked back to life with renewed vigor, and God, was it too much to ask to not start bawling in front of her father? She was twenty-seven, not *just* seven. For an awkward minute that lasted roughly an ice age, they stood in her living room, her father with his hands in the pockets of his uniform pants and her with her heart smashed to pieces.

And then her father crossed the space between them to wrap his arms around her, and Zoe burst into tears.

"Okay, now. Go ahead and get it out, kiddo. It's okay."

"I'm sorry," she sobbed, another round of cries tumbling out of her as her father smoothed her hair with one hand. "I found out I lost the Collingsworth Grant and then you got so mad at me and then Alex got hurt in this fire. . . . I saw it on the news and I thought . . . I thought he was . . . I was just so *scared*. . . ."

She bit her lip to stop herself from babbling further, but it didn't help. The tears flowed along with a half-sobbed version of what had happened, and her father held her close, the familiar comfort of his Old Spice cologne surrounding her as he simply listened. Finally, her cries became uneven breaths, then quiet sighs, and her father pulled back to look at her.

"I'm sorry you didn't get the grant. I'm sorry . . . well, for lots of things. I know I'm just your old man," he said, just as calm and matter-of-fact as ever, even as he pulled a handkerchief from his pocket to wipe the tears from her face. "But maybe we should talk about what happened earlier a little more."

"You seriously want to talk to me about what happened with Alex?"

"Not all of it," her father confirmed, his jaw giving a quick twitch. "But there are some things that I need to say."

Zoe frowned. "Like what?"

"For starters, you should know that Alex wasn't placed at Hope House by accident. He was placed there for community service because I requested it."

"What?" Her shock knocked the word from her mouth on a chirp, but her father answered it directly.

"The recommendation seemed like a win-win. He'd screwed up and needed to get his head straight, and I knew you'd make him earn it. Plus, I'm not going to lie to you, I wanted you safe. Donovan's as loyal as they come. I knew he'd look out for you once he got over having to do community service. I just didn't think . . ." Her father trailed off, running his hand over the back of his neck. "I guess I'm just a thickheaded old man. You're my daughter. Alex is one of my firefighters. I didn't put two and two together the way I should've, and when I saw you two together tonight at the firehouse, I reacted poorly."

Zoe blinked to try and get the information all the way past the holy-shit roadblock in her brain, but after the fourth try, she gave up. "So you put Alex with me because you knew I *wouldn't* give him preferential treatment?"

Her father nodded. "Alex is a great firefighter, kiddo, but the last thing he needed was to slide out of yet another dilemma. If I couldn't be the one to help him get his act together, well, I figured you were the next best thing."

Jesus. All the blinking in the world wasn't going to help her diffuse the shock of this. "I thought you didn't believe in me."

"I owe you an apology for that, too," he said, his eyes going soft. "I don't suppose you'll really understand this until you have kids of your own, but no matter how old you get, no matter how smart or strong, you're still my daughter. I let my worry for your safety get in the way of what really matters. I guess old habits die hard, but that doesn't change the fact that I should've supported you better."

Zoe thought of how her father had sent Alex to Hope House in the first place, then lent her the support of his entire firehouse, and all the quiet ways her father *had* helped, in his own way. "You did. You are right now."

"Zoe, listen." Her father paused for a deep breath. "You're an adult, and the last person you probably need advice from is your father, especially on your love life—"

Ugh, no. "Dad, please. I don't want to talk about this. I don't have a . . ." She swallowed hard, forcing her lips to shape the word. "Love life with Alex. I couldn't even cope with him getting through a week's worth of shifts. He's too reckless, and I don't know the meaning of the word. It's just not meant to be."

"I'm not so sure I agree with you there. I watched you get pretty reckless to save your soup kitchen," her father said, and the words sent another pang through Zoe's gut.

"Exactly. And look what it got me."

"What it got you was knowledge, experience, and the support of your community. Yes"—he cut off her brewing protest with a single look—"the money would've helped, but I know you better than to think you won't dust yourself off and find a way to get Hope House everything it needs to flourish, and I think you know it, too."

Zoe opened her mouth. Closed it. Opened it again.

Yeah. She had nothing. "You believe that?"

Her father tilted his head, his mouth twitching into a wry smile. "I believe in you one hundred percent, and I'm not the only one. Alex rallied for you even before I did. I might've reacted badly when I saw the two of you together, but Donovan's a good man, one who clearly cares for you. And you deserve that. Both of you."

"I'm scared," Zoe admitted. "The job is so dangerous, and it ended your marriage to Mom after all that time. What if I never get over being afraid?"

"Being a firefighter is dangerous," her father said slowly. "But being afraid to follow your heart is dangerous, too."

She stepped into the comfort of his hug, the ache in her rib cage giving way to a shaky breath. "But what if I take the risk, only to lose?"

Her father squeezed her tight, holding her up in steady support. "I think the more important question is, what if you don't?"

Chapter Twenty-Seven

Between his head feeling like it was chock-full of old rubber cement and his shoulder locked up tighter than a CIA safe house, Alex was pretty sure this morning ranked up there in his Top Ten Most Fucktacular.

He didn't even want to get started on the jagged hole in his chest that, while metaphorical, still hurt worse than everything else combined.

"Good morning, sunshine. Are you decent?" Cole stuck his head past the door to Alex's hospital room, just in time for Alex to give him a one-fingered salute.

"I take that as a yes," Cole said with a smile, and God. Nothing would *ever* rattle him. "I saw the doc in the hall. He said you're clear for takeoff, huh?"

Alex nodded, running his hand over the sweats and T-shirt O'Keefe had dropped off when he'd gotten off shift a few hours ago. "Yeah. He just came in and did the last of the concussion protocol, and the nurse went over all this stuff with me." He gestured to the pile of papers he'd barely listened to her review.

"Any update on your guy from the fire?" Cole asked,

and Alex's gut squeezed hard despite the news he'd finally wrangled out of one of the nurses.

"Yeah. He spent the night in the ICU while they stabilized him, but it looks like he'll end up being okay."

Cole's brows lowered in confusion. "I might be off the mark here, but isn't that a good thing?"

"It is," Alex said, his heart starting to pound as hard as his head. "I just wish I hadn't hesitated. I should've done my job better."

"Bullshit."

The single-word affirmation had Alex's stare whipping up toward his best friend. "Excuse me?"

"You heard me," Cole said. "You didn't hesitate yesterday because you weren't doing your job, Alex. You hesitated because you *were*. You knew I needed backup on that hose, and you knew that even though Jones is learning fast, he couldn't do it alone. Freelancing your way down the hall on a maybe wouldn't just have been reckless. It would've been dangerous."

"But it didn't turn out to be a maybe," Alex argued, a nauseous pang working up from the waistband of his sweats. "I should've trusted my instincts."

"And that's just what you did, you big dumb-ass." Cole's delivery carried a complete lack of anger or heat, stunning Alex into silence. "Your instincts told you to do your job and back us up. When the game changed and you saw that guy for sure, you acted, and we did ours to back *you* up. Yeah, the job is full of risks and what-ifs. But you know how to deal with those. Now more than ever."

Alex sat still for a minute, absorbing Cole's words, and shit, the guy was right. "Yeah," he agreed slowly. "I guess you're right."

"So how long before you come back to Eight for real this time?"

Alex held up the papers in his lap. "I'm on restricted

duty for a couple of weeks, 'til my follow-up CT scan, and I'm not supposed to drive. But other than that . . ."

Cole nodded, dangling the keys to his Jeep from his forefinger. "I've got you covered. What do you say we hit Scarlett's for some late breakfast? You must be starving."

His brain shifted from one heartache to another. Jesus, he missed Zoe. "Nah. They brought me breakfast here earlier." Never mind that he hadn't even touched the tray. The only thing Alex wanted was the one thing he couldn't have.

You need to snap out of it. With how stubborn that woman is, gone is gone.

"You want to talk about it?" Cole asked, crossing his arms over his white T-shirt.

"Talk about what?" Okay, so his attempt at denial was half-assed at best, and Cole knew him well enough to see it for what it was, but still. All the talking in the universe wasn't going to change the fact that Zoe had left.

And no matter how much Alex wanted her to, she wasn't coming back.

"Well, let's see." Cole held up one hand, and Alex braced for round two of the Everett Inquisition. "For starters, you've never *not* been hungry for Scarlett's breakfast in your life. Two, I know you spent the night in the hospital, but you look like hammered shit. And lastly . . ." He paused, easing up on his volume by just a notch. "I'm here driving you home instead of your girlfriend. So really, dude. The *I'm fine* thing? Not gonna fly with me."

Alex blew out a breath, and screw it. Now was as good a time as any to get rid of the crummy feelings he'd been jamming back all night. "Zoe decided to break things off."

He forked out a highlights-only version of the events leading up to the fire call, then another of the conversation with Zoe that had followed. Cole listened without a word in response, although Alex knew it wasn't for lack of attention or opinion.

Finally, Cole ran his palms down the front of his jeans. "Damn. I'm sorry, man."

"I am too." Alex's impulsive side told him to just forget it, to blow off all these sticky emotions and skip forward to find the next moment to really live in. Instead, he said, "Do you remember a couple of weeks ago at Bellyflop, how you said maybe it was my karma that put me in the kitchen with Zoe?"

Cole nodded. "Yeah."

"It wasn't."

"How can you be so sure?"

"Because," Alex said, his gut knotting up to match the throb in his shoulder. "I've never done anything good enough in my life to deserve her. Even if she couldn't stay."

Grabbing his paperwork, he swung his feet off the hospital bed, eager to just put this place and this day behind him. Cole reached for the door, sliding it open so Alex could cross the threshold.

Zoe stood two inches in front of him, her hand poised to knock.

"Oh, jeez!" Her bloodshot eyes flew wide, her face clearly showing signs of a sleepless night, but Christ, she was still beautiful. "I, um. I was going to knock."

His heart slammed against his sternum, and finally he managed to say, "I see that."

A beat passed, then another before Cole said, "I'll just wait for you at the nurse's station down the hall, Teflon. It's good to see you, Zoe."

Alex nodded a quick *thanks* to his buddy before turning back toward Zoe in the otherwise empty hallway.

She pressed her lips together, eyes downcast. "I heard the man you rescued is going to be okay. That's really good news."

"Yeah," he agreed, trying like hell to read her expression. A flare of emotion burned through her eyes as she glanced up from the floor. "And you look better. You know, almost fine."

He pinned Zoe with a quiet stare, a glimmer of hope sparking out from the very center of his chest despite his efforts to remain cautious. "Is that why you came here? To see how I am?"

"No. I don't know. I thought . . . I mean, I came here to . . . What I really wanted to say is . . ." She stopped, her honey-colored brows settling into that look of determination that told Alex she was dead set on getting what she wanted.

"I am in love with you, and I thought you should know."

Holy. Shit. "You what?"

Zoe moved forward, her words falling out in a rush. "I know what I said last night, about being too afraid to risk. But you were right, Alex. I can't live my life in a bubble. Not when what I really want is to live it with you. Yes, I am scared out of my mind at the thought of losing you. But I'm even more scared at the thought of not ever having you. If you still want me, I want to take the risk. I want to be with you. I want—"

"Zoe, stop."

"Oh God. What?" A look of panic streaked over her face, but Alex quelled it by closing the space between them. He pulled her in tight, and yeah. No matter how high the sky-dive, no matter how tough the climb or rough the rapids, *this* was the biggest thrill Alex ever wanted.

"You don't have to convince me," he said, brushing a kiss over her shock-parted lips. "I love you, too. I don't want to be anywhere other than with you."

"Really?" she asked, her smile lighting up her face.

"I'm a no-bullshit kind of guy, remember? If I tell you I love you, I mean it for keeps."

"Well, good." Zoe's smile became an ear-to-ear grin.

"Because even though it's a day early, I was hoping we could still have that breakfast date with my dad."

Alex pulled back, but only far enough to give her a quizzical look. "You think he'll be okay with this? You are his only daughter."

"Let's just say I think he's got *both* of our backs. And anyway, we've got some celebrating to do."

"I'd hardly call me getting released from the hospital after a scrape or two something to celebrate," he said with a laugh, but the excitement on Zoe's face snared his attention.

"I'd beg to differ, but your clean bill of health isn't the only thing we're celebrating."

"What else is there?" Alex asked.

Zoe's whiskey-colored eyes started to glimmer. "Well, in all the commotion yesterday, I missed a phone call from Emily Collingsworth. In fact, I didn't even see her message on my cell until this morning."

Alex said a silent prayer of thanks that he wasn't still attached to the pulse monitor, because he probably would've destroyed the thing from the sheer amount of *no way* pumping through his veins. "The grant lady?"

"I think she'd get a kick out of being called that, actually. Yes, the grant lady. She and I had a lovely talk this morning. We actually spent about thirty minutes on the phone."

"Zoe," he warned, and she lifted her hands in concession.

"Okay, okay. I'll get to the good stuff. Mrs. Collingsworth is obviously part of the committee that reviews the applications for her foundation's grant. She called to tell me that while Hope House wasn't chosen for the money, she was very impressed with the plans we set forth in the application, and the support we rallied within the community to raise awareness of the program. She wants to meet with me next week to talk about some smaller charity projects and other financial assistance Hope House might qualify for.

She felt really confident we'd be able to make the changes we proposed in the application if we put our minds to it."

"That's amazing," he said, and his chest filled with happiness at the look of sheer hope on her face. "It's everything you wanted."

But Zoe shook her head. "Not everything. I want you, too, Alex, right here next to me. Without you, I never would've had the nerve to get reckless."

Alex leaned down to kiss her, unable to hold back his cocky smile. "Just you wait, Gorgeous. If it's reckless you want, I've got nothing but time to give it to you."

Books by Bestselling Author
Fern Michaels

___The Jury	0-8217-7878-1	$6.99US/$9.99CAN
___Sweet Revenge	0-8217-7879-X	$6.99US/$9.99CAN
___Lethal Justice	0-8217-7880-3	$6.99US/$9.99CAN
___Free Fall	0-8217-7881-1	$6.99US/$9.99CAN
___Fool Me Once	0-8217-8071-9	$7.99US/$10.99CAN
___Vegas Rich	0-8217-8112-X	$7.99US/$10.99CAN
___Hide and Seek	1-4201-0184-6	$6.99US/$9.99CAN
___Hokus Pokus	1-4201-0185-4	$6.99US/$9.99CAN
___Fast Track	1-4201-0186-2	$6.99US/$9.99CAN
___Collateral Damage	1-4201-0187-0	$6.99US/$9.99CAN
___Final Justice	1-4201-0188-9	$6.99US/$9.99CAN
___Up Close and Personal	0-8217-7956-7	$7.99US/$9.99CAN
___Under the Radar	1-4201-0683-X	$6.99US/$9.99CAN
___Razor Sharp	1-4201-0684-8	$7.99US/$10.99CAN
___Yesterday	1-4201-1494-8	$5.99US/$6.99CAN
___Vanishing Act	1-4201-0685-6	$7.99US/$10.99CAN
___Sara's Song	1-4201-1493-X	$5.99US/$6.99CAN
___Deadly Deals	1-4201-0686-4	$7.99US/$10.99CAN
___Game Over	1-4201-0687-2	$7.99US/$10.99CAN
___Sins of Omission	1-4201-1153-1	$7.99US/$10.99CAN
___Sins of the Flesh	1-4201-1154-X	$7.99US/$10.99CAN
___Cross Roads	1-4201-1192-2	$7.99US/$10.99CAN

Available Wherever Books Are Sold!
Check out our website at www.kensingtonbooks.com